ISLE OF WOMAN

ISLE OF WOMAN

Geodyssey: Volume 1

PIERS
ANTHONY

A TOM DOHERTY ASSOCIATES BOOK

NEW YORK

ISLE OF WOMAN

COPYRIGHT © 1993 by Piers Anthony Jacob

This book is printed on acid-free paper.

A Tor Book
Published by Tom Doherty Associates, Inc.
175 Fifth Avenue
New York, N.Y. 10010

Tor® is a registered trademark of Tom Doherty Associates, Inc.

Library of Congress Cataloging-in-Publication Data

Anthony, Piers.
Isle of Woman / Piers Anthony.
    p.   cm.
"A Tom Doherty Associates book."
ISBN 0-312-85564-8 (hardcover)
I. Title.
PS3551.N73I83   1993
813'.54—dc20   93-25511
                                      CIP

First edition: September 1993

Printed in the United States of America

0 9 8 7 6 5 4 3 2 1

CONTENTS

ISLE OF WOMAN

THIS is a work of fiction, based on research on the derivation and nature of the human kind. For this purpose, the words "human" and "mankind" mean the species, male and female, while the word "man" will generally refer to the male alone. The validity of the theory of evolution is assumed. Those who believe in creationism may take this volume as what it is: a work of fiction based on certain assumptions.

Opinions differ about when mankind evolved from the primates—in crude terms, apes—but a case can be made that the first human being was the one who walked habitually on his hind feet. The several primates developed differing life-styles while in the trees, with some walking on all fours above branches, while others swung below branches. The faces of the ones above faced forward while they were on all fours, while the faces of the ones below faced forward while they were vertical. This made it easy for the hanging apes to drop occasionally to the ground and walk on their two hind feet for a few steps, though they usually put down their long and powerful forearms to brace themselves on their knuckles.

As the environment changed, and the forests diminished, one species of hanging primate came to range more widely on the ground between trees, finally giving up knuckle-walking in favor of full bipedalism. This had the coincidental advantage of freeing the powerful forelimbs for carrying, something other creatures did not readily do. The hind limbs grew stronger and the back straightened, making it easier to stride efficiently for increasing time and distance. One signal of the human capacity for long-range striding is the bulging buttock: a massive mound of muscle used to propel a human forward or up, and to assist in turning and balance.

Evidence from assorted disciplines suggests that mankind diverged from the pygmy chimpanzee about five million years ago. These two species have a number of things in common, such as their association in groups, bands or tribes, their high intelligence compared to most other species, and their extreme sexuality. Both differ from other creatures in having females who come into heat only partially if at all, and whose time of fertility is concealed, making them constantly available for sexual activity. But the special rigors of the ground brought many changes leading eventually to our present condition. This book will sample that history, touching on aspects throughout the timeline.

Obviously there was no single man or woman experiencing the whole of human development and history. But there were individuals, similar to others of their kind. We shall, as it were, follow one man and one woman and their families from the dawn of history through to the near future. Their appearance and situations will change as they go, but their identity will always be clear. They are much like us, and their development in life parallels that of our species.

Fair warning: though this is an extended story, a number of its assumptions are controversial, and in some cases more recent discoveries may disprove those assumptions. The object is not just entertainment; this is also a "message" novel, and the message is not pleasant. Each chapter is preceded by a map of the world, with the general location of the setting marked. There are also introductory and concluding discussions for each setting. Those who prefer to stick to entertainment may skip the maps and discussions as well as the Author's Note. The volume will then resemble a collection of stories featuring two widely ranging families.

CHAPTER 1

FOOTPRINTS

The earliest clear evidence of our kind's upright stance was found in the hardened ash of a volcano in east Africa dating a bit over three and a half million years ago. Three sets of footprints extended about seventy-five feet, going north, before being eradicated by erosion. The shape of the prints and pattern of pressures are typically human. These folk walked like men. The largest may have been male, about five feet tall, weighing perhaps a hundred pounds. The next may have been female, a little over three feet tall, perhaps fifty pounds. The third was a small child.

These were made by folk called Australopithecus afarensis—*never mind the pronunciation, which is changing from right to wrong—one of whom the anthropologists called Lucy. They have no names and no real language, just a collection of a few useful words. They may seem more like apes than men, at this stage, but that may be deceptive.*

THEY came near the fierce mountain and saw the mountain's breath spread across the plain, turning it gray. It was safe to cross, because the mountain was not roaring today, but it was nevertheless a marvel.

The man walked straight ahead, intent on his mission: to find something to eat. He was big and strong, and his fur was thick and even, showing his health. The woman followed just behind, keeping a wary eye on the child. Though she was much smaller than the man, her fur too was sleek and her body lithe. Her chest was flat, signaling her fertility, for she had weaned her son a year ago. She also gazed around, fascinated by the changed scene.

It was just at the end of the dry season. The creatures of the plain had grazed the grass down to the roots and moved on. Soon the big rains would come; already there were light showers. Meanwhile the mountain sent out its breath, which resembled the smoke of a great fire when it emerged, and the ash of that fire when it settled to the ground. She saw the tracks of animals in it: birds, rabbits, antelopes and even giraffes. A recent shower had made little holes in the powder wherever the drops struck. Some tracks had already been covered, and also some beetles. She saw a deserted bird's egg, and the outline of animal dung dusted with gray.

The child took to the powder immediately. He stretched forth his little legs and stepped in the new prints made by the adults. Sometimes he went to the side, making his own little prints, then returned to the safety of his father's tracks. He chortled. The woman smiled, taking pleasure in his pleasure.

She heard something. She turned to her left and paused, listening and looking. It was only guinea fowl, spooked by their approach.

The man grunted peremptorily, and the woman resumed her motion. They passed on beyond the ash-covered region, and the ground resumed its normal colors.

They were in luck: some distance farther along they found a patch of ripe gourds. The plant had been withered by the mountain's breath, but the fruits remained firm. The man cried out, and others of their band came to gather the food. The man picked up several, and the woman took two more, and the child one. They carried these back to the band's camp.

The woman and the child began to tire, so the woman employed a familiar device: she made a grunt of sexual suggestion. The man reacted as expected: he set down his burden, allowing her and the child to do the same, and drew her into him for a bout of copulation. The other members of the tribe paused, considering; then several others paired off, liking the notion. Sex was always a satisfactory interlude.

The woman relaxed, letting the man support her. He held her upright, facing him, her feet off the ground. He sniffed her genital region, excited by the odors there. Then he let her slide down to make contact with his erect penis. Most creatures approached their females from the rear, but the upright posture enabled these ones to be frontal if they wished, and often they did wish it, liking variety. The woman was like a doll in his embrace, allowing him any liberty he chose to take. It had been several hours since their last coupling, so he was quite amenable to her suggestion. He bounced her around, squeezed her, and kissed her fur as his member drove deep into her. This might have seemed like rough play, but she was tough and he was vigorous rather than violent.

By the time he was done, both the woman and the child were rested. They picked up their burdens and resumed their trek. The other couples were also breaking up, satisfied. Sex had no significance beyond the pleasure of the moment and the continuing association it signaled.

They came to the tree where the woman's sister labored, watched by other women of the band. They reached her as the great brightness of the sun settled behind a distant hill, setting the clouds ablaze. The sister was of similar size, with smooth light fur, but differed in two respects. Her breasts were prominent, their nipples poking out through the fur of her chest. And she was sexually nonreceptive, because she had already been fertilized. This was why the other woman was kept busier now: it was, in part, her job to protect the security of the family by making sure their man had no reason to respond to any outside woman. Had the family lived apart from others of their kind there would have been little problem, but in a band with several receptive females fidelity could be strained. Two women were enough, in this case, because their cycles of availability were complementary: while one was pregnant, birthing and nursing, the other was receptive. By the time her sister got a baby started, the original woman was ready again. In that manner the two kept the man to themselves, and benefited from his superior ability to forage and to protect them from both outsiders and other men in the tribe. They shared food, when necessary, with others, but not sex or child caring.

They were part of a band that traveled as a unit, but when children grew up the males went out to join other bands and mate with their women. A man was entitled to as many women as he could succeed in taking and keeping from other men. The women in turn preferred to have as much of a man to themselves as they could, and sisters or close friends cooperated in that design. It was almost impossible for a single woman to hold a single man, because of her infertile periods while nursing her small children, but two or three cooperating women could manage it.

Half the babies were lost in their first year, and some fell prey to accidents or illness thereafter, so it was necessary to sire several to be sure one would survive. On average, a woman was sexually receptive about half the time. She was less fertile than other female creatures, so that it could take her a year to conceive. That was what made it possible for only two women to keep one male, if they were correctly phased. If both conceived at the same time, they would lose him, because neither would be able to entice him with sex. Neither the man nor the woman thought of it exactly this way, but this was the mode that enabled the fledgling species to survive.

Indeed, the sister's labor was complete: she held a furry baby boy. There was a red mark on his little forehead, but it did not matter, for he was healthy. Now the man had two sons, by two sister women. It was good.

In this manner the tracks leading toward the full human species proceeded. Yes, they are our ancestors. Normally when the male is considerably larger than the female, he has more than one mate, so their social conventions were probably not the same as ours. Three million years can change things, however. Because he was born as the blazing sun set, and had a birthmark sharing this color, we shall call the new baby Blaze.

CHAPTER 2

TOOLS

Two million years before the present, Australopithecus *had given way to* Homo habilis *(HO-mo HAB-i-lis), "handy man," larger and with a bigger brain. He lived in the Great Rift Valley of east Africa. He was, as far as we know, the first of our kind to use tools regularly and effectively. But of the four kinds of tools this sequence shows, only one is what we normally think of as such. And—he wasn't the only descendant of* Australopithecus *extant.*

EMBER was four years old. She was bold for a girl, and liked to use her hands. She was always grabbing onto interesting sticks and

15

colored stones and trying to form them into fun patterns. But most of all she was intrigued with fire. Her mother had to watch her constantly when they were near a recent burn, to stop her from trying to take hold of an ember and scorch her fur. Thus her name. She had in time learned caution, but not enough; she still wanted to pick up bright embers, trying to wrap them in leaves to protect her fingers. She also had a small liability: there was a slight tremor or tic of her left cheek that appeared in times of stress or concentration. It was hardly evident ordinarily, but her mother was aware of it when the child nursed, and at other times. She hoped that Ember would grow out of it before others noticed. Fortunately the child was so active, moving her head so frequently to focus on things, that she seldom stayed still long enough for it to be obvious.

Yesterday there had been a burn on the land. It had crossed the prairie and the near valley, destroying their shelter and driving them into the water of the lake for safety. It had burned itself out during the night, but it had not been a comfortable time. Now the women of the band were out foraging for roasted mice while the men were out searching for a new place to make a safe retreat. This was, in a sense, a reversal of the normal order, for now the women were hunting meat while the men sought a homesite. It happened when it made sense.

Ember and her mother walked along the lake shore. It was safe here, because if a dangerous animal came they could wade into the water and the creature would not chase them. The fire had burned right up to the water and stopped. Now the land was covered in black ash, and pockets were still crackling. Ember was eager to go to them, to satisfy her fascination, but her mother stopped her with a terse reminder each time she started to stray. "No!" Ember had learned that word early, as well as her name.

They reached a section the fire had missed. Here the grass remained green and the trees retained their foliage, though some at the edge had been wilted by the heat. Right at the edge, hemmed in by a channel leading from the lake, was a large crackle-section. Oh, wonderful!

But they waded into the lake to avoid this, disappointing Ember. She hung back, staring at the puffs of smoke drifting up, wishing she could go and grab at them. What wonderful stuff fire must be, if she could only get close to it!

However, she did spy a pretty little stone with bright veins making patterns through it. She quickly picked it up and put it in her mouth for safekeeping. It tasted stony.

Then they spied something alarming. A big cat was crouching in the brush. But it wasn't after them. It had brought down a giraffe and was chewing on it.

They quickly retreated, keeping quiet. Ember knew that silence was essential in the presence of danger. She was frightened. She felt her cheek quivering. She almost swallowed her stone, so she poked it into her cheek for safekeeping.

They returned to the shore beyond, casting wary glances behind, then ran back to the place where others were gathering. This was beside a cache of stones they had gathered and deposited here before the fire. They had similar caches scattered strategically around the lake, so that there was always a source of tools or weapons near where they might be needed.

"Cat! Cat!" Ember's mother cried, pointing. Then: "Giraffe." She made a gesture as of something lying on the ground.

That was clear enough. Several men picked up stones, carrying them in their crooked arms, and moved toward the place. Ember's mother went along to show them the way, so Ember went too, staying close.

They entered the water by the crackling place and made themselves as quiet as possible. They came to the cat. It was a single one, not a pride. It looked up at them, blood on its monstrous fangs. It growled warningly.

But they were several, and it was one. They had the protection of the water, which the cat would not enter by choice. They could attack it with impunity, and they were hungry.

The first man flung a stone. His aim was good, and the missile struck the cat on the flank. The cat jumped up, snarling. It made as if to charge them, but stopped at the water's edge.

Reassured by this, the others flung their stones. Ember wondered whether she should throw her pretty pebble. She hoped not, because she wanted to keep it. Two stones missed, but two more struck. The cat screeched and turned, snapping at the stones, but getting nowhere. Then, as the men advanced toward the shore, throwing their last rocks, the cat realized it was overmatched and retreated, reluctantly. One more stone caught it near the tail, and it bounded away.

Ember knew that was a good thing, because the men had been

bluffing: they had used up all their stones. But the cat didn't know that. So it had given up when it was at the point of victory, because no man would have stepped onshore while that fearful predator was there. They would not even have approached it, had they not been very hungry and had the protection of the water.

Then men took hold of the carcass and dragged it to the water. There it floated, making it easier to move. They hauled it along until they reached the crackling place. Then they dragged it out and rolled it right into the heart of the crackle.

There was a horrendous sizzle and big cloud of vapor that delighted Ember. The fire was trying to eat the giraffe! But it couldn't; it could only burn it, making a special smell. The smell of burned mouse, only bigger.

There was a cry from the lookout. "Ape!"

Everyone looked. There were many apes coming, attracted by the commotion. They wouldn't have come while the cat was there, but it was gone. They wanted to know what was happening here, and whether there was anything good to eat.

The men moved into the lake. Some went to fetch some of the stones they had thrown. But though the apes were dull, they knew about stones. They charged over in a mass and swept up the remaining stones and hurled them at the men. Each ape was much larger than each man, and had much stronger arms. The men retreated back into the lake and ducked down as the stones came.

Ember took a breath and held it and went down under the water. She heard splashing near her, but didn't know whether it was from a man or a stone. The stones could not hurt anyone under the water, but it was hard to stay down long. Ember had to come up to breathe.

She saw that the apes had used up the stones and lost interest. They were wary of the crackling place, not understanding fire, and they didn't like the smell of the roasting flesh. So they moved on, disappointed. They were strong, but stupid.

The men came out. The giraffe was still cooking, and the smell was very strong now.

They brought out the special stones, the ones with the sharp edges, and as the fire died down they used these to slice across the hide so they could pull it off, and to slice across the meat so they could get pieces. They passed these around, and Ember and her mother got to bite into the meat. It was tough, and not as good as fresh fruit, but after the fire they hadn't found much fruit.

Then Ember and her mother walked to the new place the men had found, beyond where the fire had been. It was a big tangle of thorns and nettles and stingy plants, but there was a hole in it for them to get through. No bad animals would come for them here! Ember settled down with her mother, huddling close for warmth as the night cooled, and others lay close on either side. Tomorrow they would make a better shelter, and hope it didn't burn soon. But the fire had helped feed them today.

Ember was satisfied. She took the stone out of her mouth, which she had preserved despite eating the hot meat, and tried to focus on its prettiness. But it was too dark now for her to see, so she put it back in her mouth for tomorrow.

This day's activities show the manner Homo habilis *used his tools and his wits to survive in a sometimes hostile environment. He entered the water to avoid the prairie fire, and used the water also as protection from large predators, such as* Megantereon, *a saber-toothed cat the size of a lion. He used available fire to cook the body of* Sivatherium, *a short-necked giraffe that stood seven feet tall and had antlers. He used thrown stones as weapons, and chipped stones as knives for carving flesh or fruit, and maintained caches of such stones in scattered places so that supplies were usually handy. He used thorny brambles to make safe shelters. Thus water, fire, stone and brambles all were tools. He was smart enough to take advantage of the situations in which he found himself, so he got by though he was by no means the dominant creature of the region.*

The "ape" was a cousin, a parallel hominid, the vegetarian Australopith-ecus boisei: *as big as a modern man, and strong, but relatively stupid. He prospered for perhaps a million and a half years, far longer than* Homo habilis, *but was in the end a nonsurvivor. It may be that when the climate changed he was no longer able to forage effectively, while the "handy man," on the fringe, was able to scrounge his way along and survive.*

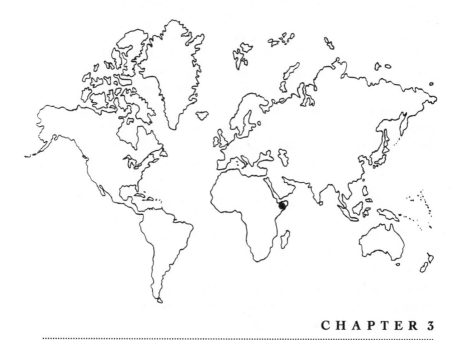

CHAPTER 3

FIRE

Homo habilis *gave way to* Homo erectus *(HO-mo e-REK-tus), "upright man," about one and a half million years ago. He approached modern human size and had a larger brain than his predecessor, and was well equipped to survive. Indeed, he was to conquer the world. About one million years ago the Sahara desert of northern Africa greened somewhat for a time, allowing* Homo erectus *to pass north and spread across Europe and Asia as well as remaining in Africa. But it seems that his evolution continued most progressively in Africa.*

21

There is some evidence that this man used fire, but it is inconclusive. Did he use fire intentionally, or did he avoid it, or did he take advantage of it when he had a chance? Perhaps a few people found ways, in special circumstances.

BLAZE was eight years old and ready for something better. The fiery birthmark on his forehead set him apart from the other children of the band, making him the object of a certain distrust and sometimes ridicule. His older half-brother Ashfoot had protected him somewhat, but now Ashfoot was thirteen and a man. He had gone out alone with a spear and run down a small deer and killed it. It had taken him two days, pursuing the animal day and night, following its tracks by moonlight and guessing when he had to, but he had done it. So Ashfoot was a man, and had joined the camp of the single men, and was no longer near enough to help Blaze. Ashfoot could go out to seek a woman of another band when he felt ready. He had proven himself. But how could Blaze do the same? His main interest was fire—and fire was supremely indifferent to him.

Today fire was near, however. It was burning in a nearby valley, after a storm. That was funny, how fire came from water, when water always stopped fire. But Blaze thought he knew how it happened. Sometimes there were fire flashes in storms, as if the water was casting out the fire in its mist, and these fire flashes in the air might start the fire on the ground. Then it would burn until it encountered water, or ran out of dry grass to eat. Whenever there was a fire, Blaze went to investigate, on the pretense of looking for fleeing game animals. His sharp eyes found such animals often enough to make this claim legitimate. But actually it was the fire itself that fascinated him. He never dared get too close to it, for it was hot and fierce and unpredictable, but he explored it as well as he could without getting burned. He had become a private expert on its ways.

He took his small spear, which was a dry stick he had sharpened against a stone and baked in the sun, making it hard. He had used it for small game, but lacked confidence in it for anything larger than a rabbit. It was mainly for defense, to point at a predator and keep it at bay. Maybe it couldn't kill a big cat, but it could damage an eye or gullet, and that might be enough. He hoped. He also kept an eye out for climbable trees, and tried never to be far from one. Trees had always been the friends to his kind, because few bad predators climbed them.

He crested a hill and paused, looking down into the shallow valley beyond. There was a shelter there, not big enough to house a band, but obviously of human design. It must be a foreign hunter, because none of Blaze's band lived separately. He would have to go back and tell the others of this intrusion, because this was home territory.

But before he could move, a woman came out of the shelter and saw him. She signaled. She wanted him to go to the shelter.

Blaze was in doubt. She was adult and he was a child, so he should obey. But she was a woman and he a boy, so he didn't have to. He had to answer only to his mother. Also, this woman was foreign, so might be an enemy.

Then another figure came out. It was a boy somewhat smaller than Blaze. No—it was a girl, because there was no bulge of substance between her legs, no penis. The fur was smooth throughout.

The woman did not signal again, but waited for him to obey. Blaze stood, trying to decide what to do. But the girl did not hesitate. She walked toward him, spreading her hands in the signal of friendly meeting. It was remarkable for a girl to approach a stranger; usually they were very cautious.

As she approached, he saw that she was nicely formed, with even limbs, light fur, and a pretty face. She seemed to be about his own age, though smaller. She smiled, showing even teeth. Her prettiness was marred only by a little twitch on her left cheek, as if she were trying to shake a fly loose in the manner an animal did. She stopped when she was close and tapped her chest. "Ember," she said, using the word for the remnant of a fire.

Suddenly he knew he liked her. "Blaze," he said, tapping his own chest, using the word for bright fire.

She smiled again, recognizing their affinity. She reached out with her open hand, the fingers curving up in invitation.

Blaze reached out and took the hand with his own, accepting it. They stood that way for a moment, gazing into each other's eyes. He saw now that hers were green, a shade he had seen only once before: when he looked into still water and saw his ghost image. He touched his cheek with his free hand, pointing to his own eye, then to hers. "Green."

She nodded, agreeing, and smiled a third time. This time he smiled with her, accepting the expression as he had her hand. They had met only this moment, yet he had already found more favor with her than with any girl of his band. Maybe she had been teased about that cheek, just as he had been about his forehead.

She turned and walked toward the woman, gently tugging him along. He went with her, oddly enjoying her presumption.

She led him to the woman, who had waited stolidly throughout. "Blaze," Ember said, indicating him. Then, indicating the woman to him, "Mother." As if that hadn't been obvious.

But then Ember tugged him on to the entrance of the shelter. He saw that it was not well made, being more like something a woman would throw up for overnight. They looked in. There was a man lying there. He was still, and there was the smell of blood. He had been injured, and now was perhaps dying. Flies were buzzing.

Now Blaze understood their situation. Ember's father could no longer protect them, and they needed help.

He would return to the band's camp and tell them. Men would come and decide what to do. They would help the man if they could, and if he died, someone might take Ember's mother. That depended on how well she could work and gather, and whether her body was appealing.

Blaze faced back the way he had come. "Camp," he said, pointing.

"Camp," Ember agreed. Then she kissed him on the ear.

Blaze was over the ridge and out of sight of the family before he realized just how much he had liked that kiss. Ember had shown that she liked him, though she had seen the mark on his forehead. No girl had done that before. Of course the boys and girls of the band didn't kiss each other much anyway, since none of them would grow up to mate with each other. The boys would all go out to find the girls of other bands, and would become members of those bands, while other men would come to the home band to find girls. Blaze wasn't sure why this was so, but did not question it.

In a sense he had gone out and found a girl of another band. But it didn't mean anything, because he was not yet a man. Still, at this moment, if he were to choose a girl, Ember would be the one.

Soon he reached the camp. "Man!" he cried, pointing back. "Down." He made the gesture of lying on the ground. "Woman. Girl."

This was important news. Three men followed him back to the neighboring valley. Blaze was afraid that the foreign family would be gone, and he would be blamed for giving a false alarm. But the shelter remained, with the woman sitting outside it, and the girl beside her.

Blaze went a little ahead, so they could see him, and know that these were friends he was bringing. "Blaze!" he called, to make it certain.

The men checked. One went in to touch the wounded one. He emerged, shaking his head negatively. "Gone," he said.

The woman nodded. She had known it. So had Ember, who looked unhappy.

The men considered the woman. One gestured to her to stand. She did so. He walked around her, studying her contours. He tugged on the longer fur of her head, and pinched her buttock. She was healthy. She should be an asset to the band, especially since she had a healthy child with her. He nodded affirmatively, looking at the others. They nodded, agreeing. The woman would do.

The man pointed toward the camp. He gestured, indicating that the woman should go that way. She started walking.

Ember came to Blaze. She walked beside him. He knew she was glad that his band was accepting her and her mother. Now they would not die unprotected.

❂

As it happened, the woman was fertile, making her interesting to the men of the band. She was not young, but she was new, and therefore novel, and her odor was attractive. She was not committed to a member of the band, so they all wanted to mate with her. But she had to be chosen by one, and agree to stay with him, and his existing mate had to agree too. That was the way of it. As it happened, most of the women did not wish to share with a stranger; that was why they stayed together in the band, with women they knew, and accepted the suits of foreign men singly or in compatible pairs. However, one man's mate had died; he had been about to depart to look for another, but now he took this one. She accepted him, and he lay her on a mat and sank his hard penis into her immediately. By that token she was his; all who witnessed the act knew it.

In a moment it was done. The woman got up, and now the other women acknowledged her. She would not be harassed by them or by other men. Her receptivity remained, stirring the desire of the other men, but they had no recourse; she served the desire of only the one. Soon that desire reappeared, for he had not had a woman for some time, and he copulated with her again. No one thought much of it, but

Blaze found the act fascinating, and wished he knew how to do it. But his penis hardened only by its own will, not his; and in any event he had no girl with whom to experiment. He envied the boys who had the ability to try it, even if they had access only to girls who were beneath the age of maturity and so lacked interest.

Meanwhile the fire still burned in the neighboring valley, and animals from that region were passing through this region. Unfortunately they were grown and healthy, impossible to bring down in the open. Only when foolish ones got caught in the dead-end gully could they be trapped and attacked and killed. Several men had staked out that valley, lying hidden, waiting for an unwary animal to make that mistake, but the local animals knew better.

Blaze had an idea. If the fire could come here, it might drive the animals into that gully. Then there could be much fresh meat. The fire normally chose its own course, heedless of the convenience of men. But could there be a way to change its course? He wanted to find out.

He set out, as he had before. Then he heard something. Ember was following him. He could warn her away, for she was after all a girl, but he didn't. He let her catch up with him and they went on together. He gave no other signal, because it would only lead to teasing by the other children, but the fact that he allowed her to accompany him was significant. It meant that they were friends, and the others took note, just as they had when the man had copulated with the new woman. It was important to know who associated with whom, for in the event of trouble friends stood up for friends. Boys normally stood up for boys, and girls for girls, but it was not absolute.

Ember, it turned out, had good legs, and was able to keep up with his rapid stride. Women learned to move well, because foraging was not always conveniently close. If there was hunting to be done, the men set camp near that, and the women simply had to range farther for the berries, fruits, nuts and tubers they specialized in. Ember was free now because her mother was busy taking up the continuing attention of her new man, and had to stay close to the camp where her man was, or else go out with him. Once his jealous early desire passed, she would join the foraging women. At present the others were sharing their foraging with her, and she would share hers with them when they needed it. A child was not expected to forage with strangers; she had to be with her mother, until she became a woman and was taken by a man. Probably

Ember was not eager to remain in the camp while her mother was active in a way Ember could not share, as she did not know the other children. So she stayed with Blaze.

And Blaze was very glad to have her with him. He felt a kind of propriety, because he was the one who had found her and her mother, but it was more than that. She liked him, and was willing to show it. Their eyes matched. Their names matched. Did she like fire as he did?

They skirted the valley where Ember's father lay. The creatures of the field and forest would chew up the body and scatter the bones, and the smell would be bad for awhile. It was best just to let it happen. Next year when the band passed this way again, there would be little if any trace. Few would even remember, or care if they did. But he saw Ember looking sad, and understood why: she had lost her father, who perhaps had treated her kindly.

They came to the fire. It had passed this region and gone elsewhere, but a number of fallen branches still crackled and there were clumps of smoking vegetation.

"Oooo," Ember breathed, her eyes shining. Now it was clear that she was just as interested in fire as he was. Joyed by this discovery, he hugged her and kissed her ear, returning her expression of the prior day. She laughed and hugged him back. That felt very good.

Then they explored the remnants of the fire. Ember found a branch that was burning on one end, and clear on the other. She touched it, tentatively, then put both hands on it and picked it up. She held the smoking torch, chortling with her accomplishment: she was holding fire!

That was exactly what Blaze had been considering. If such a branch were taken away from the fire, would it keep its own bit of fire with it? He didn't know, but he thought it might. So he looked for another burning branch, and found it, and picked it up. Then he spoke. "Camp."

Ember looked disappointed. She set down her branch, ready to return. Then she saw that Blaze was not setting his branch down; he was carrying it with him. "Oooo!" she repeated, thrilled, and picked hers up again.

They carried the two burning branches back to the camp. Not much was happening there; most folk were out foraging or hunting. Then they went on beyond, where some animals grazed. There were several buffalo, a flock of large birds, and an elephant. Ideal prey!

Beyond the animals was the gully, invisible from here and deceptive in its shallow origin, but a trap at its deep far end. The wind was blowing toward it. Blaze knew that the fire liked to follow the wind. If this worked—!

"Fire," Blaze said. He put his stick down on the dryest mat of grass he could find. Smoke went up, but nothing else happened. The stick had died down, and the fire in it was weak. It didn't like to be away from its burning field.

Ember set her stick beside his. Then she got down on her hands and feet and put her face close. She blew. What was she doing?

Ember blew again, and again. She gestured Blaze to do the same. But he hung back, perplexed.

More smoke went up, and there was a crackle from one of the sticks. The fire was coming back to life! He realized that she was making a wind for the fire, and the fire liked it, so it was responding. He had never thought of that.

Now Blaze got down beside Ember and added his breath to hers. The ends of the two sticks got hotter, and the smoke increased. Ember took some straw and put it on top of the sticks, and blew again.

The fire expanded, creeping in a bright line across the sticks. He could see its minute progress, and realized that Ember did too. She had the same sharp vision he did, that it seemed that most other people lacked. He adjusted his blowing, to get the maximum effect on that glimmering bit of flame.

Suddenly there was live fire, blazing up. They had done it! They had made the fire return from its hiding place within the wood. Now it was spreading into the dry grass. The wind fanned it, and it laid back its ears and dug deeper, getting brighter. The two sticks, too, were blazing up again, restored by the fire around them. They liked this, for they were back in a burning field.

The animals winded the smoke and began to get nervous. Blaze saw that they would move away to the side, avoiding both the fire and the gully. "Here!" he cried, picking up his stick and running to head them off. Ember followed with her own stick.

They got ahead, because the animals remained uncertain and were milling around rather than moving purposefully. Animals weren't as smart as people. They put down their sticks and blew on them again.

This time it was easier, and the flame came more readily. In a moment they had another fire starting.

The animals veered away from it and finally headed into the gully, the seemingly safe place. Then the watching men jumped up, calling to others: "Hunt! Hunt!" The hunt was on.

Blaze looked at Ember and smiled. She smiled back. They had done it! They had brought the fire and used it to make the animals go into the trap. The band would eat well for a long time, after this hunt was done.

It might have been this way. But such use of fire would have been a sometime thing, with Homo erectus, *dependent on fortunate circumstances. Mostly they had to hunt the old-fashioned ways. Bright individuals like Blaze and Ember might have had inspiration, but the more conservative adults were slow to catch on, and slower to change their ways. It has ever been thus.*

At this stage there was no concern about the welfare of the animals. They were there to be hunted. They looked out for themselves.

CHAPTER 4

ISLE

Homo erectus *spread out and became acclimated to various regions of the world. In Africa he evolved into modern mankind between 200,000 and 100,000 years ago. Exactly when and how this occurred is unknown, and conjectures differ. One conjecture is the aquatic hypothesis, one form of which is presented here. The theory is controversial, and anthropologists may be bitterly divided on the subject, but it does explain some things that otherwise seem almost inexplicable.*

At the northeast end of the Great Rift Valley in Africa is a triangle of lowlands cut off by the mountains of what is now Ethiopia, the Afar Triangle.

31

Within this is the Danakil depression. In the past this was once Danakil Island; at this time it may have been merely a shore region cut off from the rest of Africa by mountains and barren lands. We shall call it the Isle of Woman.

The full-blown aquatic hypothesis has mankind settling the region between four and eight million years ago, when there is a gap in the fossil record. Thus man developed in a place that has not been carefully explored for such fossils. Changes in climate over the millennia required man to adapt to new conditions, and increasingly he had to go to the water for food and protection that was inadequate elsewhere on the island. At those times when the island rejoined the land, or became a lowlands coastal area, groups of men went back out into Africa and down the fertile highway of the Great Rift Valley, accounting for the abrupt appearances of the advancing forms of man. Australopithecus afarensis, *found in that Afar region perhaps by no coincidence; then Handy Man, Upright Man, and Thinking Man, all found along that valley.*

Intriguing as this is, it is not the case in this narration. There is a question whether there really is that much of a fossil gap, because the line of man may have diverged from that of the pygmy chimpanzee only five million years ago. Many aspects of the nature of mankind can be explained by other means. Instead we have here a more limited variant, wherein the human being evolved as a strider on the plains of Africa until perhaps 200,000 years ago. At that time one shore-dwelling contingent was trapped in the Afar region, and it was this isolated group that suffered the shifts of habitat and life-style that led to anatomically modern man. The women had been foraging increasingly in the water, and wading into it to avoid danger on the land, and now this trend intensified.

The time mankind spent in the water led to some dramatic and some subtle changes. Much of the rest of the body hair was lost, and subcutaneous fat substituted for warmth, making this the fleshy "naked ape." Because increased mass and fat helped survival in cool water, women became larger than they had been, and more solid in the lower portions. Their legs and hips may have been what by today's standards would seem ludicrously corpulent. Babies became chubby. Mankind still had hot chases on land, so he developed sweating as a cooling mechanism. This meant that he never strayed too far from freshwater sources, such as springs or rivers, either.

With increasing brain size, the human head expanded in proportion to the body. Babies were born with larger heads, making birthing more difficult, and they took longer to become self-sufficient. This increased the importance of the

*mother, and of the family unit. More adaptations were necessary. These
continued at the region that may have defined the present physical nature of
man: the Isle of Woman. Perhaps it was, more than figuratively, the birthplace
of mankind.*

EMBER was out in the morning with several other girls and a
woman, foraging for oysters in a distant bay. When they filled the
woven basket on the beach, they would carry it back, and the tribe would
have roasted oysters that evening. They took turns diving down in the
shallow water and feeling carefully for the hidden creatures. One girl
always watched while the others dived, because these waters were not
necessarily safe. If a shark came, she would give the alarm and they
would scramble out to the beach.

Ember had just found a good oyster, using her sharp vision, and she
brought it up—to hear an alarm of another nature. "Man! Man!"

Of course that meant strangers, because the men of the tribe needed
no cry of alarm, and in any event would have been called by name. Two
of them. This could be good news or bad news, depending on the origin
and intent of the men. Some tribes stole women from other tribes, and it
was hard to do anything about it without risking ugly fighting.

Ember stood beside Clamshell, a girl of thirteen whose breasts had
bulged voluminously in the past year, signaling her readiness for
mating. Ember's own breasts were more modest, but of course she was
only twelve and they might grow some more. She peered up at the men
on the beach, feeling the facial tic starting just when she least wanted it.

Both were shaggy in animal cloaks, their beards giving them a
ferocious appearance, but it was evident that they were young. They
carried wood spears and stone knives. They might be hunting, but if so,
they had to leave, because this was the local tribe's territory.

"Who?" the matron Crabshell demanded challengingly. She was
Clamshell's mother, and she accepted trouble from no women and not
many men. She was of course standing chest-deep in the water, as were
the girls. If the men tried to enter the water, all of the women would
swim quickly away, screaming for help. Men could generally swim faster
than women, because they had longer arms and more muscles on them,
but they would not be able to catch up before the men of the tribe heard
the screams and came to the rescue.

The taller man tapped his chest. "Tusk," he said.

The shorter one followed suit. "Scorch." Ember saw that he had what looked like a bad burn on one arm, for which he might have been named. It was ugly, but he seemed to be able to use the arm well enough.

"Why?" Crabshell demanded next.

For answer, each man lifted his cloak, showing his penis. That was answer enough: they had come looking for women. That made them considerably more interesting to the girls. Normally a man showed his penis only to other men, or to the woman with whom he meant to copulate. In this context, it meant that either of these men was willing to do so with any of the women here, which meant in turn that both men were single and hoped the girls were too.

Crabshell nodded, unsurprised. "Wait," she said to the men. Then she turned to face the three girls. "Clamshell. Ember." She pointed toward the village.

The two girls swam to shallow water, not directly toward the men, then stood and waded on out. The men remained where they were, but watched closely. Clamshell, aware of this, stepped out on the beach and shook herself clear of some of the water, causing her flesh to ripple from chest to buttock, giving the men a good view. Ember found herself embarrassed, and made no such display. Perhaps if she had had Clamshell's flesh, she would have done so. As it was, she was conscious of the slenderness of her hips and legs, a disadvantage when the water was cold. Often she had to go to the village fire for warmth, or get under a cloak, instead of standing comfortably in the water. Fortunately her fascination with fire compensated, and if anybody objected, Blaze stood up for her. Since Blaze had become the keeper of the fire in the last two years, no one else could object.

They ran toward the village. Now Ember had the advantage, for her slender body could run more lightly and swiftly than Clamshell's full one. Even when she was carrying her oyster. Clamshell also had to hold her breasts in her hands to stop them from bouncing and banging uncomfortably, and that handicapped her running. Soon she was breathing hard and falling behind, while Ember was just getting pleasantly warm. She slowed to accommodate her friend, having made her point in the usual way. Of course when it came to impressing men, Clamshell had a future, while Ember didn't, yet.

They reached the village. This consisted of several shelter domes fashioned of stones, sticks and bones, with animal skins stretched over the tops. In the center was the hearth, where Blaze kept the village fire burning. Other boys fetched in wood for it, but Blaze saw to it that the wood was properly used. He never let the fire go out, not even when it rained, for it would be a difficult chore to fetch more fire. They would have to get it from a neighboring village, which would mean giving up something of value, or find free fire burning out somewhere. That was almost impossible after a rain. So Blaze had a structure he used to cover the central part of the fire, keeping the rain off, and he knew just how to tend it so that it survived. Sometimes Ember helped him, for she loved the fire too. She loved Blaze; he treated her well despite her inadequacy of body. She smiled at him as they approached, and handed him her oyster. Had they been mated, this would have been his due; as it was, it was another signal of their closeness. She didn't care about the mark on his forehead, and he didn't care when her cheek twitched; they shared a keen vision for details, and knew what counted and what didn't.

"Man! Man!" Clamshell cried, relaying the news. "Penis!" She made a finger at her crotch, pointing down, in the standard signal for maleness. Because she had done it as well as saying the word, others knew that she had seen the penis herself.

Oho! That got everyone's attention. There were men showing penises, looking for women to mate with. The men of the tribe were interested, because any men who found mates here would join the tribe and strengthen it. The single women were interested, because some of them might find men now. The women with babies were interested, because soon there might be more like them. The children were interested, because this was a rare occasion. Even the nursing babies, gripping the long hanks of their mothers' hair as they floated in the water, seemed interested for a moment.

Four men gathered. Ember led them back, for she knew where it was, and there was no point in having Clamshell try to do it. Ember could run almost as swiftly as a man.

She brought them to the place where the two foreign men waited. The men talked. Then the two visitors were escorted to the village, where things were already being set up for the occasion. First ritual food was served: bits of roasted ox meat. Only a token, not a meal—but hunger wasn't the point. When the visitors ate with the men of the village, they were bound to do the village no harm, and the villagers would not attack them. It was peace between them, for this occasion. If their business together did not work out, the visitors would depart peaceably.

After the food, the visitors stated their business: "Woman." As if that had ever been in doubt.

The elder men of the tribe nodded. This meant much more than merely acquiring mates. The visitors would have to join the tribe. They would have to prove themselves worthy, for the tribe wanted no liabilities. Each of the village men had come similarly to the tribe, joining its women and assuming its identity. Once they made this commitment, they would hunt and fight for this tribe, not the one from which they had come.

But they would join only if they found mates here. The head tribesman stood and faced the nearby water, where all six eligible girls stood chest-deep, their breasts making the water curve around them. The headwoman signaled, and the girls waded out to stand at the edge of the sand. Ember was at the end of the row, being the least endowed. Indeed, at this moment she was glad of it, because she didn't want to mate with a man yet. She preferred to remain a girl longer, and keep her friendship with Blaze. In fact, she wished she could mate with Blaze, and not just because he had green eyes like hers; but they both knew that that was impossible. Not only would he have to find a woman of another tribe, at age twelve he was too young. Ember had matured faster, as girls generally did, so she was now a young woman while Blaze remained a stripling boy. It would be several more years before he was ready.

She saw the eyes of the two men studying the girls. The eyes lingered longest on Clamshell, unsurprisingly. They hardly touched Ember.

"Turn," the chief said. Then they turned, showing their backsides. Ember knew that she was similarly deficient from this vantage. Her feelings were mixed. She felt bad because her body was not full-fleshed, yet hopeful that she would not be chosen. Of course a girl could turn down a man's suit, but that was not a good thing to do, for men did not come by that often. A girl who waited too long might never be chosen, because younger girls would become more attractive, and that could be disaster.

Tusk spoke. "Yes." He was satisfied that one of these women was for him.

"Yes," Scorch echoed, and the girls turned back to face the men. He too had found his woman. But the matter was not yet done. Who were the ones? Ember wondered apprehensively. Surely neither man would have chosen her. But now she remembered that both had seen her run, so knew her health and capacity in this respect. If they were choosing by endurance instead of appearance—but of course she could decline, if she had to. Probably she wouldn't have to.

The headwoman made a down signal to the girls, and they squatted on the beach, watching the proceedings.

The headman turned to the men. "Prove," he said.

Tusk stepped forward. "Strong," he said, lifting his right arm to show his muscle. Indeed, he looked strong.

Aha! They could use a strong man. The headman looked at the standing villagers, who now formed a considerable throng; everyone was interested when newcomers joined the tribe, and when girls found mates. Even the young men who would in due course be leaving to find their own mates: the new men, once they were part of the tribe, would share their information about the available girls of their tribe, and what abilities that tribe might be looking for. That could make a big difference to someone like Blaze, who was not muscular but who could handle fire. Sometimes a tribe would make it easy for a newcomer, or would arrange to have its most attractive women available, if it really needed someone with a particular skill.

The headman glanced around and caught an eye. He nodded, and Logroller came forward. He was strong from hauling in logs for shelters and for burning in the central fire.

The two men lay on the ground and bent their forearms up at the elbows. Arm wrestling was popular among men, though Ember had never understood why. They put their hands together and slowly increased pressure. At first Logroller had the advantage, but then the youth and muscle of the other man began to tell, and the balance went the other way. But as it seemed that Tusk would win, it stopped, and they disengaged without finishing.

This mystified Ember. "Why?" she asked Clamshell in a whisper. "Tired?"

Ember doubted it. Neither looked tired. Now the headman himself was lying down and lifting his forearm to the visitor. They went at it again, and Tusk seemed to be prevailing. Then, slowly, he gave way, and then his arm went down and he lost.

But the headman wasn't as strong as Logroller! He governed by common sense and the regard of the tribesmen, not by physical strength. How could he have prevailed?

The two men got up and dusted off sand. Both were smiling. Tusk was acceptable to the tribe; he had proven himself in two ways.

Suddenly Ember understood: Tusk could have won, but had chosen to lose. Because he wanted to join the tribe, and he wanted to get along. He had shown that he was strong—and then that he deferred to the headman of this tribe. He would not use his strength to make trouble.

"Why?" Clamshell asked in return, realizing that something was going on.

"Nice," Ember said. "Strong. Good."

"Oh." Clamshell was not the brightest girl, but she could appreciate this. A strong man who was nice made a better mate than one who was brutal. Some of the tribe's couples were happier than others.

Now it was Scorch's turn. He was slender and did not have much muscle. "Fire," he said.

That was interesting. Blaze tended the village fire, but one day he would depart. Then who would do it? There was an art to fire tending, and no one wanted a clumsy or careless fire tender. If Scorch was good, he would be welcome.

The main threat to fire was water. A good fire man knew how to protect his fire from rain. Scorch would be tested.

Now Blaze got involved. He took burning sticks from his fire and made a new fire some distance to the side. Scorch took this fire and built it up into a better one. Then he dug down into the dirt and sand, making a hole, and put some of the fire down in that. He made a deeper channel away from it. Then he arranged some wider sticks in a crisscross pattern over the center of the smaller flame. This had the effect of stifling the fire somewhat, and it sent up lots of smoke. A number of villagers were mystified. But Ember saw Blaze nodding, and she too knew what Scorch was doing. He was preparing for rain.

Then the headman signaled to the six girls. "Water," he said.

The oldest girl understood. She went to get a large water-carrying shell. The others followed. They dipped their shells in the sea and brought them up brimming. Then they ran in a line toward the new fire, where Scorch stood protectively astride it. It must have been hot for his legs, but he didn't move.

The first girl passed the fire, and dashed her water at the man. It splashed all over him, but didn't douse the fire. The next one came, aiming at the fire, but Scorch moved his body and intercepted most of it, again saving the fire. He was agile, and though the next two girls wet him down farther, the fire still blazed. Finally Clamshell and Ember came up. Clamshell aimed her water at his face, but Ember aimed hers down between his legs, to get at the fire. Because he was distracted by Clamshell's water, he couldn't stop Ember's, and she scored directly on it. There was a tremendous hissing, and smoke and steam billowed up.

But Scorch got down and blew into the hole he had made—and in a moment a flame showed. The fire still burned, down in the protected hole. The water drained away along the channel, unable to reach the fire. He had survived the "rain." He was an adequate fire keeper.

Now it was time for the men to choose. The six girls lined up again. Tusk approached the line, and indicated the oldest and prettiest of them. Ember heard Clamshell's intake of breath; she had hoped he would choose her. Ember was surprised he hadn't, for he had certainly looked closely.

The chosen girl stepped forward, accepting the suit. She put her arms around Tusk and kissed him. Then she led him toward her section of the main shelter. They would consummate their union and henceforth be a couple.

Now it was Scorch's turn. He walked along the line of five girls, and chose Clamshell. But she, seeing the awful ugly burn on his arm, hesitated, then demurred. She would not step forward. Ember knew that this was a difficult decision for her, but Clamshell was so well endowed that she could probably get a man who suited her better.

Scorch was evidently disappointed, but he could not force her to accept his suit. The girl had to agree. After a moment he moved to the side and selected the next plumpest girl. But she, too, demurred. That scar was just too ugly, and Scorch was neither large nor muscular. He had saved his fire, but he just wasn't impressive enough in other respects. Not to the girls. Ember saw the headman and headwoman grimace at the turndowns; they knew the value of fire, and wanted Scorch in the tribe. But they were not going to demand that one of the girls accept the suit.

Ember's heart was beating violently. Was he going to choose her next? She didn't want to turn him down too. It wasn't that the scar bothered her; that was a problem with fire tending. It was that she didn't want to lose Blaze, even though she knew that her love for him was hopeless.

Scorch bowed his head. He turned away. He was not interested in any of the three remaining girls. He would go on to another tribe, one that perhaps had a greater need for a fire tender.

Ember's relief at not being chosen shifted within her. This tribe *would* need a new fire man, and Scorch was competent. Whoever took him would always have access to the fire. She knew she couldn't have Blaze. Wouldn't it make sense to take Scorch?

But he hadn't chosen her. She was too thin, and she didn't have full breasts, and she wasn't eager to mate yet anyway. So she was out, and it might be a year before another man came looking for a woman, by which time she might be ready. But it was unlikely to be a fire man, and in any event one of the other girls would probably take him first.

Scorch was probably the closest she could come to the fire, without mating with Blaze. She would be glad to wait for Blaze, but couldn't; they were of one tribe, and had to separate. So she came to a frightening decision, and acted on it before she could lose her flash of courage.

"Scorch!" she cried.

Surprised, he turned and looked back. Ember stepped forward.

There was a general murmur of surprise and dismay. This was not the way it was done. He had not chosen her. Worse, she saw Blaze, appalled; he did not want to lose her any more than she wanted to lose him.

Scorch was staring blankly at her. She knew he was seeing what the others saw: nothing much. But there were ways. She could not choose him, but she might be able to make him choose her.

"Ember," she said, tapping her breastbone. "Fire." She gestured to the village hearth, to indicate that she related to it.

There was a flicker of interest in his face. She encouraged it. She performed the Woman Show. She did not have the body for it that some did, but she was limber and she knew the motions, having practiced them many times with other girls. She skipped on the sand, and whirled, and jumped, trying to make the motions lithe, demonstrating her health. She unbound her hair, letting the seaweed tie drop, so that her brown tresses swirled around her. She thrust out one hip, and then the other, using the positions to make her lower form seem more ample than it was. She took her two modest breasts in her hands and squeezed them up and together, making them seem larger. The Woman Show, accentuating desirability. Then she spread her knees and thrust her pelvis forward, indicating readiness for copulation. She turned around and lifted and parted her buttocks, showing that she could handle a penis from either side. The Woman Show, getting specific. She raised her arms and waved them, emulating the leaping tongues of a fire: a man who tended a fire should like a woman who related well to it. The activity warmed her and made her feel more confident. Then, breathing hard, she stopped, and stood in front of Scorch. She fixed him with a direct stare, half-smiling. She could not have made her interest more plain.

Scorch was studying her closely now, reconsidering. Behind him and peripherally, she saw the expressions of the villagers: satisfyingly awestruck. They had not known she could do the Woman Show so well. They thought of her as a child, despite her technical eligibility. No more!

Still he hesitated. He raised his scarred arm, as if inviting her to be repulsed by it.

"Fire," she repeated. "Burn." She showed a smaller burn on her left hand, from the time she had misjudged a hot coal. She showed another on her arm, a scar she had always tried to conceal before, because burns were not pretty.

That did it. Scorch smiled. He gestured, indicating Ember as his choice.

Relieved, she stepped into him, embracing and kissing him, fulfilling the ritual. She pressed against his midsection, feeling his penis hard behind the fold of the cloak. Yes, she had made an impression! Then she led him to the shelter.

In a kind of daze she saw the others of the tribe, their faces showing their mixed feelings. The four remaining girls were surprised, relieved, envious and appalled. The mated women were disapproving. But a number of the men were nodding appreciatively. That gladdened her. She had played at being a woman, and had succeeded in becoming one. Best of all, the headman was grinning; now the tribe would have a good new fire man.

But Blaze's face was frozen in numb horror. He had had foolish dreams, as she had; now they were gone. What would he do? She hurt for him, and for herself; but she had done what she knew was best.

They entered the shelter. Tusk and his mate had already completed their first mergence, and were lying relaxed. Both their jaws dropped when they saw Scorch and Ember. Then they got up and left the shelter, so that the new couple could be alone. Privacy was not essential for the act, but it was considered helpful for the first time.

But they paused a moment before stepping out, turning full face toward Scorch and Ember. Tusk's penis was hanging low. Then he donned his shawl, covering it.

This was part of the ritual. That penis had obviously been used. The first mating had been accomplished.

Ember's place was a mat of dry grass and leaves, comfortable enough for one but not for two. But surely comfort was not on Scorch's mind at the moment. Ember had heard that the first time was usually uncomfortable, but that it was always better subsequently. She was prepared; it surely would not be worse than the burns she had suffered.

She looked at him, standing there. He looked at her. She saw that he wasn't much older than she, perhaps only two years. He was not experienced, of course. Maybe he had believed that none of the girls would accept him, and was as surprised by her action as she was herself.

She knew how it was done, having seen it many times. The mechanics were simple enough. Indeed, it could be taken as an amplification of the Woman Show.

Still Scorch did not act. He seemed not to know what to do. That gave Ember confidence. She put her hands to his wet shawl and drew it off. Still he stood, still bemused. His penis had lost its strength. It was as if the notion excited him, but the reality frightened him.

Ember knew exactly how that was, for she was experiencing it herself. Her cheek was quivering. But his weakness gave her strength. She knew that it would be a phenomenal humiliation for them both if they did not mate now. She became bolder. She embraced him, squeezing her slender body against his, and kissed him. She made some of the motions of the Woman Show, in miniature.

He began to respond, seeming in a daze. She knew how that was, too. She had thought no man would choose her, and he had thought no woman would accept him. She had *made* him choose her, and now she would make him complete their union. Because it did need to be done, lest they both become the objects of ridicule. There had been a coupling three years back when there had been a suspicion that the man had not adequately performed, and his reputation had suffered until finally he had had to make a fully public demonstration. Ember did not want to experience anything like that, especially since others would think she was the cause, being too young and thin to be sexual. So she brought him down to the mat, and led him through it, playing with him as she had seen other women do with their men, making him react. More important, she smiled as if she thought him wonderful, and kissed him frequently. Men, too, needed to believe they were desirable, she realized. Gradually his response increased, and finally he became hot and hard and shoved into her with vigor. It was uncomfortable, but no more so than she had anticipated, and very soon it was over.

Then he looked at her with surprise, realizing that he had done it. He had been awkward and nervous, and now was neither. "Ember," he said. "Good."

"Good," she agreed, though for her it had been an act of achievement rather than pleasure.

But he argued. "Scorch. Bad. Ember. Good."

It was *her* he was complimenting, rather than the sex! Inordinately pleased, she drew him close and kissed him with special passion. She was, indeed, getting to like him, partly because of his uncertainty.

At that point another person entered the shelter. The timing could not have been better! It looked as if they had been ferociously passionate throughout.

Scorch appreciated the coincidence. As the kiss broke, he turned toward the intruder, spreading his legs to show his spent penis. Thus the signal had been made, to the first person they encountered after the mating. The union was complete.

The intruder was the headwoman. She nodded. Perhaps she had been concerned that Ember would not be able to perform satisfactorily, because of her youth. Such a failure would not have reflected well on the village. That doubt had been abolished.

They got up and went out. A feast was being prepared. Everyone would have a good time. Two girls had found mates, and the tribe had gained two good men.

But she saw that Blaze did not join in the festivity. She had hurt him, she knew, and she felt bad about that. She was sure he understood why she had done it, but still she felt the grief of it. She had taken the closest approach to Blaze she could manage: another young fire tender. Yet it was in its way a betrayal of their love.

The next day Blaze left the tribe. Ember did not see him go. That hurt her worse. She had hoped at least to smile at him, to remind him that she still loved him, for what that might have been worth. Now he was gone, and she felt guilty as well as grieved. She had made what she believed was a good choice, but not the *best* choice, because it was impossible to have Blaze himself.

The woman of the Isle made the necessary shifts. She staggered her babies, having one every year or so, the new one nursing as the older one was weaned. To accomplish this she had to become both fertile and sexually appealing while still caring for a child, so that her man would never stray. So nature reversed the ploy. Instead of expanding her breasts only at the time of birthing and nursing, when her infertility formerly made her sexually unappealing, she maintained them from the time of sexual maturity onward, and they became the opposite: a signal of sexual availability. Her mystery of fertility and her continuous sex appeal made it possible to have her man's constant assistance. Even when she had one or more children with her, and when living in a group containing a number of other nubile women. It was a biologically clever ploy.

Thus the human life-style as well as appearance was startlingly different from those of other hominids, here on the Isle of Woman, though the genetic changes were minor. From this point on, this would seem a species apart from all other animals. Skin mostly bare, and breasts always full. Physically it had become fully human.

In time the Isle rejoined the mainland; and modern mankind moved out. The sometime use of crude clothing by Homo erectus *became regular use when* Homo sapiens *was on land, making up for the lack of fur. With that steady covering came the conventions of modesty, further setting the species apart from all others. Where mankind went in Africa, he went now as conqueror, because of his superior organization and ability to plan ahead. When the Sahara desert alleviated, about 120,000 years before the present, the children of the Isle moved out into the larger continent. That ushered in a significant new stage, for there were other advanced hominids who were not about to give up their territories by default.*

SITE: THE LEVANT   **TIME: 45,000 B.P.**

CHAPTER 5

ART

Africa has touched or come close to the landmass of Eurasia in three places: the Strait of Gibraltar south of Spain, the Sinai Peninsula northeast of Egypt, and near the tip of the Arabian Peninsula. Mankind may have had the opportunity to cross at any of these places, and may have done so. The third is especially tempting, because that's where the Isle of Woman was. But we have evidence of crossing only in the Sinai region. The fossils indicate that modern man was in the Sinai and the Levant—the Holy Land—90,000 years ago. Herein lie several significant mysteries.

47

Europe and western Asia were occupied by Neandertal (Ne-AN-der-tal)
man, a center of controversy beginning with the spelling of his name. He seems
to have evolved directly from Homo erectus, *who had colonized Eurasia on*
the order of one million years ago, and was specially adapted to cold climate
and rough terrain. Central and eastern Asia were occupied by another product
of Homo erectus *we shall call Archaic man. These varieties of humanity had*
had several hundred thousand years to settle into their territories, had brains
and bodies just as large, and were well established. The Levant and perhaps
the Fertile Crescent—modern-day Iraq—became a region of contact among
the three variants. So perhaps it is not surprising that modern mankind took a
while to proceed farther. But he seems to have waited about 50,000 years, and
then abruptly exploded into the territories of the others, sweeping them aside in
a relative trifle. Why did he wait so long, and then move so decisively? In
addition, he seems to have had no better technology or organization than the
others did—and then abruptly improved it dramatically. This could account
for his sudden expansion, but merely substitutes one mystery for another. Why
the surprising change? He also seems to have developed all *the arts at this*
time, and been highly artistic ever since. Why not before?

The key seems to relate to language. There is no evidence that the prior
forms of man had any real language, though they may have had considerable
vocabularies. What was needed was syntax: the set of rules by which words are
combined into sentences. This seemingly minor advance did not come readily,
taking tens of thousands of years to develop, but it had an enormous impact on
communication, and on man's culture, and ultimately his destiny. Words were
symbols, and they had been used for a long time, but syntax enabled man to
manipulate those symbols and to generate phenomenal structures of compre-
hension. With the advent of complex communication, humans could share
knowledge with others, and pass it along from one generation to another. This
multiplied mankind's efficiency in many areas, particularly technology: his
tools and weapons became more sophisticated, giving him a significant
advantage in competition with nonlanguage folk. That technology enabled
him to conquer the world.

This leaves two of the mysteries. Since it seems that man's physical
development, including that of the brain, was complete by the time he left the
Isle of Woman, why did it take so long for him to discover how to use that brain
more efficiently? And why did the arts flower simultaneously? What did they
have to do with speech and technology? Coincidence seems unlikely; nature
always has a reason.

Perhaps the answer appeared about 45,000 years ago, in the Levant. It is also possible that it happened earlier, in Africa, near Lake Victoria, and spread from there to the Levant, but that evidence is not yet solid. The place and time are not that important; what counts is why.

BLAZE was using a sharp stone knife to carve a plump female human figure from soft wood when the girl approached. "May I join you, Blaze?" she inquired, employing the confusingly rapid and complicated succession of words these folk did.

He glanced at her. She was brown-haired and pretty of feature, though as yet lank in the body. "Bunny," he said, nodding affirmatively.

She looked at the carving. "You are doing well."

He laughed. He could not begin to match the proficiency of the women or children of this tribe, any more than he could speak as they did. He could only try to emulate them, inadequately.

"Tell me how you came here," Bunny said.

He smiled wryly. She well knew that he had been dragged in on a travois, unconscious, four years ago. She had been one of the children watching. "Bad," he said.

"No, I mean before then. You were young when you left your tribe—younger than I am now. Too young to seek a mate or to survive on your own. What impelled you to set out unprepared?"

He caught the key words in her flow of dialogue: young, tribe, mate, survive. She was asking for his background. He had not tried to speak of it before, being embarrassed. But her interest was flattering.

"Girl," he explained. "Love." He crossed his hands over his heart, augmenting the word. "Man. Mate."

"I understand," Bunny said. "You loved a girl but she took another man. You had to go from there."

"Me choose hard," he agreed, trying to emulate her flowing expression. "Me walk alone. Me join tribe."

Bunny could not contain her merriment. She had always been a happy girl, somewhat mischievous and presuming. In that, she reminded him painfully of his lost love. Indeed, she was thirteen, about that girl's age when he had lost her. How young that seemed, in retrospect!

"Now you had a difficult choice," Bunny said carefully, coaching him.

He tried. "Now you had—"

She tittered. "Now *who* had?"

Oh, yes. "Now *me* had. Hard—"

"Now *I* had," she said firmly.

He shook his head. "Bunny. Me not know. Stupid."

"No, Blaze," she said earnestly. "You are not stupid. You are doing better than any of the other immigrant adults here. No one else can speak as we who were raised in this language do. You are making progress. You are good. You must keep trying."

He spread his hands, still baffled by her elaborate and rapid spiel of words. He knew she was making sense, for he had seen other children and their mothers transmit the most complicated instructions, but his ear could not assimilate more than snatches of it.

Bunny sighed. "I'm sorry. One thing at a time. You can get it, I know. Say 'I.'"

That much he thought he could do. "I hard. I walk alone. I join tribe."

She smiled. "That's better. You had a difficult choice. You could try to survive alone, or you could try to join another tribe."

The nuances of her syntax were beyond him, but the essence came through when she rephrased his words. He continued his narrative.

Neither of his original alternatives had seemed feasible. He was a fire tender; he lacked proper experience hunting or gathering. He had brought a bit of fire with him, so he would always have a hearth, but that was not enough. He had to try to join a tribe.

But it soon had been apparent that no nearby tribe had need of a novice fire tender, and none of their girls wished to mate with a twelve-year-old boy. Especially not one with an ugly red burn mark on his forehead. Blaze had to give it up and try to make it by himself. He got hungry and tired, and finally had no strength left to walk farther, and then none to sit up. His last memory was of the grass at his cheek as he lay facedown beside the trail leading to nowhere.

"And when you woke, you were in our tribe," Bunny said brightly. "I remember when they dragged you in. We thought you were dead. But all you needed was food and water."

"Food," he agreed wanly. "Water. Not why."

"You did not understand why our men had brought you," she agreed. "It was because they were out fetching babies. They saw you were young, and since they hadn't found any babies that day, they brought you in instead."

For this was an unusual tribe. It had started long ago with the rejects of other tribes—men who had not been accepted for mating. The ugly, or incompetent, or old—some of whom had been cast out by their tribes because they were no longer sufficiently useful. They had been expected to die, but some had survived and formed their own band. There had gotten to be about twenty of them, culled from all across the region. Then a woman had come. She was young and reasonably attractive, but had been cast out because she was barren. She wanted more than anything else to be a mother. She thought that perhaps if she tried harder, she could get a baby. So she tried, with every man of the band who was willing. She was able to try several times a day. But she didn't get a baby, despite an effort that continued for years.

Then one of the men brought in a baby that had been left out to die. It was a boy several months old and he seemed healthy. Perhaps his mother had died, so there was no one to care for him. The woman fed him with water and fruit juice and mashed nuts, and he lost weight but finally managed to survive. The woman was pleased. She had a son. The band had a child.

After that they fetched in any babies they found. Most of them died, and the tribe ate the meat. But some survived. In time there was a fair number. There were also other women, some old, some ugly, but they were willing to work and they had knowledge that helped more babies to survive. The haphazard band had become a tribe, of sorts.

As time passed there were more surviving children, male and female. Because there were no nursing mothers, they were raised together, with several adults always watching over them and supervising their feeding. The children quickly learned the words used by their diverse "parents" and began communicating among themselves. At first they were satisfied with the individual words, but then something strange happened. They began making up words of their own that the adults didn't understand, because they seemed to be meaningless. But somehow they served to put the regular words together, making them more versatile. The children played games, finding ever-more-sophisticated modes of communication. It got so that if an adult wanted to organize something complicated, he conveyed it to one child with attendant gestures and demonstration, and that child then went and spewed out a rapid series of words and not-words to the others—and all of them understood precisely. It was a marvel.

For example, once there had been a rare find: a large animal had been accidentally killed in a distant valley. Men from two groups had spied the fresh carcass. One man had trudged home and taken the time necessary to indicate the situation. Since his tribe was not far away, there was no immediate rush. But the other group had been this one, and there had been a boy along. He had had a notion, run swiftly home alone—and all the other children had understood him immediately. They had indicated to the mystified adults what was required, conveying extreme urgency, and the entire group had traveled swiftly to the site. They had plunged in, carving up the body and hauling the sections away on travois, while the children spread out to watch for members of the other tribe. When the men of the other tribe approached, the children gave warning, and the procedure was hastened. When the others arrived, the entire beast was gone. Rapid and accurate communication had enabled the home group to prevail. They had eaten well for some time thereafter.

As the children grew to maturity, their facility continued. Now, as decision-making adults, they increased their power. They converted the haphazard group into a tightly organized tribe. Their communication seemed magical. They discussed strategies among themselves, and devised shortcut signals, so that a single hoot across the forest could mean that there was something worth getting, and convey its nature. Sometimes they managed to steal meat from other tribes, by making highly organized raids. When other tribes tried to retaliate, they found nothing, because lookouts spotted them and indicated exactly how many were coming on what path, and when they would arrive.

For all that, the children, together with their maturing members, were fun-loving and creative. They laughed often at things that left the others blank. It seemed that there were verbal games that only they understood. They made sketches in the dirt, discussing them in detail—and after that they were able to separate and come together at another place by several different routes, simultaneously. Blaze had seen it happen, and remained mystified.

"We draw maps," Bunny explained. "We devise routes, and agree to go to particular places at particular times, and—"

"Times?" Blaze asked, catching a word he knew he didn't know.

"A morning, or noon, or night, or another day," she said. "Or noon plus the distance the sun travels a finger width. Timing is essential, especially when we have to fight. We review what happened yesterday, and plan for tomorrow."

But it was too much for Blaze. His mind simply couldn't grasp their weird concepts. How the sun traveling a finger width related to fighting hostile tribesmen would always be a mystery to him.

"But not to your children," Bunny said wisely. "When a baby grows up with us, he learns our way. Somehow it seems to happen when children are little; they must learn then, or they never do. So our nursing mothers do not go out to forage; they stay with the nursery, so their babies can learn from the others. This makes it harder to bring in as much to eat, but it must be. We make up for it by being more clever in the foraging and hunting we do."

Indeed they were more clever. When a hunting party went out, the men had better weapons, because craftsmen were better at making them. Whatever one person knew, he conveyed to others, and this resulted in superior technique. These folk were like a species apart, much smarter than anyone elsewhere.

"Would you like to have children like that?" Bunny inquired.

"Me—child—smart?" he asked, working out her import. "Yes." Certainly he would like to have children of his own who could be like that. He appreciated the wonders of their cleverness, and wondered why this intelligent tribe tolerated dull folk like him in its midst. True, he tended the fires well, but any of the clever ones could do it as well or better, because they had comprehension he lacked.

She looked him in the eye. "Then be my mate, and I will give them to you."

"Me—mate—Bunny?" He laughed, dismissing it as humor. He was too stupid to join this tribe, and she was too young.

But she did not laugh with him. "I must mate with a man from another tribe, but I prefer not to take a stranger. I have known you four years, since I was nine, and in all that time you have been reliable and gentle. I like you, Blaze, and I want you for my own. And if you like this tribe, as I know you do, you can remain in it for the rest of your life, by mating with one of its women. With me. Why not do it?"

He stared at her. She seemed to be serious! "You—child," he said. "Me—ugly." He touched his off-color forehead.

"You think the mark of your profession makes you ugly?" she asked. "That for your ugliness!" And she kissed him on the forehead, right on the mark.

He was amazed. He just couldn't believe that this child could be ready for anything like this. He had never thought of her in that way. But now he realized that her eyes were green, and that in her approach she resembled the one he had loved. Could it be? She had always been alert and bright and humorous, but she had never teased. When she spoke seriously, she always meant what she said.

"As for me," she said, "I will dance for you." She looked back over her shoulder, catching the eye of a boy about her own age who seemed to have been waiting for the signal. He began to pat his hands on a drum, which was an invention of the smart folk. It was a section of a sapling tied into a circle, with an animal hide fastened tautly across it. *Boom-boom-boom-boom,* a regular and pleasant beat.

Bunny got up and went into the Woman Show. It was as if Blaze's lost love were doing it; the memory was painful yet exciting. She turned and leaped, and flung out her hips and her hair, and the flesh of her body shook in ways he had not before appreciated in connection with her. She had indeed grown into a young woman, and now she was showing it. She was beautiful.

But there was more to it than that. Bunny was not naked, she was clothed, wearing a woven skirt. Her motions were not random or impromptu, but choreographed. Her feet touched the ground in time to the beat of the drum—and now others had appeared, and were humming, also to that beat. As the folk of this tribe made attractive wood carvings, or finely pointed stone knives, or intricate pictures in sand, so too did they dance. She was showing her art. When she spun, and her skirt flung out, showing glimpses of her upper thighs and genital section, she excited his sexual interest—but he also appreciated the aesthetics of it. The motions and the beat, together. He knew that his appreciation was only a shadow of that felt by any of the regular folk of the tribe, but it still enhanced the effect.

By the time Bunny finished, a crowd of others had gathered. They were all enjoying the show, though none of them hoped to mate with her. That was another aspect of it: enjoyment for the sake of nothing else.

She made a final turn, and came to stand before him. "Now, don't embarrass me before this audience by refusing me," she told him. "I have publicized my desire for you. Will you take me?"

Blaze realized that he had been foolish to hang on to his impossible former love. He would probably never receive a better offer than this present one—and he had not even had to go to her. She had come to him. She had arranged this elegant proposal, drawing on the uncanny ability of her kind to plan ahead and coordinate with others. Blaze was immensely flattered. He now appreciated how easy it would be to love her. He was already experiencing the first great surge of it.

But over her shoulder Blaze saw one detail that saddened him. The boy—the young man—of the drum, who had done Bunny's bidding so well, was staring with emotional pain. He had done what he had to do, to please the girl he loved but could never mate with. Now he was suffering the agony of her loss. How well Blaze understood!

Thus the possible answers to the mysteries: when unique circumstances caused a group of babies and children to be raised in a communal situation, their single-word speech evolved into something like a pidgin, and then into a creole, on the way to becoming the first full-fledged language. This is a process that still happens when there is an assemblage of people with different linguistic backgrounds. First they communicate by means of a pidgin, which is a simplified form of a language consisting mostly of vocabulary with elementary grammatical rules. This is crude, but it gets the job done. Their children, however, raised speaking the pidgin, quickly evolve more sophisticated structure, developing a creole. This can be effective in itself, with the nuances and competence we expect in a recognized language. No one teaches these children these rules; they seem to evolve naturally, as if humanity has an inherent set of rules that emerges in the absence of an already established language. So all that is required is a vocabulary and children.

Apparently the way the brain processes language is established early, from infancy to several years of age. The fundamental paths are set up according to the available material, and do not change thereafter. If a child is raised alone, without exposure to language, his brain becomes set in an alternate mode, and he can never learn to speak with facility. The wiring is simply wrong. Thus it is not surprising that humanity did not develop full language early. As with a dry field that remains untouched until there is a spark that starts a fire, then burns vigorously, the process is not automatic. The potential is there, but not the realization. When chance, after perhaps 50,000 years, provided a suitable vocabulary to a group of children in the formative stage, they reshaped it into something more. Always before, babies had been constantly with their mothers, normally one at a time, so that they could nurse regularly, and their mothers were out foraging. There was no permanent community of children. Once that occurred, and language developed, it continued, for subsequent children were exposed not to isolated words but to the full language of their parents. The nature of the human mind was literally changed. There was nothing inevitable about it, any more than there is about the striking of a spark that ignites a fire.

What about the arts? This was tied to language, not as an effect, but as a corollary. In order to develop language, mankind's mind had to be reprogrammed to be able to manipulate symbols. When that sophistication was achieved, there turned out to be a broader application of that ability: the appreciation of art. To draw another analogy: at one time our ancestors had color vision, then lost it, and later regained it. The ability to perceive color is an obvious advantage to those who eat fruit; with it, a person can go immediately to that one fruit out of a dozen that is ripe, instead of wasting his energy picking green fruits. Color perception thus became a survival skill, because if the number of ripe fruits is limited, those people who are slow will go hungry. But once that ability was developed for the immediate selfish purpose of snatching the best fruits, it also enabled that person to see and appreciate the beauty of the sunset. A form of art became possible, as a corollary. Similarly, the development of the ability to manipulate word symbols efficiently, for complete language, opened the mind to all the other symbolism available. The arts: sculpture, painting, music, dance—and, within the language, the larger symbolism of storytelling. All gifts of that first great breakthrough that made mankind become modern in mind as well as body. Thus this was perhaps the most significant single breakthrough of the species—and it never showed in the body.

CHAPTER 6

VOYAGE

"With full language came improvements in all the works of modern mankind. The arts flourished, but it was technology that enabled humans to expand their territory. The other primate species were physically stronger, and had prior possession of the land, but they could not compete against the superior weapons and organization of the invaders. Thus by about 40,000 years ago (there is doubt about the date, but this seems like the most reasonable case) our kind was making inroads into what had for 50,000 years been forbidden territory: the country to the east. At this time the ice age was in full force and still intensifying; glaciers covered northern Europe, and there were

57

small glaciers in mountainous regions farther south. Thus mankind followed
the warmer terrain to India, southeast Asia, and on to the island chains
beyond. The glaciers took up so much of the world's water that the sea level was
hundreds of feet lower than it is today, and there was more land exposed. But
finally they ran out of land, and had to cross open water, uncertain whether
there was any haven beyond.

W HY are we going away?'' Crystal asked as they carried baskets of
dried fruit to the great raft. She was four years old, and curious
about everything.

Ember used the question as a pretext to rest, briefly, for her basket
was heavy and she was sweating. She had always been physically healthy,
but had mated perhaps too young, and it had taken her two years to get
pregnant. Then her first baby had been stillborn. Crystal had been born
when Ember was sixteen, and done well, but food had been short and
Ember had had to nurse her until just recently. The same had happened
throughout the tribe, and the birthrate had declined, for normally a
woman did not conceive again until she weaned the prior child. The
tribe needed more territory and better hunting and gathering, so that
food became plentiful again and the women got less lean.

But Ember did not care to have her daughter understand just how
grim the picture was. The mere contemplation of it made her cheek
twitch. What point, to tell the child that not only did they face possible
starvation, they faced destruction as a tribe? For the hostile Green
Feather Tribe was advancing across the island, intent on putting an end
to the People Tribe. There was no doubt about what they would do, if
they could, for they had proclaimed it: kill the men, enslave the
children, and divide the women into three camps. One camp for the old
or ugly, who would be hobbled by having the tendon of one foot cut,
and who would then work as directed or starve. One camp for the
desirable young women who were willing to serve whatever men chose
them, their children by those men becoming members of the Green
Feather Tribe. One camp for desirable young women who refused to
serve, and who would therefore be bound, hobbled, raped, and fed only
as long as men desired them for further rape. No, Ember would not tell
Crystal that her father would be killed outright and her mother raped
and maimed, or that Crystal herself would be put in a camp for children

where she would be worked to death if a Green Feather family did not choose to adopt her. That perhaps she was already too old for such adoption, because she would cry about the loss of her family, and refuse to be consoled by any other family. So she might simply be thrown into the sea and forgotten.

"This land is worn," Ember said carefully. "Its animals and birds are almost gone, and so are its fruits and nuts and tubers. We are living mostly on shellfish. It is time for us to find a new land, where there is plenty to hunt and forage."

"But where is there any other land?" the girl asked. "The Bad Tribe has the land behind, and there is no land ahead. Just the sea."

"There is land ahead," Ember said. "We can not see it, because the sea is wide, but it is there. We know because one of our small rafts was lost in a storm, and the wind blew it far away across the sea, and it came to new land there. Then the men managed to paddle back here to tell us of it." She did not express her own severe doubt about that land, because of four men originally on the raft, two had been lost in the storm, another had expired on the way back, and the lone survivor had been found far out, raving. The only thing that lent credence to his story was the seed of a strange fruit found on the raft, like none known before. But Ember suspected that he could have been blown to one of the islands of the chain, back behind their own, inhabited by other tribes who perhaps found strange fruits. Not a new land at all.

"Will it be fun?" Crystal asked.

Fun? Ember dreaded it! She had seen how angry the sea could be, and she feared to face it herself. The men went out daily on the small rafts to spear fish, staying close to land, but even then the sudden storms could catch them. It was the consensus of the tribal elders that the current should carry the rafts across in the course of three to five days. The storm had taken the one small raft across in one day, but that was not the preferred way. Sometimes a lunar month went by without a real storm, but sometimes two storms occurred in a day. It would be a horrible gamble, braving the sea for five days, out of sight of the land. The very notion of losing sight of land appalled her.

"It may not be fun, but it is necessary," Ember said, as carefully as before. "We shall have to make the best of it." And hope that they all did not die.

"I think it will be fun," the child said brightly. "Daddy says we'll have a house on the raft, and even fire."

Ember smiled. "Daddy is right, of course. It should be fun." Oh for the innocence of childhood! She remembered when she had been Crystal's age, going out gathering with her mother just after a fire had burned the land, and encountering a dangerous animal, so that they had had to retreat to the water. She had been delighted at the time, but now realized how risky that had been. Her own mother had shielded her not only from danger, but from the knowledge of danger. Now Ember was doing the same for Crystal.

They picked up their burdens and resumed their walk. They followed the path down to the harbor where the three big rafts were. These were quite different from the little ones; in fact they were enormous. Two were already in the water, while the men were still making the third. They were of stout bamboo, lashed together with tough vines. They looked like the mats used on the floors of their houses. That was not surprising, because the mats were made of small bamboo; the principle was the same. When these went to sea, they would tow the small rafts along with them, to use as shuttles between the big ones, and for fishing. If they didn't have to take apart too many of the small ones to provide cord for the last big one. So far they had gotten by without doing that, but they were getting pressed for time and materials.

They walked down to the shore, and then out on the stepping-stones leading to their raft. Ember went first, making sure the footing was secure. When she stepped on the edge of the raft with her burden, the surface of it hardly gave way. The bound bamboo poles were each the thickness of her fist, and their air-filled segments made them light and strong. They were much better than wood for this purpose. It was impossible for such a raft to sink, and almost impossible for it to be battered apart. But savage waves could still wash things and people off the surface and into the sea.

They crossed the floating mat to the cabin in the center. This too was made of bound bamboo, with smaller poles bound between a frame-work made of larger ones. The cabin seemed small, but was actually large enough for more than twenty people to sleep, snugly fitted. Each raft would hold more than thirty people, but the others would be outside paddling most of the time. If a storm came, those others could cling to the projecting poles of the cabin. They might get battered by the water, but they wouldn't get washed overboard. These rafts had been designed with survival rather than comfort in mind.

"Oooo, fun!" Crystal exclaimed, delighted by the cabin. She ran into it and out again, and peeked at Ember around a corner.

Ember set down her bag and took out the fruits, placing each carefully in the bamboo trunk built into the cabin. The water could be seen below the floor, and that was intentional: any rain or wave would flow right on through, instead of collecting on the raft. The tribe had had experience with rafts for generations, and knew many tricks like this. But no one had ever before made rafts this big, or tried to float them this far. Ember's worry warred with her awe of the accomplishment, and her worry was winning.

There was a cry from the shore. "Ember!"

She set down the last of the fruit and went out. "I am here!" she called back. It was a messenger boy of about ten. He was Sand, so named for the color of his hair.

He crossed the stepping-stones and came onto the raft. "Boo!" Crystal cried, jumping out from behind the cabin.

Sand stiffened, stepped back, and waved his arms as if about to fall overboard, while the child laughed. He was a good sport. Then he entered the cabin, where Ember was arranging the fruit to fit tightly, wasting no space. She knew that they might have to survive on the raft longer than they planned, so they needed plenty of food. They would be fishing, of course, but fish were chancy while fruit was sure. With luck, they would catch lots of fish, and have fruit left over when they reached land. With luck.

"Hide—I'll find you," the boy said to Crystal. She disappeared with a giggle. Then, to Ember, he murmured, "Bad news. Scorch is hurt."

A chill passed across her as if a cold wind had stirred. Scorch had gone out to collect special wood for the voyage: dense, slow-burning varieties that were hard to douse with water. They did not want to lose their fire in a storm! What had happened?

"Green Feather," Sand said in a low tone, so that Crystal could not hear. Then, to be sure, he turned his head and called, "Are you ready? I'm going to find you!" And back to Ember: "They are coming in fast. They surprised him. He killed one and got free, but with a spear in his back. We drove them away, but he is bleeding. He is at the center house."

Ember strode from the cabin. "Play with Crystal," she said tersely. "Give me time."

He nodded. He ducked out and around the corner. "I'm going to find you!" he called again. There was a hidden titter.

Ember paused at the edge of the raft. "Don't fall in the water, Crystal," she said. "I will see you when I bring the next bag." She crossed the stones and hurried to the main house of the village.

Scorch was lying there, with two women trying to help him. There was blood-soaked material beside them. "Oh my love!" Ember cried, getting down to hug him as well as she could without hurting him. "Are you all right?"

"I am now," he said bravely. "It's not serious."

She soon saw that it was intermediate: the spear had glanced off a rib and torn through the flesh of his side. It surely hurt terribly, and he had lost blood, but he would not die. If he didn't get a death-dealing fever.

"We need to get you by a fire," Ember said. Because there seemed to be less illness by the fire. Sometimes wounded men got a fever that killed them, but less often when they were kept hot from the outset.

They got him to the fire and built it up so that he was bathed in the heat. Ember cleaned the wound and put bandages on him, binding them tightly enough to stop the blood. "It was my best day, when you chose me as your mate," Scorch said as he relaxed for sleep.

Ember kissed him, then hurried back to reclaim Crystal. Scorch was a good man, and he had not disappointed her. She could have done much worse, gambling as she had on a stranger. She knew now that a man of fire was not necessarily an ideal mate. Scorch had grown with time and added responsibility, and was well regarded in the tribe, and a good father too. Yet somehow she retained her longing for the ideal man she might have had, the one who was not merely good, but perfect. For the one she had loved but had not been able to have. She did her best to conceal that secret longing from Scorch, but feared that he suspected it. She felt guilty about it, but even in this hour of Scorch's injury she could not quite abolish her foolish dream.

She met Sand and Crystal near the shore. They had finished their game and were returning to the village. "Mommy! You forgot your bag of fruit!" Crystal cried.

So she had. But now it was time to tell her daughter the truth—

gently, with reassurances, so that she wouldn't panic. Ember braced herself for the words.

○

Next day Scorch was stable. It seemed that the bad fever was not attacking him, but he was weak. He would have to rest for several days while his wound healed.

But the Green Feather Tribe was offering no respite. They were aware that the People were planning to escape, and they didn't want it. They wanted children to adopt and women to use. They also wanted to be sure that the People didn't ally with some other tribe and return to drive the Green Feathers from the island. They also wanted the big rafts, which would aid their own fishing. So they were coming right on in to complete the conquest immediately. They would close in on the village in the afternoon, because they would be traveling in the morning. They knew that the People needed several more days to get ready, but could leave as early as tomorrow if they left their third raft unfinished.

Which was the problem. Two rafts were almost ready, and could be pushed out to sea soon. The third was not ready. They needed more time to complete it and load it with food. They could not stand and fight; the Green Feathers were too numerous and vicious. What could they do?

"Go to the senior meeting," Scorch told her, when she acquainted him with the situation. "Tell them that only fire will stop the enemy. We must burn the grass, the forest, even our own village, to keep them at bay while we escape. And when we are gone and they come in, they will have nothing but ashes. Tell them I will rouse myself and do it."

"You can't do it," she protested. "You are too weak."

"I can do it," he insisted. "I know how to set the fires, as they do not. I can read the wind and the vegetation, to make a wall that will burn them."

"But you will use up your last strength," she said. "You will be caught by your own fire, and die."

"No," he said.

"Don't tell me no," she said. "I know the fire too. I know your injury. I will not let you sacrifice yourself."

He saw that he had not fooled her. "I must, Ember," he said. "To save

you, and Crystal, and the People. If I do not, much worse will happen.
You know I must do it."

She knew he *would* do it, if she did not prevent it. "I will do it," she
said firmly. "I will set the fires, and still have strength to return. You
know this is better."

He seemed to want to argue, but she cut him off by leaving. She went
right to the senior meeting, where the nine senior men were consulting.
"I bring word from Scorch," she announced. "We must use fire to stop
them. If we set fires now, they will burn toward the enemy, and spread,
and safeguard our retreat to the rafts."

"But fire will burn our village too," a senior objected.

"Scorch says that it will—but that this means that the Green Feathers
will inherit only ashes from us."

The men exchanged glances, nodding. They liked that notion. None
of them were from the Green Feather Tribe, because it had come from
elsewhere, attacking and destroying the local tribes. The tribes these
men had left behind had been taken by the Green Feathers. Even if the
People had the strength to stand their ground, they would not admit any
Green Feather men, or allow their own men to join that tribe.
Destruction was the only answer.

"But can Scorch do it?" one man asked. "He is injured."

"He can not," Ember replied evenly. "But I can. I know the fire too. I
will set the island ablaze."

"But you are a woman!"

"Smaller loss if I am captured," she retorted.

"Perhaps," one said, with a flattering doubt. "Do what you must. We
shall see to the evacuation. We will be at sea by dusk, though
unprepared."

"See that my child Crystal goes with her father."

They nodded. They knew that this was no routine mission that Ember
was about to undertake. Her chances of returning safely were not ideal.
If she did not do so by dusk, she would be stranded. No one needed to
remind her what that would mean.

Ember wasted no time. She made up a good firepot nestled in a shell,
with several stout slow-burning leaves to hold the coals in, and plenty of
punk in the middle. She took several slender dry sticks, and a bag of dry
moss, so that she would not have to forage for flame material in the
field. She donned a stout harness to hold a pack containing these things.

She knew she looked much like a man now, because of the way her stout jacket-cape covered her breasts, but that was good. She intended to do a man's work today.

Ember set out as the villagers hurried to get the last preparations done. Another woman was carrying the remaining fruits to the raft. Crystal was with Scorch, and would be taken onto the raft when he was. Anything they could not load by dusk would be left for the fire to destroy.

She held a bit of material up to test the wind. It was starting to stir, going out from the warming land to the sea. That was the wrong direction, but she knew it would change by dusk. She merely had to get far enough away to be sure the fire would not close on the village too soon. Then it would turn and drive on the Green Feathers, who would have to flee it. It would have to cross over some of its own ashes, but the rising breeze would lift it to the treetops that had been dried by its first passage, and instead of a grass fire it would be a tree fire, much worse. It would do the job, if she got it started in the right places at the right time.

She started the first fire near the shore, so that the enemy would not be able to go around it and reach the village too soon. She got down and brought out her smoldering punk. She blew on it, and got dry leaves burning. Soon there was a fire, slowly expanding. Slowness was the key; she needed it to grow to its prime later, when the enemy would be trying to pass this section.

She moved inland, starting fires at appropriate intervals. There had not been recent rain, so this part was relatively easy. The wind was rising moderately, stirring the fires to greater effort, and they would soon link together and form a wall.

Then the wind reversed course, unpredictable as it often was, and the fires started to pursue her. Fire could move rapidly when it chose. This was good, because it meant that she would not have to go farther inland; the fire would take itself there faster than she could go.

But when she turned to cut back to the village, secure behind the expanding line of fires that were not yet burning in that direction, she discovered that it had grown too well. The wind had whipped an arm of flame between her and the village already. She would have to go the other way, outside the forming fire wall, and that had its own special risk.

She hurried, hoping she would be lucky. But she was not. As she crested a hill and started down toward the shore, she saw men. They were between her and the sea, and the fire was behind her. She was caught.

She knew what to do. She turned and ran directly for the fire. But the men pursued her, and they were faster; she saw that she couldn't make it to the fire first. One caught the back of her jacket and hauled her up short. So she tore open the fastenings and tried to get out of it, so as to leave him with nothing more than the jacket. But this was a mistake, because it bared her breasts, which were still large from her recent years of nursing.

There was an exclamation of surprise. What they had taken to be a boy was a woman. The boy they might simply have killed outright; the woman they would not. Another man caught her as she tried to leap away, hauled her back away from the fire, and threw her to the ground. Now the other two came up, staring at her big breasts. They spoke in an alien tongue, but she knew what they were saying: here was a treat. Do with her what men do with women. If she resists, knock her unconscious or bind her. She would be good, perhaps, for several days of fun before she expired from mistreatment.

She pretended not to resist. But they took no chances. One man held her head down to the ground, trying to kiss her without getting bitten, while another caught her feet and held them apart. The third stripped away his breechclout, then ripped away her skirt, dumping it and the pack carelessly beside her. Then he got down on her as the other let go of one of her feet. So now she could kick with one leg, for what little good that might do her. It would probably just increase the man's joy of the occasion.

They had not bothered to grab her hands, being more interested in her face, breasts and legs. Despite her desperation, she had a stray thought: was this why women had several aspects of interest to men, instead of just one? So that they could entertain two or three men simultaneously? No—so they could *distract* three men while fighting for survival! For Ember realized that their diversion had given her a chance to fight back.

She flailed with seeming helplessness, which the man seemed to enjoy, but it was not aimless. While the one played tag with her face and left breast, and the second held her foot and ran his hands up toward her knee and thigh, and the third set his hardening penis for penetration, her right arm found her pile of clothing and the harness. She plunged her hand into her pack and found the firepot. She got her fingers around a cushioning leaf and drew it out with the central punk. It was burning hot, but she ignored that. She brought the burning punk down behind the man as he stretched his body flat on hers. She felt the curve of his thigh, finding her place as carefully as he was finding his.

Then she rammed the punk into the crevice of his buttocks, questing for his testicles. She rubbed it in as hard as she could.

The man bellowed and convulsed. The action caused his member to plunge into her, but not with any joy. His crotch was burning! He leaped off her, screaming, in his distraction kicking the man behind him in the head so that he fell back and let go of her leg. The man at her head, amazed, not realizing what had happened, let her go for an instant. Perhaps he thought there was an enemy attack. He was right, but not in the way he supposed.

Ember rolled over, scrambled to her feet, and plunged away. By the time they reacted, she had a good lead. Her nakedness gave her an advantage, because she was smooth and unencumbered, while they were burdened with clothing, surprise, and a burn that might have made running awkward.

Nevertheless they gave chase. But this time she was able to reach her target before they caught her. Maybe they thought they had her pinned against the sea, and expected her to try to turn aside. But she never paused; she plunged into the water and swam out beyond the surf. The waves were steep, being whipped by the wind, but she had swum this sea all her life. The shallow water was her friend. It was only the deep water, beyond the embrace of land, that she feared.

They let her go, realizing that further pursuit was pointless. In a devious way they had actually done her a favor, because her first impulse had been to go for the fire, dying in the heat of her namesake. They had prevented her, and now she had found life instead in the water.

She swam back toward the harbor—and saw that the men had not after all given up. They were wading in the shallow water, to get around the fire, so that they could catch her as she returned to land farther in. They knew she could not stay out beyond reach forever.

Ember smiled. There was a reason she had entered the water where she had. The People had known that the enemy would try to avoid the fire by wading around, and had prepared for it. They had set assorted traps at low tide, knowing that the rising water would conceal most of these. So she stayed deep, and watched.

The first man tried to avoid wetting his feet by stepping across the beach just beyond the edge of the fire. Suddenly he paused, slapping at his ankles. He had encountered one of the nets of stinging nettles placed there. He backed off in a hurry. Those nettles were not lethal, but the stings were most uncomfortable for some time.

The second man waded deeper, carefully avoiding the region of nettles. Then he too cried out: he had stepped on one of the hidden spikes. The spikes were embedded in the sand with just their sharp points exposed, a menace to bare feet. It was difficult to get by them carefully, and impossible rapidly. He too backed off.

The third man, wincing as he walked, was the most determined. He waded deep, then swam around or over the stakes and came back to land inside the fire. He watched for the nettles, and waded to shore in a clear lane. He stepped onto land—right where an old trunk concealed a nest of hornets who had already had all they cared to take of human intrusions. He splashed back into the water in a hurry, in the process tangling his ankles in nettles and landing on a spike. His loud cries announced all three.

Ember smiled. The men might in time make it past the fire, but not quickly and not without further discomfort. The defenses were effective.

When she was out of sight of the men, she swam to shore at a safe place, and followed a safe path back to the village. Work was proceeding apace, with men using stout hand axes to chop the bamboo for construction. "The fires are set," she reported. "The traps are working. But some men may get through too soon; we need to be on guard."

"We *are* on guard," a senior told her. "Children watched you return without revealing themselves. They would have cried alarm if they hadn't recognized you."

Ember was relieved to know that. She went to see Scorch before settling back down to useful work.

"You look awful," he said, before she could say the same about him. "You're naked and scratched and bruised."

"I had to swim back," she said.

"More than that, I think. What happened?"

She knew better than to try to conceal things from him. "The wind changed, and the fire got behind me. It cut my work short, but I had to go ahead of it to get back. There were three Green Feather men—"

"Did they rape you before you got away?"

It occurred to her that this might be a sensitive issue with him, as it was with her. But the truth had to be told. "Yes and no. They caught me and stripped me, but I got hold of the burning punk and rammed it into the butt of the one who was on me. I burned my fingers, but I burned him worse. He did not enjoy getting into me."

He stared at her. "You—as he was—?"

"Yes. It was the hardest thrust I ever had. No offense. But his attention was elsewhere. I think he will have trouble pooping for awhile."

"You raped him back!" he exclaimed. He took her hand, seeing the tender fingers. "You put the punk up his—the fire—"

"Well, I tried to. But he didn't stay long enough for me to finish the job." She smiled, hoping he would smile too.

Instead he laughed. "Only a fire woman could have done that! You fixed him with fire!"

"Yes. Then I got away."

He sobered. "If it had been me, they would have killed me immediately. You got away because you distracted them."

"Yes."

"You did my job, and returned to me. I'm so glad I didn't lose you. Let's not tell others the details."

"No details," she agreed, relieved. She had been raped, and had avenged herself, and had told her mate. As far as others were concerned, it had never happened. That was best.

Ember went back to work hauling fruit, while men struggled to complete the third raft in time. But it simply was not possible to get all the poles properly bound. They ran out of good cord, and had to stop with the raft undersized. It also lacked a cabin. But twenty people volunteered to ride it, and they agreed that during the voyage they would switch off with others, so that everyone had his turn with the more comfortable complete rafts.

The fire burned nicely, and as the wind shifted and intensified it made a beautiful display in the center of the island. But the alarm was cried: the enemy had managed to get around it, and was closing in on the village. The People had to evacuate immediately and get on the rafts, before the enemy got close enough to catch the rafts and prevent them from leaving.

Ember made sure Crystal and Scorch were on a raft. Then she returned to the shore.

A senior intercepted her. "You are too late for anything more. They are already closing on the village."

"Not too late for my purpose," she said grimly. "I will join you in a moment."

Then he understood her intent. "Then hurry," he said, following his own advice as he went toward the rafts.

Ember went to the village, carrying another fire-shell, and went to the center. "Everybody get out of here," she called, just in case anyone had been missed. "I'm going to finish it!"

There was a cry. Ember looked—and saw a foreign man at the outer edge of the village. The enemy was already here!

There was another cry. Another man, coming in from the side. She was about to be trapped, again. Perhaps by the same men she had foiled before. She knew that this time they would not give her any chance to fight or escape, and they would make sure she suffered a great deal before she died.

But she had the same remedy as before. She brought out the punk and set fire to the central house. It was of bamboo, thatched with straw, and years dry. It blazed up immediately. She touched a straw torch to it and ran to the next house, and the next, sowing fire in her wake.

Now there were cries of dismay from the Green Feather men. They had thought they had captured the village intact, and now they were losing it as well as the People.

Ember ran on, making her trail of fire. It was time to return to the rafts. But how could she get past the men? They had lost the village, but they hadn't lost her.

She surprised them. She ran inland, leaving the burning village behind. She entered the forest and quickly lost herself. Now she was between a fire and a fire, and soon enough those fires would meet and merge. But she knew the pattern of fire, and knew where it would travel last. She made her way quietly along that route, back toward the sea.

When she reached it she saw that the rafts were already moving out. They had not waited for her. They couldn't, because they had to get away from the men of the Green Feather. They could stop anyone from swimming to them, because the People could simply spear swimmers. But if the Green Feathers had any rafts of their own here, they could mount a more effective attack. So the paddlers were ranged along the edges, and the rafts were slowly coursing toward the open sea.

Ember slipped into the water and began to swim. She was tired from her exertions of the day, but this was the swim she had to complete. She stroked for the rafts as rapidly as she could.

The sea breeze was in her face, and the waves were pushing her back. She had to slow as her arms grew fatigued to the point of numbness. She could not, after all, get there.

She made a final effort. She cried out, and waved an arm, trying to attract the attention of someone on a raft. But she was afraid that no one would hear or see her, or that if they did, they would think she was one of the enemy. Now all she could do was try to hold her place, and hope.

There was a shout. Someone had spied her! But her flare of hope was quickly damped: that shout had been from the land. It was the enemy!

Now a man set off from the shore, swimming toward her. They were going to haul her in after all, so they could torture her to death. They knew that she had set the fires that deprived them of even a remnant of their victory.

She could simply let herself drown before they got her. All she had to do was give up. She was near it already. But somehow she couldn't. She had to hang on to the last, even if it did merely put her into the dread hands of the enemy.

The Green Feather man came toward her. She recognized his face: he was one of the three she had foiled! He gave a grim cry of exultation and stroked the last few body lengths to her. She was so tired she could not even try to swim away. She knew she should push the air out of her lungs and duck her head down under the heaving surface of the sea, depriving him of her final pain. But she merely watched him, like a bird trapped by a snake. He reached out—

A spear came from nowhere and struck him in the chest. He looked surprised as the blood stained the water before him. Then he drifted away.

Ember turned her head. There was a small raft approaching, with a spearsman standing on it. They *had* spied her! They had sent out a raft. She, distracted by the swimmer, had not been aware of it—and the swimmer, distracted by her, had not seen it either. She would be saved after all.

There was a second man on the raft. He caught her hands and hauled her up until she lay sprawled across the center, unmoving, just breathing. Then both men set to work with paddles, going toward the big rafts.

They reached it, and other hands lifted her to the more solid surface. She came to rest in the cabin, in the center of a crowd of people. She was beside a man who was lying on his back. A child was sitting by her other side.

"We were scared for you, Mommy," the child said, taking one of her hands.

"That we were," Scorch agreed, taking the other.

Ember let her consciousness go at last, knowing she was safe.

When she woke, it was dark. She knew they were well out to sea, because there were no sounds of land. No birdcalls, no crunching of gravel underfoot. Just the slopping of the waves against the raft. It was restful. But now she needed to attend to a natural function. The one the rapist should find excruciating.

Her mate and child were asleep on mats on either side of her, as were most of the other folk. Ember got up, finding a lane between sleepers, by the dim light of the central fire. She walked along it and out of the cabin, where dim moonlight showed the way. Men were still paddling on either side of the raft, slowly. She walked to the rear where there were two structures: the steering assembly and the privy enclosure.

There was a man holding the long steering oar, keeping the raft more or less on course. He was asleep, but it didn't matter; the oar handle was under his arm, and any shove on it would wake him. The privy was unoccupied, for which she was glad. She entered it, hoisted up her skirt—someone must have put it on her after she passed out—hung onto the rail, and squatted over the dark water. Her innards let go and there were splashes below her. Then she scooped up some water from the side and washed herself off.

She was feeling a bit queasy, but she knew why: she had been on the heaving raft for several hours, and her equilibrium was suffering. It would pass. Sickness on the water was to be expected; that was why no one had eaten much before setting off, lest the food be wasted before the sickness passed.

She straightened out and walked back across the raft. She saw that there were six paddlers, evenly distributed by type: two seniors, two adults, and two older children. The adults were both women. She realized that the shifts would change frequently, so that no one became too fatigued to bounce back soon. They had a long voyage, and strength was valuable. The paddlers were not stroking hard, just trying to keep some forward progress.

"I should be paddling," Ember said. "I haven't done my share."

There was a general laugh among the paddlers. "Go back to sleep," one woman told her. "You did more than any of us, driving off the enemy with fire, and you almost drowned. It is our turn now."

Ember realized that the woman was right. Ember would not be much use on the paddle; her arms were still sore with fatigue, and her body was not much better. She did need to get more rest.

She returned to her place in the cabin, lay down, took Scorch's hand in one of hers and Crystal's in the other, and fell promptly back to sleep.

○

Dawn woke her next. Sunlight was slanting through the crevices in the cabin. Crystal was up and playing with other children, and had evidently been fed. There was something about this forced closeness of the tribe that Ember realized she liked; folk who hadn't interacted much before were doing so now, and folk were helping folk at every turn. They all knew this was no easy voyage they had embarked on, and that there was a more than reasonable prospect for death at sea for them all. If they were ever going to get along well with each other, and do each other good, this was the time. It made for an excellent sense of community.

Ember felt better, if not good. That last session in the sea had taken much out of her, perhaps because it had started her on the path to acquiescence of death. She still wasn't quite used to the notion that she was after all alive. And still not certain that life for her or any of them was fated. It was also strange living on the raft like this. Her queasiness of stomach had eased, but she saw several others looking distinctly uncertain, and every so often one would go to the edge and vomit into the water.

Scorch was still asleep, and the fire was low. There was her job. Ember added fuel to it, carefully, so that it was in no danger of dying out, without wasting wood. But when she was able, she would take her turns with the paddle. Because she wanted to reach land again as much as anyone did. If it could be done.

The shifts with the paddles kept changing, and so did those with the sleepers. The pallets were constantly being vacated and reoccupied, because there were not enough for everyone at once. But there was another kind of shift, she realized: couples were going into a curtained-off corner of the cabin for a time. For sex, which was usually private. If those sleeping nearest that section heard anything, they pretended not to. Ember realized that this was best.

A senior entered the cabin. "Ah, you are awake," she said to Ember. "Are you recovered?"

"I am ready to take my turn paddling," Ember said.

The woman smiled. "Not yet, I think. You remain weak from yesterday. When you are strong enough for that"—she nodded meaningfully at the private corner—"then, perhaps, the paddle. But if you are able to serve food for those who are hungry, now—"

"That I can more readily do," Ember said, relieved.

"Not much, for each," the woman cautioned.

"I understand." All too well.

Then a man brought in a fair-sized fish. He had evidently speared it, using a tethered spear. "There's a school," he said, pleased. He set the fish down by the fire, and went out to try for another.

Ember fetched a stone knife, about to set to work on the fish, but one of the older girl children came in. "I can do that," she said. "I know how."

Perhaps she did. Ember gave her the knife, and instead unpacked some of the dried fruit. But she kept an eye out, and when the girl faltered, she guided her. This was the way the young learned. When the fish was ready, they put it over the low fire for cooking.

People came in, attracted by the smell, and Ember and the girl served them fruit, and after awhile, fish.

Scorch woke. Knowing his need, Ember went to help him get to his feet. She steadied him as he walked out to the privy rail, and as he squatted. Then she helped him walk back. He was recovering, but she felt his weakness. Her stiffness was wearing off with activity, but she had merely gotten fatigued. He had lost blood, and that would take more time. She was so glad he was recovering!

As they re-entered the cabin, she saw his look fix for a moment on the curtained corner. She made a mental note. And later in the day, when that alcove was free, she took his hand and glanced meaningfully in that direction. "They won't let me row until . . ." she murmured, leaving out a great deal more than she spoke.

He nodded. Ember looked at the girl who had helped her in the morning, who was now working on her third fish of the day. "Call me if you need me," she said. The girl nodded, pleased to be left in charge of the fire for awhile.

Ember steadied him again as they went to the corner. Then, inside, she whispered in his ear. "Do you remember our first time?"

He smiled, remembering. "But you—I would not want to hurt you, after yesterday." He meant more than her fatigue.

"You could not hurt me, if you wished to, today," she replied. She meant more than his weakness.

So she took him through it, this time not because he was hesitant, but because he was weak. She lay beside him, holding him close, facilitating it for him in the ways women knew, and in due course he completed it. It was perhaps just as well that he lacked real force, because she had been bruised internally, however satisfying the reason. She kissed him ardently, because this time was as important to her as the first had been, in its different way. Because it meant he had truly forgiven her for being raped. Intellectually he knew it was not her fault, but she had feared that his penis would have a different idea, showing how his primitive heart felt. Now she knew it was all right. Which was of course much of the reason he had wanted to do it now: to show her that. The rowing was merely a pretext, for them both, to do what otherwise might better have waited. He was a good and kind man.

If only she could as readily abolish that other secret longing she had for one she could never have mated with. Scorch did not deserve to have less than her whole heart. But try as she did, she could never quite eliminate that secret.

The curtain parted. "There you are!" Crystal said. "Doing it again."

"Doing it again," Ember agreed. "Because we love each other." Children in a family learned by observation, as was proper. Then she gently disengaged, helped Scorch don his jacket and breechclout, and got back into her skirt.

Scorch reached out and tousled his daughter's hair. "One day, when you are big, a man will come for you," he said. "And you will give him the same pleasure your mother gives me."

"Of course," Crystal agreed matter-of-factly.

Thereafter Ember did take her turn on the paddle, and the effort worked out the last of yesterday's fatigue and overwrote it with today's fatigue. It was good.

✿

The voyage continued, the first day passing into the second. Ember spent as much time inside tending the fire as she could, because the sight of the endless sea outside still frightened her. They were steering by the sun, going east, the way the lost and found man had said the land was. But he had been blown by a storm, then come back on devious currents, and gotten lost and incoherent before being rescued; how could he be sure of the direction? He said he was sure, and others chose to believe him, but Ember's doubt would not be quieted. So she avoided it, as much as she could. She took her paddle turns at night, once she was sure Scorch did not mind, so that she could not see the vastness of the sea. The vastness of the night sky was all right; she had always enjoyed that.

The second day moved into the third. Still no land, increasing her tension though it was really too soon for it. The sky clouded over and a light rain fell. That helped, because they were able to catch more fresh water in broad shells, replenishing their supply. The occasional fish stretched their food.

When the clouds cleared, another problem developed. Ember and several other women set to work fashioning a net from leftover pieces of cord to shade folk from the burning sun. There were no trees here, and the cabin didn't help those working elsewhere on the raft. They expanded the net, lacing it with cloth and small lengths of bamboo from disassembled mats to make it opaque, and it helped—only to have a wind spring up and try to blow it away. They had to tie it to the edges of the raft. But then it tended to interfere with the arm motions of the paddlers. Paddling was fatiguing enough without such hindrance. They tried to prop up the center with a bamboo pole, but it wouldn't stay in place. Ember finally had to kneel before the center paddler and hold the net just clear of him. But it grew hot under the net, and she had to remove her jacket so she could sweat freely. Then she became aware of the man's gaze, fixed on her breasts, which were almost under his nose. There really wasn't anywhere else for him to look, but it made her feel awkward, because normally a woman did not put her breasts that close to a man unless she wanted him to touch them. It was natural for a woman to be bare above the waist in the heat of the day, but the present fullness of her breasts did attract some attention. She knew he was getting a reaction, which perhaps distracted him from his paddling. But neither of them was free to change the situation, or even to acknowledge it. So she found the conditions of the large raft awkward in more respects than she cared to state.

On the fourth day Ember and Crystal took a turn fishing. They went out on one of the smaller rafts, with a senior woman. The day was calm and they were not going far out, so it seemed safe. It seemed that the crowded folk got along better if each could be given some time away from the main mass, and the small rafts were ideal for this. There were six of the little rafts, two to each large raft, and each would hold up to four people. Or in this case, two adults and three children. The other two children were rambunctious boys who normally kept their mother so jealously busy that it was difficult for her to have time for their father. So they were being given the treat of a special fishing trip, while their parents went to the private alcove.

Ember and the woman paddled on either side, while the three children sat in the center and peered eagerly around. To them it was an adventure, going out alone; they had already become jaded by the dullness of the main raft. Progress was slow, because neither Ember nor the older woman had much strength or energy; both had been kept busy throughout the voyage. There had always been something else that needed doing. If it wasn't paddling or preparing food or seeing to a man, it was trying to find a place to sleep, or waiting to use the excretion rail, or trying to clean off salty sweat with salty seawater. Or working with the shade net, which Ember now preferred to avoid. So it was good to get even this far away, for awhile.

"Big fish!" Crystal exclaimed, peering down into the water. She lay prone, with her head over the edge, so she could see better. The boys hastened to follow her example.

Ember looked, and saw it. Indeed it was big—too big to catch with their little net. But maybe a man could spear it from one of the big rafts. She waved, trying to attract attention: "Big fish!" she called, and pointed.

But the fish, evidently warned, turned and moved rapidly away. Too bad; it could have fed a number of people.

They stopped paddling when far enough out, and prepared the fishing net. It was finely woven from fibers normally used for rope, and indeed at the edges it twined into stout cords. The technique was to lower it gently into the water, spread it out, and then abruptly haul it up when a suitable fish crossed over it. This required patience, because the fish were wary of anything new or strange. But in time they would come, especially if some bits of food were set floating on the water above it.

But just as the fish were becoming curious, the boys, bored, started splashing the water. Ember gritted her teeth, realizing that sharp words would not help the situation; the children needed their distractions too. She caught the eye of the senior woman, who evidently agreed. Fishing was merely the pretext; the point was to get away from the temper of the main rafts.

Ember looked around. Now all three large rafts were visible, like three villages on a plain. Men were working on the third, trying to redo the cords binding it together, so that it would be stronger. Because it was incomplete, lacking the larger, firmer outer pole on the fourth side, it tended to lose cohesion. Fortunately it had not been subjected to any bad stress. The next day should bring them to land, if their course was right. If the fisherman had spoken truly. If there were no storm.

"Big fish!" Crystal cried again, pointing. Her sharp little eyes were often the first to spy things. In that, she took after Ember, who would have been more alert for fish had she not had to worry about so much else.

It turned out to be a huge fish—larger than the little raft. A thrill of nervousness made Ember grip the edge of the raft hard. If such a fish were to turn on them—

"Perhaps we have been out long enough," the senior woman murmured.

"But we haven't caught any fish!" one of the boys protested.

"That's because you scared the little ones away!" Crystal said, with some justice.

"Did not!" the boy retorted.

"Did too!"

"It was your ugly face did it!" the other boy said, and both laughed.

Upset, Crystal turned to Ember, but the senior woman interceded. "See if you can scare the big fish away, so it doesn't eat us." That got all three children involved in the new project.

They returned to the big raft. The huge fish moved elsewhere. Ember was relieved. She doubted that it would be smart to tackle that one, even from the main raft. The open sea had creatures never seen by the shallow shore. Probably that was just as well.

❂

On the fifth day there was still no sight of land. The mood of the people was tightening. All the adults and some of the children knew that it was time, and that their supplies were dwindling. They could stretch out their stored food another day, perhaps two, if they caught more fish. But their bags of water were also depleted, and the salt water was no good. For that they needed rain.

The turns at paddling became shorter, because the paddling was getting faster, verging on frantic, and people were wearing themselves out. No one spoke of it, lest the smaller children catch on, but they were getting seriously worried. They could never make it back, even if there were not a hostile force on their island. They had gambled by heading straight out into the sea to an unseen land. If they found no land, they would die adrift on the sea. But maybe it was just ahead, waiting to be discovered. If they just moved a little faster . . .

A haze appeared, thickening into a cloud. Maybe there would be rain! They assembled their shells and water bags, ready to catch any that came. If only it did come, instead of flirting with them before drifting elsewhere, as other clouds had done. Once they had even seen a cloud raining on the horizon, but all they got was a faintly cool outflow of air, hardly even a breeze, and no fresh water.

But this time it was serious. The cloud expanded and turned dark. In fact it became stormy, being the edge of a larger cloud just now coming into sight. They were going to get too much rain!

They prepared two ways. Women and larger children sat out with their shell bowls and bags, to catch the water, while the smaller children retreated to the cabin and found good handholds on the bamboo. The men set about securing everything they could, especially the precious paddles. Then they, too, searched out good handholds, knowing that anyone who got swept off the rafts would be forever lost.

The storm closed rapidly on them. The wind struck first, sending the remaining children scurrying for the cabin. It intensified, making the hair of the women fly straight out from their heads. "Get in!" Ember cried. "This is too much for us!" But it was also too strong for them to dare let go.

The moment there was a lull, they got up and scrambled for the cabin. It was full. The next gust of wind was tearing across the sea, making the water disappear under the froth of decapitated waves. Ember caught hold of the edge of the cabin, and other women grabbed on beside her. Then the wind shoved them all against the wall. Someone screamed as she lost her hold. The scream faded behind. Ember thought she heard a splash.

The wind caught the cabin. The raft lifted, seeming about to fly out of the water. Children screamed. Then it settled, wallowing in a forming valley. Ember stared out over the sea, and saw a range of waves coming at her, each eager to take its shot at the raft. But as the first wave approached, the raft floated up its steepening slope, up and up, until it seemed about to topple over on its back like a dead turtle. There were more screams. Frothy water spilled from the mountain peak and flowed across the deck, bubbling. It coursed into the cabin. The screams intensified. One of them was Crystal; Ember knew her daughter's voice even amidst the cacophony. Her heart ached to go to the child, but she knew it would be folly to try.

The raft crested the water mountain and plunged down the opposite slope. Now they had to do it all over again! But Ember realized that they had seen the worst of it, because all that was to come was more mountains like the first, and they had handled that one. The storm could not sink them! Of course she had known that bamboo would never sink, but now her belief was strengthening.

The rain came down. It pelted them, the drops stinging where they struck bare skin. Ember thought of opening her mouth to get a drink, but she didn't dare, for fear the wind would blow down inside her and hollow her out like a gutted fish. All she could do was hang on.

The rain became sheets of water, cold and cutting. Ember ducked her head and jammed her eyes closed. Her hands felt numb, but they were locked in place; she knew she would die if she ever let go. She lost orientation; she seemed to be in the center of a tumbling stream, with all the raft and sea whirling around her.

How long it lasted she did not know. It seemed forever, but she had experienced such storms on land, and knew that their fury was usually soon spent. She knew she had been through worse storms—but then she had had the security of firm ground and trees and rocks, rather than insecure water. What might be moderate on land had been a terror at sea.

She found herself part of a small pile of women. She tried to let go of the pole, but her fingers would not unclamp. She had to shove one arm forward, breaking the grip, then do the same with the other. She stood on the deck, brought one hand to her face, and used her mouth to unkink the hooked fingers. Then she looked into the cabin.

It was a heaving mass of women and children. The women in the center had grabbed the children, and the women around the edges had grabbed the center women, and the mass of them was anchored within the cabin. They were bedraggled, but all there.

"Mommy!" It was Crystal.

Ember reached out for her, and pulled her from the mass. Then every child was going for its mother, and the mass disintegrated. There at the bottom was Scorch, anchored by two older children, with another woman's child in his arms. He looked up at Ember, surprised. "Well, I started with ours," he said, somewhat awkwardly. He handed the child up to her mother, who seemed to have gotten similarly mixed up.

A quick survey established that all the children had found their mothers except one. A two-year-old boy was gazing blankly around, confused and shivering from the recent soaking. Suddenly Ember knew who had been lost to the storm.

"Crystal, we must share," she murmured. Then she strode across to pick up the little boy. "You will be with me, for now," she told him. Then she looked for his father.

She found the man untying the paddles. He didn't know. How could she tell him, while holding the boy?

She started to turn away, to find someone else to tell him privately. But the boy recognized him, and cried out. Ember had to go to him. "I will hold him, for now," she said, giving him a straight stare.

The man's expression changed from recognition to surprise, and then to a neutral mask. He left the paddles and went to the cabin. Ember knew what he would learn there: the worst. All she could do was shield his child from the horror of it, for awhile.

But there was more horror coming. People were pointing out to sea. There was no land in sight. In the distance was one of the other rafts—and a tangle of floating debris.

The third raft had been torn apart. Only the unsinkable bamboo poles remained, and some floating fruits. No people.

○

The sixth day was bright, and the paddling was easy. But the gloom of the loss of twenty-one people was as bad as the gloom of continued isolation. Had they merely been the first to go? No children and only one young woman had been lost, but the sacrifice of the strength of men and wisdom of seniors was a crippling blow to the People.

Ember gave out the last of the stored fruit to those who were paddling. The children were whining with hunger, but only the paddlers could get them all to food and safety. If they lost their ability to move, they would all die of hunger. At least now they had some fresh water; several men had been able to hang on while holding water bags, and the deluge had filled them.

The day was waning. Ember looked out toward the east, hoping to see what she knew she would not. She saw others doing the same. Now it was not bright hope, but desperation; if there was nothing but more sea out there, they were doomed.

"Maybe I can see it," Crystal said.

Why disillusion the child? "Maybe you can," Ember agreed. "Let me hold you high so you can look." She heaved her daughter up until she was sitting on Ember's head, then precariously standing on her shoulders.

"Oooo, I see it, I see it!" the child cried.

"What do you see," Ember asked, suspecting that this was a game. "A cloud?"

"A little bit of land," Crystal said. "I think."

Was it possible? Ember doubted it. "Can you point to it? So someone else can see it?"

"Yes. Over there." The child pointed slightly north of east.

It might be just something floating on the water. But Ember followed up, just in case. "Crystal says she sees something," she reported to the others. "In that direction." She pointed.

In a moment five people were peering into the dusk. "I see a seabird," one said. "Where does it roost?"

"I think there is something there," another said. "Maybe an outcropping of rock."

"With the waves splashing over it," Crystal agreed.

"Yes." The man turned to Ember. "Understand—I can not be sure. But it could be. If only there were more light!"

"It could be a barren isle," another man said.

"But let's go for it," the first said.

The paddlers oriented on it and worked more vigorously. They were driven by hope, knowing that the morning would most likely show it to be illusion.

But as the night progressed, there came the sound of it: the crashing of surf. There was something there. But was it what they needed?

Ember leaned back against the wall of the cabin, one arm around Crystal, the other around the little boy, who still did not realize why his mother wasn't with him. The more attention he got elsewhere, the less traumatic it would be. The boy's father was staying clear because he knew his own grief would give it away. So he was rowing, trying to wear out his awareness along with his body. Ember, having come so close to losing her own mate, and also so close to having him lose her, understood.

"That is land!" a voice exclaimed. "Real land! I can smell it!"

Or had she dreamed it? Ember went back to sleep.

But in the morning it was true. The dawn came over a shore extending north and south as far as anyone could see. There were trees growing thickly on it, and birds flying above them, and hills beyond them. It was an island large enough to support their population.

Ember's tight internal reservations let go, and she wept. She was not the only one to do so.

It turned out to be a huge land, larger than the island they had left behind. There were creatures unlike any seen before. Some were large running birds, while others were giant hopping rabbits. A hunting party even encountered a monster standing twice the height of a man, with a massive tail and huge front claws, and a head with a tremendous nose that flexed like the body of a snake. They wasted no time in killing it, hurling a dozen spears into it before it twitched into stillness. The meat had an odd taste, but was solid.

Truly, they had found the promised land.

Indeed, it was more than an island they found, perhaps 40,000 years ago. It was what is known as the Sahul Shelf, a land bridge linking Australia and New Guinea. They had crossed about a hundred miles from Tanimbar, an island at the end of the long chain extending three thousand miles south and east from Asia, to reach land near the present Aru Islands, then part of the new continent. From there it was easy, and they quickly spread across it and went on to the islands of the south Pacific. Other waves came, and their descendants became what are known as the Australian aborigines. They flourished until the recolonization of the region by Europeans in relatively modern times.

CHAPTER 7

NEANDERTAL

Thirty-five thousand years ago, having advanced through much of the rest of the world, mankind was finally conquering Europe. This was forbidding territory, because of its mountainous terrain and savagely cold climate. But the population was expanding, and it was only natural to migrate into the remaining wilderness. As it happened, this particular region was still occupied by Neandertal (Neanderthal) man, and there were occasional encounters between the two cultures. How did modern humans fare against these brutes who had brains as large and bodies which were considerably more

85

*powerful? Mankind prevailed, but perhaps not in the fashion once believed.
This sequence takes place in what is now southern France.*

BLAZE pulled his hood down across the mark on his forehead,
watching his breath fog. It was cold in the mountains, and winter
was coming. They would need a big supply of dry wood for the main
hearth. The other men of the tribe were busy hunting, so Blaze went out
alone to prospect for suitable wood.

This was rugged country. There were no level sections; the slopes
were continuous, leading up toward bare crags and down toward
winding valleys. In between it was mostly forested. There had been
plentiful deadwood, but in the course of the past few years this had been
collected and burned. Now it was necessary to range farther, seeking a
region where the dropped branches and fallen trees had not already
been cleaned out. When he found enough wood, he would tell the
others, and a party would be organized to haul it into the village.

Blaze thought about his mate, Bunny, who was still lovely in his eyes
after eight years and three surviving children. She was now gravid with
the fourth, and working at weaving another blanket to keep it warm.
The first baby had died, but the second had survived and was now five
years old. They had named him Stone, to avoid what had turned out to
be the bad magic of the first name, Fire. It seemed that Blaze's son was
not fated to be a fire tender. But there was a good future in the crafting
of stone, so that would do. The other two were girls, already taking after
their mother, being pretty, coquettish, and talkative. He had only one
regret about the relationship, and that was that she wasn't his first love.
It wasn't Bunny's fault that he had longed for what could not be. That
she was not, quite, his perfect woman.

A stone turned under his foot. Blaze, foolishly lost in his thoughts,
misstepped and took a plunge down into a ravine. His arms flailed
ineffectively, and he struck the ground, bounced, and slid down into a
dry riverbed. The slope was so steep that he could not stop himself. He
reached the base at speed, saw that it was actually a drop-off into a bed
of boulders, spun onto it—and felt terrible pain as one leg caught on
something. He screamed and blanked out.

Some time later he woke to agony. He tried to move, and discovered
that his foot was caught in a crevice, and that his leg was strained. Even if

he could wrench himself free, he would not be able to walk. He would have to try to crawl—and he wasn't sure he could make it out of the ravine. He was probably done for, because the others would not know where to look for him, and indeed would not have the time to search the entire region. It would be night before they realized that he had not returned, and they might not be concerned until the following day, because sometimes a man did stay out overnight when the search was long.

Unless he could summon help. If the hunting party happened to be within range of his voice—

He called, and called again, and again. There were echoes down the ravine, but no one answered. They were not close enough.

But there was another way. He gritted his teeth against the pain and struggled to get his hand to his pack. There was the symbol and essence of his trade: his smudge pot. The source of his fire, which he always kept smoldering. Because without it he would have to go to a great deal of trouble to evoke a new fire, if something happened to the home hearth. That would be a horrible loss of esteem for a fire man.

He brought out the pot, which had been fashioned from surplus stone chips and exterior wood braces, bound into the shape of a cup. Within it, couched in a bed of ashes, was the smoldering punk. He gathered what grass and leaves he could reach and formed them into a little pile. He found a bit of dry moss and set it in the center. Then he brought his punk to it and blew up its flame.

As he blew, he got a strange feeling. It was as if he had done this before, once, with someone. With a woman, or a girl. Someone he loved. Yet he could not quite remember. It did not seem to make much sense. There was only the fleeting familiarity, the awakening of emotion along with the flame. Perhaps something he had dreamed.

The pile of material ignited, sending up a small cloud of smoke. Blaze continued to blow on it, making it burn more strongly, and more smoke appeared. He reached as far as he could, fetching in any bits of wood or root or stem he could, and added them to the little fire. Still more smoke went up.

He carefully repacked his punk in the pot and covered it, returning it to his pack. It had done its job. He was sending out his signal.

But soon he had used up all his fuel and the fire was dying. The smoke was thinning as it diffused, becoming invisible as it cleared the ravine. Was it enough? Would anyone see it or smell it? He feared that no one would.

The sky was clouding up, obscuring the sun, so that he could not mark the passage of time on his fingers. A storm was building, and at this season it would be snow. Probably a lot of it. That would finish him, because not only would it bury him and freeze him, it would cover any possible traces of his trek through the forest. He was bundled against the cold, but he would not be able to withstand this, caught as he was.

"Bunny," he breathed. "Stone. My wife, my son. I love you both, and my daughters too. You will have to do without me." It was sad to think of it, because another man would not want to mate with Bunny now. Not with her three or four children. She would have to survive by herself, and this was the worst time. They might free her for another man by killing her children, but she wouldn't accept that, and in the end she would die too. All because of Blaze's foolish misstep.

There was a sound. Something was coming! Blaze called out, because if it was an animal this would scare it away, and if it was a man this would bring him in.

The sound became clearer: the tramping of a man's feet. Rescue!

Then the man's upper body showed above the edge of the ravine, and Blaze knew horror. That wasn't a human man, it was the hulking outline of a beast man! The deadly enemy of all true men. A creature to be killed when encountered—but it required a group of at least three well-armed and -prepared men to do it, because none could match the speed and power of the beast.

Blaze realized that his ploy to bring help had brought disaster instead. The beast man had seen or smelled the smoke, and come to investigate, for they used fire too. Indeed, sometimes they roasted and ate their own kind. This time it would be Blaze they ate.

Blaze had lost his staff in the fall, but he still had his good bone knife. He would try to get in a strike before the beast bashed him into oblivion. Even if he had been on his feet in full health, well armed, his chances alone against the beast would have been slight; as it was they were nil. But he had to make the effort.

The beast man stepped over the edge and slid down into the gully, maintaining his balance in a way that Blaze hardly believed. Physically, these creatures were amazing. Their faces were brutish, with their low foreheads, receding chins, and protruding jaws, but their dexterity was matchless.

Blaze held the knife ready. All he would be able to reach was a leg. The beast men, though massive, were shorter than real men, but Blaze was lying on the ground. Probably the beast would simply sidestep the thrust, then kick the hand, breaking it. Perhaps he would kick the head first, ending it there.

The beast man reached the bottom of the gully, then tramped across to Blaze. He reached down with one hand.

Blaze struck. But his motion had hardly started before the beast caught his wrist, his reflex so swift that Blaze had not even seen the motion. All he knew was that his wrist was caught in a bone-crushing grip. The knife fell from paralyzed fingers. So much for his one effort.

But the beast did not break his arm with one twitch, as he could readily have done. He merely held Blaze helpless. He grunted, pointing to the last of the fire with his free hand. When Blaze did not respond, the beast grunted again, imperatively.

He didn't know about fire? That was impossible; the beasts used it themselves. Maybe not well or consistently, but they certainly knew what it was, and had no fear of it. Of all the creatures of the land, only true humans and beast men were attracted to fire.

The beast grunted a third time, and now his cruel grip on Blaze's arm tightened. He was demanding a response.

"Fire," Blaze gasped. "I made it."

"Fhurh," the beast grunted, his grip relaxing slightly. He was trying to say the word!

"Fire," Blaze repeated, enunciating clearly. If the monster was intrigued by a bit of fire, would he postpone killing Blaze? Or did he want a bigger fire made, so he could roast his prey?

"Fire," the beast said, getting it more clearly. His kind could speak, but had a different and far inferior language. Blaze understood that they spoke only single words at a time, being unable to assemble them into larger concepts. Then the beast pointed to Blaze's trapped leg. He grunted once more.

"Caught," Blaze said. "Hurt."

The beast studied the leg, seeming fascinated by it. Then he spoke: "Home."

"Home?" Blaze asked, bemused. That sounded like a legitimate word.

"Home." The other hand came down, catching Blaze's thigh. The beast began to haul on the limb.

This motion put pressure on the other leg, the trapped one. Pain flared. Blaze screamed.

The beast let go of him. He peered at the caught leg. Then he put his two hands on the caught foot and yanked it out. Blaze screamed again.

The beast waited for him to subside. Then he looked at the leg, which was swelling.

"I fell," Blaze explained unnecessarily. He knew the beast couldn't understand, and wouldn't care anyway. He was just curious. "Now I can't walk. Hurts."

The beast nodded in a surprisingly human way. Then he picked Blaze up and put him across his massive shoulders. It was as though Blaze were a child.

He clenched his teeth to avoid screaming again, because this time the pain was not as bad as before; his leg was turning numb. And because he somehow had the impression that the beast was not trying to hurt him. So he relaxed as well as he could and let himself be carried.

The beast man tramped down the valley of the gully, then up the side where it sloped less precipitously. He carried Blaze tirelessly, not seeming to notice the burden. He moved rapidly on across the land, knowing where he was going.

The wind was rising. The storm was coming across. The first flakes of snow were coming down. Blaze realized that even if he didn't die to feed the beast, he was lost, because the snow would still cover any traces. Even if a hunting party searched for him, and realized that he had been in the ravine, it would not be able to follow beyond it. There would be no swift vengeance for his death.

Despite the discomfort and continuing pain, he faded out, perhaps sleeping. Every so often he woke, to find himself still being carried. He knew that time was passing, because the storm was intensifying and the day was darkening. The beast man ignored it all.

Then, seemingly suddenly, they were at the mouth of a cave. Blaze was set down inside it.

After the dull pain of his jolted leg subsided, he looked around. In the fading light he saw two other figures: a beast woman and a beast child. The child was curled almost into a ball and looked miserable.

This was the beast's family! His mate and cub. He had taken Blaze home—the beast home. As food for them?

Yet the beast could have killed him, hacked him to pieces, and brought only the best chunks here. Why had he taken the trouble to bring Blaze here alive?

Why else but to roast him for their next few meals! He had been easy prey. Meat kept better while it was alive.

Blaze shrugged. What difference did it make? At least it would be a swifter death.

But there was no fire. That was odd, because not only did the beast men use it, they might even know how to make it by striking sparks from stones. Yet it was evident that there never had been a fire here.

Blaze tried to sit up. His leg radiated pain, and he fell back with a groan.

The beast man squatted. He took hold of Blaze and heaved, lifting him and setting him against the wall so that he could sit. Despite the great power of this act, it was also surprisingly gentle.

The beast woman gazed at him. She was squat and massive, not as muscular as the male but probably a good deal stronger than Blaze, even when he was in health. Then she advanced on him.

Now it was coming: she would wring his neck and pluck out his eyeballs. Maybe the eyes would be morsels to feed the beast child. Blaze decided not to try to fight; the sooner he died the better off he would be.

But the female put her hands on his leg, instead, touching the swelling and pressing in toward the bone. The contact hurt, but not greatly. Her touch, too, was gentle. She seemed to be exploring the extent of the damage. Then, satisfied that it was not extensive, she retreated. She fetched a hide from a deeper recess and set it on him as a blanket. Then she offered him a dried fruit.

Blaze was amazed. Her exploration had been for information, not to harm him. Her hands had been competent rather than clumsy. Now she was giving him warmth—and food.

These creatures seemed not to mean him any evil. They had shown no hostility. Instead of killing him, they were taking care of him.

He accepted the fruit, and chewed on it. It was tough, but the juices came in the course of chewing.

The child stirred. The female lifted him and put his face to her furred breast, nursing him. Blaze saw that the little one was shivering despite being well covered.

The child was ill. That made something clear. The beast men normally traveled in bands, as did mankind. These ones must have left their band, or been put out of it, because of the sickness of their child. Sickness was a mysterious thing, sometimes jumping from one creature to another. So this family had to live apart, until their child got well or died. That was the way of it among people, and evidently among beast folk too.

Yet what of Blaze? He was in his fashion also ill. Why should they add to their burden? They had enough trouble taking care of their own.

Yet there were stories he had heard, which he hardly believed, about beasts taking care of isolated babies, and sometimes even helping humans. As if the beasts were too dull to realize that these were enemies.

Or as if they had compassion for anything that was hurting. So they tried to care for a sick human the same way as for a sick beast child. It was not the most intelligent thing to do, but it was pointless to expect intelligence in beasts.

Where this would lead, Blaze did not know. But if this family was offering him life instead of death, he should respond in kind.

Blaze knew what to do. He reached into his pack and brought out the firepot. "Fire," he said.

The beast man moved. He stared at the pot. "Fire," he repeated, understanding. But then he shook his head in a clearly negative way.

He didn't want fire? Yet he would be an unusual beast man if he mistrusted the use of it. There must be a confusion. "Fire," Blaze said. "Warm. It will make the cave warm. For you. For your child." He tried to make a warm gesture. He pointed to the little one. "Warm." For heat was what was needed, more than anything else. Time spent in the heat of a fire could make people well. He had seen it many times.

The man tapped the cave floor with a strong finger. He shook his head. He made a choking sound.

Perplexed, Blaze put his hand down on the floor and scraped it with a fingernail. Suddenly he understood. This was lime rock—and in the presence of fire, it gave off choking, caustic fumes. He had long since learned not to use lime-rock stones to fashion an interior hearth.

The beast family had come to the cave for protection from the weather, but had known better than to start fire here. So they endured the cold. But their sick child, however hardy he might be ordinarily, needed more than blankets now. He needed the steady, healing warmth of fire.

And Blaze was the one who could arrange it. Because he was a fire keeper. He knew how to nullify that lime rock.

"Rock," he said, trying to make himself understood. "Stone." He cast about, and found a loose stone. He picked it up. "From a river. Big. Bring it here. Different kind of stone, for a hearth. For the fire."

They gazed at him in almost human perplexity. But he kept at it, making gestures of stone, of flowing water, and fire on the stone. Finally the man understood him somewhat—at least well enough to know what he was asking for, if not why. Would he do it?

The man went out of the cave. The woman finished nursing her child and set him back down on the floor. The child was still shivering, despite being warmly covered. It was the kind of chill that came from inside, that no clothing or blankets could cure. Only sustained fire.

Blaze leaned back against the wall and closed his eyes. There was nothing he could do for now, so he hoped to sleep.

○

He woke as the man returned, carrying a monstrous slab of stone. He set it down on the cave floor between Blaze and the woman. Blaze was awed again at the creature's strength. He tried to slide the slab over a bit, but couldn't budge it. This was not only big enough, it was flat, even slightly indented, making it ideal. It was from a riverbed, a stone other than lime rock, that would not fume when heated. The man had understood better than Blaze had thought.

"Fire," he said, tapping the top of the rock. "Here."

The man went out again. In a moment he brought dry straw and leaves and twigs of wood. He knew what a fire required. He was trusting Blaze to know what he was doing. That was a trust well placed, for this was Blaze's area of expertise.

Blaze brought the punk close to the straw. He got his face close to it and blew. The punk brightened. Then the straw caught. A flame crept through it. He put more on, carefully, and the smallest twigs. Then he put larger twigs. The fire expanded, and no fumes came. The beasts sniffed the air as if expecting to choke, but were reassured.

The beast man brought larger pieces, and Blaze added them as appropriate. Soon there was a small blaze. His namesake. The smoke was finding its way to the ceiling and out.

The woman brought the child near the fire. The clean heat reached out to them. Blaze had given them a gift in return for their hospitality. That gladdened him.

Blaze repacked his smudge pot. Then he lay back, exhausted by the injury and the effort, and slept again.

He woke to the continued blaze. The cave was warmer despite the accumulating snow beyond its entrance. The light of the fire illuminated the cave.

The beast woman was now tending the fire, feeding it sticks as required, letting it neither rage nor die down. The child was lying close enough to be warmed, and looking less miserable.

The woman saw that Blaze was awake. She grunted. She held a tuber out. It had been scorched in the flame.

She was offering him more food. Blaze reached out and took it. He brought it to his mouth and tasted it. It was edible. He bit off a fragment and chewed it. Soon he finished it. Then, satisfied, he fell back and slept again. The warmth and rest were doing as much good for him as for the child.

When he woke again it was morning. Snow was piled high against the entry, shutting it off from the wind. Instead of making the cave colder, the snow made it warmer, because of that. Blaze understood the effect; it was evident that the beast folk did too.

Now he had to urinate. He didn't want to do it in the cave, but he did not believe he could get to his feet and walk outside, for several reasons. What was he to do?

The beast man had been sleeping deeper in the cave, not needing the heat the way the others did. He got up, went to the entrance—and forged on out, shoving the loosely packed snow out of his way. His power continued to surprise Blaze, though he had always known that the beast men were much stronger than humans.

In a moment the man returned. He had gone out to urinate himself! Blaze sat up. "Piss," he said, gesturing to his crotch.

The beast man glanced at him, surprised. Then he nodded. Apparently it hadn't occurred to him that a true human would need to do such a thing too. He came and picked Blaze up, forging on out with him. The sharp chill of the outer day was fierce after the warmth of the cave. The man set him down in the snow.

Blaze winced as his bad leg came down, but he was able to stand on the good one, bracing against the deep snow. He opened his garment and urinated. "Done," he announced.

The man picked him up again and carried him back into the cave. They seemed to understand each other well enough.

The woman had more edible tubers. She gave one to Blaze to eat. Then she nursed her child again.

The day continued. The man brought in wood and more tubers, keeping them supplied. The woman tended the fire, ate, nursed, and took herself and the child out to urinate or defecate. The child had been looking better, but was shivering again when she brought him in. He still couldn't handle the terrible cold of the outside. Not until he was well.

But maybe Blaze could help him there, too. He had a needle, just about his most precious possession, next to the smudge pot. He had some fiber thread, and an awl. One never knew when repairs to clothing might be required, and such repairs were important. In fact, vital, in weather like this.

He lifted the blanket he no longer needed. He curved it around his body, to judge how it might make a jacket. Sewing was not his specialty, but he understood the principle. The beast folk wore clothing, but it was crude, leaking warm air at every corner. Mankind had fitted clothing, and that made a big difference, because it did not leak air. A fitted jacket would solve the child's problem.

Yet it was too complicated to make a jacket from an original hide. Bunny could have done it, but Blaze was not sufficiently skilled. It would be better to improve the child's existing jacket.

Blaze tried to explain to the others, but it was hard, because they used only words, not language. They had a word for everything, including things he did not, like each part of a tuber, but they did not assemble these into sentences. The closest he could come, after establishing the terms, was "Child. Jacket. Good."

When they did not understand that, he became bolder. He pulled himself around the fire, using his hands and good leg, approaching the child. The woman watched him warily, but did not protest. Blaze had, after all, shown no evil intent, and had enabled them to have the lifesaving fire.

The child was now sitting up, facing the fire, wearing his jacket. Blaze came to sit beside him, then took his left arm, slowly. The child did not protest. Blaze took the loose sleeve and creased it so that it was snug around the little wrist. Then he took his sharp stone awl and forced it through the material of the hide, making a tiny hole. He brought out his needle, strung some fiber thread, and poked it carefully through the hole. He had to work at it, but he got the thread through.

He made a knot, then made another hole, passing the needle and its trailing thread through. He continued this, until he had circled the arm. He drew it snug, tied off the thread—and now the sleeve remained snug, leaking no air.

The beasts looked, not comprehending what this meant. Undaunted, Blaze moved around and tackled the other sleeve. In due course this, too, was tight.

Then he got another notion. He took his own hide, brought out a cutter stone, and used it to slice out a section. He formed this into a hood, and sewed it to hold the shape. Then he took it to the child, set it on his head, and sewed it to the top of the jacket. This took time, but he got it done.

That was about all he could do. He was out of thread, and his bone needle was getting dull. But he knew that next time the child went out, he would not get chilled the way he had before.

His laborious sewing had taken up much of the day. Blaze realized that he had distracted himself, taking his mind off his leg. That leg was still swollen, but the pain was easing. He was recovering.

He needed to get out to urinate and defecate. The tubers fed him, but his digestion was not as hardy as that of the beasts, and his body was letting him know. So he tried to see what he could do for himself. He braced himself against the wall and managed to climb to his foot, keeping his weight off the other. Then he hopped out into the snow. He was mobile again!

He did his business and turned to re-enter the cave. Then he had an idea. He searched the region and spied a dead sapling that had not yet been taken for the fire. He stripped this down, making a crude staff to replace the one he had lost. Now he was able to use it to take some of his weight, enabling him to walk instead of hop. It was a significant improvement.

He started back toward the cave—and saw the others come out. The man was foraging for wood, and the woman for tubers. She was holding the child, and this hampered her.

Blaze sat on a rock, bracing himself. "Child," he said, extending his arms.

The woman hardly paused. She brought the child to him. Blaze was pleased to note that the child was not huddled and shivering. The wind was down, and late afternoon sun was shining, so that it did not seem as cold. But it wasn't just that. The tight jacket and hood were conserving his warmth. Blaze knew how efficient a fitted jacket was, because his own was fitted. Perhaps the beasts were coming to understand that now.

Blaze held the child on his lap, keeping him secure. The child was more alert than he had been, and was gazing around at the things of the outside.

"Mother," Blaze said experimentally. The child's head turned to face the woman. She was now foraging with surprising efficiency. She did not cast aimlessly about; instead she moved to a particular spot, plunged her hand down through the snow, worked her fingers, and came up with a tuber. As if she knew exactly where it was.

As Blaze watched, he realized that she *did* know exactly where the tubers were. She never missed. She must have noted their positions in the ground before the snowfall, and now was collecting them when she needed them. She had a better memory than Blaze did, by far.

"Father," he said. The child's head turned again, to face the man. He was locating dry wood the same way: proceeding directly to a spot, then bringing up a stick without hesitation. Now Blaze remembered how the man had brought him in: not only with enormous strength, but without hesitation about the route, though there were no visible markers. The snow had been falling, but it hadn't made any difference. The man knew his way without markers.

Blaze realized that these creatures seemed stupid because they could not speak in sentences and seemed to lack ability to reason things out. But they knew everything by name, and perhaps also by location. Perhaps they could never get lost, because they remembered everything they saw. That accounted for their excellence as foragers. They weren't stupid, just different.

"Father get wood," Blaze said.

"Father—wood," the child repeated.

He was doing a sentence, of sorts!

"Mother get food."

"Mother—food," the child agreed.

Could the child learn what the mature creatures could not? How to truly speak? Blaze was excited.

The man brought in a good pile of wood for the night. The woman brought in a sufficient supply of tubers. Then she came to take the child back. The child was starting to shiver, after this time spent out in the cold, but it had been longer and better than before. The jacket was effective.

Now Blaze returned to the cave, using his staff. He settled himself in his place, feeling better mentally as well as physically. The beasts were helping him, but he was helping them too.

Next day the child was improved. Blaze talked to him some more, teaching him simple sentences. Did he really understand them, or was he merely mimicking? "Child—mother," Blaze said. The child went to his mother. But that could simply be because of the second word. So he couldn't be sure, yet the notion was intriguing. Maybe a beast child raised among people would learn to speak fully.

"Child—stone—white," Blaze said. And the child picked up a white pebble from among the darker ones laid out. He bared his big yellow teeth. He did understand!

"Friends," Blaze said, hugging the child.

They whiled away the day, talking and playing with stones. The man and woman went out to forage, satisfied to leave the child with Blaze. Things looked very good.

But on the third day the child was worse. His shivering returned, and this time neither the jacket nor the fire could ease it. He lay there, neither eating nor speaking, and his breathing became panting. When the woman tried to pick him up he mewled with pain.

Blaze looked at the others. None of them knew what to do. The illness was stronger, making the child weaker, and they had no way to fight it from outside. They just had to wait, and hope.

In the morning of the following day Blaze's swelling was going down, but the child was no better. He would not nurse, and hardly seemed to wake. They waited all day, watching the child fade.

By the next morning the child was dead. His little body was cold. The woman hugged him, but could not bring him back.

The man went to the back of the cave and used a stone to dig a hole. The woman gathered up the small collection of little stones that the child had played with. They laid the body in the hole, and the woman put several of the stones on it. Perhaps they were also to amuse the child. She added a tuber, for the child to eat. Blaze knew that the child would never play with the stone or eat the food, but he felt better seeing those things there.

Blaze felt the need to make his own offering. At a loss, he cast about for something meaningful. Then he thought of it. He brought out his precious needle and laid it on the little jacket, near one of the cinched sleeves.

The man scooped the gravel back into the hole, burying the body. The woman placed the rest of the stones on top, decorating it.

They returned to the fire. There was nothing else to do.

Blaze realized that the couple had no further reason to stay here. They could now return to their tribe, and probably make another child. He knew that their kind had only one child at a time; probably the woman was unable to have another until the first one was old enough— or gone.

This meant it was time for Blaze to go too. His foot was now taking weight well enough, and he should be able to find his way back to his camp. It might take two days, because he had been carried some distance, but he could do it.

But the beasts did not go immediately. Instead they gathered more wood and tubers, piling both up within the cave. Blaze realized that they were doing it for him! They did not really need the fire for themselves, and they could forage whenever they were hungry. They were making it possible for him to be comfortable for some time without them.

Not only was this a nice gesture, it showed that they did something he had doubted they could do: they *could* plan ahead. They knew what he would need, and were providing it.

Blaze did not have any adequate way to express his gratitude. The beasts had saved his life by bringing him here, even as they lost the life of their own child. The beasts were good people.

When the chore of provisioning was done, the two organized for their own trek, which might be a long one. They stepped out of the cave, and paused.

Blaze heard a shout. "Beast men! Kill them!"

Blaze launched himself up and out of the cave. There were members of a hunting party from his tribe. They must have seen the smoke and tracked down its source, then found the tracks in the snow. "No!" he shouted. "No, leave them alone! These are my friends!"

"Blaze!" a man cried. "We thought you were dead!"

"These kind folk saved me," Blaze called back. "They took care of me when I hurt my leg. Now stand back and let them go; I owe them my life."

Amazed, they stepped back and lowered their spears. Blaze turned to the beasts. "Friends," he said. "No hurt."

Somewhat warily, they looked at the party of men. There were eight there, armed and ready. Too many to fight, especially when one beast was a woman. They hesitated.

Blaze walked out toward the hunting party. "Move away. Show them you mean no harm. Let them go. Let them go!"

Reluctantly, the men retreated farther, leaving a clear avenue. Still the beasts were unsure, perhaps fearing treachery. No, that was surely too complicated a concept for them; they simply distrusted the band of enemy men, sensibly enough. They did not understand what Blaze was telling them.

"Walk with me," Blaze said. He gestured forward, then stepped out himself. "Walk."

The man took a step, and then the woman did. Blaze used his staff to help him walk. He led them past the hunters and on to the open forest. Then he stopped. "Go in peace," he said. "We will not hunt you. Friends."

They moved on. Blaze stood and watched them go. The other members of the party came up to join him, but did not pursue the beasts.

"Now I'll tell you all about it," Blaze said. "Right after I douse the fire in the cave." He did not mention the burial, for fear someone might disturb it.

It was good to be alive and back with his own kind. He was eager to rejoin his family. But he knew he would never forget his days with the beast folk—or let his family forget.

In the course of a few thousand years—an eyeblink in terms of prehistory— the superior technology and organization of modern mankind drove Neandertal man to extinction. At the time of this story Neandertal had been largely ghettoized in the mountains. The contacts may not always have been hostile, but the limitation of Neandertal's range to the least hospitable regions meant his inevitable decline. Some late Neandertals did begin to improve their technology, but it was really too late. By about 35,000 years ago they were gone.

Some believe that modern mankind derives from Neandertal. This is quite doubtful. The three varieties of mankind—Archaic, Neandertal and Modern —coexisted for up to 100,000 years as separate species, each in its own section of the world. The other two species may have lacked the aquatic phase of development, so have been furry all over, never developing clothing as sophisticated as modern mankind's. Their women may have developed their breasts only when nursing, and remained infertile until their chests became flat again. That would have limited their rate of reproduction. There are hints that their life-styles differed significantly from that of modern mankind's, as their extremely rugged bodies suggest. But also their brains. Neandertal did have a brain which may have been larger than ours, but it was different in structure. It seemed to have more in back and below, while ours had more in front and above, the cerebral cortex. This suggests that we improved our powers of reasoning, especially related to language (try working something out without talking to yourself in your mind!), while he improved his powers of perception and memory. Neandertal didn't need to reason things out, when he already knew where everything was, and remembered perfectly how to do what he did. You might think of him as the ultimate conservative: if it was good enough for his grandfather, it was good enough for him. Yet compared to other creatures except modern mankind, he was a genius.

Surely Neandertal man was not a beast. But in the end the reasoning powers of mankind, armed with full language, proved to be more effective for survival than physical strength and memory.

CHAPTER 8

CAVE

The art of mankind flowered everywhere, but most of it was in perishable forms that did not survive for us to appreciate. The fancy sewing is gone, and the sand painting, and most of the wood carvings. The songs and dances left no physical records. Only some of the stone weapons—there is art in craftsmanship too—and "mother goddess" figurines endured. With one noticeable exception: some of their paintings were preserved in unlikely places.

Yet physical records are not the only kind. We know there was music, because we retain our love for it, and for dancing. There was also storytelling,

103

which sharpened our imagination and polished our appreciation of evocative language. The arts are still with us, helping to define our nature. This is a story of the Magdalenian culture of Europe, about 17,000 years ago.

CRYSTAL was so excited she could not stand still. "I saw it! I saw it!" she cried, dancing in place.

Ember paused in her work and smiled at her ten-year-old daughter. "You must tell us all," she said. "Tonight, by the main fire." She was working by a lesser fire now, smoking the meat left over from the last significant kill. Dried meat didn't taste as good as fresh meat, but it stored much better, and was a protection against lean spells. It took time to do it right, neither burning nor spoiling the meat, but she had an excellent eye for it and knew what she was doing.

Her remark made the girl pause. "All? I couldn't!"

Ember understood the problem. There would be all the children of the tribe, there to listen to the stories told by the men. Crystal was shy. But Ember knew that her child had a flair for expression, and a marvelous experience to relate. This would be good for her. She was not afflicted with the nervous facial tic that too frequently vexed Ember herself, so would not suffer public embarrassment. "You will manage," she said confidently. Indeed, she would speak to Scorch, to be sure of that. Scorch knew what to do.

❂

In the evening the tribe relaxed around the good fire Scorch kept. The men settled down to polishing flint and ivory, while the women worked on garments and ornaments. The entertainments were nominally for the children, but everyone listened. It was the good time of the day.

A man played a tune on a bone flute, and three of the older girl children danced to it, stepping and whirling around the fire so that they were outlined against its light. They were supposed to be careful about how much of their bodies they showed, being properly modest, but first one and then the others stripped away their jackets on the pretext of being too warm. Then, bare-breasted, they spun so that their skirts flung out, showing their legs up to the thickening thighs. Some older women frowned, but kept silent. Soon enough these girls would be finding mates; that was the idea.

Now the storyteller made an announcement. "Tonight Crystal will tell us about her adventure."

Ember gave her daughter a shove, so that she stumbled to the fire. There were thirty pairs of eyes on her, stopping her tongue. She couldn't say a word. She was on the verge of becoming a woman, but she looked thin and frightened. Ember remembered how she had been at that age. Yet soon enough she had become bold, and got her mate, and had seldom regretted it. All Crystal needed was encouragement.

Then Scorch got up. He put his hand on his daughter's shoulder. "We'll tell them," he said. "We went up to the cave on the morning slope—"

There was a titter from somewhere in the audience.

Crystal nudged him. He looked at her. "What's that, child?" he asked as if perplexed. "I didn't hear you."

She forced out a word. "Evening."

"Oh, that's right. It's on the evening slope. I had forgotten. So we walked up the ridge—"

There was another titter. Crystal nudged him again. "Streambed, Daddy," she whispered.

"I can't hear you," he complained.

"Stream," she said louder, flushing.

"Oh, that's right! The streambed. So we splashed up through the water—"

This time there was open laughter. Scorch was known as a funny man, and he was not disappointing the children. Crystal had to nudge him a third time. "It's dry," she said. "You know there's no water."

"No water!" he exclaimed. "But it's a streambed! Are you sure?"

He was teasing her, but she liked it. "Daddy, it was just this morning. There's nothing but rocks."

He shook his head. "It's a good thing your memory's better than mine. So we climbed down from the streambed into this hole—"

"There's a big mound of rubble!" Crystal said, exasperated. "Covered with ferns and brambles. Why can't you tell it right?"

"How should I tell it?" he asked plaintively.

"Say how we went there because they needed more fire," she said. "More torches and lamps, so they could see to paint. Tell them how we carried bags of fat for the stone lamps and put them on the floor, so there would always be enough. And how we saw all the paintings of animals, and—"

"No, you tell them, Crystal," he said.

"But I can't—"

"Yes you can."

"I'm—I can't talk before everyone."

"Yes you can. You've been doing it."

"But I'm scared!"

"No you aren't. Not anymore. Tell them everything." He squeezed her shoulder encouragingly.

Crystal looked out from the fire and realized that it was true. She was already talking before the group. He had tricked her into it.

Ember nodded. Scorch was a good father, even if he had not been her dream man. She could not complain.

Crystal plunged in. "We went down this slope and into this cave. There were all kinds of things there. The trunks of small trees, and branches, so they could make ladders to go down deeper in, and rope piled in coils, and someone was making a—a—"

"Scaffold," Scorch murmured.

She flashed him a smile, and continued her story.

Crystal was really impressed by the cave. It was such a big hole in the ground, and there was so much happening there. She felt really privileged to accompany her father this summer. The cave was very special, and they didn't let just anyone in. Because of the magic. Someone had tried to protest that the presence of a girl would spoil the magic, but Scorch had scoffed at that. "There's already a woman in there," he remarked with a certain wry smile Crystal didn't understand.

Crystal helped him set up some lamps. They took pieces of stone from the rubble, finding ones with indentations suitable for fat. They put in the fat, and then put in fiber wicks. When they had several, Scorch stood. "Now we must test one," he said.

He lit a lamp, getting the fat to melt and get into the wick, and finally to catch fire and sizzle. It smoked awfully, but in a moment it settled down and made a nice even flame. Then he led the way into the main part of the cave.

Crystal was awed by the size of the great chamber they entered. It was absolutely huge, the biggest room she had ever seen. As her father held up the lamp, its light showed the white wall, looking like an enormous angry white cloud, with billows and curves and shadows.

Along the base of that cloud, where the darker land seemed to begin, were animals. First there was a small russet horse just about to leave the cave. Then there was an aurochs, crudely drawn: its belly almost dragged on the ground and its two horns looked like thin straight sticks. That must have been drawn a long time ago, by someone who hadn't really learned how to do it, working by the dim daylight near the mouth of the cave. But farther in were more competent aurochs, with muscular bellies that did not drag, and grandly sweeping horns. What a magnificent display!

They picked their way across the uneven floor toward the narrow holes that led deeper into the earth. Crystal saw that under the large aurochs were smaller animals, as if a group of them were fleeing a fire. They were aurochs cows and calves, horses, deer, and even a bear. They were all wonderful in their realism; the flickering shadows made them seem alive, about to move or around the cave.

But something bothered her. "Daddy—how did they reach up there?" she asked. "To paint the animals?"

He smiled. "They had to stand on trees," he explained. "With cut-off branches for their feet." He gestured, so that she understood that it was a ladder, with each branch a step. "Sometimes a beam put crosswise, held up at each end by cut-off trunks. It wasn't easy."

She believed it. She wished she could have been there to watch them. But she knew that these pictures had been made before her time. Now the artists of the tribe were going farther back in the cave, to find walls that hadn't already been done.

They reached the entrance to the next chamber. Beside it was the biggest of all the aurochs, larger than life-size, its head and horns reaching over the opening. It was a guardian of the secrets beyond, she realized. As long as it was there, no bad things would get in.

Now Crystal followed her father through a winding corridor that was narrow at the bottom and wide at the top. The ceiling formed a white vault. Animals were painted all along the upper section, some of them right above where the two of them were walking. The first animal was a

massive brown cow with a black head, her muscles and bulges right there
in relief, as if she had been walking by when solidified into stone. There
were other cows, and horses.

The way narrowed, then opened out again, and there were more
animals. Then at the end was something astonishing: "A horse!" Crystal
exclaimed. "On its back!"

"So it is," Scorch agreed, smiling. "I thought you would like it."

"What's in the next chamber?" she asked brightly. "Upside-down
bulls?"

"You may look if you wish," he said, giving her the lamp. "Put this
down here, so that it will be there at need." He gave her one of the unlit
lamps.

Thrilled to take the lead, Crystal held the lamp very carefully, for the
last thing she wanted to do was lose its light, and went on around the
wind in the narrowing passage. There was a two-colored horse on the
outer curve behind a fat bison. The bison seemed to be looking right at
her!

The passage went on. She tried to follow it, but it got so narrow that it
was impossible. How she wished she could explore the rest of it! There
might be so many more chambers with wonderful animals. All she could
do was sigh, set down the spare lamp, and work her way back as she had
come.

But she paused, remembering something Scorch had said. Then she
pushed forward again, hoping she did not get stuck. She reached into
the passage as far as she could and made a crude sketch of a woman with
her fingernail. It didn't show, but she knew it was there. She had added
her art to this phenomenal gallery, where no one else could ever paint
over it. And she had put into the cave the one thing it lacked: a human
woman. Now it was complete.

"What—you didn't go to the end?" her father inquired with mock
surprise. "I thought you would want to see the painting of your
mother."

"She's there," Crystal replied.

He glanced at her, surprised. She smiled. She had reversed the ploy,
and managed to tease him back.

They worked their way back, admiring the herd of horses on the south
wall. They returned to the huge hall of the bulls, fetched more unlit
lamps, then went down a passage leading south. This was much more

constricted, and in places they had to get down on their hands and feet to get through. All along the sides were small pictures of horses.

Then it opened out into a beautiful chamber. It was much smaller than the hall of the bulls, but larger than the one with the upside-down horse. The upper walls were yellow-white. There were the painted heads of seven ibexes, with their enormous horns, all of them facing in the same direction.

But now Crystal had work to do. Because she was small, she had to set down her lamps and scurry back to fetch more. This was why her father had brought her: to make his work easier. But of course he had known that she had been itching for years to get to see the fabulous caves, and never would be allowed in them once she became a woman. So he had made this one chance for her, giving her the experience of her life.

She made several trips, carrying two lamps each time. It was nervous work, because all she had for light was her father's lamp at the end of the passage, and a lamp in the hall of bulls. Between them it got dark indeed. But she did her job without complaint, justifying her presence. Perhaps someone had said that she would panic and not be much help, and Scorch had stood up for her. She meant to justify his faith. So she made three extra trips, until there was a total of eight lamps.

When she was done, she rejoined her father and they moved on. Now she saw another panel of animals, mainly horses and bison. Then farther along there was a larger panel, with a herd of horses running back toward the entrance, and one great black cow going the opposite way. The horses were beautiful, and the cow magnificent. She was even sticking out her tongue!

But the cave had not yet ended. They went on into a narrowing, diminished passage. They had to stoop, and then to crawl on hands and knees, wriggling through crevices. Crystal had to go back to bring forward the collection of lamps, making several more trips.

At last they were in the farthest recess. Here, in a low cave, were pictures of cats. They were not as fancily drawn as the bison and horses, but that was understandable: there was hardly any room here to work. Nevertheless, the scenes were dynamic.

One showed a lion about to mount a lioness, to mate with her. Crystal of course knew all about mating, having seen her parents do it often enough. People did it from behind or face-to-face, depending on how friendly the woman felt. Animals always did it the unfriendly way.

Indeed, the lioness's ears were flattened and her mouth was snarling. But she was going to have to let him do it, if she didn't want to get chomped. That was how it was, with animals, and she understood sometimes with people too.

Another scene showed several lions arguing about food or something. One was growling; the sound lines by its muzzle showed that. Its tail was switching in the air, and it was jetting urine, marking its territory. That was the way cats were, certainly!

But Crystal had a question as they left the lamps and started back. "Daddy—why?" she asked hesitantly.

"Why do we paint the pictures? It is for the hunt. Each time we get ready for a big hunt, we paint a picture of the animal we want to catch. That gives us power over it. Sometimes we want to be sure an animal can't hunt *us,* so we paint it too. See those spears in the back of that lion above the mating pair? After a lion killed one of us, we painted it there, and riddled it with spears in the picture, and after that no lion has killed any more of us. They know we have stopped them with our picture."

Crystal's face brightened. So that was why! The cave was the secret to successful hunting! She knew it worked, because they had managed to kill all the kinds of animals shown in the pictures. It was certainly worth all the trouble.

Still, she had another question. "Sometimes several men go to the cave," she said. "I know most of them aren't painters or builders. So—"

"That is not for any woman to know," he said gravely.

"But I'm not a woman," she protested. "Not for another year or two, at least."

He considered, and she knew he was teasing her again. "Will you promise to forget everything when you do become a woman?"

"Oh, yes!" she said eagerly, with her fingers crossed.

He pretended not to notice. "Then I will show you the secret place."

He led her back to the chamber with the big black cow and beyond. Then he went to the side, and there was another passage. There was a knotted rope descending into the darkness. "There is the ceremonial chamber," he said. "Can you climb well?"

"I think so." The dark hole frightened her, but she was determined to learn everything she could, knowing that she would never have another chance.

He set the lamp in a kind of harness on the end of a second, lighter rope. "I will climb down. Then you lower the lamp to me. Carefully, so it doesn't burn the cord! Then you will climb down into the light."

She nodded, her mouth dry. She would have changed her mind, but lacked the courage to do that. So one fear canceled the other.

He took hold of the rope and swung on down, disappearing into the hole. After a time that seemed longer than she knew it was, he called back from the depth. "Now, Crystal."

She lifted the cord and held the burning lamp over the edge. She let the rope slide slowly through her fingers. The light made changing shadows as it descended. It was as if ghostly spooks were trying to find their way out of the hole.

Then it steadied. "I have it," Scorch called. "Now you come on down."

She caught hold of the top knot on the heavy rope, as she had seen him do, and put her feet down. They found a lower knot, and then one lower still. She moved one hand down, and then the other. Then she clung tight and lowered her feet. It was awkward, because she wasn't used to this, but she quickly found the next knot down. Knot by knot, she dropped into the hole, until she was amidst the light and saw the floor. She reached it and let go.

"This is where we hold our ceremony and make our offering, each hunt," Scorch said, moving the light to show the nether region. "Here by the wounded bison."

She saw the picture of the bison, its belly transfixed by a spear, its guts coming out. Before it was a crude sketch of a man; there was no mistaking it, because of the plain penis. This was a battle between man and bison.

Beyond the man was another figure, one she had not seen before: a woolly rhinoceros. Between them was a bird. On the opposite wall was the head of a horse. All around were cryptic markings.

"This is all I can tell you," Scorch said. "Except that the cave does continue, but there are no more pictures, and we don't try to go to its end. It isn't safe. This is the only place we need."

Crystal nodded. She had seen the ultimate secret of the cave. It was more than enough.

Then he held the lamp high while she climbed the rope back up. Her arms, already tired from the descent, got stiff with fatigue, but the

horror of getting trapped in this hole drove her on, and she hauled
herself up and over, panting. Now she urgently wanted to escape the
cave, afraid that the ceiling would collapse on them, or that the river
would come again and wash them into nowhere, or that the light would
fail and they would lose their way and never find their way out. All these
fears loomed, now that her curiosity was settled. Perhaps the spirits of
the hole had found her and were harrying her, determined to punish
her for spying on their secrets.

Then she drew up the thin rope with the lamp, almost burning her
fingers in her nervousness. Her father climbed up, and her fear
diminished; *he* had no concern. He was strong, and he knew the cave,
and always had fire with him. He was male.

They came back to the chamber with the seven ibexes, and then to the
hall of the bulls, where other men were working on what she now
recognized as a ladder for the hole. How well she understood the need
now!

At last they emerged to the blindly bright light of day. Scorch put his
hand on her shoulder. "You did well, Crystal," he said. Suddenly all her
fears were forgotten and she felt wonderful.

Ember felt wonderful, too, hearing the story. She had known that her
daughter, being insatiably curious about stones, had desperately wanted
to see the secret cave while she could. She had urged her husband to
take Crystal there. Once she had presented her case, he had understood, and then he had acted. He was a good man, once shown a proper
course of action. So he had done it, giving the girl the complete tour on
the pretext of needing assistance delivering new lamps, and it was
evident that it had impressed her greatly. Crystal had seen the secrets of
the stone, and it had given her a new horizon.

Crystal finished her story, gave her father a hug, and came to join her
mother. She was flushed and happy with her experience and her effort
of narration. It was the first time she had told a story before the fire, and
she knew she had done it well, once she got into it. All the children and
most of the women had paid close attention, for the cave was a mystery
to them too, being man's business. It was as if they had all gone down
into the amazing chambers, and seen the bulls and horses and cats, and

then the deep hole where the lone rhino lurked. Now they all knew about the seven ibexes and the upside-down horse.

Ember put her arm around Crystal's shoulders, hugging her. "You did well," she agreed. Indeed, she was proud of her daughter for conquering her fear of the cave, and then of the audience by the fire. Crystal had grown doubly, this day.

Thus it is that we know of the paintings of ancient man, because those that were protected deep in the caves survived to modern times. There were a number of caves, and each had its particular style of art, and its periods of use or occupation. The cave described here is Lascaux, in south-central France; it is perhaps the most famous, but not unique. Thus we know that this was no fluke; Magdalenian man's art flourished throughout, and surely appeared in many places other than cave walls. This one surviving evidence of it is the proof.

Storytelling too remains in our nature. We love stories, whether they are told around a fire or come through a motion picture screen. Given our choice, we would spend more of our time absorbing stories than we would doing anything else—which is why television is so popular. Stories are relaxing exercise for the mind, entertaining us while reinforcing our human nature. Perhaps the simplest definition of mankind is that he is the storytelling animal.

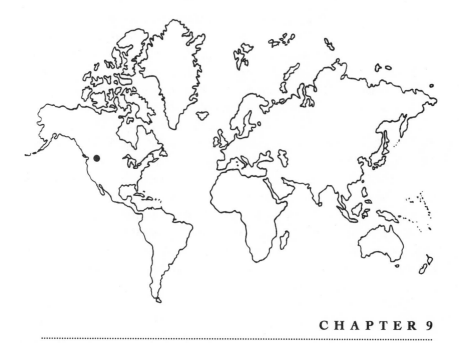

C H A P T E R   9

CAT

There have been claims that man colonized North and South America as early as 40,000 years ago. The expanding polar caps of the ice age took up so much water that the sea was anywhere up to four hundred feet below its current level, and as with the Sahul and Australia, the Bering land bridge made it possible to cross from Siberia to Alaska by foot almost anytime between 100,000 and 10,000 years ago. But it seems unlikely, not only because the archaeological evidence is scant and questionable, but because there was no evidence that eastern Siberia itself was inhabited that early. How could mankind reach America before he reached the broad region he had to cross to

115

get there? If anyone came then, it was more likely to be Homo erectus—*and
there's no credible evidence for that, either. So the more recent period of
15,000 to 12,000 years ago seems to be it, because we have plenty of evidence
for that. Perhaps the record will change with future discoveries.*

*It seems to have started with a tiny population breaking through the
retreating barrier of the glaciers and passing from Alaska through western
Canada to the United States and points south. These few tribes, encountering
what seemed like unlimited resources, expanded rapidly to fill both continents.
They hunted the biggest game animals, by preference, such as the mastodon
and mammoth, until they were extinct, then went on to the next largest species.
There seemed to be plenty to go around, at first.*

THE People were moving to new territory, because the hunting had
turned bad where they were. But they needed food while they
traveled, too. Bunny and their daughters were out gathering. Meanwhile
Blaze took Stone out on a hunt for small game. There should be rabbits
or prairie chickens in the brush, if they got far enough out from the
camp and were quiet. At eleven, Stone was big enough to start thinking
about doing for himself, mastering the manly arts, so that he could
become ready for marriage. So this time the boy was leading the way,
and he would have the first throw of the spear.

It was in fact a kind of a contest, to see whether the men of the family
could bring in more food than the women. Bunny and the girls almost
always found something, but Blaze and Stone hoped to find more and
better. Meat was always better than nuts and berries or boiled roots.

But there were few signs of significant life. They moved swiftly
through mixed pines and oaks and open terrain until noon, spying only
small flying birds, lizards, and insects. It was as if the game had been
warned about their approach, and moved elsewhere. More likely there
had simply been too many people passing this way, leaving the smell.
The animals were learning caution, and the mere whiff of man could
send them quickly away.

Stone was getting impatient. That wasn't good; hunting was mostly
patience. They might have done better to have stopped an hour ago,
climbed a tree, and waited to see if any animals came by. Rabbits were
plentiful, and generally came out to forage as soon as they thought it
safe. But this was a learning experience for the boy—and possibly they
would after all find something. One could never tell, on a hunt. That

was part of the thrill of it: the gamble against the unknown. Certainly Blaze was not going to say he would have preferred to remain at the camp and keep the fire. They wouldn't need a fire unless there was meat to roast.

The forest thinned, then cleared, and an extended open, level area appeared. And there within it was a small herd of animals grazing. They had looked for small game—and found big game instead!

Stone looked at him. Blaze nodded. "You were right, son; this is a major discovery. Can you identify the animals?"

The boy squinted against the brightness of the day here. "I think—camels."

"Camels. Not our favorite prey, but quite good enough. There's a lot of meat on each animal. So what is our best course now?"

Stone considered. "Camels are too big for just one or two men to bring down. We need to bring the tribe."

Blaze rubbed the scar on his forehead, pretending to be perplexed. "But what of your practice kill?"

"It must wait, for the good of the tribe."

He had answered correctly. "Then how should we proceed?"

"If we both go back for the tribe, the camels will be gone by the time we return in force. So one of us must stay here to watch them while the other goes back. Then if the herd moves, he can stay with them, and leave signs for the tribe to follow, and we will still get the camels."

Right again. The boy was shaping up well. "Then which of us will go?"

The boy considered longer this time. Blaze knew why. Stone relished neither the notion of returning from half a day's trek alone, nor remaining out here in the wilds alone. He had undertaken this hunt with his father, expecting at least to have the company and support in case he blundered and needed to be extricated. Either role would deprive him of that competent backup. This was not mere juvenile foolishness; there were dangers in the field, making pair hunting advisable. He had a man's decision to make.

"I will go back," he decided. "I am younger, and maybe can move more quickly." Then, realizing that this might not be diplomatic, considering his father's age of thirty-two, he added: "And you can better handle the herd, if it starts to move, perhaps turning it back toward the tribe."

"I agree," Blaze said, smiling. He did feel better about remaining out here himself, instead of trusting his son not to panic. "I will wait, and try to turn the herd, if it moves. I will delay taking other action, in the hope that you will return in time to make your practice kill."

"I will go now," Stone said appreciatively. "I will run, and be there well before nightfall. But they may not come until morning."

"Unless we are lucky, and you meet hunters partway back," Blaze agreed. "I will make a fire if I need to. But don't run too long; alternate with walking, to keep your strength, and pause if you suspect any danger. Safety is better than haste."

"I will move safely," the boy agreed. Then he was off, running lightly on his young feet.

Blaze smiled, watching him go. This was another test of manhood, perhaps as good as spearing a rabbit. They had come a long way, and would have been tired by day's end, just walking. Running would hasten fatigue. But worse than that would be the fact that Stone was alone. It took courage to be alone, until a person became sure of his powers.

He walked on around the edge of the clear region, seeking the cover of trees, watching the camels. He did not know a lot about this particular animal, except that it had once been more common and hunted more widely. It was a stroke of luck to find even a small herd here. It was odd how the populations of animals changed. Perhaps the herds traveled to new regions, in the way that mankind did.

His foot caught on something, and he stumbled and fell flat on the ground. His first concern was whether he had spooked the herd by his carelessness. Only when he saw that he hadn't did he check himself. He had not been hurt. He had seriously injured himself some years ago, because of carelessness, and had taken several days to get back to the tribe. In fact he had survived only because of the sufferance of members of a normally hostile foreign tribe. He did not want to repeat that experience.

He continued circling, until at last he was beyond the herd. Now he saw that there was a neck of open land passing between forested hills. That avenue led to a much larger grassy plain beyond. If the camels entered that, it would be impossible to catch them. But it should be easy to prevent it, because they had to go through this narrow section, and he could spook them back if he needed to.

But already they were moving this way, with what looked like an ungainly stride. They were long-legged, scoop-necked beasts, each with a single hump on its back. But perhaps their aspect was no stranger than the monstrous mammoths, with their noses stretching right down to the ground.

He had to stop them. So he ran out into the center of the avenue, crying out and waving his hands. He was smaller than they were, but it was the nature of grazing beasts to flee anything they did not understand. He wanted to make them turn and run toward the camp of the People, or at least mill about and remain in the smaller field.

But the camels did not react in the manner of deer or horses. They did not turn; instead they veered slightly and ran faster. They were trying to get around Blaze and escape to the larger plain. It was as if they knew that they were better off defying his bluff than remaining in the smaller field.

If they wouldn't spook, he couldn't stop them. Blaze ran to cut them off, but already they were passing him. In desperation he fitted his spear thrower to his spear and hurled it at the last of the animals. The best he could hope for was to wound it, so that perhaps they could follow the trail of blood and locate the creature. At worst he would miss entirely. Then he would have to start back to the camp, to intercept the hunting party before it got all the way out here, and explain that he had failed to hold the prey. That he had wasted their time and hope, and risked his son for nothing. That prospect hardly appealed.

His throw felt good. His excitement and concern lent strength to his arm. The spear sailed across—and struck the belly of the camel. He had scored!

The animal screamed and staggered, the spear lodged in its gut. Blaze ran to grab that spear, trying to shove it in and inflict more damage. But as his hands closed on it, the camel lurched forward, and the point broke off. Blaze was left with the pointless shaft.

The camel ran on, stumbling but keeping its feet. Blaze could not tell how bad the injury was. Some animals could run for days after being speared, while others died soon after the strike. How would it be with this odd creature? All he could do was follow it, and hope it fell before too long.

The camel slowed, and the rest of the herd left it far behind. The camel walked, still moving faster than it seemed to. Blaze's hope faded. He had made a phenomenally lucky throw, but only a perfect shot to the heart could have brought down an animal of this size.

Then the beast fell. Just like that, it was on the ground. Blaze had brought it down after all!

He hurried up. The camel tried to rise, but could not regain its feet. It glared balefully at him. It occurred to him that the creature was in pain. It would be better to kill it, so that it would not suffer further. What was the best way to do that?

Probably it would be best to slit its throat, so that it would quickly bleed to death. But that head remained disturbingly active. When he tried to approach, the beast squealed and struck at him with its teeth. They were not predator's fangs, but they looked formidable enough. It did not seem prudent to risk getting bitten. So, with regret, he let it be. Maybe it would die soon on its own.

He sat down to wait it out. "Camel, if I had a choice, I wouldn't kill you," he said. "I wouldn't hurt any living creature. But I have a wife and three children to feed, and times have been lean. The rest of the People are no better off. So we have to hunt, to survive. The women gather, and that keeps us from starving, but to prosper we need meat."

The beast did not seem mollified, so he continued. "I'm really not a hunter. I'm a fire tender. I know all about fires. Indeed, I have fire with me now, in a pot in my pack. I can start a fire anywhere, and use it to cook food or to warm a shelter. So I don't normally go out to kill creatures. But my son is coming of age, and I have to guide him to manhood, so we went out hunting together. I wasn't going to throw my spear at all. He was going to do it. But then we saw you and your herd, and you are much bigger game than we expected. My son went back for help, and I stayed here to be sure you didn't get away. Then when you tried to pass me, I had to act. I really didn't think I had a chance to bring you down. It was sheer luck, really."

Still the camel did not look appreciative. "Well, I suppose the world looks different to you. But if you had to eat meat, and you spied our tribe, I suspect you would try to kill some of us to eat. We're all just trying to get along, in our separate fashions. So—"

Blaze paused. Had he seen something? He had been looking around as he spoke, knowing better than to be careless. The day was late, and he did not relish having to spend the night out here in the open. He had expected to find a good tree to climb in, secure from nocturnal ground creatures. They weren't all predators; there were porcupines and skunks who had quite effective ways of keeping others at bay, and sometimes they acted before fully checking the situation.

He waited. If there was something, it would show again in due course. It might be merely a squirrel coming down from a tree, or a rodent coming out of a hole. But he had to be sure of its nature before he could relax.

He realized that if there was something near, it had been warned by his silence; it knew he was alert for it. So he resumed speaking. "So it is just a matter of roles. Right now I have the role of the hunter, and you have the role of the prey. But perhaps your spirit will come back in the body of a wolf or even a man, and when I die, my spirit will return as a camel. Then you will be hunting me, and it won't bother you any more than it does me." He paused, reflectively. "Which is to say, it *will* bother you, but you will do it anyway, to feed your cubs. Maybe in the past you were a hunter, and now it is your turn to be the prey, so that your spirit has complete experience. Who is to say what is right, when we all act according to our natures?"

He glanced at the camel, and discovered that it was either dead or near death. Its head lay on the ground, and it did not seem to be breathing. So it had not suffered long, despite the lack of a throat cutting. It was now a carcass suitable for butchering.

But he was not alone with the body. There was a rustle, closer than what he had imagined before. Blaze gripped his spear shaft nervously and looked quickly around.

Now he saw it, slinking through high grass. His gut tightened. That was no wolf or bear; that was a cat. A big one. Which meant that it would not be enough for him to kill the camel; he would have to guard the carcass too. In fact, he would have to watch out for himself, because the largest of the cats did not necessarily avoid mankind the way wolves did. If they were hungry enough, they would attack a person too.

He saw the cat again, and this time also the white of a tusk. A sabertooth. The worst. It must have smelled the blood or heard the commotion, and come to investigate. Now it knew that there was plenty of meat here, and it would not leave without getting part or all of it.

Were there other cats? Blaze saw no signs of them, and indeed, if there had been a pride, they should have come in to force him to retreat. But one cat alone would hesitate to meet one man, because it could not be certain of the victory. A man with a good spear was as formidable an opponent as a cat with tusks. It didn't know that his good spear had been blunted; that now all he had was the shaft. It didn't know that his weapon was not enough.

Blaze considered. He had a series of choices. He examined them in sensible order.

He could stay and defend the carcass, or he could leave it. If he stayed, the cat would try to come in and take a bite, and he would try to stop it, and it might then turn on him and attack. If he left, he would be safe, but the cat would get the carcass by default, and he would be a failure.

If he remained and fought the cat, he might beat it back, or it might drive him off. If he had had a good spear, he might have hurled it into the cat and at least wounded it. As it was, he would probably just annoy it, and get killed.

Then he had another thought, a worse one: suppose he made such a show of ferocity that he drove the cat away, and it did not return? Then where was it most likely to go?

To find his son Stone. The cat could readily sniff out that trail, and as readily overhaul the boy. Stone lacked even a spear shaft. He would be easy prey.

No, the issue had to be settled here.

There was another alternative. He could make a fire. All beasts feared fire. That would keep the cat at bay, without actually driving it all the way away.

Blaze looked around, and realized that there was very little wood nearby. He saw only a few twigs. Not enough to last. Long before nightfall it would die out.

Nightfall? That was when the real problem would begin! He could stave off the cat by day, by jumping around and threatening it, so that it thought he was stronger than it was. But at night it would be more alert than he was, and would see better than he did. His vision was acute by day, but poor by night, even compared to that of other men. The cat's advantage lay with darkness. He would not dare sleep, but even if he remained vigilant, it could sneak up and suddenly pounce, catching him by surprise and bearing him down. If this issue were not settled by night, he would have to flee the carcass, because otherwise he would die.

So the fire did not matter. It would be a losing ploy. It would merely back off the cat long enough to make the cat's victory certain. He had to kill the cat first; then he could make a fire for warmth and protection from anything else. With the cat dead, he would be able to forage more widely for fuel, so as to have the fire last the night.

But how could he kill the cat, with only the shaft of his spear? Even if he could cut the stone point out of the camel's gut, he would not be able to fasten it firmly to the shaft; that was a special art, requiring cutting of the end of the shaft, and precise fitting, and binding with fine, strong cord. He lacked that art; he was a fire worker, not a spear maker.

But suppose he could sharpen the end of the shaft to a point? Would that suffice to kill the cat?

No. The wood simply was not strong enough to penetrate the hide and sinew of a large animal, and reach a vital organ. It might bruise the creature, and embed splinters, but sharp stone was needed to kill it.

Unless he could ram it into the creature's mouth, and down its throat. That should stop it! Because the lining of the throat was not tough.

But the cat would not simply stand there and open its mouth for him. It would sneak up and pounce, and its tusks would plunge through his flesh, crippling him. Then it would kill him at its leisure, perhaps letting him suffer longer than the camel had.

Unless he tricked it. If he lay down, pretending sleep or death, so that it thought him easy prey, then roused just in time to put the spear in.

Could he do that? Before darkness?

He doubted it. He could lie down, but the cat would probably be too canny, and would wait until darkness anyway. Cats were good at waiting, because they could not run down their prey the way wolves could. They had to wait for it to get close; then they jumped out and caught it with a sudden, brief burst of energy. Somewhat the way people did.

Blaze sighed. There seemed to be no help for it. His only real chance to fight the cat before dusk was to go out after it. If he couldn't fight it by then, he would have to desert the carcass.

He hefted his spear shaft and walked boldly out after the cat. There was a rustle as it moved away; it was not sure what to make of this. He turned to pursue it. It moved on around the carcass in a large circle, refusing to be driven away, but also refusing to fight. Yet.

Blaze followed. "Come and fight me, cat," he cried. "All I have is an imitation weapon. Turn and fight, because I can not hurt you from behind."

Still the cat refused to oblige. It was too hungry to allow itself to be driven off, but not sure enough to stand and fight. So it compromised.

Blaze was tired, but desperate. He had to make the cat turn on him! Then he might live or die, but the issue would be settled. So he broke into a run.

The cat moved faster, readily staying ahead. But it seemed nervous. Surely only a man with a good spear would dare to provoke such an encounter! He saw that it was quite lean, with ribs showing; it was hungry, and had been so for a long time. Just as the People were. Lean hunting affected all the predators. That was why they were contesting so determinedly for this one carcass: the one who got it would survive, and the one who lost it might die. They didn't have to kill each other directly; hunger would do that to the loser. The one who gave up the carcass without a fight, as much as the one who lost the fight.

Blaze kept running, though his breath was coming fast. Mankind was a long-distance mover, while catkind was a short-distance mover. He could keep this up longer than it could, tiring it. He thought. He hoped.

He had to slow, being unable to keep up the pace. But the cat slowed as soon as he did. It was less stressed at the moment, because it had merely loped while he was running. But it was tiring too. Its short-range advantage was giving way to his long-range advantage. It did not know that if it simply ran away into the forest and hid until dusk, it would win, because he would not be able to fight what he could not see. It thought it had to remain in contention without a break.

He slowed to a stride. But no slower. He could maintain that pace indefinitely. The cat could not. The longer this continued, the greater the shift in advantage would be.

But he knew that before it lost its remaining strength, the cat would turn and fight. He was not at all sure he would beat it. Because if it came at him at the wrong angle, or too swiftly for him to orient his spear, it would be on him, and its tusks and claws would destroy him in a moment. This was a challenge he would never have made, if he had not been desperate. If the hunger of the People did not depend on it.

At least he was saving his son, because even if he drove the cat away now, it should be too tired to make the longer quest for Stone. He had deprived it of its long-range stalking, by making it use up its strength running around the carcass. That was one victory, even if he lost the rest.

The cat moved to the side, away from the carcass. Was it giving up? Blaze doubted it—and in any event, he wasn't sure his son was far enough away to be safe. So he didn't *want* the cat leaving, yet.

So he pursued it, lurching after it. The cat snarled, showing the teeth behind its tusks. What a formidable array! Blaze feinted with his shaft—just as the cat moved forward. The end of the shaft touched a tusk and glanced off. The cat jerked back.

Blaze realized that it had done the same thing he had: feinted, trying to back him off. Trying to make him make a mistake, such as putting his foot in a hole and falling on his back, leaving his belly open to attack. The cat was as smart as he was, in this situation. The only reason he hadn't fallen for it was that he had already started to push forward, and couldn't reverse that quickly. So he had instead backed off the cat, by accident.

But the next confrontation could as readily go the other way, and that could be the end of him. The cat didn't want to fight him any more than he wanted to fight it, but it was hungry and had to get at the meat. It would leave him alone, if he simply walked away. Just as he would leave it alone, if it walked away—in any direction other than the one in which his son had gone.

But it wasn't going. It didn't know that his son was out there. It did know that there was plenty of meat right here. So it intended to have that meat.

That thought gave Blaze a notion. Suppose he hacked off part of the carcass and dragged it some distance away, leaving a share for the cat? Then it could eat, and he could relax, because it would not come for him or the main carcass once it was sated. It might even drag that share away, and he would not see it again. There would still be enough left for the People. That would avoid the risk of a fight he wasn't sure of winning.

He walked away from the cat, not turning his back; it was more like a sidle, with the shaft ready. He returned to the carcass. He held the shaft in the crook of one arm and brought out his stone knife. He could carve off a foreleg; that had enough meat to hold the cat, and was light enough for him to drag.

But as he bent to the task, the cat came in, snarling. It thought he was feeding, and that he would eat the whole thing. So it wouldn't let him do it.

"Get away!" he cried, brandishing the shaft.

The cat backed away, but not far. The moment Blaze sought to address the leg, the cat advanced again.

He tried working two-handed: holding the shaft aloft with his right, and using the knife with his left. But the skin of the camel was tough and baggy, resisting the stone blade; he needed to hold it firmly in place in order to cut into it. He also needed to look at what he was doing. And if he got through the skin, what about the sinew, flesh and bone? He would never get that leg separated, working with only his left hand while watching the cat.

Meanwhile, even as he contemplated the situation, the cat advanced again. Perhaps it was realizing that the spear shaft had no point, so was blunt. That his weapon might not hurt it at all, even if it scored.

Blaze realized that he would not be able to sever the leg. It would be difficult if he were able to put his full attention to it, and it was pointless to try with less. He was likely to get pounced on. He was unable to explain to the animal what he had in mind. Had it been another man, from a hostile tribe, he could have made a deal. Maybe.

But if there was more here than the cat could eat in a few hours, why not simply let it feed on the main carcass? After a few hours it would move away, sated, and there would still be plenty left for the People.

No, that was no good either. Because the cat would naturally go for the best parts first, and leave the rest of it chewed and soiled. That would mean that much of it would be wasted. There might even be cat urine or feces on it, because the cat would try to mark the carcass with its scent.

So he couldn't share, either way. He still had to defend his kill.

Blaze got back to his feet. Oh, he was tired! But so was the cat.

He resumed the stalking of his opponent. "Come at me, tuskface! Gape your mouth and charge me, so I can ram my pole down your gullet. Do it now." Because dusk was closing, shifting the advantage. He couldn't ram what he couldn't see.

But the cat was too smart for that. It moved to the side, still not certain he was bluffing. So he lunged at it with the staff, trying to poke it and provoke it into an attack.

And made his mistake. He misstepped when the cat dodged, and he stumbled, and fell forward. The cat whirled and was on him in an instant, pouncing with its jaws gaping, those two terrible tusks thrusting down. That was the way it killed its prey: by leaping onto the animal's back and plunging the tusks into the neck. The neck of most animals was weak, being vulnerable to any kind of strike.

But even as he fell, Blaze was lifting up his shaft to try to fend off just such an attack. The jaws closed on the wood instead of his body. But the striking forepaws caught his jacket, their claws sinking through it and into his flesh.

He got his legs under him and heaved himself up, violently, knowing that he would be finished in a moment if he did not get away. The shaft shoved broadside at the animal's body and head, preventing the head from getting into striking position. The claws ripped out of Blaze's flesh but retained their hold on his clothing. As he struggled free, the stitches gave way, leaving the bulk of the jacket to the cat.

And now the cat made its mistake. It thought it had hold of Blaze, and when he pulled away from his jacket, hauling the shaft with him, the cat chomped on the jacket. Cat and jacket rolled on the ground in a fierce fight.

Blaze turned, swung his shaft around, and oriented the end on the struggling mass. "Hey, tuskface!" he called again. "Over here!"

The cat was already realizing that something was amiss. It withdrew its claws, got its footing, and crouched, ready to pounce. It opened its mouth—

And Blaze rammed in the pole. This time he scored. It entered the cat's mouth just as it was opening and the body was launching into the air. The cat's own leap carried it onto the shaft.

The shock almost jarred the shaft from Blaze's hands. But he secured his grip and shoved forward as hard as he could. The pole did not actually go down the cat's throat; it jammed against the back of its mouth. But its somewhat sharpened point was lodging in something, and the cat was in trouble. It clamped down on the pole, reflexively, trying to bite it, to destroy it. Instead of being smart by scrambling back as fast as it could.

Blaze kept shoving, and the cat kept biting. Then the shaft wedged in a little more, getting past some kind of barrier, and the cat was in worse trouble. Now it tried to retreat, but couldn't hold its footing. Blaze just kept jamming the pole in until the cat screamed once more and collapsed. Something vital had been punctured.

He kept the pole lodged as he got his knife and cut across the cat's throat. This time the cut was effective, and the blood flowed out. The cat was done for.

Blaze stepped back. He had won, but as much by luck as planning. He hoped he never faced such a challenge again.

Now he felt more tired than ever. The fatigue that had been masked by his desperation had returned with full force. But he couldn't rest yet. There might be other predators coming in.

He staggered out and fetched wood. He brought it back to the two carcasses as darkness closed. Without the immediate threat of the cat he could range farther, and get enough to last the night. That was important, because already the chill of it was setting in.

He took the added precaution of harvesting all the tall grass he could, in a circle around the site. It would help start the fire, and extend it some, but that was not his reason. He wanted to prevent the fire from spreading, when he slept. Because a fire out of control would be as bad a threat as the tusked cat had been.

He made the fire, keeping it small. It was mostly for warmth, and partly to warn away other animals, and partly to signal the People, if they came during the night. He doubted that they would, but they might, if they were sure of their way. A large enough party, with torches, could travel well by night, because then the air was cool.

When the fire was right, he sat down by it, really appreciating its warmth. There was something about a fire that fascinated him, no matter how many times he saw it, and that also comforted him. How often he had lain with Bunny by the fire, having sex with her there. She was twenty-nine years old now, beyond her youth and full sex appeal, but he still found her satisfying. How he wished she were here with him now!

He slept—and dreamed instead of another woman. He did not know her name or tribe, but he knew her nature: she was a fire tender, loving the fire for itself. She was his own age, and beautiful and ardent. His dream woman. He had always dreamed of her, even before mating with Bunny. Her eyes were green, like his, and she had burn scars on her fingers, and there was something wrong with her cheek. She was insatiably curious, wanting to know all about everything. He had never met such a woman, but had always longed for her. In fact he had acceded to mating with Bunny because her green eyes reminded him of that phantom woman he loved. Certainly Bunny was good enough for him; in retrospect he concluded that she was the best of all the women he had encountered. He would have congratulated himself on the wisdom of his choosing—except that she had chosen him. But she could not compete with his oddly imperfect fantasy woman. He felt guilty about that, but it was so.

He woke, finding the fire dying into embers. The feeling of the dream woman grew stronger. He added wood and shaped up the fire so that it burned better, and the image of the woman faded. She was a creature of the dying fire, somehow, not of life.

As dawn came, so did the People. There was a cry as they spied him. Stone was there, with four hunters. They *had* traveled by night, perhaps sleeping during part of it, so as to arrive in time to hunt the camels.

Now they stared at the two carcasses, amazed. "And you said you weren't a hunter," one said.

"Well, I couldn't wait for you," Blaze replied, smiling. "And I had to set an example for my son."

They laughed, knowing that it had required skill and determination to accomplish what he had, but mostly luck. It would do.

"I knew you would do it," Stone told him. "And so did Mom. She said you wouldn't let a camel get away."

The hunters smiled to themselves. They would be the last to deny it. They had women and children of their own.

Thus seeming plenty quickly became scarcity, as one species after another was hunted to oblivion. Mankind showed no judgment and no restraint. Mastodons, giant beavers, horses, camels and saber-toothed cats joined many species of fish and birds in extinction. What seemed so wonderful to a tribesman—the finding of a small surviving herd of camels—was actually another step in the impoverishment of the variety of species on the continent. But this was only the beginning. It is possible that this destruction of potentially useful species accounts for the Western failure to domesticate animals such as horses, camels, and elephants that contributed so much to mankind's power in Eurasia, and thus left the tribes of the Americas vulnerable to conquest. The dog was domesticated, but little else.

CHAPTER 10

TOWN

Ten thousand years ago, in the mountains of the region known as the Fertile Crescent, mankind was beginning to utilize wild grains such as wheat and barley in a more thorough manner than before. This was not a sudden change; it took time to shift from the primary dependence on hunting and gathering to actual cultivation. Nevertheless, as this supplementary source of food proved to be reliable, so that fewer people died of hunger, the residence of the communities using it expanded. Indeed, agriculture was to make possible an enormous increase in human population. Soon the hunter-gatherer cultures

131

were being crowded out of their ranges, much as the Neandertals were crowded out by the moderns.

Thus came into being what we call the Natufian culture, a precursor of what is called the Neolithic Revolution. The setting is the Levant, where full language may have evolved 30,000 years before this. The town is an outlying province not far from Jericho of biblical fame, perhaps the world's first full city.

CRYSTAL was outraged. "Something's been eating my flowers!" she cried. "See, they're chomped off, down low on the stems." She pointed the damage out to her mother.

Ember nodded in that parental way she had. "Perhaps an ox."

"But, Mother, there's no hoofprint!" Crystal protested. She was fifteen, and knew what was what. She had guarded these flowers, pulling out encroaching weeds, so that when they bloomed she could pluck them and take them in to beautify their home. She had always had a taste for beauty, whether in flowers, paintings, or in stories.

"Perhaps rats," her mother suggested. Her cheek was twitching just a trifle, which meant she was up to something.

"They are chewed off too high," Crystal said, fathoming the error.

"You must post a discouraging spell," Ember said.

Crystal considered. She was not at all certain of the efficacy of spells. Certainly none she had tried had worked very well. But she was untrained in them. "Do you think the priestess would come out and do a spell?" she asked.

Ember smiled. "She might, for you."

The girl reconsidered. The priestess might indeed to it, but not for mere flowers. Spells were reserved for important things. So she would have to see to this herself. "I'll come out tonight and guard them," she announced. "Because in one or two days more will be ready to bloom. After that it won't matter."

Ember shrugged tolerantly. "Do as you wish. Check with your father first. But now we must harvest some barley."

They got to work, picking the small ripe seed heads and collecting them in their baskets. They had to harvest only the uppermost seeds, because the ones below were unripe and not suitable. Crystal shared her mother's acute direct vision, so was good at this. It was tedious work, but they made it fun by singing as they labored, with the other women joining in. They developed some really nice harmonies, so that Crystal was almost sorry to finish.

They brought their baskets in to the pounding women, who used their skill with wood mallets to beat the grains separate from the tough husks. Each family's basketful was done separately, and the grain returned to that family, with shares taken out for the pounders and for general use. The pounders, male and female, were so skilled that it was better to have them do it, and yield the shares, than to try to do it oneself.

She did check with Scorch when they returned to the town. He was as usual tending the central hearth. Each family hut had its own small hearth, of course, but it was sometimes more efficient to roast acorns and large carcasses on a big one, then share out the portions. Hunters had brought in a gazelle, which was now slowly cooking; there would be satisfaction tonight. However, ordinarily the communal hearth was maintained simply as the eternal flame, the source of all other fires in the town. Ceremonies were held around it.

Her father glanced at her in that way he had. "You are insatiably curious, Crystal, just like your mother," he remarked. "One day that could get you into trouble."

"Don't treat me like a child!" she retorted, though she knew the remark was well intended. "I'm a woman. Just like my mother." She inhaled to make the point.

"Indeed you are," he agreed, casting a frankly assessing gaze across her torso. "Your mother was younger than you when I first mated her."

He had turned it on her. "Well, I just haven't found a man as good as you," she said, trying not to flush with mixed pleasure and chagrin. If she got much older without finding a man she liked, she might have to visit the big town of Jericho where there were many more men. But she detested big-city ways; those folk thought they were better than small-town folk, ludicrous as that was. "So is it all right if I go out tonight?"

"I will go with you," he offered.

"No! I want to do it myself. I'll take a spear and a knife. I can handle the kind of animal that eats flowers."

He nodded, resigned in much the way of her mother. "You are grown. If you can face the darkness alone, we must let you." But he looked uneasy about it, and she knew that he would be watching out for her, listening in case she should scream in the night.

"Thank you, Father," she said, and kissed him. She had almost always been able to get her way, if her desire was basically reasonable.

He returned to his work without comment.

○

That evening Crystal went out to the edge of the barley field, where her chosen flowers grew. She did it under the cover of the last remaining daylight, knowing that the night marauder would not be close then. Of course it might not show up this night, either, having already gotten many of the flowers. But if it did, she would be ready for it. She hoped. She had a short wood spear, a small stone knife, and her hollow bone firepot and unlit torch.

She made a nest for herself in the nearby tall weeds and settled down for what she feared would be a long wait. She was well garbed, because it would get cool in the night. Her woven shawl covered her body from shoulder to knees, and her gazelle fur skirt covered all of her legs and feet when she settled down. The firepot was covered so as to give off no light and so little smoke as to be unnoticeable, but it was warm, and helped heat the air under her skirt. She should be comfortable.

Now she had to be absolutely quiet. She could sleep if she wished, but had to be ready to wake the moment there was the sound of any creature approaching. Her eyes adjusted to the light of the half-moon, so that she could see well enough. If the animal proved to be big, like an ox, she would jump out and frighten it, for they were timid creatures despite their size. If it turned out to be small, she would try to spear it, though she was only a girl and not well versed in weapons. Either way, she would discover what it was, and give it a real scare. For she had a device that should be effective against even a carnivore: her firepot. Both her parents were fire workers, the one for the village, the other for the home. They had taught her the use and control of fire. So she could quickly produce her glowing punk and touch it to her torch and make a blaze of light.

Time passed, and the sounds of the night came. Some were all right, like the chorusing of frogs and crickets; in fact she wanted those sounds near her, because their absence would signal her presence to the animal. Others made her nervous, like the rustling of what might be a snake. Probably it was just a rat, though. She also saw a large bird swoop silently by, perhaps an owl. But there were no sounds of heavy treading, such as a grazing animal might make.

Soon enough it got dull, then downright boring. Without realizing it, Crystal drifted to sleep. But she had the sense to remain still and quiet.

She woke soon; the moon had not moved far. There was heavy motion in the field! It was coming toward her. Her ploy was working. She felt under her spread skirt, making sure of her torch and firepot, ready to bring them together. But not till she knew just what kind of creature she was dealing with.

The tramping of feet came closer. She didn't dare turn her head to peer directly, lest that motion make her visible. Unfortunately her peripheral vision was poor—just like her mother's. But in a moment the animal would come into her line of sight, and she would know.

Then the moon moved behind a cloud, and the darkness closed in too thickly to give her the necessary view. Oh, didn't that douse her fire! She could still hear the animal, but couldn't see it in the gloom of the ground.

Still, she could tell where it was by the sounds, and the loss of moonlight also made her invisible to it. She could light her torch the moment it chomped her flowers, and illuminate the marauder. So the moon really didn't matter. She was going to give that creature one big surprise, and it probably would never bother her flowers again.

It kept coming closer, tramp, tramp. She tried to figure its size and species by the pattern of the footfalls, but couldn't; they were irregular, and the thing paused often, perhaps sniffing the air. She knew that animals had keen noses, but the human smell here wouldn't tell it anything, because the flowers were right by the path they followed to reach the barley field. That always smelled of human.

Finally it was right there, so close she heard its breathing. She could see only a vague hulk, a darkness against the darkness. It loomed over her flowers, and she heard a stalk being crunched.

It was time to act. She thumbed the cover off her firepot and poked the head of the torch into it. Then she brought both out and blew. The torch flared to life. "Ha!" she cried, thrusting the blazing brand forward.

There stood not an animal but a man. His mouth was open with surprise. Then he reacted in the manner of a hunter: he leaped forward, bringing his spear to bear.

Crystal screamed and tried to scramble away. But she was sitting cross-legged on the ground, and couldn't move well until she got to her feet.

Then the man was on her, his arm bearing her back. The torch flew from her hand. Crystal screamed again and tried to push him off, but his hand caught her cape at her chest and shoved her down again as he brought his spear around. She felt his strength, and knew that she had no real chance. He was going to kill her.

The realization had a peculiar effect on her. She became passive, her fear fading. It was as if she were already dead, so it didn't matter. She was beyond pain or caring.

Then he paused. The hand moved at her chest, pressing her breast beneath it. He had discovered she was female. Men didn't usually kill women. Not right away.

That snapped her out of her stasis. She inhaled, so as to scream again, but he moved his hand up to cover her mouth. She thought to bite his fingers, but hesitated; that might only make him react in fury, and then he would run his spear through her after all. So she waited to see what he would do, before deciding what she would do.

He pondered a moment, then came to a decision. He got to his feet, and hauled her to her feet. Was he going to rape her? Now she could scream, but still she hesitated. She wasn't sure why.

He bent and put his shoulder to her stomach. Then he heaved her up like a log, draped across his shoulder, so that her head was halfway down his back and her legs dangled down his front. He tramped back the way he had come, carrying her.

She thought once more of screaming, and once more did not act. She knew this was crazy. The man was hauling her away from the town, to who knew what fate, yet she had stopped protesting. Her mind was coming to terms with the situation. She realized that he had been as surprised as she by the encounter. First he had sought to kill her as an enemy; then, realizing that she was a woman, to silence her; then he had decided to take her home. Maybe to ask his mother what he should do with her.

She smiled, thinking that, though it wasn't funny. She was in trouble, and her life was in danger. At any point the man's uncertainty could be resolved in favor of simply killing her and being done with it.

The moon came out again, but it didn't help much, because all she could see was where they had been. But this was uncomfortable; she would prefer to be on her feet, no matter where they were going.

So she did something crazy. She spoke to him. "Hey, man, put me down. I'll walk."

He stopped, listening. Did he understand her? She wasn't sure what tribe he was from, as there were a number of nomad groups in the area. He might understand, or might not, or might be somewhere between.

He leaned forward and set her down. She shook herself, and rubbed her belly where she had been chafed. Now she could make a break for it. But he would simply catch her and put her back on his shoulder.

So she did another crazy thing. She smiled at him, though aware that he might not be able to see her expression, and slowly moved into him. She embraced him, and reached her face up toward his. When he did not bring his face down, perhaps being too surprised, she moved her hands up to the back of his head and pushed it down from behind. Finally she got it in range, and she kissed him on the mouth.

He seemed stunned. Good. Now he might view her as a person instead of a captive. So he wouldn't hurt her.

"Let's go," she said. "Where do you live?"

He spoke his first word. "Home." He pointed.

So he did understand her. That helped.

She walked in the indicated direction. After a moment, he did the same. Now it was as if she had just decided to go with him, instead of being captured.

"What is your name?" she asked. "Mine is Crystal."

He considered, then answered. "Name—Carver."

"Carver," she repeated. "You cut up animals?"

"Wood," he said.

"You are a wood gatherer? For fire?" This was getting almost positive. The more she engaged him in dialogue, the less likely there was to be trouble.

He hesitated again, then reached into his jacket. He brought out an object.

Crystal was afraid it was a stone knife, but soon realized it wasn't. It was a stick. He held it toward her, and she took it. She ran her fingers over it. The thing was irregular, as if carved—

Carved. He carved wood. And this piece of wood was in the shape of an animal. Perhaps a gazelle. He had carved a figure. He was an artisan!

"It's beautiful," she said, returning it. For though she could not see it, she could feel its intricacies. She had been trying to impress on her captor the fact that she was a person; now she was discovering that he too was a person.

In due course they reached the camp of the nomads. This consisted of several conical shelters fashioned from cut saplings and overlapping furs. Crystal could see only their tops outlined against the dark sky, but knew the type. She had never thought much of the nomads, knowing them to be primitives. But they were a major source of animal hides, because they lived by hunting rather than by farming. The men of the town traded with the nomads several times a year, giving up good wood and stone tools for hides, and sometimes woven basketwork.

Carver brought her to one of the rude shelters. Sure enough, there was an old woman, sitting by a low fire. "What's this? What's this?" she exclaimed, spying Crystal.

"I found her," Carver replied awkwardly. "She was screaming, so I took her with me."

"That's a townswoman!" the woman cried. "What did you think we would do with her?"

The man stood silent, evidently not having thought that far ahead.

Rather than have the man think of something, Crystal spoke for herself. "He was taking my flowers. I watched to see who. I thought it was an animal."

"Flowers," the woman said. She gestured at the shelter. Now Crystal saw in the firelight that the door flap was decorated with flowers. "He brought them for me."

Crystal turned an appraising eye on the man. This barbarian carved figures in wood and brought flowers to his mother. He was not the savage she had feared. Still, she argued her case. "I was saving those flowers for *my* mother. Or rather my father. He works all day with the fire, and doesn't see the countryside as much as he would like. So I bring him flowers, when I'm out harvesting grain."

The woman heaved herself to her feet. "Let me look at you, girl." She approached and ran her hands over Crystal's body, squeezing her on the arms, breasts, hips and thighs. Crystal realized that she was either blind or very weak of sight, at least in the night. "You're a pretty one. They will miss you."

"I didn't mean to come here," Crystal said.

"Take her back," the woman told Carver. "Before the town sends men to overwhelm us in vengeance. Get her back before morning, so we don't get the blame."

Carver hesitated. "I like her," he said after a moment.

"Well of course you do!" the woman snapped. "She's got a good body and a good face. But she wouldn't like it here. We'd get little good use of her. See, her hands are hardly callused, and her teeth aren't stained. She doesn't know how to chew hides. Take her back to her own kind."

Crystal was not inclined to argue with this assessment. All she wanted to do at this stage was get home.

Carver nodded regretfully. It was evident that he was indeed impressed by Crystal's appearance, and perhaps by her kiss, but had little knowledge of women.

The man started walking, and Crystal hastened to join him. "Thank you, Mother," she called back over her shoulder.

It took time to cover the distance to the town, because the moon had faded out and there was no good path. Carver was better able to see than Crystal was, perhaps because he was familiar with this country, having hunted in it by night. She kept blundering into brush and even trees. Her jacket and skirt kept snagging on branches and brambles, and her arms and legs got scratched. She stepped in a hole, took a fall, got snagged again, and her skirt got ripped off her body. She recovered it, but couldn't repair it in the dark, so had to carry it. Finally Carver had her put her hand on the tail of his jacket, so she could follow in his footsteps while he picked out the way.

As they approached the barley field, points of light appeared. These turned out to be torches. "Those are townsmen, maybe looking for me," Crystal said. "You must go back now, before they see you."

Glad to be freed, Carver started back. Then he paused. "I wish—" he started, but couldn't finish his thought.

"I am not your kind," Crystal reminded him. "I can't chew hides."

He put his hand in his jacket. He brought out the carving. He shoved it at her. "For you."

"Why, thank you, Carver," Crystal said, touched. "I will cherish it."

He started back again. But now the light of torches appeared between him and his route home. The townsmen had surrounded them and were closing in, not yet knowing the identity of the two figures.

"Carver, wait," Crystal cried. "I don't think you can get through, and they won't understand. Stay with me, and I'll try to explain." Because the man had turned out to be a decent sort, and she didn't want him hurt.

They waited until the torches came within hailing range. "It's me, Crystal!" she called. "I'm all right."

"Who's that with you?" a townsman called back. "Did he hurt you?"

"No, he just—showed me his home," Crystal explained. "Let him go; he's all right."

"He raped you," the man said, coming close enough to see her bundled skirt, which she was holding before her in a haphazard attempt at modesty. "We'll kill him."

Carver made ready to bolt, knowing he was in trouble. But Crystal knew it would be futile. If he tried to run, they would riddle him with spears. "No," she told him desperately. "Stand still. I will protect you."

But she knew by his nervous look and the determination of the closing townsmen that he would not stand still and they would not let him go. She was about to be responsible for a needless killing. Carver's poor ailing mother would have no one to support her. So Crystal did one more crazy thing.

She dropped her loose skirt and flung her arms around Carver, holding him in place by sheer determination. She turned her head to scream at the others. "No, he's mine! I love him! I will marry him! We had a tryst!" She gripped Carver tightly and hauled up her bare legs, wrapping them around his torso. He staggered, trying to keep his balance, hardly understanding what she was doing.

The townsman's jaw dropped. "It's that way?"

"Don't you dare touch him!" Crystal cried. "I'll bring him home to meet my family now. He'll join us. He has a skill we can use. He can carve figures." She hiked herself up on the man and planted a kiss somewhere on his face.

There wasn't much the townsmen could do except accept her word. They agreed to let her bring the stranger to the town. Crystal picked up her skirt with whatever aplomb she could muster and wrapped it around her hips. She held it in place with one hand, and used the other to lead Carver toward the town. "It will be all right," she told him. "You'll see. Once they know you're tame, they'll let you go home to your mother."

But it turned out to be less simple. Scorch and Ember were understanding, having pretty well figured out the situation, but couldn't speak of it openly because it would make a liar of their eldest daughter. The town did not just admit outsiders without challenge, especially not nomads. There was a solid core of unbelievers in the town who thought Crystal was just protecting the nomad to cover her shame for being raped, and they wanted to settle that shame the honorable way, by castrating and killing him and defiling the corpse. She didn't dare let him out of her sight. But she was dead tired and had to sleep. So she had to have him sleep with her, in the family hut, behind the hearth.

The hut was vaguely like the shelters of the nomads, but larger and better constructed, with linings of stone rubble. They were sunk half a body length into the ground, with stout posts supporting the roof. Instead of animal skins they had reed matting, and the sleeping section was raised above the packed-dirt floor. This was much better than a sewn-skins shelter!

Behind the hut was a privy trench. Crystal took Carver there and used it herself, just as if they were lovers who had no secrets from each other, because she knew that others were covertly watching. She insisted that he use it too, while she watched, because she feared that if she allowed him decent privacy he would instead try to flee the town, and get killed. She had been his captive; now he was hers. Until the townsmen were satisfied of the legitimacy of the association.

Reluctantly, he performed. Then she took him back inside and to her mat, and made him lie there with her. "My people do not understand," she murmured in his ear. "They want to kill you. You must pretend to love me, until they lose interest. Then you can go home."

"I do like you," he said. "I could love you." Indeed, she was becoming aware that he was aroused, and would want to have sex with her if she didn't discourage him quickly.

"Yes, but you wouldn't want to leave your people and live here, would you?" she asked pointedly.

"All I want to do is carve," he said.

"Oh, that's right—I must return your carving." She fished in her jacket for it. "It isn't right for me to keep it, when you didn't get to go home."

"No, that is for you, because you are nice. I know you saved my life."

She was touched again. "You're nice too, Carver. You bring flowers to your mother, and you brought me back."

"I didn't mean to take you," he said apologetically. "I just didn't know what to do, when you turned out to be a woman. I thought you would rouse the town against me."

"I understand," she said. Indeed, now she did. "Look, I'm awfully tired. I've got to sleep now. Don't go anywhere without me, because the townsmen don't like strangers."

"I sleep too, in the daytime," he said.

So they slept. He did not try to rape her, and she appreciated that.

In the afternoon Crystal woke to the sound of talking, and realized that her parents were having a dialogue with Carver, who had gotten up but not left the house. She did not mean to eavesdrop; she just was slow to wake, being partially conscious for awhile, and gradually realized what she was hearing. Then she just lay there and listened some more.

"No, we are not lovers," Carver was saying. "She just said that to stop them from killing me."

"She always did have a soft heart," Ember said. "She gets angry if someone even hurts a flower."

"Well of course," he said. "Flowers are beautiful." Then, after a pause: "I should not have taken her flowers. I did not realize—"

"How could you know?" Scorch asked. "Flowers are for anyone to pick."

"But these are special," Carver said. "They bloom at night, and make the shelter smell nice. I got them for my mother." Another pause. "Oh, she will be worrying! I should have returned before this."

"We shall have to resolve this quickly, so you can return," Ember said. "Crystal said you carve wooden figures."

Crystal, listening, wondered what that had to do with it. But she knew that her mother did not waste time when something was on her mind.

"Yes, I wish I could stop hunting and just carve," he agreed.

"Here is a piece of wood," Scorch said. "Can you carve it?"

"Oh, yes! Oh, this is a nice piece. See the grain of it. There is a bird in there, waiting to be expressed."

"A bird?"

"I will show you." There was the sound of wood being scraped or carved.

"My daughter said she had a tryst with you," Scorch said. "She said she loves you, and will marry you."

"No, I already told you—"

"Let me finish," Scorch said firmly. "My daughter is many things, but never has she been a liar."

"I would not call her that," Carver said. "But if she became a liar to save my life—"

"Oh, I see the bird!" Ember said. "You are bringing it from the wood."

"It was always there," Carver said, pleased. "I just had to uncover it."

"You do have a rare talent for evoking the essence of wood," Scorch said. "A figure such as this could have mystical significance. A shaman might have use for it."

"Anyone would like to have it near," Ember said. "It's almost alive!"

"I just reveal what I see. It can be anything. This wood has a bird. Another might have a flower."

"It's beautiful," Ember said.

"There is no need for Crystal to be a liar, or for you to lose your life," Scorch said.

There was a silence. Carver evidently did not understand the thrust of Scorch's words, but Crystal did. She strongly suspected that her father knew she was listening, and that his words were meant for her.

She would not be a liar, if she really did marry Carver. If her ruse became the truth. Her parents approved of Carver, perhaps because they had always liked pretty things, and it was evident that he not only liked such things, he made them. But marriage—Crystal was not at all sure she was ready for that, though she was of age.

In fact she was more than of age. Other girls married at thirteen or fourteen, whenever their breasts developed enough to attract men. Crystal had been ready in that sense for two years, and had had her chances, but still found the young men of the town to be singularly uninteresting, and the older men worse.

Yet she would have to marry sometime. Those who did not became social outcasts, and eventually full outcasts, being expelled from the town. That was not what she wanted. Now she realized that her parents were in the process of taking action to prevent it.

"Suppose you could be given work carving," Ember said. "Here in the town. All day."

"I would not care where I was, if I could do that," Carver said. "But I could not stay here. My mother—"

"Suppose your mother came here?"

"I don't think she would like it. She—"

"She depends on you," Ember said. "She does not go out much now."

"Yes. She is lame and does not see well. She weaves mostly by feel. I have to tell her the colors of the strands. Since my father died, I—"

"If you could continue to provide for her here," Ember persisted. She, too, was evidently speaking for Crystal's ears, guiding her course. Scorch and Ember would rather have her marry Carver than remain unmarried.

"I suppose she wouldn't mind. She stays mostly in the shelter. She can still use her hands, so she keeps the fire and cooks. I bring the wood and food."

"The townsmen must approve any person who seeks to join the town," Scorch said. "But normally they allow those who marry towns-folk."

"How well do you like our daughter?" Ember asked.

Carver finally got their drift. "Oh, I like her well. She is pretty, and she likes flowers. But I know nothing about the ways of the town, and—why would she want to be with the likes of me?"

"She must like you well enough to protect you," Ember pointed out. Of course she knew that wasn't it; Crystal would have protected a baby ox from harm, if it lowed at her. She took all creatures personally, and if they were not enemies they were friends.

Crystal decided that it was time for her to get up. "Hello," she said, stretching.

"Carver needs to see to his mother, who is alone and worried," Ember said.

She knew she had to decide now. The townsmen would not let Carver go unless she married him. She had known that the moment she brought him in, but had not let herself realize what it required of her. So was she ready to commit, though it forever changed her life?

Maybe this was the way her life was to be. She had not made the decision on her own, so it had been made for her. If she didn't go along with it, she might not like the next choice any better. Carver wasn't a bad man. He was talented, and he wasn't arrogant in the way of a city man. She could probably manage him, and that notion had appeal.

"Let's do it," she said.

"Do what?" Carver asked.

Crystal laughed, feeling better already.

After that it was swift. They went to the head townsman and declared that they were marrying and that their children would be loyal townsfolk. With Crystal's parents supporting her commitment, the head townsman had to accept it. He nodded, and something relaxed; the watching men no longer had a cause.

Then they walked to the nomad settlement to fetch Carver's mother, reaching it by evening. The woman was not unduly surprised. "I knew you were dead or married," she remarked, as if there were not much difference between the two.

"But we want to take you with us, Mother," Crystal explained. "So we can take care of you."

Now the woman showed surprise. Crystal realized that she had expected to be deserted by either the death or marriage of her son. So for her it meant doom, regardless.

But she was quick to accept the new order. "Take down the shelter," she told Carver.

Under her direction, he lowered the poles and carefully folded the stitched furs. They made a considerable pile. Crystal realized that this represented the wealth of the nomad family: the longer it survived, the more furs it collected, and the warmer was its shelter. Carver's father must have been a good provider.

Carver used poles to make a travois, and heaved the mass of furs onto it. He started to haul it, then realized that this wasn't enough: there was his mother.

"I'll haul it," Crystal said. She fitted herself to the harness. The furs were heavy, but her legs were good, and when she leaned forward she could haul the mass along.

That left Carver free to help his mother. The woman could walk, but only slowly, when her son was supporting her. Crystal realized that Carver's care for his mother was one of the factors in her decision to marry him. He would have similar loyalty to his wife. His good qualities were subtle but strong.

They were making the trip by night; it was really better for the woman, who liked neither the harsh sun of day nor the stares of strangers as she limped along. Better for Crystal too, because she was soon sweating despite the cooling air and slow pace. This would have been devastating at noon.

By morning they were at the town. Ember served them gruel by the fire while Scorch stared at the bundle of furs with amazement and set about wrestling them into the house.

The three of them were tired, and quickly settled down. Carver's mother was soon snoring on Ember's bed. Ember gave Crystal a meaningful glance and took up her basket: she had grain to gather out in the field. Scorch had gone to tend the main town fire right after moving the furs. The house was theirs, for much of the day.

Crystal was fatigued from the long haul, but knew what she had to do. She touched Carver's shoulder. "I know you are tired, but this is the time we must do it."

"Do what?" he asked sleepily.

She opened her jacket, showing him her breasts.

Suddenly he understood. After that he needed no more guidance. He did indeed desire her, and now that she was willing, he proceeded with a vigor that belied his fatigue. All she had to do was lie there and let him.

This was just as well, because she realized belatedly that her uncertainty about sex was a significant part of her ambiguity about marriage. She had known what it was and how to do it, but had doubted that it would really work for her. She had somehow felt that a man would find her inadequate, because her breasts were not the fullest and her thighs were not the fattest. But as she noted the thorough enjoyment of her body that Carver was experiencing, those doubts dissipated, never to return. She had worried for nothing.

Carver made a final panting thrust and collapsed. In a moment he was asleep. This was the way of a man, she knew; she had seen her father do it often enough. Crystal stroked his head and concluded that this sufficed.

In the afternoon Crystal woke to find Carver's mother tending the hearth fire. Then Crystal realized that she remained bare, with Carver's hand on one of her breasts. His mother had surely seen. Well, perhaps that was just as well; this sort of thing was expected of newly married folk.

Crystal worked her way free, got up, went to the privy trench, cleaned herself, and then approached the hearth. The woman handed her a bowl of gruel. "It is good," she said. "My boy needed to be married."

"I needed to be married too," Crystal said. "But now we must get a house, for us and you."

"Will the furs be enough?"

Suddenly Crystal realized the point of bringing the furs along. They were worth a fabulous amount! "Yes, I think so."

Carver stirred. "Crystal," he called.

"I am here," she called back.

The old woman made a crooked smile. "No, you must go to him," she murmured. "He is a young man." She faced deliberately away from the bed.

Oh. Crystal went back to her husband and doffed her jacket and skirt. In a moment she was amidst another siege of his enjoyment. She was somewhat sore from the prior session, but kept her mouth shut. She remained glad that her body not only performed as it should, but that it excited so much enthusiasm in him. They had been married only a night and a day, but already she felt competent.

In due course Carver was up and dressed and eating gruel. Now, with nice and perhaps not coincidental timing, Ember returned from her harvest. "There may be a house available," she said. "A widower is moving in with his son, if he can get good value for his house."

"The furs," Carver's mother said.

"Yes, I think so," Ember agreed.

They went out and talked with the widower and his son. It was a good house, and the widower came to inspect the furs. He was satisfied. By evening the exchange had been made; the furs were gone and they owned the house.

They moved in, with the considerable help of Crystal's family, and made their own hearth fire. It was dark again, and they were tired, so they settled down to sleep. Carver had at her again, enthusiastically, and she was glad to oblige because she knew that not only did it please him, it would soon put him to sleep.

In the morning Crystal took Carver around, introducing him, and showed the carving he had given her. There were several folk who expressed interest in having similar carvings, for which they were prepared to trade. The shaman was indeed interested, as Scorch had surmised. That meant that there would be no trouble there. Crystal nodded; Carver's skill was viable. She got him assorted pieces of wood, and he settled down to carve.

Nine months later Crystal gave birth to a daughter, whom they named Flower. This capped a generally suitable experience. Carver had done well with his carving, and his mother's weaving and sewing were competent, and they had never gone hungry. They simply traded his carvings for whatever they needed. She wasn't certain whether Carver was happier to be constantly indulging his talent, or constantly having a young woman of his own. Certainly he had taken well to town life, and seemed not to miss his former nomadic style at all. He brought her and his mother flowers almost every day, if there were any to be found.

But with the birth of her child, Crystal believed she had truly come of age. She had proven herself capable in every aspect of marriage. What better success could there be in life?

Thus, gradually, the hunter-gatherer society gave way to the settled life. The crafts of the towns supplanted those of the wanderers. The future of mankind lay with the settled regions. But nomads continued to exist, and at times had considerable impact on the settled regions.

C H A P T E R 1 1

CITY

One of the most remarkable early cities we know of was Catal Huyuk, in Anatolia (modern Turkey), founded about nine thousand years ago. It existed in one form or another for about two thousand years, and may have had as many as 10,000 people at its height. Its architecture was strikingly distinct from what had been before, and from what was to follow. Yet it was not far from the region where the hunter-gatherers still ranged. In more than one respect, it might be considered a frontier city, though it did not exist in isolation; there were a number of similar cities in the region. With such large settlements came also the politics of human interaction.

149

BLAZE spied the trading caravan near the volcano. He had an affinity for the volcano, because it was a fire mountain, though he would have stayed well clear of it had it been violent.

He strode forward to meet the trader. He had not encountered this one before, but knew their nature. The chances were good that the man would have what he wanted.

The man stopped and waited for Blaze to reach him. He was garbed in bright robes, indicating his trade. If Blaze wished to trade for such a robe, the man would take it off, revealing another below it.

"I have glass," Blaze announced.

Now the trader spoke, having identified Blaze's language. He of course spoke many languages, and knew how to make himself understood even if verbal communication didn't work. "Glass we have," he said, indicating the mountain.

"Yes, of course." Blaze came here himself to gather crude obsidian. He had a good eye for the fragments that would make the best knives. "But mine has been worked." He brought out a sample blade that his son Stone had made. Stone was clever with rock, naturally.

"Ah." The man squinted at the blade, immediately recognizing its craftsmanship. "How many?"

Blaze flashed the fingers of both hands, twice. "Twenty."

The trader nodded. They would do business. "What do you want?"

"Fine textile for my wife." Bunny was thirty-four, and showing her age, but a garment made of fine cloth would do much to enhance her.

"Textiles we have. Come." The trader turned and walked to his largest bag, which he had set down as Blaze approached. Blaze followed, wondering how badly the trader would cheat him. Still, it was better than hiking several more days to the big city, where the merchants would also cheat him.

The man opened the bag to reveal bundles of textile. Nearby sat a strikingly pretty young woman. There was a collar around her slender neck, with a rope extending from it to the bag on which she sat. The girl looked about fourteen, and was dressed in a silken gown whose near translucence showed her breasts. What was such a creature doing here?

The trader caught Blaze's gaze. "Ah, you notice the slave. Perhaps you would prefer to trade for her instead? The dress goes with her."

"Her?" Blaze asked, startled. "We mountain folk do not hold slaves!"

"Nor do you need to. Take her and free her, once she accepts you. I keep her tied because I do not know her well enough to trust her, but she has made no effort to escape. Feed her, treat her well, and she will be as fine a wife or mistress as you could ask. She is quality-born."

"I have a wife!" Blaze said indignantly. "And a son as old as this girl is. I would not—"

"For your son, then." The trader squinted, surely considering how far he should pursue this matter. "She would be just right for him. For your twenty blades, an even trade."

For his son. Blaze had never thought of such a thing. But the boy would be unlikely to find any woman as lovely as this one. And, though he tried to quell the realization, Blaze was attracted to her himself. She reminded him of Bunny, when she had been that age, lithe yet wonderful where it counted. No, it wasn't attraction, it was affinity: because she reminded him of his wife of more than twenty years, he hated to see her bound like this. What would happen to her, if the trader took her to the next town?

But this was foolishness. There had to be a catch. "I'll trade for cloth," he said.

But the trader had sniffed a better deal. "You think there must be something wrong with her. Well, there is; she cries too much. See, her eyes are red-rimmed. I do not mistreat her, I only keep her bound, so she will not run away. Yet she weeps. I don't wish to travel far with such a drag. Take her off my hands, make her happy, and she will be the bargain of the year."

Blaze was tempted again. Such beauty, for his son! Still, he knew better. "Cloth," he said firmly.

"Still you fear a bad bargain. Well, I will prove her to you. Talk to her. As long as you need. I will make camp here, so you are not rushed. Get to know her. Then, if you are not satisfied, trade for the cloth."

Blaze knew that the man believed that if he got to know the girl, he would like her increasingly, and would be unable to let her go. Traders were exceedingly canny in their judgment of people. But he was now quite interested in the mysterious girl. At least he could satisfy his curiosity.

"Does she speak my language?" he asked.

"Yes. But the city dialect."

"That might as well be foreign," he said. "I can't understand a fast-talking city man at all."

"She can make herself understood, if she chooses." He squinted cannily at Blaze. "You would not trust my translation."

Exactly. The man wanted to make a sale.

Blaze addressed the young woman, who had been listening throughout. "Woman, will you talk with me?"

She looked up, her eyes great and sorrowful. They were green, and that made him take note; his wife's eyes were green, as were his own and his children's. But it was not his eyes the girl was looking at. She saw the great fire mark on his forehead. She did not speak.

Blaze was used to this. He touched the mark. "My head is not burning up," he said. "I was born with this, and I am ordinary beneath it."

She averted her gaze.

"I might buy you for my son," Blaze said. "But I must know you are worth it."

"You are talking too fast for her," the trader reminded him. "Use simple words. Gesture." He moved away, to see about making camp.

Blaze tried. He walked around the bag, so as to face the girl directly. "Blaze," he said, tapping his head and then his chest. Then he made a gesture as of tapping her chest, without touching her. "You?"

She lifted her hand, but did not gesture. She simply put her arm across her breasts. Blaze saw that she was cold; the scanty garment was intended for display rather than warmth. It served its purpose admirably, but he did not wish to be distracted, and he found himself feeling protective toward her, as he might for one of his daughters.

He reached into his pack and brought out a light fur he used as an extra layer when the night got cold. He shook it out, then offered it to her. "Put this on." When she did not react, he approached her, lifting it. He wrapped it around her shoulders, so that it formed a small cape. He pulled the edges close in front, then took her limp hand and set her fingers around that overlapping margin so she could hold it closed. He noted that her hand was very fine, with slender fingers that were not callused. The nails were full and healthy, unchipped. This was no laborer of the field.

"Seed," she said.

"Seed?" he repeated blankly. "To grow a plant?"

She brought out her other hand. She pointed to him. "Blaze." She pointed to herself. "Seed."

"Oh. Your name." He should have realized. "Seed—talk—Blaze?"

She gazed at him another moment, then drew off the fur and held it out to him. She hooked a finger in her gown, pulling it down to expose her breasts.

Blaze was at first startled by the fine formation of her bosom, and the way she showed it. Then he realized that she had misunderstood him. "No. Talk." He touched his mouth. Then he held the fur out to her again. "Warm."

She accepted it. But her hand snagged on the cord leading to her collar as she tried to put it on. That reminded Blaze of her status: a bound slave.

He turned his head. "Trader!" he called. "Remove the collar!"

"If she runs away, you have bought her," the trader called back warningly.

Blaze brought out his supply of worked blades. He set them on the trader's main bag. "If she runs, they are yours," he agreed.

"Cut the noose cord," the trader said.

Blaze brought out his own obsidian knife, one not for trading. Seed's eyes widened. Realizing that she could misunderstand again, he demonstrated by putting it to his own neck, the sharp edge outward. He made a sawing motion. "Cut. Collar." Then he brought it slowly to her. He put it to the cord that tied the collar closed, and carefully sliced into it. In a moment it parted and the collar loosened. Blaze put away the knife, took the collar off, and set it on the ground by the bag.

He saw that her neck was chafed and red where the collar had been. He brought out his bag of drinking water and dripped some onto his spare headband. He used the damp cloth to gently wipe her neck clean. Seed sat perfectly still, though he realized that the treatment stung. He saw her pupils narrow, because his face was now close to hers. It was mildly intoxicating to be so close to such a lovely creature, but he focused on his business.

Her eyes were fixed on something, and when he finished with her neck and pulled back he realized what it was: his water bag. She must be thirsty, because the trader probably didn't concern himself overly much about the needs of a slave.

He lifted the bag. He put it to his mouth and squeezed out a swallow of water. Then he offered it to her.

Seed's hands shook as she took it. She took one swallow, two, three, before forcing herself to stop: she was thirsty, all right!

"Take more," he said. He knew where to refill it.

She understood him well enough, this time. She took several more swallows before returning the bag to him.

Was she also hungry? Blaze brought out a morsel of smoked meat. He took a bite, tearing loose a fragment, showing that it was good. Then he offered the rest to her.

She took it and chewed avidly. Yes, she was hungry.

Blaze looked around. He spied outcroppings of rock close by. "Come, Seed," he said, gesturing to the rocks. He walked to one of appropriate size and sat on it.

She followed, taking a rock opposite him. He noted how gracefully she walked. How had such a creature come to be such a captive? This was surely the child of some wealthy or powerful city man, who should have married within her class. Out in the country women had to work as hard as the men, but he had heard it was different in the city, where some led lives of leisure.

"Blaze—fire," he said, making the gesture of rising flames. "Wife—Bunny." The signal for a woman. "Son—Stone." The signal for a half-grown man. Was she understanding him? The signs were common across the countryside, but perhaps not known in the city, where many people spoke the same language. "Seed—Stone." He looked at her, arching one eyebrow in a question. How much of this did she understand?

"Seed marry Stone?" she asked.

She did understand! He had not used the word "marry," and her word was inflected differently, but in the context it was clear enough. He realized that she had understood him more readily than he had assumed, but had waited to commit herself. That made sense, because if she was to be given a choice, she needed to know what he was offering. She had thought at first that he wanted a sex slave for himself, and signaled her aversion to this by returning his fur. Of course he could have bought her and forced her, and she probably would have made only token resistance, if any. She had been hungry and thirsty; he could simply have refused to feed her until she stopped protesting. So she had not truly turned him down; she had merely expressed her preference, when she thought she was being asked. Then he had freed her, and fed her, without making any sexual demand. By such tokens he had satisfied her that he was not trying to deceive her, and did want to know her wish. So now she was talking.

"My son," he agreed. "Stone—fourteen." He showed five, five and four fingers. "I have daughters too, younger." He made fingers to show their ages. "Seed?"

For the first time she smiled, briefly. It was like a flash of color as dawn intensified. "Seed is fourteen, also."

"Stone works stone," Blaze said carefully. He brought out his obsidian knife again. "Stone made this."

She looked at the knife, and nodded. "Stone is good with his hands." Her speech organization differed from his, but he was able to pick out the key words: Stone, good, hands. He knew that Seed was doing the same as he gradually elaborated his speech. The trader was right: they spoke the same language, just different forms of it.

"Very good," he agreed. "He is a good worker and a gentle man. He would like a beautiful woman like you. He would treat you well. But you would have to work."

"Stone wants babies?" She cupped her abdomen with her hands, spread her knees, and made a downward motion, as of squeezing something out.

"Yes. We value children. We treat them well. We are a family."

"I would like to be in that family," she said. "But I must not."

Blaze had thought he was understanding her increasingly well, but now he stumbled. "Seed—wish—no?"

She looked at him, and he saw tears flowing down her face. "Blaze—Stone wish no."

He was baffled. She would like to marry Stone, but thought that neither Blaze nor Stone would want her to? How could she think that, after their dialogue? "Why no?"

She paused, then wiped away her tears with the back of one wrist. "When you know me," she said. "How I came here."

"Tell me," he said.

The telling took some time, but Blaze was hardly aware of its passage.

He saw Seed in his mind's eye, as if he were she, fourteen years old and living in the great city.

❂

It was so exciting, being chosen to compete for the great spring ceremony of fertility. Seed had done her best to win the favor, practicing her walk and her smile and studying her body in her mother's obsidian mirror. Now it had happened; she was one of the ten finalists. It was an honor to be among them, but still she hoped for more. She wanted to become the Spring Leopardess.

So did the other nine girls, of course. They ranged in age from eleven to sixteen, and all were pretty, but Seed's mother had whispered that she was the prettiest. The younger ones were not yet fully developed, Seed's mother said, so that they looked like children with bumps, and the oldest was too mature, so that her breasts sagged as if weighted by rocks. Seed had to smile at that remark. Of course there were men who liked either type, but the fertility god liked them perfect, neither green nor overripe. Everyone knew that. And Seed, her mother said, was perfect. She had the best face and figure in the city. Seed found that hard to believe, and suspected that her mother was not completely objective, but it was fun to imagine that it was so.

Seed went to the interview chamber on the appointed morning, and climbed down the ladder to stand on the floor mat. Six of the other girls were already there, and the other three arrived soon after. No one wanted to be late for this occasion, lest she lose the honor by default.

Then the girls were interrogated by the Priestess Lea, who was splendid in her leopard robe. She asked each if she came here of her own free will, and of course each said yes, and whether she had ever lain with a man, and of course each said no. Sexual experience was great and good, as everyone knew, but for this purpose, virginity was essential.

When the priestess had satisfied herself about the qualifications of the girls, she proceeded to the really important part. She had them step out of their robes and stand naked before her.

Seed was not supposed to be interested in the bodies of other girls, and ordinarily she wasn't, but in this case she was. She had to judge for herself whether she had a chance. So she glanced around surreptitiously, sneaking glances this way and that, while removing her garb, folding it, and setting it carefully on the low shelf by the wall. She saw that though the breasts of the youngest girl were slight, her body was otherwise well formed, and her buttocks were actually rather nice, flexing quaintly as she walked. And though the breasts of the eldest were quite solid, they hardly sagged when she stood deliberately straight and tightened her chest muscles, and were quite impressive. In between were several whose narrow waists accentuated their other qualities, making them seem better proportioned. Three had truly lovely faces, and four had flowing tresses that reached to their thighs and even to their knees. One girl overlapped those groups, with both face and hair. Seed had always been pleased with her even features and fine brown hair that reached to her bottom, but in this company she was by no means outstanding.

In fact, whatever aspect she studied was better represented by one of the other girls. Seed's confidence withered like pea vines in a drought. She had been deceiving herself, supposing that she could prevail because of her good body. But she refused to let her nervousness show. She kept her chin high, her belly muscles tight, and her chest half-inflated, so that at least she had no bad weaknesses.

A girl peeped. Several others turned their heads to look at her, but Seed remembered just in time that lapses in poise were faults, and kept her eyes forward and her expression serene. She knew that Lea was watching all of them, and noting who reacted to what. Still, Seed was horribly curious about what had caused the other girl to peep.

The priestess walked behind Seed. Suddenly something wedged into her left buttock, low and inside. She was so surprised that she didn't react at all, not even tensing the afflicted part. What was going on?

Then she realized that the priestess had poked her with a finger. That was why the other girl had peeped! It was another test of poise, a pretty direct one. Seed had gotten through it mostly by accident.

"Now form a line and walk," Lea said.

Seed fell in behind the eldest girl, and others fell in behind her. They walked around the chamber in a circular path. Seed saw that the girl ahead had a flexure of hip and bottom that was bound to score. She tried not to be too obvious in her emulation of it.

"That is all," the priestess said abruptly. "Dress and go home."

All? Seed saw that the others were as surprised as she was. But she

kept her face composed and walked to her clothing. She suspected that
the interrogation was not over, and that they were still being judged. So
she dressed efficiently but without undue haste, maintaining her poise.
Then she started to walk to the ladder—and paused.

She was not the first or the last to complete her dressing. Three girls
were ahead of her, and one was starting up the ladder. Two were
approaching it.

Seed walked instead to the Priestess Lea. She made a formal little
bow, and waited. It was bad form to speak to a priest or priestess; one
had to respond when they required it. But one could signal an interest
in being addressed.

"What is it, Seed?" Lea inquired after a moment.

"Thank you for the interview," Seed said. "I appreciate being
considered."

The priestess nodded curtly. Seed turned without further speech and
walked to the ladder.

Then the other girls realized their error. They had been about to
depart without paying their concluding respect to the priestess. Fortunately they were able to salvage it; none had actually left before Seed's
action. But Seed had made a coup by being the first to recognize the
courtesy.

She went to the ladder, now being the first to use it. She climbed,
evincing no haste, and stepped out on the roof. She did not look back.
Decorum, poise, composure throughout—these were the hallmarks of
the successful candidate. She hoped.

She made her way to her own house, in the residential section of the
city. The entrance hole was open to the sun so the chamber could air
out. She turned and put her feet on the ladder, climbing down into the
room.

"How was it?" her mother asked.

Now at last Seed was able to relax. "I think I made no mistakes," she
said. "I didn't look when a girl peeped, and I didn't peep when the
priestess poked me, and I remembered to thank her for the interview.
But when we were naked, I knew that anything I have, someone else has
better. So I think I won't be last, but neither will I be first."

Her mother bustled her into a less formal dress, questioning her
rapidly. At each answer, her mother commented. "Yes, that peep

eliminated that one," she concluded. "She lost her poise. How many did she poke?"

"I think only two, though maybe others who didn't peep. But why didn't she poke us all?"

"Because she had already eliminated most of them. She poked only the finalists."

"But that would mean—"

"Yes. And you were the first to thank her. That gives you an advantage. I think you won it, Seed."

"Oh, I couldn't have!" Seed protested, flustered in a way that surely would have disqualified her at the interrogation. "I was not outstanding in anything, really."

"A woman is not fashioned from a single trait," her mother reminded her. "If you were second best in everything—"

"Oh, surely I was in the middle on most things."

"But if you were last in nothing, and first in poise and politeness, you could have been first overall. You may be sure she had made her decision by the time she dismissed you. I think you have won."

"Why didn't she tell us, then?"

"She must consult with the head priest. He could refuse her choice, if he had reason. They are great rivals for power, you know. He might do it just to embarrass her."

Seed did not argue further, because it would have been impolite, and because she hoped it was true that she had won.

Her mother proved to be right, for the next day the priestess announced her selection, and it was Seed. She basked in the applause and envy of the other girls. She did her very best to project a modesty she did not feel. She had won!

At the appointed time Seed went alone to the shrine wing of the city, where the Priestess Lea instructed her in the protocol of her role.

"As you know, the bull is our symbol of male potency," Lea said.

"Oh, yes, the Great Bull is the god of our city," Seed agreed brightly, eager to demonstrate how well she had been taught. "He brings us good crops and makes us strong."

"Yes. This is why the high priest wears the bull horns during ceremonial occasions. But it is the leopardess who is fertile. His potency counts for nothing if it does not meet her fertility."

"And if the potency and fertility do not meet, our crops will fail,"
Seed said.

Lea nodded. "So it is essential that every part of the ceremony be
properly performed. I must see that you do your part, or it will reflect
on me. I chose you because I believe you are best able to accomplish
what I wish."

"To make the crops flourish!" Seed said.

The priestess smiled. "That, too." She paused, then stared hard at
Seed. "You are remarkably poised for your age and experience."

"Thank you," Seed said, trying to prevent the unpoise of a flush of
pleasure.

"You will need it. You must swear not to reveal what I am about to tell
you to any person not of the priesthood."

She was going to learn secrets! Wonderful! "Oh, yes, I swear. I will tell
no one, not even my family."

Lea nodded, smiling grimly. "Do you understand the broader aspects
of your role?"

"I will represent the leopard goddess in the ceremony," Seed said
promptly. "I will have my first sexual coupling, with the bull god,
represented by the priest, and that mergence will bring the good crops.
And if I should get a baby, the next season will be even better."

"This is the ceremonial role, yes," Lea agreed. "Only a virgin may
perform it. I was the representative of the goddess, when I first
bloomed, and when I got a baby not only were the crops good, I became
a priestess. When the head priestess became infirm, I assumed her role.
It may be that you will perform similarly."

"Oh, I hope so!" Seed said.

"But the timing must be right."

"Time?"

"This is not known generally, but it is not mere chance that causes a
woman to get a baby. She must receive the man's potency at a certain
time. Even then it is not certain, but it is far more likely. We must
discover the one day of the month that is right for you. The ceremony
shall be scheduled for that day."

Seed was amazed at the nature of the secret. Only one day? She had
never thought of such a thing.

"There is more," Lea said. "This is something you must not say even to one of the priestly persuasion. The gods do not necessarily answer our calls, even when our ceremonies are perfect in every way we can fathom. In fact, it may be that the gods do exactly as they please, regardless of our inducements."

Seed was horrified. "But we need the crops! How can the gods ignore our need, if we do our best to please them?"

"We actually know very little of the ways of the gods," Lea said seriously. "Perhaps they humiliate us on occasion merely to remind us of their power. But here is where the human aspect comes in. If we arrange a perfect ceremony, and the crop nevertheless fails, what do you suppose will happen?"

"It could not be a perfect ceremony, if it fails," Seed said. Then she remembered what the priestess had just told her. "Or—that is what people will say."

"Precisely. It will be considered imperfect by definition. So what will happen?"

"The highest priest or priestess will fix the blame," Seed said slowly. "The wrong part will be eliminated, and the ceremony done again."

"And who will receive the blame?"

"Why, I don't know. I—" She broke off, a horrible realization coming.

"Now you appreciate the risk," Lea said. "If the high priest makes an error, do you suppose he will proclaim it?"

"No, he will blame someone else. And that could be me."

"That could be you—though you are innocent," Lea said. "Seed, you are not only a marvelously lovely girl, you are intelligent. That is why I did not want to choose you. But I could not choose a lesser girl, this time; you were too clearly the best." She shook her head. "How I wish you had jumped and screeched when I goosed you! But you would not be spooked."

"But I wanted to be chosen! It is the greatest honor!"

"Seed, it is not yet too late. You could be disqualified, and so avoid the ceremony."

"Disqualified!"

"There are ways. If you were to be intercepted on your way home, by an ignorant brute of a man, and raped—"

"Raped!"

Lea sighed. "I see you will not be moved."

"Of course I will not be moved!" Seed said hotly. "I will fulfill my role in the ceremony, and all will be well!"

"I hope so," the priestess said. "It has been well the last three years, and perhaps will be so again."

Despite her fervor, Seed found the doubt contagious. "Why do you suspect it will not be well this time?"

"Because we are in a persistent drought," the woman answered. "We must have rain, or the crops will be poor. There is no sign that rain will come."

"But surely the ceremony—"

"Only if the gods wish it. And I fear they do not."

"Why?"

"Because the high priest has had the role ten years, and there has been no baby. We can not assure fertility in one year, or in two, but in three or four or five we have normally been successful. He has been too long. I believe that his potency is suspect, and that no girl will conceive by him. I fear that the drought is a sign of the gods' displeasure. We must replace the high priest—but he refuses to go."

Seed worked it out. "I will not get a baby, no matter what, because the bull is not sufficiently potent. And if I do not, and the rain does not come to make the crops grow, then I will be blamed though the fault is not mine."

"That is my concern. Seed, you have much to offer. It would be a shame to see you unfairly disgraced. But a lesser disgrace now could free you from that risk. Let a stupid girl replace you, and take that ill chance."

"No! I would not—cheat."

Lea sighed again. "Spoken like the perfect candidate for priestess. I think I knew you would not renege. But at least I have acquainted you with the risk. At any rate it is not certain; the weather may change, or you may after all get a baby. Either would save you. Now we must ascertain your day, to give you the very best chance."

The priestess questioned Seed closely, and ascertained her day. Seed did not understand the intricacies of that calculation, but was satisfied that Lea did. As it happened, that time was only three days away. There would barely be time to schedule the ceremony.

On that day, Seed was exquisitely garbed in the ceremonial leopard-pelt robe, open at the front to display her breasts and pelvis, demonstrating her nubility. The Priestess Lea used red rouge to heighten the color of her lips, and pale powder to lighten the rest of her face and cover blemishes, and dark paste to make her eyes shine out of pools of night. She did the same with Seed's breasts, so that they became like alabaster with dark nipples. She used an obsidian blade to trim the ragged fringe of her pubic down, making it perfectly even. She painted Seed's fingernails and toenails red, and polished her teeth so that they glistened white. She brushed out Seed's hair with some kind of preparation, so that it spread out like a voluminous cape, seeming twice as thick and full as it ever had before, and its surface glistened. She set a circlet of precious copper on her head, and bracelets of brightly colored and polished cowrie shells from some far sea on her wrists and ankles. Finally she hung a collar of woven leopard hair about her neck. From it dangled a lead pendant shaped in the likeness of a leopard giving birth to a bull. It fell just between the separation of her breasts, and swung when she walked, colliding with one breast and then the other, calling attention to both. Satisfied, Lea showed Seed her reflection in a water mirror whose dark pan enabled her to seem to look right through it and see herself as a stranger. Indeed, she was the loveliest strange woman she had seen in all her life. The very sight of herself, clothed as she was with all the symbols of fertility, excited her desire to achieve that fertility. Surely it would have much greater effect on any man, who was by nature already eager to explore the mysteries of fertility.

The priestess peered up through the entrance hole in the shrine. "There is a cloud," she said. "Perhaps the weather will turn after all."

"I hope there's a deluge to soak us all, right while he's in me," Seed said. "And not a moment before."

Lea smiled. "I hope so too, dear. That would certainly demonstrate your fertility."

Now it was time. They mounted the ladder and stood on the plastered roof. The nine other girls were already waiting on adjacent roofs. They were the honor retinue for the leopardess of the season. Each wished that she could have been the one chosen. Had she known before what she knew now, Seed might have been satisfied to see one of the others win. But this was her duty, and she would carry it through.

They fell in around her. Each was garbed in flimsy clinging linen robes that became translucent when viewed from shadow toward light, showing how well they too represented the fertility of the female form. If a company like this did not incite the gods to enormous fertility, they were surely beyond satisfaction.

They reached the edge of the city. Three ladders had been set against the outer wall. Lea and Seed used the center one, while the suite of maidens used those on either side.

At the base stood the complement of men, the honor guard for the maidens. Each wore a bull-hide robe and a skirt made of bull leather. They formed around the maidens, before them, after them, and to the sides, and marched up the broad lane toward the ceremony field. The nine girls formed an oval within that enclosure, surrounding Seed and Lea.

Seed knew the ritual well, having been rehearsed on it many times. But now it was as if she had never been tutored. Her mind went blank, and she seemed to float in the center of a flock of birds, knowing nothing of her destiny. How glad she was for the immediate presence of the priestess, who knew exactly what to do. So she moved along, guided by Lea and the formation around her, keeping her place.

Now, in her detachment, Seed focused on the event to come. She had blithely repeated the rote about the potency of the bull and fertility of the leopardess, but of course she had never touched a man sexually. Suppose she got together with the Bull Priest Boro, and it didn't work? That her anatomy simply didn't fit, or something, so he had to give up in disgust? Suppose she froze, and became hard as a plaster wall, and all her decorations availed nothing?

"Do not be concerned," Lea murmured. "Just relax, and let him do it. It is not possible for you to fail, if you are there."

"How did you know what I was thinking?" Seed whispered, surprised.

"You forget that I went through this myself," the priestess replied. "I was terrified, at this point, but I made myself limp like a rag doll, and later I was told I performed beautifully. No one knew my inner incapacity. No one will know yours."

"But *you* know!"

"Be assured that I will keep the secret—as will you. The men must never know that we are not as self-assured as we are beautiful."

"They must never know," Seed agreed gratefully.

They came to the main barley field, where the ceremony was to be held: as close to the crops they wished to influence as possible. A large altar of wood and mud brick had been made in the center, and on it was a thick mat. Beside it stood the High Priest Boro, wearing a great bull-hide cape and a headdress of bull horns. The ceremonial costume made him look magnificent.

But Lea was glancing at the looming bank of clouds. Seed understood her concern exactly: the gods were showing their readiness to participate. But if they were not pleased with the ceremony for any reason, they would withhold their rain, and the crops would not be good. If Lea's suspicion about Boro was correct, the gods might well be annoyed enough to make a more substantial demonstration—such as sending a drought that would destroy the crops entirely. Because of the bull priest's inability to put a baby in the leopard maiden.

Seed could understand the gods' frustration. Fertility was not a single thing, it was a pervasive complex of things. Through all of nature male sought female, and female brought forth more of their kind. How could a ceremony be perfect, if the male's potency lacked substance? She could only hope that the great bull god and leopard goddess would give the priest one more chance, and bring the vital rain this season.

Indeed, the clouds were thickening. They seemed likely to bring rain before the day was out. Perhaps they would even fulfill her dream, and bring it at the moment of her participation. Then all would indeed be well.

"Now I must join the invocation," Lea murmured. "When I signal, you mount the altar and lie on it. Wait until I join you there before you get up again. That is all you truly need to do."

How wonderfully simple she made it seem. All this ritual reducing to a simple lying down and getting up, when signaled! Surely Seed could do that much without error.

The ceremony began. Boro made a speech, addressing the gods and begging their indulgence. Then he turned to Lea. He brought out his penis. "Here is my potency," he proclaimed. "Where is your fertility?"

"She is ready," Lea responded. "Leopard maiden—come to the altar!" She gestured to Seed.

The circle of maidens around her opened to make an avenue between her and the altar. Seed walked forward, hoping she wouldn't stumble or do something similarly gauche. She quelled her impulse to hurry, and instead focused on her legs, making her hips move from side to side and the lead pendant swing, rebounding from her breasts. She saw the young men staring at her, and knew that every one of them envied the priest who was to penetrate her. That was an exhilarating thought! She was, at this moment, the ultimate symbol of fertility.

She reached the altar, stood by it, turned, sat on it, then leaned back until she lay flat against it. Actually it was humped, so that her pelvis was highest, for ready access. She let her thighs spread and her legs touch the ground on either side. Her arms fell down so that her hands touched the ground also. Her leopard robe opened naturally to expose her full torso. Here she was, in contact with the earth at four points, her breasts pointing at their angles to the sky, east and west, her head north, and her pelvis south. She was as ready as she could be.

The bull priest approached. He got down on her and set his hardened penis at her pelvis. Suddenly he thrust, and she suffered a sharp pain. She bit her lip to stop from crying out. But he did not stop there. He drew back somewhat, only to thrust again, and again, repeatedly so that she could not count the times, each one seeming harder and deeper than the prior ones. She had not realized that it would be like this! Was something wrong?

Then at last he shuddered to a stop. He lay on her, his weight squeezing out her breath, making her gasp. Finally he lifted himself, and he was gone from on her and in her. It was over.

She lay where she was. Indeed, she would not have known what else to do. Her pelvis was raw and stinging, and something was tickling her, as if she had wet herself.

Lea came to her. "Rise, child," she murmured. "You have done your part."

"But I hurt!" Seed whispered. "And something—"

"Use this." The priestess gave her a soft, spongy cloth.

Seed used it to wipe her smarting pelvis. She was shocked to discover a red stain. It was blood!

"It is all right," the priestess said. "You did well."

"But there can not be blood," Seed whispered. "Not at this time of my month."

"This one time, there can be," Lea said. She drew the robe around Seed's torso and guided her back to her escort of maidens.

Seed distracted herself by looking again at the sky. What she saw dismayed her. The wind had shifted, and the looming clouds were dwindling, retreating the way they had come. There would be no rain. She had after all failed.

The march back was a blur. Seed was dimly aware of the priestess tending to her, cleaning her up, making her comfortable. Of eating something, and sleeping.

The next day she felt better, and in three days she was all right. The priestess explained that with some girls the first penetration was painful, and there could even be bleeding. But that was no shame; instead it was unequivocal evidence that she had been virginal. It was one of the things the priestess had checked for when selecting candidates for the ceremony. It was best for them to be not only virginal, but able to prove it by this means. In this manner she reassured Seed. But she seemed pensive, as if she feared something.

On the third day it happened. There had been no rain, and the sky was so clear it was obvious that there would be none. The building promise of rain had been destroyed at the ceremony.

"Because the leopard maiden was not a virgin!" the high priest proclaimed. "She spoiled the ceremony, and the gods were revolted."

"That's not true, that's not true!" Seed cried when she heard of this.

"I know it is not true," Lea said. "It is a lie he is telling to cover his own failure. It will not fool the gods, but I fear it will fool men. The worst has happened. We must get you out of here."

"No! I must go and defend my honor!" Seed cried in deep distress.

"Child, it is not so easy. Do you think he will allow you to refute him? Even if you could make yourself heard, you would not be believed, for you are only a girl while he is the dominant priest. But he will not take even that risk. He will seek to have you killed."

"Killed!" Seed cried, appalled. "I am innocent!"

"Indeed you are. But this is politics. I had hoped it would be all right. I thought he would not dare do a thing like this. But when the weather turned so abruptly, it was a signal from the gods that no one could mistake, and he had to act. He reversed it, shifting his blame to you, and I fear that he can get away with it. If I try to defend you, I too will be in peril, because I selected you. In that way he can also eliminate the threat to his power that I represent."

Seed knew that the woman was not lying to her. "Oh, what can I do?" she asked tearfully.

"I have prepared for this," the priestess said. "As I prepared last year, but did not have to do it. I have made a deal with a trader. He will take you as a slave girl, to be sold to some man far from the city. He will make his profit, and your life will be saved. It will not be the good life you deserve, but perhaps neither will it be bad."

"But I know nothing of the lands beyond the city," Seed protested.

"You will learn. And do not give up hope. The matter is not at an end; I will safeguard my power, and when the priest makes a mistake I will pounce like a leopardess and destroy him. Then I will be able to bring you back, and vindicate you, and in that way vindicate myself. Your exile need not be permanent. Just take care of yourself as well as you can, and I will summon you when I am able. This I promise, by my honor as the priestess of the leopard."

Seed believed her, and knew that this was her only feasible course. She let herself be garbed in a linen robe and nothing else, in the manner of a slave girl, and that night followed Lea out over the roofs and to a secret ladder. There was a man waiting. He took her and guided her to his stash of goods, and put a blanket over her. Then he fetched a collar and tied it snugly about her neck, and tied the other end of its anchor cord to a bag of goods. Then he heaved up his other bag. "Now you will stay here or walk," he said gruffly, in strongly accented city language. "If you walk, you can carry or drag your burden, but you will not escape it. If you keep the pace, I will feed you; if you do not, I will not. If you try to run away, I will beat you. If you behave well, I will leave you alone. If you please me, I will sell you to a good man. If you do not, I will sell you to a bad man. Now do as you decide." He set off into the night.

Seed knew that she had descended into the most menial of lives. But at least it was life, instead of death. She picked up her heavy bag and trudged after him.

The trader was true to his word. He was not, she discovered, a bad man, merely a tough one. He did not rape her or even mistreat her. After he had made his point, and she obeyed his directives without question, he gave her a bit of bread and some water, and let her sleep. When she tired the next day, and he saw that she was truly trying to keep up, he slowed his pace, and then he made temporary camp by a stream and allowed her to bathe and rest. He seemed not even to watch when she drew off her inadequate garment and washed herself, but she knew that he would be after her in a moment if she tried to run away. She also suspected that he did not sleep as soundly as he pretended, and at night she neither approached him nor tried to move too far away from him. He did not feed her enough, but she realized that he feared that only her hunger truly bound her to him. She was docile and uncomplaining, knowing that things could get worse than they were.

Yet she could not stifle the tears. She had had such hopes of life, and now she had only fears. Her future was a terrible blank. Would she ever see her loving family again?

On occasion they stopped while the trader traded. There were isolated hovels scattered across the land, and sometimes travelers stopped to do business. Seed kept to herself at such times, trying not to be noticed, and the trader allowed it. He wanted to get her farther away from the city before selling her.

Several days out the trader spied a lone man, a hunter by the look of him. "Hunters treat their women well," he said. "I will try to sell you to him. If you make a bad impression, he will not buy you. Then I shall be displeased."

"Will I be worse off with a bad man, or with you?" she asked.

He laughed, surprising her. "If you truly fear him, and I believe that your fear is merited, I will allow you to discourage him without penalty. But do not try my patience."

So it was that she came to talk with Blaze. "Now I would like to have you buy me for your son," she concluded. "But I know you will not do that."

❂

"Why not?" Blaze asked, amazed. "You have told me your story, and I think I understand enough of it to appreciate your situation. Why do you think I should not wish to buy you, or that my son would not want you?"

She brushed her long hair away from her face with the backs of her fingers, a gesture he was coming to like. "Now you know that not only am I not a virgin, I am in disgrace. It is possible that I am indeed at fault in some way, and the gods are punishing me, and will bring misfortune on anyone who tries to help me. I may even carry a baby that will never be your son's. I have no training or skills useful in your kind of life. I am, it is said, beautiful, but I have nothing else to recommend me to your family. I see you are a good and kind man. Therefore I have told you my story, so that you will know me for what I am and can avoid being hurt by my presence.''

"But at what cost to yourself? Won't the trader be angry with you, if I do not take you?''

"Won't the gods be angry with me, if I bring mischief to a family that does not deserve it?'' she countered. "Better that I suffer alone.''

Blaze was profoundly moved by her speech, for he could see that she was sincere. "Oh, Seed, we of the mountain pastures understand about the ways of boys and girls, and place no great store by virginity. We require only that a woman be true to her husband in body and spirit. We do not worship the gods in the ugly manner of the city folk, so they will not hurt us for rescuing you from that. If you have a baby already, we will raise it as our own, for we freely adopt the children of others when there is need. All I ask is that you try sincerely to learn our ways, and to do what you can without shirking, for our life is harsher than that you have known. And that once you marry my son, you be faithful to him until such time as your marriage severs, and not seek some other life. This is the way of our people.''

She stared at him, seeming unready to believe. The tears had never wholly left her face; now they streamed copiously.

Blaze stood. He held out his arms to her. She launched herself into them, and sobbed into his shoulder. No further discussion was required.

Blaze did not need to deal directly with the trader. The man already knew. He was gathering up his bundles and the twenty obsidian blades, deciding to make camp somewhere else.

They set off for Blaze's home, leaving the trader to carry both his bags. Blaze did not have the fine cloth he had come for, but he was satisfied. Seed was much the better bargain, he was sure.

He thought she would have to rest often, but she kept the pace well enough. He realized that she had been forced to carry a heavy bag; now she was walking free, and it was easier. Still, she had the aspect of a delicate creature, and he decided to camp for the night early. He chose a stream he knew, where there were fish. It did not take him long to spear one, while Seed went into the brush to urinate. He did not watch, for if she ran away, it was now her right. He made a fire and roasted the fish, giving her a good share.

Then, as the night closed in, he had to explain something. "I must douse the fire, because it is not safe to leave it untended at night in this region. I have been traveling alone. I have only the one extra fur for shawl or blanket. I will share it with you, but you will have to sleep close to me, for its warmth and mine. I have no designs on your body, which I prefer to save for my son. I merely want to keep you warm. Do you understand?"

"You have bought me," she said simply. "You may use me as you wish. I will not tell your son."

"I did not buy you. I freed you. If you run away I will not pursue you. I am not watching you."

"But I have watched you. I saw that you trusted me."

"Yes. So now I merely explain my purpose so you will not misunderstand."

Her face brightened. "You do not want me with you naked."

"That is the way I do not want you," Blaze agreed. "If I should forget myself in the night and touch you inappropriately, wake me and I will stop, with my apology. Normally it is my wife I hold."

She came to him, and he clasped her and spread the blanket fur over them both, and relaxed for sleep. He had selected a rise in the ground free of ants and shielded from the wind by a stout tree, but the chill of the deep night could be harsh. At first she was tense, and he knew she had not quite believed him, but gradually she softened, and then she slept. He smiled to himself, and drifted off.

He dreamed, later, that a pretty young woman was kissing him. He woke to discover it was true. His situation came back to him. He drew his head back. "Did I forget myself?" he asked, embarrassed.

"No," she murmured. "I kissed you."

"Why?"

"Because you did not require it."

"Perhaps that would make sense to my daughters," he said with a faint laugh, and went back to sleep.

In the morning she remained snuggled against him, breathing softly and evenly. He lay there for a time, though he would ordinarily have gotten up and made ready to travel while the land was cool. Though she had not complained, she had been tired, and she needed more rest. He thought of Bunny, when he had first known her, lithe and soft as this young woman was now. What joy he had had of her, in that flush of youth! Now he was thirty-seven, an age when many men were dead. Yet instead of being dead, here he was with the loveliest creature he could remember sleeping in his arms. He was increasingly glad he had happened across her, because he had worried about his son's prospects. Now they were secure. What a strange turn their lives had taken!

After awhile Seed woke. "Oh, it is past dawn!" she exclaimed. "I must be up, or the trader will—"

"No more," he reminded her gently. "It is my son Stone you will answer to, after this."

"I know I will like him." She began to untangle herself from him and the blanket fur.

"How can you be sure of that?" He helped her to get free. Her gown had twisted, so that one breast showed; there were crease marks on it from the pressure of their contact.

"Because he is yours." She met his gaze for an instant, and averted her eyes. Then, as an afterthought, she straightened out the garment.

Blaze smiled tolerantly, as if unconcerned, but he was in sudden turmoil. Her glance had suggested that she would not have protested, had he chosen to do more with her than sleep, and indeed might be inviting it. And her words—she would like his son, because she liked him. This young woman, no older than his son, and not much older than his eldest daughter—she was hinting at something. A girl might indeed flirt with the father of her husband; he had seen it in other families. What disturbed him was the way that suggestion had struck right through to his fancy. Suddenly the idea of such contact with her could not be casually dismissed. His desire had been touched.

They walked that day, and camped again near a stream. Blaze could have made better time alone, taking a more direct route, but he tempered his pace to accommodate hers, and took a route that intersected suitable streams so she could drink and have water to wash with. Wash she did, not trying to hide from his sight, and he could not avoid seeing her without being obvious about it. So he pretended nonchalance, as if she were one of his daughters. But he could not convince himself. Then she went through her hair with a wooden comb, letting her nude body dry. Oh, she was exquisite!

She came to him in the dusk as he made a suitable place to sleep. He smiled. "Tonight I can let the fire burn; the wind is down and the terrain is safe. You should be warm enough beside it."

"Douse it," she said.

"But last night was a special case. There is no necessity now. And tomorrow we shall be home."

She met his gaze, in the way she had in the morning, but longer. "I know. Please. I will not tell your wife."

She was actually proposing it! "Seed, I could not do that! You owe me no such thing. Just be good to my son."

"I will. He will never doubt. I will never betray those I know. But I have not met them yet. There is only this night. I beg you, Blaze, douse the fire."

He stared at her. "You don't understand. I wish you to be chaste for Stone."

"I am not chaste. That much I will tell him." She drew at her garment, showing her perfect breasts.

Oh, the temptation! He thought again of Bunny at that age. "But why, Seed? This makes no sense at all!"

"Because this one time I would like to do what I alone want. To be good to a man who is kind to me. It is the only time in my life, perhaps."

He shook his head, determined not to be swayed by the wiles of a girl barely older than his daughters. "I will not douse the fire." He lay down.

"Then I will pretend that I slept by it." She drew off her gown and lay down with him.

"Seed, I am not yet so old as to be immune to a lovely woman. I can not resist you if you tempt me further," he said, embarrassed by the admission. "Please go to the fire."

"Only this night," she whispered, and kissed him firmly on the mouth. "Then forever secret."

His arms went around her of their own volition. "I never asked you to do this."

"I would have done it, if you had asked." She kissed him again, and her hands went to his clothing, to work it open. He could have stopped her, but did not.

"I told you I did not want you naked," he reminded her.

"Maybe you did not mean it." It was really a question, a plea for reassurance. If he denied it, he could still head this off.

"I did not mean it," he echoed. "But I did not act."

"Had you raped me, I would have made no resistance," she said. "Because you bought me, and were kind to me, even before you decided. Had you asked me early, I would have wept, but done it, because I owed it to you. Had you forgotten yourself in the night, I would have let you, and not wept, because I saw that you cared for me enough to spare me when you were awake. Had you changed your mind this morning, and even gazed at me with desire, I would have done it then, because I realized that I wanted this of you. Now you have shown me that you will not, and I must discard all pretense and beg you. So I plead with you: this night, and never again. It shall be as if there was never this night. Please, in your kindness, share this with me."

"In *your* kindness you offer what you know I should not accept. My son, my wife——"

"I know. It is wrong. Yet I must do it. I must seize my only opportunity to act on my dream." She kissed him again, and this time he kissed back.

"I never intended this," he said after a moment, knowing that his continued protests were futile.

"Nor did I." She got the rest of his clothing open or out of the way, and squeezed close to him. Her body was like the animation of a goddess, more than perfect in its youth and grace and desire.

"Only this night," he said, helplessly echoing her words. "Then secret."

"Only this night," she agreed.

He let go of his resolve. He clasped her to him and kissed her savagely. His hands slid down her body, across her back, her tiny waist, her plump buttocks. He kissed her mouth, her cheek, her neck, and her mouth again. Then his urgency became unendurable, and he slid into her and erupted, pulse after pulse, kissing her throughout.

"Yes, yes," she breathed, clinging to him. "This time it doesn't hurt."

Spent, he relaxed. "Because you wanted it," he panted. "You were ready for it. I was too fast, but you were ready."

"I am still ready. This time it was wonderful."

"Because I am not a corrupt priest sacrificially raping you," he remarked dryly.

"Yes. Because you are a warm and caring person. But it is too brief. Is there—I have been told that with the right man—can there be more?"

He understood what she was searching for. He had been too swift in sating his passion, leaving her aroused but not fulfilled. It was not fair to leave her like this. "There can be more, if you wish it. More for you."

She gazed at him, her eyes great and green and lovely in their closeness. "I wish it—if you do."

"There are ways to make a woman respond. I will show you some, and you can tell me what pleases you." The fact was that despite his sating, her allure was so strong that he did not want to give it up.

"Yes, show me. I want to learn from you." Then, after a pause: "For your son."

So she could know how to please his son. Could he believe that rationale? He decided to make the attempt at belief. "Your breasts. Let me kiss them."

"My breasts?" She was surprised. But then she moved, wriggling, hiking herself up against him. She brought her breasts to his face. "Kiss me, my lover."

He kissed her breasts. They were wondrously silken soft. He stroked her buttocks and thighs. They were as wondrously sculptured and firm. Gradually she melted, discovering the appeal of this kind of attention. She put her hands on his head and drew it in to her, giving him first one breast and then the other, making him lick the expanding nipples. "Oh, yes, my love, oh yes," she murmured, over and over, caressing him with her words.

He had thought his penis dead, but it came to life again. She found it and fondled it, learning rapidly. Then she slid down again, on him, and set it in her. She kissed him, and squeezed her breasts against his chest. "Again, my love," she murmured. "Again, my love, my love."

He began to thrust again, and this time she moved with him, making his strokes firmer and deeper. Nature had taken over the instruction. Realizing what she wanted, he slowed and let her make the pace. He found her lips and kissed them continuously. This time it was her urgency that mounted and finally climaxed, leading him into his second. "Oh, my love, my love!" she gasped in the throes of it.

"Oh, my love, my love," he echoed guiltily.

Finally it subsided. She was spent, as well as he. But their words continued. "My love, my love," they said together. There was a special thrill to it, though he suspected that the words were a worse violation of his marriage commitment than the sex. All this was wrong, yet had compulsion because of its forbidden nature.

He got the blanket pelt back on them, and used her gown too, for added cover. They remained embraced, relaxing into sleep at last.

He woke in the night, dreaming again of kissing a young woman. But this time he knew her identity. It was Seed, and he loved her and desired her. His groin stirred.

She woke, feeling it. "Yes, my love," she whispered. "Never stop, my love." She moved to accommodate him, and she remained slick and ready. She pressed her breasts against him, and kissed him wherever her mouth reached.

He thrust, long and slow, and felt her answering contraction. He found her mouth with his own, and her tongue with his own. His buildup was slow, because he had already done it twice this night, which was a thing he hadn't managed in a decade.

But he realized that this time it was his passion that led the way, rather than hers. She was doing it merely to please him. He hesitated.

She felt it immediately. "Do I not please you, my love?"

"You do. But this is teaching you nothing. It is merely sating my lust."

"But I want you to sate it!"

"At least let me teach you something more," he said, compromising with his guilt. "Let me show you another way it is done, so you will know."

"Anything you wish, this night, my love," she replied. "I want whatever you want."

"Then turn around. Face away from me."

"Away?" She disengaged, and rolled over. Then she presented her back to him. "Take me this way," she said, realizing how it worked. "And hold my breasts, my love."

He entered her from behind, feeling her glossy hair against his chest, her soft buttocks against his crotch. He embraced her, getting both arms around and putting his hands on her breasts, which seemed fuller than ever. He felt her react as he gently squeezed and stroked, and that made him react in response. He thrust, and she matched him with a push back. He squeezed, and she inhaled, making her breasts fill his hands. He kissed her hair and her shoulder; then she twisted her torso, turned her face, and managed to meet his kiss with her mouth. In that contorted yet ideal position they climaxed again, she following soon after him. "My love, my love," she whispered, relaxing.

This time they did not disengage. He got his lower arm out from under her body, so she could lie straight, but kept his other arm around her, holding a soft warm breast. They slept. From time to time he woke, finding himself fallen out of her and his hand elsewhere; he stiffened and got back into her, and took her breast again, not trying to climax, just liking the closeness, and slept once more. "Yes, yes, my love," she murmured sleepily.

At last the dawn came. Blaze found himself still holding Seed's evocative breast and pressing into her cleft from behind. Now he knew how far he had transgressed, and the guilt surged. He should not have done it at all, and instead he had done it three times, and remained connected between times. He had truly shattered his vow of marriage, and with a child the age of his child. The worst of it was that he had told her he loved her, over and over.

She woke, seeing the dawn. "Oh, it can't be over already!" she exclaimed.

"Forever over," he said grimly. "I don't know how I could have done it."

"No, not over," she said urgently. "It is still the night. The sun is not up. There is no color. There is still time."

"Time?" he asked, knowing what she meant.

She drew away, turned, and came back at him. "Quickly, quickly, my love, before the night is gone!"

He did not argue. He kissed her, and stroked her hair and body, and got into her, thrusting and thrusting, until he climaxed yet again. "My love, my love!" he gasped.

"My love, my love, my love!" she cried passionately, squeezing the last of the ecstasy out of their embrace.

Then the dawn brightened with color. They separated. "We must wash," she said with radiant regret. "It is over."

"It is over," he agreed, his emotions confused yet intense.

"We must never speak of this."

"Yes."

"I will love your son, and you will love your wife."

"Yes."

"We will never again touch each other as man and woman."

"Yes."

"But will you tell me one thing, truly?"

"Yes," he said heavily. "I did mean it when I said I loved you. I do love you, though the gods smite me. But it must be over."

"And I love you. I have learned so much. But it must be over." She glanced sidelong at him. "But may I do one more thing, before we wash it all away?"

He opened his arms. She stepped into them. They kissed, deeply. Then they broke. They went to the river and washed in the chill water, together.

"I will say only that I had a love, and learned from him, and lost him," she decided. "That much is true."

Suddenly he realized why he had fallen into this. It wasn't just her phenomenal beauty. It was her green eyes, matching his own. She had animated his secret love, the one he had always desired but never encountered. Bunny was a wonderful woman and wonderful wife, but there had always been that secret longing for his mysterious true love. That love was not Seed, but in the night she had seemed to be it, and he had done what he had to. That understanding made him feel better. Perhaps Seed, too, had such a secret ideal, which he had briefly animated.

By the time they were clean, both were shivering blue, and sex was far away. But the glances they exchanged showed that their love had not been similarly vanquished. Their forgetting could never be more than pretense.

They dressed, and set out again. They both knew what they had to do.

✣

By evening they reached his home. Bunny was roasting acorns while Stone chipped at another obsidian blade. Both were watching as Blaze and Seed approached. They were surprised to see him with a companion.

He was forthright. "I gathered chips and found a trader. But I did not trade for what I expected. I got this young woman."

Both were silent, studying Seed, who stood perfectly still. But there was a squeal from inside the house, as Blaze's daughters realized that something was happening. In a moment they piled out: ages twelve, ten and five. They stood staring, uncertain how to react.

"This is Seed, from the city," Blaze said. "I brought her for you, Stone. To be your wife."

"My wife!" Stone exclaimed, astonished. The three girls tittered. They found the notion of their brother suddenly getting married hilarious.

"She is your age, and comely," Blaze said. "It is time you married. She will be good for you. Walk with her, talk with her. I believe you will like her."

Stone looked at his mother. She nodded. He got up, awkwardly, holding the blade.

Seed stepped toward him. "Your father says you make these excellent blades," she said, trying to speak so he could understand. "That is a good talent." Then she smiled, showing her beauty.

There was a murmur of awe from the girls. Stone looked as if struck by a sudden stiff wind. "I—yes," he said, and smiled back, unable to do otherwise.

"Please show me your country," Seed said, exactly as if she had not trudged through it all day.

"Yes." He walked out, heedless of direction, and she gracefully paced him. Blaze knew she was tired, but there was no evidence of it.

"Girls, go with them," Bunny said. "Introduce yourselves."

"I'm Doe," the eldest exclaimed.

"I'm Weasel," the second said.

"I'm Mouse," the third said.

"How did you get to be so beautiful?" Doe asked Seed as they walked away from the house.

"I grew up," Seed replied. "As you are about to."

"Oh, I hope so!" Doe said as the others tittered. They moved on away from the house.

"From the city?" Bunny inquired of Blaze, focusing on her acorns. Her voice sounded unconcerned. That was a signal of trouble.

"I wanted to get linen cloth, for you. But he offered her to me, and when I declined, he said I might want her for my son. And—"

"And she was beautiful and woebegone and young," she concluded. "And you had a soft heart."

"The trader read me as well as you do," he confessed. "So I talked with her, and got her story, and she was willing."

"Surely she was," Bunny said with a certain muted edge. "She read you as readily as the trader did."

"I believe her story," he said doggedly.

"And what was her story?"

"She was chosen to be the virginal sacrifice at their spring fertility ceremony. The priest deflowered her, then when rain did not come, blamed her for being unchaste. She had to flee for her life. The trader took her, and threatened to sell her to a bad man if she did not please a good one."

"Then he saw the perfect mark," Bunny said. "And she knew better than to fail to impress you."

Unfortunately accurate. Bunny had always cut to the quick of things. "I believe she will be good for Stone," he persisted. "You know he lacks the nerve to go out after a woman himself."

"She will govern him completely. She has already won him."

Blaze realized how impetuously he had acted. "Did I do wrong, Bunny?"

She did not look at him. "Did you?"

She suspected! "What do you mean?"

"If I were a hearty man, and I had to travel alone with a creature like her who longed for comforting, I know what I would do."

"She has green eyes," he said. It was his admission of guilt.

Now she looked at him. "You have never expunged your fantasy woman."

"I never have," he agreed, ashamed. "But she does not exist, and you do."

Now she smiled. "Yes, I do." She had forgiven him, perhaps.

"Next time, I will get you good cloth."

"Surely you will." She removed the acorns from the hot stone. "You will be hungry. You did not have food for two."

"I speared some fish."

She brought out flat bread. "When they return, we shall tell the neighbors."

He nodded agreement, chewing on the bread.

Soon the group did return. Stone and Seed were holding hands, despite the interference of the girls. Seed looked demure, and Stone's face was set in a mold of wonder.

"Will you marry my son?" Bunny asked Seed.

"Yes," the girl replied shyly, to a background of more tittering. "I like him."

"Then we shall go to tell the tribe. All the rest of us." That included the girls, who had showed signs of preferring to stay. "There is bread." She indicated it. "See that the fire does not go out." That was Bunny's way of telling her son that the family would not be back for some time. He seemed blank to the message, but Seed was not. She glanced at the home, and made the suggestion of a smile.

Blaze and Bunny set out for the next house, pitched about one shout away. "She knows what to do," she said when they were clear.

"Surely she does," Blaze agreed somewhat lamely.

"Do what?" Mouse asked, as her older sisters smiled without answering.

"You are right," Bunny said. "She is what he needs. He will be the envy of the other young men—and older ones too, perhaps."

"Perhaps." Everything his wife said had a double meaning now, and not just because of the presence of the three girls.

"But they will marry tomorrow, so that none of the other men will seek to win her. She is for him alone."

"For him alone." He was agreeing never to touch Seed again. That had always been his intention, but his wife needed the confirmation.

They came to the other house. Bunny nudged him. "Our son Stone has found a woman," he announced. "They will marry tomorrow, at our house."

"Who?" the other man asked, surprised. "I have not seen him with anyone."

"She is not from our tribe," he clarified. "She is from the city."

"The city! Can she forage?"

"She will learn."

The man was quiet, not wanting to speak openly of foolishness.

"What is her appearance?" the woman asked.

The daughters tittered. "Adequate," Bunny said.

The woman was silent, suspecting that this meant, at best, plain. Both of them evidently suspected that this was some desperation measure. Could the boy have had some foolish liaison, and gotten a foreign woman with a baby, and been threatened with reprisal if he did not marry her? Sex before marriage was common, but a marriage like that was less than ideal.

They walked on to the next house. "We may surprise them tomorrow," Blaze murmured, beginning to enjoy this.

"Oh, will we surprise them!" Doe agreed, appreciating the joke.

"How?" Mouse asked.

"They think she's ugly like an ox cow."

Mouse squealed with laughter.

They toured the settlement, ignoring the masked looks of surprise, pity and contempt. The neighbors would be there for the marriage, pretending that it was a joyous occasion. After that, Seed would be accepted in the tribe.

It was dark by the time they approached their own home. Stone and Seed were sitting by the hearth fire, talking in low tones. She looked more confident, and his expression of wonder had spread from his face to the rest of his body. Oh, yes, she had educated him!

"They've done something," Weasel whispered conspiratorially.

"Maybe twice," Doe agreed somewhat enviously.

"What did they do?" Mouse asked.

"Why should I tell you?" Weasel demanded.

"Don't tease her," Bunny said.

Weasel grimaced. "You know. Sex. Like Mommy and Daddy."

"Stone?" the child demanded unbelievingly.

The other two burst out laughing. By then they were close to the house, and had to stop conjecturing.

"She will share your bed, until you make a house of your own," Bunny told Stone. "Tomorrow the neighbors will come to see you married."

Stone, dazed, nodded. Then his attention returned to Seed.

They concluded the evening and went to their beds. The young couple was on one side of the chamber, and the old couple on the other, with a pile of supplies between. The three sisters were across the back, close enough to listen very carefully while they pretended to sleep. Sex was nominally private, which meant that those not engaged in it were required to ignore it. By the time they got to be of age, they had a fair notion of its frequency and mechanics. That was the way children learned, after all. Anything they missed could be filled in by the appropriate parent before they actually performed it themselves. That was why Mouse had been incredulous about Stone; she knew he had never before done it. She would have liked to watch him mess it up.

Blaze dreaded this night, and not because of the ears of his daughters, who were long since bored with adult business. Bunny might be cold to him, showing her unexpressed anger at his lapse, or she might be loving, and he might find himself unable to perform. He had been amazed at the night with Seed; he had never done it that frequently with Bunny. It might be several days before he was able to rouse himself again.

She chose to be warm. "The presence of young ardor excites me," she whispered. "Come, my husband; pretend that we are young."

He thought of Seed twining across Stone, and his ardor returned. He embraced Bunny and surged into her. Did that thought of Seed make him in essence unfaithful? He wished he could abolish the notion, for he feared that Bunny could somehow hear it. Indeed, he needed to forget that one night, and make it as if it had never existed. But he knew he would never forget it.

Meanwhile, he could hear his son panting as Seed brought him to fulfillment, surely not for the first time this night. He was glad of that, for a complex of reasons which included the distraction it provided for the girls and the confirmation that the lovely young woman's last sexual experience was legitimate. He tried to persuade himself that he had no wish for it to be otherwise.

In the morning the neighbors arrived. Seed, true to mountain custom that Bunny had impressed on her, remained hidden in the house until all were assembled. The neighbors and the daughters stood in a half circle before the house. Blaze stood at one side of the house hearth, and Bunny at the other. Stone stood directly in front of the hearth, in the center of the half circle of neighbors. He looked appropriately uncomfortable.

The tribe shaman stepped out of the crowd. "What man is to be married?" he inquired.

Blaze stepped across to clap his hand on Stone's shoulder. "My son

Stone," he said. "He is of age, and ready to assume the duties of marriage."

"What woman will he marry?"

Bunny ducked into the dark house. In a moment she brought out Seed, who was cloaked from neck to feet in a heavy robe of furs. Her brown hair was brushed down across her face, concealing it. She was completely anonymous. "My daughter Seed," Bunny said. Everyone knew that the woman was not really her daughter, but when the woman's own parents could not be present, such a substitution could be made. This was ordinarily a sign of trouble, because it suggested that the woman's parents did not approve the marriage, or were unaware of it.

"Do you choose this woman of your own free will?" the shaman asked Stone.

"Oh, yes!" Stone agreed with an enthusiasm that caused several glances of perplexity. That did not sound like a forced marriage!

The shaman turned to Seed. "Do you choose this man of your own free will?"

"Yes," she said.

The shaman turned to the audience. "Does any person have objection?"

"Yes," a man said gruffly. "We have not seen the woman. How do we know who she is?"

"Maybe she's great with baby," came a voice from behind.

The shaman turned back to Seed. "We must see your face, to be sure of your identity," he said. This much was a normal part of the ritual.

Seed lifted her hair away from her face with the backs of her fingers. Suddenly the neighbors knew she was not ugly. There was a muted murmur of appreciation.

"And your body," the hidden voice called.

This was part of a ritual that was seldom invoked, because of its implication. If Stone had had a regular girlfriend, and decided to marry her, it would have been understandable. But to have a woman appear from far away for sudden marriage suggested something else. Could she be pregnant by some other man, and Stone had to pretend otherwise? What a story might lurk there! "You do not have to show your body," the shaman said. "Just your face."

There was a murmur of disapproval as more neighbors sensed a scandal. A woman who already carried a baby when she married offered no guarantee that the baby was that of the man she married. Her husband could claim it as his own, and the child would be accepted by the family and the tribe, but everyone would know there was doubt.

"Has my daughter been challenged?" Bunny demanded, looking properly outraged.

The shaman was not eager to embarrass anyone. "No."

"Yes!" cried the voice, eager for that embarrassment. "Show your fat tummy!"

"Then she must answer it," Bunny said grimly. "Seed, show yourself."

Seed put her hands to the neck of the cape, drawing loose the bow there. Then she paused, as if unwilling to complete the exposure. Blaze realized that Bunny, who had mischief in her soul, had coached the young woman perfectly.

"Show it!" the voice cried greedily.

Seed abruptly flung off the cape. She was completely naked beneath it. Suddenly the full luster of the most beautiful body in the region shone forth, the effect heightened by the glistening oil Bunny had applied. Full breasts, full hips, full thighs, a remarkably slender waist, and an almost flat abdomen. She turned in place, showing full buttocks too. She completed her turn, and smiled.

There was a concerted sound of awe that increased as she moved, and climaxed with her smile. Then a titter from a daughter, finally able to reveal the joke, followed by growing, appreciative laughter from the assembled men. The challenge had not only been answered, it had been destroyed—and the startled husbands had been treated to a sight their wives would never have permitted, had they realized. For now every husband had been most forcefully reminded of what his own wife lacked.

"Is there any further objection?" the shaman inquired as the hubbub slowly faded. Even he could not suppress a smile. There were no objections. "Then I declare this marriage sealed. Retire to the consummation."

Seed turned in to Stone, wrapped her arms about him, and kissed him. Then they walked around the hearth and entered the house. Every man was staring at the bride's naked motion. Bunny picked up the fallen cloak and hung it across the entrance, darkening the interior and obscuring the activity inside. Of course it could hardly be any mystery; no one could imagine any man hesitating even an instant.

Now it was time for the feast. Food and brewed ale appeared. The group fell to, talking with animation about what had just been seen. Men clustered around Blaze, and women around Bunny, and children around the girls, all demanding to know where they had found such a creature for Stone. This was one marriage ceremony that would never be forgotten.

❂

The months passed. They made a house for Stone and Seed, near the original house, for the new couple was young and needed help and advice. Blaze was away from the house much of the time, searching out other stones for working, and wood for the hearth, which required a lot because of the need to heat some stones for working. He also assisted in moving the tribe's goat herd from one pasture to another; they needed every man and some tame dogs to keep the unruly creatures on the route. But he had reports from others, so knew what was going on.

Stone worked on the obsidian fragments, chipping them into quality blades that would be good for trade. He had a touch that no other had; the glass just seemed to respond to him. Seed learned to forage by going out with Bunny and the girls. She was not a fast learner, having had no prior experience, but she did her best and never shirked. It was clear that under her beauty and her city ways she was a girl much like any other, and that she very much wanted to please this family into which she had married. It turned out that the family was willing, somewhat as Stone was willing to be pleased by the attentions Seed paid to him.

But as Seed learned, she changed in two significant ways. One was physical: she had a baby in her, and though at first this was only slightly evident, as time passed it became strongly evident. That was good news; the line would carry on into the next generation. The other was emotional: she became pensive at odd moments; sometimes she wept, though she tried to conceal this from the others. Stone did not understand this, and indeed she never wept in his presence. But there was a sadness about her that seemed to grow as her baby did.

Finally Bunny took a hand. She took Seed out foraging alone, and talked to her. In her experienced woman's way she fathomed more than the younger woman had wanted to tell. Then she talked with Blaze.

"She has three problems. She told me two."

"Can you deal with them?" he asked guardedly.

"How is the herd doing?" she asked irrelevantly. But he knew better than to challenge it, because her seeming irrelevancies had a way of becoming abruptly relevant, farther down the path.

"Not well," he admitted. "The drought makes grazing sparse, and we have to move the goats more often. If good rain does not come, they will grow lean even as the pastures give out. We shall have to slaughter too many."

"And we can't yet take them to the winter pastures," she said.

"They will be barren too." The summer was late, but it was not good to travel before the land cooled.

"What will we do, if this continues?"

"We will have to migrate to another land, where there is rain. But I fear that other tribes will be doing the same, and there will be complications."

"Stone has good talent with the obsidian, and you with the fire. Could you find employment in the city?"

"The city!" he exclaimed, appalled. "That is not our life!"

"The country is not Seed's life, yet she is living it."

"She misses her people!" he said, understanding her point. "That is one of her problems."

"Yes, she is homesick. Her family hardly knows where she is or how she is doing. She would like to see her mother again."

"But we could not go to the city, just for that!"

"There is another way to see it," Bunny said. "We would not do well, going to the city unprepared. But she is *of* the city; she could teach us its ways. Then perhaps it would be better."

"We are mountain folk!" he protested. "The city would stifle us. All those people, knowing so little about real life!"

"But if the weather does not turn, we must go somewhere, and I think there will be problems wherever we go. The city might be the least of evils, if we have abilities those people respect, and if one of us knows its ways."

The prospect remained disturbing, so he changed the subject. "That is one of her problems: missing her home, her family. What are the others?"

"She carries a baby, and she is not sure of its father."

"Stone is a good young man! He will treat that baby well." But he knew that this was not her point.

"She first had sex with the high priest of the city. It might be his baby. She fears that it will look like that priest."

Blaze nodded. That could indeed be the case. Or, worse, the baby could have a blaze on its forehead. That would be true disaster. "But there is nothing to be done about that," he said. "We must simply wait for the baby, and hope it looks like Stone."

"Yes. In truth, most babies look the way their parents choose to think they do. It seems likely that it will seem to be of our family. It will be one of us, regardless."

"So that concern will resolve itself, in due course," Blaze said, relieved that Bunny had settled the matter in her mind. "What is the third problem?"

"Have you seen how careful she is to please Stone?"

He laughed. "She would please him even if she didn't try! She would please any man."

"Yes. But she tries almost too hard."

This was becoming uncomfortable again. "I have hardly seen her in these months. What I know of her I have learned from you and the girls. Why should she not do her utmost to be a good wife?"

"Most women tire of such catering, after the marriage settles in. Haven't you noticed?"

He looked at her. "I have never had any complaint about you, Bunny."

"Because you were always willing to accept what I offered. You never expected me to be your lost dream woman."

"There *is* no dream woman," he said without real force.

"Perhaps. But I think Seed has a dream man."

"A dream man? Not Stone?"

"She is in love with one she will not name. This is the thing she will say to no one. So she caters ardently to Stone, to prove to others and herself that she has no other love." Bunny met his gaze briefly. "As you have always done with me."

"As I will continue to do, for you have always been more than worthy of me." But she had made the problem clear.

That started a path of thought. There was no mystery about why he had succumbed to Seed's allure; even had he not always dreamed of an unknown, perfect woman, Seed's great beauty would have made him desire her. But why had *she* desired *him*? She had been grateful for his kindness in her adversity, but all he had asked of her was that she be good to his son. She had sought repeated sex with him, when her only prior sexual experience had been negative. That had not seemed to make much sense, for the desire of women was not like that of men. Now he saw an answer: she feared that there could be a baby from the priest, and she did not want it. So she had tried to get a baby elsewhere. She had been increasing the chances that the baby would not be the priest's.

But why would she love Blaze, when there was no further point? It could only be because she saw in him the shadow of her ideal man, just as he had seen his ideal woman in her. He was old enough to know his own foolishness and not be governed by it, but she was young. He still felt the pull of her, despite his resistance. He still desired her, and not merely for sex. She came often to his thoughts when he was alone, and not only then. Now he knew that her feeling was the reflection of his. They had tried to separate after a single night, and had not succeeded. But none of this could ever be spoken.

"She is a good young woman," Bunny said after a fair pause. "You made an excellent purchase. It is not her fault that age has not yet worn down her fancy. Time and children may do much, however."

"I have tried to stay well clear," Blaze said somewhat lamely.

"Too hard, perhaps."

How well she understood him! "What would you have me do?"

"Sometimes the image is more interesting than the reality. Do not avoid contact. Be close to your son's wife, as you are to him. Learn from her, as she has learned from you."

"Learn from her?" He would not ask what his wife thought Seed had learned from him.

"About the city. The way they speak. I think we shall need that information."

Blaze realized that Bunny was prepared to move to the city, and that he would have to prepare himself also. The idea disturbed him, but if the weather did not turn, it might have to be. The city evidently had ways to survive a drought, perhaps by vigorous trading for food from far away, but the mountain folk had no established trading lines.

"I think you should be the one to tell her of our discussion," Bunny concluded.

"I can't do that!"

"That we fear we may have to move to the city. That decision must be yours."

"That will please her," he agreed wanly. As he considered it, he realized why Bunny wanted him to tell Seed. Because then her pleasure at his presence would have an explanation.

And perhaps her love would fade as she saw that Blaze was an ordinary man. The same for him, as he saw how like his daughters she was. He loved his daughters, but had no sexual inclination toward them. Bunny had concluded that separation wasn't doing it, so was trying proximity. He hoped she was right, because he felt guilty for his illicit feeling, knowing it was irrational and that it could only hurt others he loved.

He went to his son's house that evening. Stone was by the fire, working on a blade, painstakingly chipping to make it right. Much of his skill was simply patience; if it took half a day to get it right, he did not begrudge the time. He smiled as he worked, liking it, and perhaps thinking of his wife. Blaze could readily appreciate that.

"I came to talk to Seed," he said.

"She went for water," Stone said. Every woman made daily trips to the nearest spring to fill the family bags with fresh water. She would be back soon.

"Then I will talk to you," Blaze said, sitting on an adjacent mat. He realized that he had not done this in some time. In trying to avoid Seed, he had also avoided Stone. "You know we have a drought."

"I know. I'm glad I am working here, instead of trying to herd balky goats."

"If it does not ease, we will have to move."

"Where would we go?"

"Either to a new land—or to the city."

"The city!"

"You have a talent that will serve as well there as here. Instead of giving your blades to a trader, who then takes them to the city, you would have them there directly. And Seed knows the city."

"I would not leave my family." Stone was thinking of his parents and sisters, rather than his wife and coming baby.

"We would go too. We could learn its ways, as Seed is learning ours."

Stone looked up. "Seed—she is wonderful. But sometimes she weeps, when she does not know I am near."

"She misses her family."

Stone's eyes widened. "Yes! Why didn't I realize?"

"Because she did not want you to. She feared that you would think she was dissatisfied with you."

"If she wants to go to the city, I will go to the city," Stone said simply. "I would do anything for her. My life changed, the day you brought her to me."

How well Blaze understood his son's feeling! "You became a man, when she arrived."

"Yes. I did not truly live, until she came."

"My own fire skill should be useful in the city," Blaze said. "Your mother can adapt to anything. Your sisters can learn."

"Still, it is not a good life for real people."

"Perhaps the weather will turn."

They waited, not talking further. Soon Seed returned, bearing two heavy bags of water suspended from a wooden frame across her shoulders. "My husband, my father," she said as she saw them.

Blaze looked up at her. Her belly was well swollen, and the rest of her body had fleshed out somewhat to match. She was no longer the infinitely desirable slave girl. Then his eyes met hers, and it was as if a fire spark jumped between them. The love was still there, undiminished.

"I came to talk to you," Blaze said, breaking his gaze away. How could he ever get beyond this illicit emotion?

Seed reached the house entrance and set down her burdens. Then she brought out another mat and kneeled on it, facing them both across the fire. "Is something wrong, my father?" It was an honorary title, customary among mountain folk, signaling dutiful devotion. Sometimes such signals were correct, but not in the proper way.

"The drought continues, my daughter. We must consider moving. It may be that it is time to give up our mountain life and go to the city."

Her face froze. Blaze realized that she did not dare react, for fear of being disappointed.

"Do you think there would be a place for all the members of our family there?" he asked.

"Oh, yes," she breathed. It was almost as if she added "My love."

"Would you be willing to teach us the ways of the city, as we have taught you the ways of the goat herders?"

"Oh, yes!"

"Thank you, my daughter." Blaze allowed his gaze to meet hers again, and again the spark jumped. He saw that her eyes were shining, and not with tears of sorrow. "I shall tell the others."

"I will do everything I can, my father," she said. "But I must remind you of one thing: I can not yet return to the city, because the high priest would have me killed."

"Maybe if you concealed your identity," Blaze suggested. "They would not recognize you as the wife of a mountaineer."

"I suppose, if I cut my hair," she said dubiously.

"Don't cut your hair!" Stone cried, dismayed. Blaze privately echoed the sentiment; her hair was one of her beauties. He didn't want to see any part of her sacrificed. Sometimes he had to fight his urge to reach out and stroke that hair, as he had when they had lain in the love embrace.

"Maybe some other way," she said, her excitement at the prospect of returning warring with her caution.

Blaze stood, not daring to remain any longer lest his formal mask crack. "Then we shall begin to learn, though we hope the weather changes."

"I did not realize that you missed your home," Stone said to Seed.

"My home is here," she replied.

"I want you to be happy."

"I am happy with you."

She was ritual-perfect. Blaze walked away, knowing that Seed would soon make Stone forget any qualms he had about anything. But probably she would no longer weep when she thought he did not hear.

❂

A few days later the weather turned. Rains came, and repeated, turning the pastures green. The extra goats did not have to be slaughtered, and it was not necessary to migrate.

But Bunny did not change her mind. "Weather is treacherous," she said. "It can turn again. We have been warned, and we must prepare."

So Seed taught the family the ways of the city, as the next month passed. Every evening, when the work of the day was done, she would settle herself somewhat heavily by the hearth and discuss another aspect. One evening she told them of the way its houses were, each connected to all the others, and how they used ladders to get from one to another and to get inside by climbing down from holes in the roofs.

"But why not use the entrance on the ground?" Doe asked, perplexed. Her breasts were filling out, and it was evident that she would soon be ready for marriage herself.

"There *are* no entrances on the ground," Seed said, to general amazement. "The city sits by the marsh, and the snakes are always there, so there are no doors and no low windows. The only entrances are in the roofs."

"But isn't that a lot of trouble?" Weasel asked. "How do visitors get in?"

"We don't want visitors at night. They might be mount—I mean, unfriendly people. So we take up the ladders and keep them out, with guards walking the roofs. In the day we put the ladders out, and everyone uses them."

"This is weird," Doe said.

Seed smiled. "To city folk, sleeping in open houses is weird."

"What about when you need to poop?" Mouse asked.

"You use the leather bucket."

There was a general titter. "You poop in buckets?" Weasel asked. "Then what do you drink from?"

"Water bags. Then in the morning you take the bucket to a courtyard and dump it out. You also take the ashes from the hearth and dump them on top, to control the smell." Seed looked at Mouse. "But you can poop there directly, if you want. Just poke your bottom over the edge of a roof and let it fall."

"I want to poop from the roof!" the child exclaimed, delighted. "Plop! Plop!"

"Maybe wait till someone walks by below," Weasel suggested. "Then *ssssst!* on their heads."

They all laughed. But Blaze was not at all easy about living in such a place. Its customs were strange indeed.

When they had the general idea of the layout of the city, they worked on the language. It was a variant of their own, but had devious nuances, and the accent was horrible. But the girls considered it a challenge, and worked to get it right. Blaze and Bunny labored at it more doggedly, finding it harder to fathom. They found it easier to settle on a few common terms that they could manage without heavy accent.

But the weather continued good, and their concern faded. What point, learning odd material, if there would never be need for it?

"Stay with it," Bunny told Blaze. "You might have to visit the city anyway, sometime."

"Even if I'm the only one?" he asked. "I would be alone with her."

"What would you do with her, when she's great with the baby?"

He did not care to argue the point. So when he was not otherwise busy, he would settle down by the hearth and talk with Seed. Sometimes the others were all out on other chores, that Seed was now too ponderous to undertake. If she was disappointed about losing her chance to return to the city, she did not show it. She met his gaze frequently as they talked, and smiled often. He found himself smiling back. He realized that her condition did not matter, for they had sworn off sex anyway. Only their tacit love remained, unvoiced but clearly present when they were alone.

Why had Bunny permitted this? Blaze eventually worked it out. She wanted to keep Seed happy, and knew that though Seed loved her home city, she loved Blaze more. As long as she had his continuing interest, she was satisfied. If the weather turned again, and there was another bad drought, they might still go to the city, and then Seed could be happy about that. This was an interim measure.

Even though his love for his wife had been compromised, Blaze was coming to appreciate new aspects of Bunny's trust and competence. What would have become of him had he married some other woman instead of her?

As it happened, Seed's birthing time came suddenly when the others were out. There was no time to fetch Bunny or Doe or a neighbor woman. Blaze got her to her bed, helping her the way he had helped Bunny herself, putting out clean cloth and talking calmly and encouragingly to her. But as the pains intensified she became distraught. "Oh, hold me, my love!" she cried, forgetting their pact of silence.

He put his arms around her shoulders, holding her half-sitting in the way she wanted. She clung to him with the strength of pain and effort. "My love! My love!" she screamed as the water burst.

"My love," he murmured in her ear, stroking her fine hair, and she relaxed for a bit.

Then Bunny arrived. Without a word she went to work, making competent what Blaze had made incompetent, and he was able to retreat from the scene. "Fetch the women," she said as he left.

In due course other competent women were there, and after what seemed like interminable time, there was the cry from the birthing chamber. They wrapped the baby in a clean cloth and brought it to Seed's arms. Then they permitted Blaze to join them, so that he could see his grandson. He was relieved to see no blaze on the tiny forehead.

"What—?" Seed asked, seeming to wake from a sleep.

"Male," he said. "You have a son, Seed, and I have a grandson. The women got you through." So that just in case she had not realized it, in her delirium, she would know now that they were no longer alone.

Bunny helped her get the baby in position for nursing. The other women had already set about cleaning up the blood and fluid. It had not been a bad birthing, as such things went. That was another relief.

In a moment, Seed was asleep, the baby still at her breast. Now Stone arrived.

"You have a son," Blaze said. "You are a father. Your wife is all right. I must go and tell your sisters."

Stunned, Stone nodded, staring at mother and child. Blaze departed for his own house. He hoped Seed had not spoken any more guilty words during the birthing, but he couldn't be sure. Perhaps Bunny had cautioned her.

⊙

Stone named the baby Tree, signifying that he would not make the mistake of requiring his son to emulate either his grandfather in fire tending or his father in stone chipping. The baby was healthy, and seemed to favor his mother, leaving questions about his sire moot. Everyone was pleased. Seed brought him to visit his grandparents and aunts often, but after the initial interested fussing by the girls, this faded. Bunny was often busy, so many times Seed was with Blaze as he worked at the hearth. They continued to go over the material of the city, and Blaze felt that he was coming to know it so well that he would be able to make his way through it and within it if he needed to. The idea of going there was growing in him, because of his increasing competence to handle it. He also realized that if his presence helped make Seed satisfied to be a mountain woman, her presence would help him appreciate the city. It was a two-way effect, as Bunny must have anticipated.

Seed was beautiful again, her body almost as slender as before, her breasts and buttocks larger. Her hair still shone. Even bundled in goatskin furs in winter, she attracted the covert gaze of any man in sight. Her possession of a son increased her assurance; she had proved herself and knew it. When she nursed him in the field, even some women shook their heads, wishing they could have breasts like that. Men privately joked with Stone, enhancing his status: if he ever got tired of being married, and wished to find another placement for his wife . . .

Still Bunny encouraged Blaze to meet with her, studying the city. Stone never questioned it, perhaps because Seed still had him totally captivated. Blaze was after all old, almost forty; he might not live much longer, and so it was good for him to know his grandson while he could.

○

When Tree was almost two years old, and walking, the drought came again. The goats grazed the pastures down, and the question of migration loomed again. The irony was that to the south and west the rains were good. The city was prospering, its barley fields promising a bountiful harvest. Blaze concluded that its head priest would be in no trouble.

Then came a surprise. A trader came through with a message: the priestess wanted Seed to return, secretly. He showed a piece of linen with a mark on it that Seed recognized as the stamp of the Leopard Priestess Lea. That meant it was authentic. Seed was excited.

"How can you know?" Blaze asked. "Anyone could have sent such a message. Maybe the priest himself, so he can locate you and get rid of you, so you can never embarrass him by giving him the lie."

"No, this is Lea," she said. "Her stamp proves it."

Blaze was not the only doubtful one. So Seed clarified it for the full family. Every man or independent woman in the city had his stamp, which was different from any other; no two were the same. He used it to prove ownership of his property, or the authenticity of a message he might send. He kept the stamp with him, or hidden in his house chamber; no one else could use it. When he died, his elder son inherited the stamp and all the family assets marked by the stamp. Such things were very important in the city, and stamps were never carelessly used. "So Lea is the only one who could have stamped this cloth," Seed concluded. "And I am one of the few outside the city who could even recognize it as hers. I know she sent the message. It must mean that the situation has changed, and she can restore my reputation in the city, vindicating me."

"But why should you return secretly, then? That suggests you are still in trouble."

"Something must have happened that places the high priest in peril," Seed said. "So that I may be able to help her defeat him when the crisis comes, by testifying as to his lie about me. I *was* virginal for him." She reached out to take Stone's hand before he could get distressed. "Not for you, my husband. But I have given my body to no other man since I came to you." That much was true.

"Can this priestess be trusted?" Bunny inquired warily.

"Oh, yes, she is a good person. She saved me from death when the priest betrayed me." She turned again to Stone. "She sent me to you, with the aid of the gods, I know now."

With a brief dalliance on the way, Blaze thought. He still could not bring himself to regret it, though it complicated her existence and his.

"Then it seems that our time of decision is suddenly upon us," Bunny said. "You have learned the ways of the city well, Blaze?"

"Well enough, I think," he agreed. "Yet I had not learned of the stamp, until now."

"I did not think to mention it," Seed said. "I have no seal myself; my father in the city has ours." Then she frowned prettily, concentrating. "If we go there, you must have a stamp, my father. With a unique design."

"Like his forehead!" Doe suggested. She was now fifteen, older than Seed had been when she came to the family, and she had fleshed out nicely. But she had not yet found a young man to her liking, perhaps preferring to remain with the family awhile longer.

"Stone can make a stamp out of obsidian," Weasel said. She was now thirteen, and had also fleshed out, but not as dramatically.

"I can try," Stone agreed, contemplating his father's forehead.

"First we must decide whether to go," Bunny reminded them. "This is a serious step. You girls would lose your friends, and be among young men you have not seen before."

"Boys!" Doe and Weasel cried together, not at all dismayed. So much for that caution.

They discussed it. They recognized that the prospects for another timely turn in the weather were not good; already goats were being slaughtered. They knew that even if the weather turned immediately, it would take time for the pastures to recover. And there could be another drought a year or two further along. The old way of life was becoming more precarious. That was one reason the elder girls were not finding suitable boys: a number of families had already moved out, depleting the tribe.

They decided to go to the city. They would dye Seed's hair black and stain her cheeks so that she looked older and grimmer, and she would try to speak with a nomad accent. It would not be possible to make her look plain, but she could be lovely with a different complexion. That should conceal her identity, until they learned what the priestess was about.

They traded their house and goats for supplies for the journey. It would take about eight days, as a family of eight, and there might be delay before they were admitted to the city. They might even have to arrange to build their own cell-house there, and that would require the trading of their last resources, because Seed assured them that cell building was a specialized industry in the city.

In a few days they started out. Stone and Blaze took turns carrying Tree, who could not keep the pace. All had solid bags, so that the end of each day saw them tired. Nevertheless they made good progress, and reached the river where Blaze and Seed had camped their last day together. They gathered wood for the fire, and at one point Blaze and Seed carried a log together, one at each end, their eyes linking across it.

Blaze wanted to drop the burden and clasp her to him, and knew she wanted the same. But they simply carried the log and set it by the fire, then went on about their separate businesses.

Later he was alone briefly with Bunny. "I think I would put you two together for three days and nights running, if that would wear it out," she murmured, looking elsewhere. "But I know it wouldn't."

"I never sought this," he said, also looking elsewhere. "Had I known before I met that trader—"

"No, what has happened has been on balance good—and perhaps will be better. She has been ideal for Stone. She is also our avenue to the city, when we might otherwise go hungry. If there is a price, it must be paid."

"I am glad it is you I married," he said with genuine appreciation, "for you understand and negotiate my weaknesses as well as my strengths."

"I do indeed," she agreed, smiling somewhat distantly.

They slept, Blaze with Bunny, Seed with Stone and Tree, and the three girls together. Blaze dreamed of the place they were in, and of a young woman in his embrace. *My love, my love!* He woke to know it wasn't true, suffused with guilt. It wasn't that he didn't love Bunny, but that this other emotion had come in and captivated him, like an illness that would not let go. He wished it had never happened, yet simultaneously was gratified that it had, because it had transformed an otherwise somewhat dull existence.

The worst and best of it was that he knew that Seed was similarly dreaming and thinking. She was not truly his dream woman, but she had enough of the dream elements to evoke the old longing. Surely, in time, she would tire of passion for an old man, and turn to the young one who worshipped her. Then, perhaps, Blaze's own fancy would fade like the foolishness it was.

Bunny stirred. Impulsively he kissed her. She woke. "Is it me you desire?" she whispered.

"I always desired you." Then, realizing that he was being evasive in the same way Seed was, he qualified it. "I was awake. I knew it was you I kissed."

"That will do." She turned in to him and set about the matter of sex in the way they had always done it. He was eager to desire her, for herself and to diminish the guilt, and soon that desire was there and intense. Bunny did not have the body she had had in her long-ago youth, but it still had qualities that could excite him, and she was completely knowledgeable and cooperative about his ways. There was much to be said for that.

When it finished, and they lay quietly cooling, she put her mouth to his ear. "Do you ever wonder who I clasp in my mind when I'm with you?"

He was astonished, then realized that she was teasing him. *"You* were in my mind," he said. "My thoughts stray only in your absence." And there was a gratifying truth. He had lain with Seed when away from Bunny, and dreamed of Seed when alone in body or in mind. When Bunny chose to take his attention, she could do it, as she had just demonstrated. He had never wanted to leave her, and never expected to. She was his reality.

Bunny squeezed his hand, and was silent. She must have known this too.

He slept, feeling much better.

The journey continued. The family traveled well together, having had experience when moving between the summer and winter pastures; they were after all mountain folk. They reached the volcano, which the girls and Tree were thrilled to see; they ran along its nether slopes, finding good fragments of obsidian. Stone, too, was pleased; he had been here before, but had been too busy in the past three years to make the trip. He explored, searching out special fragments.

That left Blaze, Bunny and Seed to make the camp for the night. They worked to fetch wood and erect the small goatskin tents they carried. Blaze couldn't help meeting Seed's gaze every so often, in the ordinary course of events, though he tried to avoid it. This was after all where he had first met her. How significant that encounter had turned out to be! Before that his life had been good but routine. After that . . .

Bunny paused in her practical business of gathering dry grass for beds. "Take a walk with her," she suggested.

"I have a better idea," Blaze said. He walked across to Seed. "This is where I bought you for my son. Perhaps if you reminded him of its significance . . ."

She nodded, smiling. She knew that Bunny had understood the situation from the outset; it was Stone's discovery she feared.

When Stone returned with an armful of fragments, Seed approached him forthrightly. "This is where your father bought me for you, three years ago. This is where it started, though we had not yet seen each other. Perhaps we should celebrate the occasion."

Stone was embarrassed. "I went off hunting obsidian without thinking of you!"

"Think of me now. Let's take a walk by ourselves."

Stone was glad to agree, knowing what she had in mind. They linked hands and moved in a direction opposite to that taken by the others.

Bunny shook her head. "I wish I could manage my man like that."

Blaze laughed. "You have managed me throughout! I have loved it."

"That walk with her could have been yours," she said darkly.

"Then it would have been no more than a walk. Now I will walk with you, and it will not be far afoot." He caught hold of her and kissed her.

"But there is work to be done," she demurred.

He kissed her again. "I don't consider it work. You do?"

"Blaze! In the daytime?"

"*They're* doing it in the daytime." He ran his hands over her body, squeezing the good parts through her clothing. Indeed, he found the prospect of daytime sex exciting.

She resigned herself to the inevitable and returned his interest. Soon they were on the grass bed she had been fashioning, indulging vigorously despite the daylight and their clothing.

"Maybe this was better," Bunny murmured as it finished.

"Better than what?" someone asked.

They both jumped. There were the three girls and Tree. Doe had spoken, while Weasel was fidgeting because of her sister's temerity.

"Better than making camp without help," Blaze said gruffly, putting himself together.

But they would not be shamed. "I never saw it before," eight-year-old Mouse said. "It was always too dark. Is that exactly how it's done?"

"Well, there are other ways," Blaze said. "Here, let me show you." He addressed Bunny. "Turn over, woman."

"Some other time," Bunny said, getting up as she stifled a laugh. There was a titter.

Now the girls helped with the work, and it moved faster. But all three of them were thoughtful. Blaze realized that they really were interested, wanting to know the details so that they would not make mistakes when their turns with men came. Doe and Weasel, now fifteen and thirteen, were both old enough to do it, and perhaps were getting impatient about their lack of experience. Probably he and Bunny should have done it in daylight before, letting their children witness the full course of it. But while they did not seek to hide the fact of sex, neither were they inclined to show it publicly. It was an essentially private act that everyone knew about. Also, if there had been any doubt in the minds of the children about where Blaze's interest lay, this should have put it to rest. So perhaps this inadvertent demonstration had been for the best.

Soon Stone and Seed returned, and Tree ran to Seed for nursing. This at least was freely public. Things were back to normal.

❂

They reached the city on schedule, in good order. It had actually been a pleasant journey, because of the unity of the family. Now they were all apprehensive, knowing that their lives were about to change dramatically.

The city was impressive, even awesome. It was huge. It was like a cliff made of baked mud, rising straight from the ground to well above head height. There were no apertures, just ladders leading to the top.

A man on that phenomenal roof spied them. He waved, and called something indistinguishable.

"My father, you must go and tell him what our business is here," Seed murmured. "I must act ignorant."

Blaze walked forward, alone. "Trader?" the man asked from the roof.

"I am mountain," Blaze called. "Come live in city."

"Mountain," the man agreed. "Wait." He walked away, over the roof, and in a moment disappeared.

Blaze returned to the family. "He says to wait."

"He will fetch the manager," Seed said. "That should be Crockson, if he hasn't died."

"What kind of name is that?" Doe asked.

Seed smiled. "We of the city have some odd names. He is the son of Crock, who made our earthen pots. Crock died, but Crockson kept the name, though he never made a pot. There are many like that."

"As long as we don't have to use weird names," Weasel muttered.

"Like Blazeson," Doe agreed. "Or Bunnydaughter. Or maybe Stonesister." They went into a siege of stifled tittering.

After a time an older man appeared. "That's Crockson," Seed said. "I must hide my face, because he knows me."

"No," Bunny said. "Pick up your child and look innocent. We need to know that you are no longer recognizable."

"Oh, yes, I don't look the same," Seed agreed, remembering. "And I must remember to answer to my other name." For they had realized that her own name would quickly give her away. They had practiced calling her Shrew, and the girls had finally managed to do it without laughing. She was of course nothing like a shrew. She picked up Tree, who toyed with a strand of her black-colored hair.

The man descended the ladder and approached. He was old— perhaps older than Blaze—and solid. "You mountain people?" he demanded.

"Yes," Blaze agreed. "Come live city."

"You don't sound much like a mountaineer," the man said, using the full syntax.

Blaze smiled. "Neither do you. I have tried to learn something of your speech. When I talk to my own, it is more like this." He turned to Bunny. "Woman, are you sure you want to enter this strange place?" he asked her so rapidly in their natural dialect that he knew the man would miss most of the words.

"They do talk funny," she replied the same way. The girls smiled.

The man scowled, not appreciating being made the butt of a joke. "You will have to learn our speech. I am Crockson, the city manager. Do you have any useful skills?"

"Not herding goats?" Blaze said with a smile. He suspected that city folk thought that mountain folk knew nothing else but that and copulation.

"Actually, if you are good with goats, we can use you. They know who they like and will obey. But I was thinking of more solid skills, such as hewing beams or spreading plaster."

"My son works obsidian," Blaze said. "Show him your work, Stone."

Stone brought out several fine blades. Crockson pursed his lips. "You *made* these? You did not trade for them?"

"I made them," Stone agreed.

"I recognize that type. We have been trading for them for several years. Demonstrate to our craftsmen that you can do this, and you will have a secure place here."

"And my wife and son," Stone said, indicating Seed and Tree.

Crockson hardly glanced at them. "Of course. We shall be glad to cut out the grasping trader, for these. We will supply you with obsidian and other stone. But you must produce."

"This is what I do," Stone said.

Crockson returned to Blaze. "What else?"

"I work with fire."

"Tending mountain hearths?" The question was derisive.

"Fire hot enough to crack some stone. I know the woods that will do it." He touched his forehead. "I was marked for fire from birth."

"We will test you with our coppersmith," Crockson said. "We need fire men."

"And my wife and daughters?"

"They go with you." Now the man considered the girls. "They will be willing to marry city men?"

The girls tittered. Doe smiled. She had a good smile, and became prettier behind it.

"Yes," Blaze said. "If they are good men." The girls tittered again.

"As it happens, we have several houses free," Crockson said. "We will give you two, together, for your family and your son's family. When your daughters marry, they will go to the houses of their husbands, leaving you less crowded."

This seemed too easy, but Blaze wasn't sure how to question it. Seed did, however, and she spoke, with her affected accent. She addressed Blaze. "My father, why do they have empty chambers?" The matter had to be important, or she would not have risked betraying her identity.

"I don't know, Shrew." He turned to Crockson. "Don't families live in those houses?"

The man scowled, evidently uncomfortable with the question. "There was an illness. It is gone now."

"The swamp plague!" Bunny said, alarmed.

Crockson shook his head. "It is gone. Some died, some left, some got better. So we have fewer people, and room for some more. The illness does not come often."

Nevertheless, it was apparent that there was a risk here. The mountaineers seldom got the swamp fever—but they might get it if they became city folk. Blaze wished they had known about this before committing themselves.

"We will take those houses," he said. This was after all much easier than arranging to build new ones.

"Today you move in," Crockson agreed. "Tomorrow you and your son show your skills. If you are not good, we will require you to move out."

That was reasonable, and Blaze was reassured. No one gave anything for nothing.

Blaze followed Crockson up the ladder. When Blaze reached the roof, he was amazed again. It was a different world, a patchwork of squares of baked mud, each one higher or lower than its neighbors. Some were so much higher that they had ladders. In other sections several squares rose in formations like giant steps. Many squares had dark holes in them, with the ends of ladders poking out. He realized that every square was the roof of a chamber-house, just as Seed had said. But it was a wild experience, seeing it directly.

Bunny and the girls followed him. The girls exclaimed in awe as they came to stand on the immense roof of the city. Then Stone came, carrying Tree. Seed was last; she took her cue from the girls, murmuring in awe. It was a pretense she would not have to maintain long, because all of them would soon be accustomed to this peculiar terrain.

They walked across the city, which gradually rose, so that they had to use another ladder every so often. Blaze could not count the squares; they were everywhere. Then they reached a high ridge of roofs and looked out over a lower part of the city. It was so large as to defy Blaze's imagination. His entire tribe could have lived in only a small part of it, and all the other tribes he had encountered or even heard about would hardly have filled up the rest of it. If he reckoned the possible numbers by tens, spreading the fingers of both hands, he would have to keep adding up tens for too long a time to keep track of. He felt slightly dizzy just trying to grasp the number.

Every so often there was a gap in the roofs, seeming like a pit, several houses wide. They skirted one of these, and the smell that rose from it reminded him of what Seed had said about refuse: that was indeed where the pots were dumped. In fact there were people doing it. There was considerable traffic across the roofs, as people emerged from their holes and walked across to other holes. Blaze thought of mice in a field, scooting from one burrow to another.

Somewhere in the center of the city Crockson stopped. He bent to lift a wooden panel out of the way, revealing the hole beneath. "Here is one house," he said. He stepped to the adjacent square. "Here is the other. I will send a child to show you how they are used."

"I know how to use a house," Bunny muttered.

"We do not follow mountain ways," Crockson said in a superior manner. "You must learn our ways."

They climbed down the ladder into the first chamber. It was large enough for them all to stand in. The floor was baked mud, and on several slightly different levels. The lowest panel was covered by rushes laid flat. There were no windows; only the entrance hole admitted light. One square set in the floor had ashes: this was a hearth. There was a hole in one wall just large enough for a person to crawl through on hands and knees, leading to a smaller chamber. That was all. Overall, it was dark and dank, not at all appealing to mountain folk.

Seed looked up to be sure no one from the city was close. "I can show you everything," she murmured. "But they will wonder, if you seem to know it already. The children will tell you quickly and run elsewhere before you really understand, but after that I will clarify what they don't. This isn't the best house, but it's clean. It will do."

Soon the child appeared. "Crock says you're mountain people," a boy about Mouse's age said brightly, scrambling down the ladder so rapidly that it seemed for a moment that he was falling. He landed on the floor. "That's the man's place," he said, pointing to the highest panel in the corner. "That's the woman's place next to it, lower. That's the children's place." He pointed to the panel touching the other quarter of the man's panel. "There's your hearth and oven. The mats are in the storeroom, there." He pointed to the hole. "There's some wood for the hearth, too, but you'll need to get more when it's gone. There's a water jar and a poop pot; don't get them mixed up." He giggled as he shot back up the ladder.

"That was it?" Blaze asked, bemused.

"That was it," Seed agreed. "Now I can show you the rest. Crockson won't know that the boy was so fast." She went to the storeroom hole, reached in, and pulled out a woven mat. "Put this on the man's floor panel. Of course you don't have to sleep alone, my father." Her eyes turned away as she smiled fleetingly. Blaze felt the familiar thrill of the implication that went beyond the mild humor. "You may let my mother on it if you choose. But that panel is the man's, in every house, and always kept clear for him. It would be a disgrace if a visitor came and a woman or child was sitting on it."

Blaze took the mat and laid it on his corner. It would do. Seed meanwhile hauled out a second mat for the woman's panel, and a third for the children's. Blaze marveled at the number of good mats stored here, but realized that they had belonged to the prior family, and there had been no point in taking them away. Why steal the things of dead folk? It was at best an annoyance to the spirits of those dead.

"Oh, he didn't tell us where to go for food," Seed said. "Well, we'll just pretend he did. I'll show you, as soon as we're settled here."

"Don't we go out into the field to forage?" Doe asked.

"No, the city is more organized than that. Some women go out to cultivate the crops, and some carry in the food, and then others trade for it each day. You'll see."

They set up the chamber, then went to the next to set it up for Stone and Seed and Tree. It was almost identical. "I hope that not all city folk are as similar to each other as these chambers are," Blaze remarked.

"Oh, no, they are all kinds," Seed said. Then she broached more serious matters. "I must go to see the Priestess Lea, to learn why she summoned me. And I would like to see my mother, I mean my natural mother, because—" She shrugged.

"Oh, you must see her!" Bunny said immediately. "It will be such a relief to her!"

"But I don't dare let anyone else know my identity," Seed said. "Because—"

Bunny turned to Blaze. "We must help her do these things secretly."

"We must meet with the priest and priestess anyway," Seed said. "You must agree to honor the bull and leopardess. You don't have to actually swear belief, but you must promise never to speak against the gods of the city. So if we go tomorrow as a family, I can make myself quietly known to Lea."

"Could she then tell your mother?" Bunny asked.

"Yes!" Seed agreed gladly. "She can do it without arousing suspicion. Then my mother can arrange to see me by some coincidental encounter. I just want her to know I am well, and—" She broke off, her eyes tearing.

Bunny put her arms around her. "Of course. You have been too long away from her."

In a moment Seed recovered her composure. "I must show you the trade market. We shall have to use one of Stone's blades, but it should buy us food for several days. But they will cheat us, and if I protest, someone will know I have been here before."

Bunny had the answer. "Blaze will take three older girls there. They will exclaim foolishly among themselves. But he will heed the scattered gestures of only one."

"Three?" Doe asked.

"You, Weasel and Shrew. When Shrew lifts her hand to her head, he will know the bargain is fair. The other two will gesture randomly."

It was a good device. After the first time, Blaze would know the approximate values of things, and would be able to bargain for himself.

"The merchants reckon food value in terms of days of use," Seed said. "They are very quick in their judgments. If you shop for a family of four, they can translate that into days of eating for that family. But it's different for each type of food, and of course there are other systems for other types of things. It takes time to become a truly savvy shopper. I'm not good, but I can give you general values. There are standard amounts of each food that count as a day, so once you agreed on the days, the rest is simpler. Unless they try to cheat you that way, too, because you are new."

"I will not be new tomorrow," Blaze said.

He took the three to the roof, while Bunny, Stone, Tree and Mouse remained to finish getting the two chambers in order and start a fire in one hearth. They crossed the roofs toward another section of the city.

Blaze paused. "How will we find our chambers again? I can not tell one from the other, and there are so many blank roofs."

"You will learn the address quickly enough," Seed said. "But if you do get lost, look for the mark of the stamp."

"The mark?"

She returned to the cell they had left. "See, here in the hard clay is the imprint of the seal of the former owner." She pointed to a little design on the corner of the hole cover. "You will replace that with your own device, soon. But remember this one, for now. There will be no other exactly like it."

He nodded. But he would also do his best to learn the position of this chamber, so that he would not have to check several covers.

The market was a much larger chamber, or series of chambers, with several access holes. The walls were lined with tables where assorted foods were set out. Blaze was amazed at the variety. There were fruits and vegetables he had never seen, and several kinds of grain, and sections of meat from a number of animals. There were even great jugs of white milk, each containing more than any goat could give.

"Ah, you are new here," the closest man behind a table said. "I have not seen your face before, and I certainly have not seen your daughters."

There was a three-way titter, and much waving of hands.

"I just arrived with my family today," Blaze said. "From the mountain country. There is a drought there."

"So we have heard. But we trade for things grown where there is no drought. What do you want, and what do you offer in trade?"

"I want barley and peas for bread, and fruits. I have this." He brought out one of Stone's obsidian blade.

The man's eyes narrowed but his pupils widened as he squinted at the blade. "You can have several days' supplies of food for that. How many are there in your family?"

"Eight."

"You primitives are fecund! Still, that will be enough for two days' worth of food."

From the corner of his eye Blade saw Seed's hand settle at her waist. The other girls touched their heads and thighs, covering for the real signal.

Waist level. That meant the offer was only half good enough. He would never have known, because the traders he encountered never gave so much. But of course they had to make advantageous deals at each end.

"I have had some experience with traders who have passed our region," Blaze said. "I think I might have done better with one of them."

"That may be a better blade than I thought," the produce man said quickly. "I believe I can offer three days' supply."

Seed's hand found its way to her chest. Blaze was distracted for a moment by his glance at her breathing bosom, but quickly refocused on the bartering.

"I think I will see what the next man offers," Blaze said, glancing to the far end of the chamber where the meat man's table was.

The man pursed his lips. "You *have* had some experience! I will offer you four days, but no more."

Seed scratched her head. Blaze nodded. "That seems fair to me."

The man started setting out shares of barley and assorted nuts and fruits. The girls oohed and aahed at the strange kinds; they knew apples and acorns, but not some that must have come from far away. But amidst Seed's exclamations was a gesture; her hand hovered near her breast again.

"Perhaps conventions differ," Blaze said. "When I traded at home, we got four apples where you have put three."

The merchant glanced at the table. "You are right; I miscounted." He added another apple.

In due course the transaction was completed. The girls and Blaze had cloth bags of produce, and the merchant had an excellent blade he would surely trade for more than he had given. But Blaze knew that Seed's signals had enabled him to bargain with considerably more savvy than he could otherwise have managed.

They found the way back without trouble, though dusk was closing, because Seed unobtrusively guided them. Bunny was right: the girl was extremely useful, apart from whatever else lay between them.

Bunny was amazed when she saw the amount they brought. "All for one blade?"

"Twice as much as I would have had, without advice," Blaze said.

"Every time the man made an offer, See—Shrew moved her hand," Weasel said. "Then Father got more."

Bunny had a small fire burning on the hearth whose smoke rose smoothly up and out the hole above it while heating the chamber. She used it to make barley porridge from the last of their original store, because now they had new grain to replace it. They feasted on that and fresh apples. Then they took turns using the pot in the corner that wasn't lighted by the hearth fire. They used the reed-covered section of the floor to urinate; the earth below it was porous. Blaze knew he was not the only one who found it awkward to perform such functions inside a house, but it was obviously more awkward for all of them to troop out over the roofs and climb a ladder down outside the city to reach the nearest natural ground. Again, Seed's advice was invaluable; she had grown up here, and knew all the ways of the city. "They even bury people under their squares, when they die," she remarked. "Then they plaster them over."

"I can wait," Blaze said, not managing to laugh.

Stone and Seed took Tree to their own house, while Blaze, Bunny and the girls settled in this one. The mats were comfortable enough when buttressed by goat hides, and in the dark it was almost possible to pretend that they remained in their old house with the tribe. Of course Bunny slept with him, while the three girls settled on their square.

They had entered the city and settled in well enough, this first day. But tomorrow Blaze and Stone would have to prove their skills, and the family would have to see the priest and priestess. There was much yet to learn and do.

In the morning they used the pot and mat again, each according to his need, and ate the leftover porridge. They coordinated with Stone and Seed, agreeing that Bunny would care for Tree between nursings so that Seed could quietly show the others where to go. Of course the boy had not told them this either, but they would pretend he had.

But as they made ready to go out, the city manager arrived. "I will take you to the professionals," he said. "You two men. Then the men must meet the priest, and the women the priestess."

They did not argue. Blaze and Stone went with Crockson across the roofs. Now Blaze saw there were actually paths there, much as there were on ordinary terrain, leading to ladders. People were using them, meeting each other, exchanging greetings, and turning off when they reached their destinations. Women were carrying pots to the court-yards, and men and women were going to the edge of the city and down to the ground for foraging, farming and hunting. Crockson did not pause to introduce Blaze and Stone to anyone; Blaze realized that this was because they were not yet citizens of the city. They still had to prove their merit as craftsmen or workers.

He took them to another linked series of chambers. Each had an aperture at the top, perhaps having once been an individual house, but now they were a complex of four or five with ground-level doors between them. Blaze realized that only the outer wall of houses had to be secure against snakes; inner ones could connect as they pleased. These ones had stoneworkers and something Blaze didn't recognize.

"I bring two new men, from the mountains," Crockson announced. "One is an obsidian stoneworker; the other deals with fire."

Several men looked up, interested.

"Show your skill," Crockson said to Stone.

Stone brought out several of his blades and passed them around. One man beckoned him. Stone went there, and the man presented him with an unworked fragment of obsidian.

Stone smiled. He took it to a stone worktable and brought out his chipping tools. He turned the fragment over, studying it from all angles, then applied his tools and chipped off a suitable raw blade. He set aside the main fragment and went to work on the chip, carefully fracturing off a smaller chip. It would take much of the day to produce a perfectly crafted blade, but it was clear that he knew exactly how to do it. He smiled as he concentrated.

The man caught Crockson's eye. He nodded affirmatively. He could see already that Stone was no impostor. Then he put a hand on Stone's shoulder. "You are one of us," he said. "I recognize your blades, and see that you are their author. Now we shall exchange names."

The other men approached. "Have you ever worked flint?" one asked.

"I never could get enough to work," Stone said regretfully.

"Here you will have all you desire. We import it."

Crockson gestured to Blaze. "Your son has proved himself. Now it is your turn. Come to the fire."

In the next chamber was a huge stone and brick structure with a fire inside it. "This is a mountain fire worker," Crockson announced, indicating Blaze.

"What does a mountain man know about a forge?" the man tending it demanded gruffly.

"I have never seen one, but I know its nature," Blaze said. "And I know fire."

"How would you tend this?"

"How hot must the fire be?"

"Hot enough to melt the copper from this ore."

Blaze saw that there was indeed copper ore in a hopper above the forge. "You will melt the forge before you melt that ore," he said. "You have to get it closer to the fire."

The man smiled grimly. He put on giant fiber mittens and pulled at a projection in the upper part of the forge. A stone tray slid out. In it was more copper ore. It was evidently right in the blaze, when in place.

"With the right wood, that might do it," Blaze said. "But it would be better to blow on it."

"Have you ever used a bellows?" the man asked.

"No, but I know its nature."

"Here is our bellows. You tread on it."

Blaze looked at the device the man indicated. He nodded. "I think that will do it. But one man could not maintain the effort long enough. You need two or three men, to alternate, until the copper flows."

The man smiled. "Today my assistant is away. I thought I would have to work alone. Now I have you." He glanced at the manager, nodding. He had seen that Blaze did know fire.

"Only for the morning," Crockson said. "We must visit the shrines in the afternoon."

The morning passed swiftly. Blaze loved the forge and bellows; the combination produced the hottest fire he had seen, and it did indeed make the copper flow. This was the kind of work he had dreamed of, and never expected to have. His experience of the city was proving to be infinitely more positive than he had anticipated.

By the middle of the day both Blaze and Stone were solidly committed to their city professions. Neither was eager to go to see the priest. "What does the priest have to do with business?" Blaze asked the copper craftsman. "No one is getting married."

The man shook his head. "The priest has his nose into everything. He intercedes with the bull god to make our harvests good. We have to humor him by making regular offerings to the bull shrines, and the women to the leopard shrines. We have to have him bless our babies. I could do without it, but who am I? A coppersmith. I know nothing of the ways of the gods.''

"Only men honor the bull?'' Blaze asked.

"Oh, no, women do too. And men honor the leopard. But the priest curries favor with the merchants and identifies with the bull.''

Blaze did not pursue the matter. It was clear that the priest had power regardless of the wishes of ordinary folk. That confirmed what he had learned from Seed. The priest was dangerous—unless he lost his power.

Blaze and Stone walked across the roofs to rejoin the women at their chambers. Stone was excited. "They have more good material—they know more about stoneworking than I ever knew. There is much I can learn here.''

"The same for fire,'' Blaze said.

"Half the blades I make, I keep,'' Stone said. "The others are for the city, to trade for more material and equipment. We shall do well, this way.''

"I get a share of the copper I smelt,'' Blaze said. "We can trade that for food or other things.''

"They trade for everything here,'' Stone said. "The men told me there are even pretty women who will come to a man every night for a month, for a good obsidian blade.''

Blaze laughed. "That is one thing you don't need!''

"Yes. But I couldn't say that, because Seed isn't supposed to be pretty now.''

"She remains pretty enough, and she is your wife. Say that she wouldn't like you to spend your blades that way.''

They reached their houses. "We met the neighbors,'' Bunny said. "Several boys came to look at the girls.'' There was a titter.

"I knew some of those boys,'' Seed said. "So I stayed busy elsewhere, and did not speak to them. But Doe and Weasel can do better than those ones.'' She lifted her hand to chest height, humorously indicating the rating of the offerings.

Crockson came to guide them to the priestly section of the city. "This is routine, but necessary,'' he explained. "The men will meet Boro, and the women will meet Lea. Each will make a token offering, and agree to honor the bull and leopard. Once you are accepted by the priest and priestess, you are citizens of the city. Every month you will have to make a new offering, and you will have to attend the big ceremonies, but that is all."

Blaze just hoped that it would indeed be routine. He would be satisfied if the priest did not see Seed at all.

They came to a roof on which was sketched a handsome outline of a bull. Here was the bull shrine, obviously. It rose higher than the surrounding roofs, and had a hole in the top of the short wall extending up from the adjacent roof. This was the entrance.

Blaze and Stone entered the hole and descended the ladder after Crockson. The interior was fine and clean, the walls plastered white, and the floor solid throughout. On one wall was mounted a statue of the head of a bull. Near it was an altar on which was mounted a large set of bull horns. Behind this altar stood a man robed in a bull-hide cloak, wearing a smaller set of bull horns.

Crockson went to stand before the man. He bowed his head in a signal of respect. "High Priest of the Bull, I bring two new residents."

"Are they qualified?" the priest asked.

"Yes. They are father and son. The father is a fire worker and the son is a stonesmith. Both have families."

"Let them present themselves."

Crockson stepped back and gestured to Blaze. Blaze walked to the horn altar and bowed his head, honoring the ritual as the manager had explained it. "I am Blaze, of the mountains. I bring this bit of copper as an offering for the favor of the bull." He held it out.

The priest took the copper. He looked bored. "Do you undertake to pay proper respect to the bull, according to our custom?"

"Yes."

The priest made a negligent gesture. Blaze retreated, and Stone came to stand at the altar. "I am Stone, of the mountains. I bring this obsidian blade as an offering for the favor of the bull."

The priest accepted the blade and confirmed that the newcomer would also follow the custom. He dismissed them.

"That was easier than I expected," Blaze remarked as they rejoined the women.

"He knew I wouldn't have brought you if you weren't qualified and ready with offerings," Crockson said. "Nevertheless, you must try never to annoy him."

Blaze knew how serious that warning was.

A few roofs over they came to one with a leopard sketched on its surface. The women entered this one, while Blaze and Stone waited outside with Crockson. Men, the manager explained, were generally no more welcome here than women were in the shrine of the bull. But the priestess could make an exception if the whim took her.

After an interval, Bunny's face showed at the entrance hole. "She asked whether Stone and Shrew were married according to the ritual of the leopardess. She says our marriage ritual is not valid in the city."

Crockson clapped a hand to his forehead. "I didn't think of that! She is right. There will have to be a wedding ritual."

Blaze exchanged a glance with Stone. This smelled like trouble. They did not want to call attention to Seed in any way, and this was bound to. "What must we do?" Blaze asked.

"The man must be married in the presence of his father," Crockson said. "The woman in the presence of her mother."

"I am Stone's father, but Shrew's mother did not come with us," Blaze said carefully.

"You will have to explain that to the priestess. Perhaps she will allow a substitute."

Bunny went back down the ladder. In a moment she reappeared. "The priestess says that since there is already a child, the ceremony must be performed immediately. She knows of a woman who may be willing to serve in lieu of Shrew's mother, if Shrew is also willing. I will go to talk to this woman, if you will show me the way, City Manager."

"Of course I will," Crockson agreed, relieved. "What is her name?"

"Almond. Do you know her?"

Crockson concentrated. "Yes, I believe. She had a daughter who was shamed. Yes, she might do it, because she never had a chance to see her own daughter married. She is a sad woman."

Blaze kept a straight face. Suddenly he knew that the priestess knew Seed's identity, and was sending for Seed's real mother. Bunny, excellent at keeping secrets, would let the woman know most discreetly. Almond was about to be much happier than she had been.

Bunny turned to Blaze as she climbed out of the hole. "Stone must enter, for the ceremony. And so must you. For this purpose it is permitted." Then she set off with Crockson, expressionless.

They climbed through the hole and down the ladder into the shrine. This one was far more cozy than the other; beautiful woven tapestries were hung on the walls. Between them were sculptures projecting from the walls, not of bulls but of human breasts. On another was a picture in relief of two spotted leopards facing each other. And one of a goddess, her arms and legs spread wide, her long hair streaming sideways, as if blown by a powerful wind.

The girls stood in one corner. The priestess stood before the leopard panel, in a robe that fell open to show parts of her torso from breasts to thighs. Blaze realized that she represented fertility, so she showed her fertile attributes. They were impressive. But perhaps unsurprising, considering her position. She was, after all, the one who had selected Seed for her beauty, and she had certainly selected well. An impressive body was perhaps the prime requisite for this position, though it was evident that intelligence was required to hold it for long.

Blaze had no guide to protocol here, so he used what had been appropriate for the bull shrine. He went to stand before the priestess and bowed his head. "I am Blaze, of the mountains. I am the father of the husband of the woman Shrew."

"Look at me, Blaze."

He lifted his eyes to meet hers. Suddenly he felt increasingly uneasy; he had never seen such a calculating yet understanding expression. She seemed to know everything about him, fathoming it through his eyes and his mind laid open behind them.

"I will discuss arrangements with you in a moment," she said, and looked away. In that manner she dismissed him.

Blaze stepped back, and Stone moved up to fulfill the ritual. Then Lea addressed the others. "I will meet with Blaze in the next chamber. Be seated here. Advise me when the women return."

The girls, including Seed, settled on their panel. They made a little circle around Tree, who enjoyed walking from one to another, being hugged, and released. Lea ducked through a portal, leading Blaze to the other chamber. This one was evidently a storeroom; the decorations were more subdued, and there were a number of statuettes of the hugely endowed goddess, both sitting and standing. As symbols of fecundity they were extremely apt.

"Sit, Blaze," the priestess said, taking a stool. Her robe fell farther open, showing her body to his view almost as completely as the naked statues. Blaze sat, fearing what was on her mind.

"I am gratified that Seed found such a good family," Lea said. "I see that she has a good son, a good husband, and a good love. It would have been better if the three were together."

This was even worse than he had feared. "We call her Shrew," he said lamely.

"And so will I, for now, for her identity must be concealed. You have done well in this respect. Is her son yours, as well as her love?"

Seed would not have told her that! The woman had fathomed it herself. It was impossible to avoid the issue. "I do not know."

"We must retain that doubt. Do you understand why?"

"My son must never know." He hoped she would not betray that secret.

She smiled. "That, too. But I have a more crucial reason. If Seed's life is ever threatened by the priest of the bull, tell him the boy is his."

"That might be true," Blaze said miserably.

"But only if there is no other way." She shifted her position, crossing her thighs and folding her robe across her body. She seemed not to care whether anything showed or failed to show. "I mean to use Seed as the final element in the destruction of the priest. The city has suffered the loss of one citizen in five in the past season, to the swamp fever, and he is surely liable for that. When it turns out that he blamed a fertility maiden falsely, he will be done for. I could not make the charge secure, three years ago, but now I believe I can. All I ask of you is that you protect Seed, preserving her anonymity until I can make my move in a few days. Then I will unveil her, and she will testify, and the priest will be discredited and probably killed. Thereafter she will be restored to favor, and indeed may become a priestess of the leopard."

"That would be good," Blaze agreed, not thrilled.

"And all secrets will be kept."

He knew she was threatening him and bribing him, with the same information. He hated being caught, but knew the snare was tight. He had to do whatever she required. "All kept," he agreed.

Lea rose and moved to the portal. "Bring the boy," she called.

Seed came, leading Tree. "Let me look at you," Lea said, putting her hands on Tree's little shoulders and turning him around. She tousled his hair. "Oh, there is a bug," she said. "Let me get it out. Hold still, I fear this may hurt." She ran her fingers through his hair, to the scalp. "There it is." She made a pinching motion.

Tree jumped, then cried. He ran back to his mother.

"I am sorry," Lea said. She squeezed something quickly between her fingers and threw it into a nearby pot. "Sometimes they cling so. But it is best to get them out, so they can't suck the blood."

Seed looked at Tree's scalp. It was bleeding from that spot. "Thank you," she said faintly. "I did not know."

"We shall say nothing of this," Lea said. "I'm sure things will be all right."

They returned to the main chamber. Soon Bunny returned, with another woman of her age. "Almond has agreed to serve, if you agree to allow it, Shrew," Bunny said.

Seed looked at the woman, and her knees seemed about to give way. "Oh, yes," she breathed.

"Perhaps you should embrace her, to lend realism to the pretense," Lea suggested.

Seed almost threw herself at her mother. They hugged each other with such abandon that the girls were surprised. "It would fool me," Doe remarked.

"She has always been good at deception," Bunny said.

The girls looked at her, not understanding. Then Doe, who had become quite close to Seed, looked thoughtful. Blaze hoped she was catching on only to the half of it.

They proceeded with the ceremony, which was similar to the mountain one, but without the challenge to Seed's appearance. Then Almond departed alone, wiping away her tears, and the others returned to their chambers. The day was complete.

The next two days proceeded well enough. Bunny went alone in the evening to visit Almond, to thank her for assisting in the ceremony; they could not risk having Seed do it. Instead Seed, affecting nonchalance, took a pot out to the courtyard for dumping. Blaze was returning from his day at the forge, and kept a wary eye out. Indeed, he knew that the two women had arranged their trips to coincide with his return, so that he could watch to see if any of the other folk crossing the roofs were suspicious. A light rain was starting, and the sky was darker than usual for this time, because of the cloud. Most folk were hastening to get under cover.

Everything was ordinary, with one exception. One man was watching Seed intently. Was it just because she was a pretty woman, even when she was trying to mask it? Blaze wasn't sure. They had done their best to conceal Seed's identity, so that the priest would not be warned, but if the city manager had by chance made the connection to Seed's mother, there could be mischief. One passing remark to the priest, by a man who thought nothing of it . . .

Blaze reached his chamber and stepped beyond it. "Stone," he called in a low voice. "There may be something."

Stone quickly climbed the ladder and joined him. "I see nothing." Blaze realized with mild surprise that the lad had, at age seventeen, filled out into a fairly robust young man. Marriage had been good for him. The surprise was that Blaze had not taken the trouble to observe this before.

"The man beyond the courtyard. If he tries to sidle around it to join Shrew, one of us should be near."

They separated, going at leisurely paces toward the two ends of the courtyard, as if thinking of urinating into it when the woman departed. The man did start moving around the courtyard. Blaze, looking mostly elsewhere, moved to intercept him. But the man moved more quickly, slipping by ahead, and running to catch Seed. He had something in his hand.

Blaze broke into a run, chasing the man. "Seed!" Blaze cried, forgetting himself in his concern. Seed turned—and saw the stranger bearing down on her. She screamed and tried to get out of the way.

The man caught her and lifted his arm. Now Blaze saw the knife. He launched himself, catching the man and blocking the arm before it could descend. Seed dropped to the roof and scrambled away.

The man turned on Blaze, thrusting with his knife. But Blaze had one of his own. He used it as he would when slaughtering a goat, slicing the blade swiftly across the man's exposed throat.

The man looked surprised as his blood gouted. He made no sound. He couldn't, after that cut. Then he collapsed.

Stone ran up to them. "That was an assassin," Blaze said tersely. "He tried to kill her, not to rape her. That means the priest knows. He will send others. We must hide."

"I know where," Seed said. "Stone—cover for us. Pretend we're not gone, until someone tells Lea. No one saw what happened, I think."

She was probably right. The others had been going to their homes, and not watching. Blaze heaved the man's body into the courtyard, where it landed with a soft thunk of displaced refuse. The rain would soon wash away the blood.

Seed led the way. Blaze followed, hoping that she really did know a good place. They crossed a number of roofs, and came to one he had not been to before. They lifted the cover, climbed down the ladder, and replaced the cover.

It was completely dark inside. That gave Blaze no trouble as long as he was on the ladder, but once he stood on the floor he did not know where to go.

But Seed did not hesitate. She took his hand and led him to a pile of filled bags. "This is a wheat storeroom. It links with other chambers for barley, acorns, lentils and peas. No one comes here at night, and the bags are soft."

Indeed they were. The two of them settled down on top of the broad pile, shifting some bags to make their bed comfortable. They were safe, for now.

But the moment Blaze relaxed, he remembered what he had done. "I killed him!" he whispered. "I slaughtered him like an animal. I never did that to a man before."

"You came to my rescue," she reminded him. "He was trying to kill me. I was terrified." Indeed, he felt her body shivering with reaction.

That put it into perspective. "When he threatened you, I knew nothing but to stop him. But now you are safe, and I know what I have done. I am a murderer!"

"You protected me."

He was conscious of the oddness of it: she had almost been killed, but he was the one reacting. "I should just have pushed him into the courtyard. I didn't have to kill him!"

"He was an assassin. He would just have kept coming after me. Boro knows who I am, and has given the order. You did what you had to do."

But Blaze perversely would not be consoled. "I am a murderer. What will become of me?" His future seemed as dark and blank as the chamber. Their desperate move to the city had ended in disaster.

Seed did not argue further. She caught his head in her hands and drew it in to her bosom. Her breasts were marvelously full and soft, as they had been three years before, and her embrace was wonderfully comforting. He lay there, allowing himself to be thus comforted.

After a time he could no longer ignore the irony of the situation. "Seed, I am selfish," he said. "I should be trying to comfort you."

"It is all right, my love. I have always been here for you." She embraced him more closely.

There it was. She still loved him, and wanted to be with him. Now they were together. But it wasn't right.

"You must not stay here, Seed. You must nurse your child." That was only part of it, of course.

"Oh, yes, I must," she agreed. In another year Tree would be weaned, and Seed would have another child. But in the interim the child had to be fed every few hours. Both his appetite and the pressure of the milk in her breasts required this. She would soon be uncomfortable.

"You have shown me where to hide. Go to your son."

"Yes. In the dark I can do it. You stay here and sleep. I will return to guide you to a better place. This was just the closest one."

She gave him one more intimate soft squeeze, then disengaged and went to the ladder. He heard her climbing, then heard the roof panel move. Then he heard it being replaced. He was alone.

What *was* he going to do? Surely he could not remain in the city, after this. But if he fled it, what of his family? There was no living to be made out on the range; that was why they had come here. But he was the one working; his family depended on him more in the city than it had in the tribe. They were all in trouble, because of what he had done.

Yet how could he have let that man attack Seed? She was probably right that the man would simply have come after her again, if he had lived.

Yet again, the high priest could send another assassin. There seemed to be no end to the dangers of their situation. All because Boro had somehow found out.

How had that happened? Now Blaze was able to put it together: Crockson, of course. The man had guided Bunny to Seed's mother. He had remarked how the woman had lost her own daughter. He could have mentioned to others Almond's participation in the ceremony the priestess required. Word could have circulated to the priest—or Crockson could have mentioned it to the priest himself, thinking nothing of it. The priest was surely not stupid. He could have made the connection.

In that case, Seed would be in constant danger as long as she was in the city. The priest knew that her testimony could help ruin him, so was determined to kill her before she could speak. They would simply have to flee the city, because Seed could never live safely in it.

Perhaps they could travel farther on south, and join a tribe in a region not suffering drought. That seemed to be their best hope.

Somewhat reassured by that decision, he relaxed and slept.

He woke as the panel was moved. That would be Seed returning.

She replaced the panel and came directly to him. "I nursed him well," she said. "Both breasts. He is soggy full. He will sleep till morning."

"I have slept," Blaze said. "But you should too."

"In your arms I can sleep," she agreed. "Be with me, my love."

Something else fell into place. "We agreed never again," he reminded her. "I am married and have children; you are married and have a child. We are not for each other."

She sighed. "I hoped you would forget."

"Our love has no future. It is pointless. Even though we must flee the city together, we have no business betraying our families. Suddenly this is clear to me."

"You are right. Yet my heart will not hear. I never loved any man but you."

"Is my son not worthy of your love?"

"He is worthy. I am the one who is not. You always knew that, Blaze."

He had another revelation. "Because of your experience, you felt unworthy. You thought yourself suitable only to be someone's mistress, not to be someone's wife."

"It is true. I am unworthy. You alone understand."

"Oh, Seed, you are more than worthy! You have made Stone happy. You have given him a son. You have earned your status. Now it is time to give yourself the happiness you deserve. Love Stone as he loves you. He knew your history too, yet loved you from the start. Love him back."

"I have gotten him and all of you into trouble," she said, and he heard the weeping in her voice. "I should never have come into your lives."

"You transformed our lives! Promise me that if we live, you will let yourself love him."

She laughed, not happily. "That is an easy promise to make. I think we will not live."

"Promise anyway."

There was a pause. "I promise," she whispered. "It would be easy to do. He is truly worthy."

Then he held her, and she slept. For the first time they lay embraced without desiring sex. For he knew in retrospect that he had desired her from the moment he first saw her, at the fire mountain, as a shadow of his dream woman, and she had oriented on him also at that moment, as her rescuer. Their relationship had now changed, subtly but certainly.

Before dawn she woke. "We must change our hiding place. I told Stone where we would be, so the priestess can help us."

"The priestess? Why should she help us?"

"If she makes her move now, and brings me forth, she may yet overthrow the priest. Then we will be safe in the city, under her protection."

"But the assassin! I killed him!"

"He was as worthless as the swamp fever. No one will claim him, not even the priest."

"No penalty for murder?" he asked, amazed.

"Not if Lea wins."

He shook his head in the darkness. "I do not understand the ways of the city!"

She found his face and kissed him. "That is why you think yourself unworthy to be a citizen. Promise me you will abolish that notion, if we live."

He had to laugh. She had reversed his ploy, and shown him the other side of his logic. "I promise."

Then they left the wheat chamber and moved across the deserted roofs to what turned out to be the carpentry section. Here there were stacks of curing wood, waiting for the many uses it would have throughout the city. They hid behind the piles. "No one comes here, even in the day," she explained. "Not until the wood is ready. It has to sit for a long time, drying."

"A good hiding place," he agreed. "But there is no food."

"Someone will bring some. We have only to wait. Lea will know what to do."

Blaze thought of something else. "If no one will care about the assassin, why should I be hiding?"

"Oh, I didn't think of that! I am the only one who needs to hide. You can return to your house."

Blaze shook his head. "I might as well wait for someone to come here. I should have realized before."

"I know why I did not think of it," she said. "I wanted to be with you, before I died."

"That also must be why I did not think of it," he agreed. "But now perhaps we understand each other better."

"Perhaps we do." She kissed him again. "See—the power of our bodies is fading."

"Yes, it is," he agreed, surprised. For he still appreciated the phenomenal desirability of her body, without actually desiring it.

"Yet we will always remember what we promised to forget."

"Yes. We could not forget, but we can remember."

After a time Blaze thought of another aspect. "If there should be trouble, and you fear death, you should have a knife."

"A knife?"

He brought out his. It was one of Stone's fine obsidian blades fastened to a stout wooden handle. "Stab this into someone's belly, below the chest so the ribs will not turn it. Or slice it across a throat. Then you will not die alone. Perhaps you will be able to escape."

She took the knife. "You withdraw your love, and offer me death," she murmured. "I thank you for both."

An hour after dawn showed through the crevices of the roof panel, two men entered the chamber. "We have cloaks to conceal you," one announced loudly to the chamber. "So you can go to the priestess without being known."

Blaze and Seed stepped forward. "The priestess sent men?" he asked, surprised.

"Do you think she would send women wearing leopard cloaks?" the man demanded. "That would be no concealment!"

Blaze saw the logic. They donned the cloaks and followed the men to the roof. They moved across to a new section of the city. Blaze saw that it was not the shrine section, but realized that that, too, would have been obvious. There had to be a meeting place that no one suspected.

They entered a chamber illuminated by a large wax candle. One of the men replaced the panel. Then both drew knives.

Blaze realized that they had been betrayed. These were the priest's men! "Seed—act," he cried, leaping at the closer man. His swiftness of reaction caught the man by surprise, and his shoulder collided with the man's shoulder and shoved the man back against the wall. Blaze went for the man's knife with both his own hands, and in a moment had caught the wrist and hand and was twisting the knife away.

Meanwhile Seed had surprised the other man just as much. Blaze's knife had appeared in her hand and was menacing him back. Women used knives for many things, but never in combat, and for a moment he did not know what to do. That moment was all Blaze required to complete the capture of his man's knife.

Blaze made ready to stab his man and jump for the other. He knew that hesitancy could be disastrous, because an old man and a woman could not truly expect to prevail against two young men.

"Wait!" the second man cried. "We were not trying to kill you!"

"You are from the high priest," Blaze said. He feared that he should not allow them to distract him for even a moment, but he also did not want to kill again if he could avoid it.

"We are," the man admitted. "We tricked you. But we were supposed only to disarm you and hold you here for the priest."

"The priest wants this woman dead," Blaze said.

"No—he wants only to prevent her from testifying. He will spare her life if you leave the city."

Blaze glanced at Seed. "Does this make sense?"

"Why would he be sure I wouldn't come back?" Seed demanded.

The man shook his head. "It wouldn't matter."

"Why wouldn't it matter?"

The man looked uncomfortable. "She wouldn't talk."

Something was strange. Blaze had seen that manner in a trader who thought to cheat him. "Why wouldn't she talk?"

The man did not answer. But Seed suddenly understood. "You were going to cut out my tongue!" she cried. "You were going to rape me, cut out my tongue, and send me out of the city again, with some trader who would sell me too far away to return. And the rest of the family would be banned from the city, so *they* wouldn't tell."

The man did not deny it.

Suddenly Blaze was ready to kill again. His grip tightened on the knife he had wrested from his man.

Then another man appeared in the doorway to the next chamber. He was followed by yet another, and a third. Blaze realized that their delay had indeed been fatal; they had missed their chance to kill and flee, and now had no chance. These were probably nominally servants of the bull, but actually hirelings for dirty work.

"Wait!" Blaze cried, realizing that it was time to use his last ploy. "I must talk to the priest."

"He will soon be here," one of the new men said. He glanced at the one before Seed. "You have not finished with the woman?"

"Touch that woman, and the priest will have *your* tongue cut out," Blaze said. "He wants to hear what I have to say."

The man would not be bluffed. "Tell it to me, and I will judge."

"I will tell him alone, and *he* will judge."

The man considered. He was evidently a lesser priest, with some authority. "We will wait."

Seed moved across to join Blaze. She could not know what he had in mind. She just wanted to be near him when they died. And she expected to die, because she had the knife and would not allow herself to be raped or mutilated without trying to do the same to her attacker. She had loved Blaze constantly, but he realized that she was not the same naive girl she had been three years before, and now was capable of hate as well as love. Considering the horror she faced, this was understandable.

They waited somewhat tensely, the two of them on one side of the chamber, the five men on the other. No one spoke.

The high priest arrived. He looked at the tableau, and immediately realized that something had gone wrong.

"The man claims he has something to tell you, that you want to hear," the lesser priest said.

Boro shrugged. "Then tell me," he said to Blaze.

"You will want it private."

The priest's mouth quirked. "Then set aside your knife, come to the other chamber, and tell me."

Blaze started to move, Seed beside him.

"Not the girl," Boro said. "She will remain here. Should you displease me in any way, she will pay the price."

The man knew how to bargain! Blaze set down the knife and walked to the doorway. Seed remained behind, realizing that this was the way it had to be. She was trusting him to know what he was doing, certain that he would never willingly allow harm to come to her. He climbed through the portal, which was only half the height of a man.

The priest followed him. They moved to the far side of the chamber. "That woman has a son," Blaze said.

"And a husband," Boro said. "That is your news?"

"That son may be yours."

The priest's beginning sneer froze. "Mine?"

"You know who that woman is. She was your fertility maiden three years ago. That boy is two years and three months old. He could be yours."

The man was obviously interested. He was in deep political trouble, and in the next few days, at the time of the fertility ceremony, the high priestess would charge him with failure to invoke the protection of the gods against the swamp fever. Then Seed would testify to his false charge against her, and be believed, and he could be finished. But if he could demonstrate that he had put a baby in a sacrificial maiden, his reputation and power could be salvaged.

Blaze appreciated why the priestess had said to use this ploy only as a last resort, because it would weaken the priestess's case. But if Seed were about to die or be rendered mute, this was better.

Boro's eyes squinted. "If the child were mine—what would be your price?"

"Merely to be allowed to live in the city in peace," Blaze said, realizing that the ploy was working. "The mother would of course be honored by the priestess for her part in the matter. Her husband knew her history, and would not object to the identification of the child. Her husband will have his own turn to have a child by her, in due course."

"No one would deny the paternity of the child?"

Blaze shrugged. "We have no way of knowing, for sure. But perhaps you do."

The priest put his head to the doorway. "Bring the woman's child here."

There was a scramble as someone headed up the ladder from the other chamber.

"Bring the woman here," the priest said. "Alone."

In a moment Seed came through the aperture. She was without her, knife, realizing that she could not otherwise be trusted near the priest.

"They dyed your hair and marked your cheeks," Boro said, looking at her.

She nodded. She did not know what Blaze had said.

"Your son could be mine," the priest said.

Now she realized. "Yes, High Priest."

"And if he is, what will you say of me?"

"Nothing, High Priest." Indeed she understood: she could not testify against him if she hoped to save her life or that of her son.

"What does the leopard priestess know of this?"

"She suspected, when she saw the child," Blaze said. "But she hoped it would not be known."

Boro smiled grimly. "Of course."

Soon Stone arrived, carrying Tree. It had evidently been made plain to him that Seed had been captured by the priest, and that her life was at stake.

"Bring him here."

Stone brought the boy to the priest. Boro looked at Tree's head, parting the hair. In a moment the scab on the scalp showed, where the priestess had pinched it. "She tried to scratch it out!" Boro said. "She knew this child was mine!"

"She said it was a bug in his hair," Blaze said.

"She saw the mark!" Boro exclaimed. "See!" He bowed his own head, parting the hair. There was a dark patch of skin.

"I didn't know you had such a mark," Seed said. Then, her mind still working, she added, "Too."

Blaze had to admire her quickness. She knew as well as he did that there had been no such mark on Tree's scalp. There was only the scab where the priestess had scratched. But the priest was incapable of believing that the priestess would ever try to help him in this way. He was sure she had tried to do the opposite: to expunge an existing mark.

Boro focused on Seed. "You will testify only to the age of your son, and the mark?"

"As long as I live in peace," she agreed.

The priest nodded. They understood each other.

After that it was routine. Tree was presented, and the mark shown. All the family agreed that they had not before recognized the significance of the mark, but could not now deny it. Stone seemed uncomfortable about the matter, understandably, but did not argue. He, too, well appreciated the fact that the mark was their salvation; there would be no further attempts on Seed's life, and the family would be allowed to remain in the city. He also was pleasantly surprised to discover a certain extra quality of attention in his wife. It was as if her love for him had been restrained, and now was unrestrained.

There was more that Stone did not know, but Bunny did. "It is over," she murmured when alone with Blaze, reading his manner.

"We still care for each other," he demurred. There was no need to identify the people he meant.

"But the dream is gone."

Of that he wasn't sure. "She was only a representation of the dream. Now I know she is not the dream."

"The priestess lost, but her power remains strong," Bunny said. "When the priest dies, she will be supreme."

"We shall certainly support her, when that time comes," he said. "She brought us to the city, and saved Seed's life."

"And banished a dream."

He realized that this had been one of the effects of Lea's ploy. The prospect of death had caused both Blaze and Seed to reassess their values and emotions. They had realized what had some future and what did not.

"I always did love you," he told Bunny. "Now the shadow is gone."

"I know it."

They proceeded to further erase the shadow.

At its height, the city of Catal Huyuk may have had 10,000 people. One layer followed another, as one generation built atop another, with individual houses seldom lasting more than 120 years. There is no evidence that the city was ever conquered or damaged by hostile people. Eventually the inhabitants simply moved elsewhere, and this section of Anatolia reverted to wilderness. Nevertheless, Catal Huyuk was one of the first great cities of the world, a center of trading, art and religion, and its place in history is secure. Its people's use of identification stamps or seals presaged the wider use of similar seals by the later Sumerians, suggesting a continuity of culture. Thus we may owe a great deal to this truly ancient city.

CHAPTER 12

KINGDOM

The developing cities in the Levant and Anatolia saw their full flowering in Mesopotamia, beginning about six thousand years ago. Perhaps for the first time, war between cities became feasible, and the formation of larger political states. Each city was under the protection of its own special god, and when that god failed to perform sufficiently, the city was conquered by another and its god icons taken away to reside in ignominious captivity.

The city of Lagash had been governed by a relatively benign ruler, Urukagina, who also ruled her neighbors Nina and Girsu, which was the

233

religious center. Then came Lugalzaggisi, "King of the Lands," of the nearby
city of Umma, intent on conquest.

    It has been claimed that one of the earliest activities of civilization was the
brewing of ale: it was necessary to develop competent agricultural and
manufacturing and distribution mechanisms to handle this most precious
product. Well, maybe.

O H, I hope Carver is all right," Crystal said anxiously. "He's really
    not a fighter."

"Neither is Scorch," Ember replied. "We simply must have faith that
our god Ningirsu protects us all." But the twitch in her cheek belied
that faith.

Crystal's faith did not look strong. Neither was Ember's; she knew
that when one city fought another, one god fought another, and that
meant that one god would lose. How could they be sure that their god
was stronger than the enemy's god?

They reached the temple of the goddess they served directly: Ninkasi,
"The Lady Who Fills the Mouth." Ninkasi was not the highest in the
hierarchy of gods, but she had perhaps the most devoted following. She
was the goddess of ale, and four of every ten measures of barley in the
city went to her product. Ember had worked her way up from lowly
furnace watcher to head brewer, and now was one of the most important
women in the city. She made sure that the rations of the goddess went
out to every man in the service of the city. In this time of war, that meant
almost all of them. Two big mugs of ale a day, to each. No other god
brought such regular and wholesome cheer.

The slaves were ready. "Move out the crocks," Ember said. "To the
front gate."

The slaves put their shoulders to the harness. The wagon rolled onto
the street, bearing its burden of large crocks. Progress was slow but
adequate.

"Mistress," the head slave called respectfully. "What news of the
front?"

Ember was ready. "Our brave men went out this morning. Surely they
are routing the enemy troops even now, and will soon return in good
order."

"Mistress, are you sure?" He sounded worried.

Honesty was best. "I am not sure. But our god has always protected us before, and surely he will now." She reflected a moment, realizing that this was not adequate. "I shall try to obtain a more immediate report. Failing that, I'll see if I can get us up on the wall so we can take a look ourselves."

"Oh, mistress!" he replied, awed.

Crystal smiled. She knew that women were not supposed to mount the wall during wartime, but that such things could be accomplished if properly phrased.

Reassured, the slaves moved along. They reached the front gate, where the guards were more than ready for their rations. Ember lifted her arms in a benediction for a crock, and the slaves unloaded it and carefully poured the precious ale into lesser containers. These were in turn poured into the waiting mugs of the men. Crystal counted the number served and made a note on her ledger. Each man was entitled to one and only one mugful at this time.

"What news of the battle?" Ember inquired.

"Mistress, we have none. But surely our brave and bold men are giving an excellent account of themselves."

"Surely," Ember agreed. She looked up. "What of the men on the wall?"

"Mistress, we are shorthanded because of the number of our men in the field," the gatekeeper explained. "They may not come down until the relief contingent arrives."

"We can't wait for that," Ember said. "We have the other gates to serve."

"You can fill their mugs, and they will have them when they come down."

"And how many will be mysteriously empty by then?" Ember inquired cynically. "We must serve them personally."

"They can not come down," he said. "They must maintain guard on the wall, lest the enemy make a sneak attack."

"Leave a lookout on the wall; the men can climb back up there much faster than the enemy can approach across a plain which extends to the horizon."

"It is against regulations."

Ember knew it was, and she did not want to get the man in trouble. She was angling for another solution. "Then we shall deliver the gift of the goddess to them there. Our men must be served." Without giving him a chance to object, she turned to the slaves. "Pour out the second crock and carry the containers to the top of the wall on either side. Mind you spill none, but don't dawdle. Bear in mind that you are assisting the defense of the city."

The slaves jumped to the task with such alacrity that the gatekeeper knew he had been had. He elected not to challenge it. He turned his back and surveyed the street. He would be able to report that he had seen no women or slaves on the wall. He would not have done it if he had not known how much the men needed the ale of the goddess, and that Ember was trustworthy.

Crystal followed the slaves up to one side, and Ember followed those ascending to the other side. They were greeted by hearty cheers as the men realized what they were doing. They all knew and liked Ember, the mistress of the blessing of the Lady Who Fills the Mouth.

"Heed me," Ember announced. "I want no report of anything irregular occurring here. Bring your mugs in silence."

There was a murmur of understanding. No one would speak openly of seeing any women or slaves on the wall.

The men brought their mugs, and the slaves filled them. Between mugs, the slaves looked out across the irrigated fields and the plain beyond, hoping to see returning troops.

When the measures had been delivered and recorded, the party was ready to descend back into the city. Ember gazed outward one more time, just in case she might spy the dust of a returning mission.

And she did! Just a faint stir, to the west. "Look!" she exclaimed, pointing.

Everyone looked. Soon there was no doubt. But after that it became apparent that something was wrong. The column was not in fit marching order, but strung out, bedraggled, and slow. They must have lost the battle!

Ember shook her head. There had been a time, she understood, when Sumer had been at peace. But not in her day. There was always news of one city quarreling with another. Lagash had had its own quarrels, and indeed was now the mistress of two other cities. But the present governor was a peaceful man, so had not done much with the city's defenses. Now, she feared, they were about to reap the consequence.

"If you will, mistress—off the wall, quickly," the gatekeeper cried.

Ember, Crystal, and the slaves hastily got back down to the city street. Oh, this was surely trouble!

"Mother—do you think Father and Carver are all right?" Crystal asked anxiously. Scorch had been among the troops going out, because there was always need for a blacksmith when weapons got battered. Carver had simply been of age to qualify for troop duty.

"I hope so." That was all she could say.

They trundled their ale wagon back to the temple. They were not able to serve the other city gates, in the face of this apparent disaster. "Report to the slavemaster," Ember told the slaves. "If you stay in the temple it should be all right, because the enemy likes ale as well as we do. Just make sure you are not mistaken for fighting men."

"But we want to fight on your side, mistress," the head slave protested.

She shook her head. "If your help would enable us to save the city, you still would not be allowed to fight. You know that. Weren't some of you captured from Umma in one of the routine skirmishes?"

"Yes, mistress. But we are loyal to you now, for you have treated us well."

"I'm sure you are. But I'm also sure that our commander would never believe it. Be practical: if the situation seems hopeless, we'll have to concentrate on preserving as many lives as we can. You will serve the new order. Pray to the goddess that you are well treated there."

Immediately the group of slaves broke into the litany of protection, appealing to Ninkasi. Ember was sure their prayers were sincere.

She turned to Crystal. "Fetch Flower here," she said tersely. "We shall all be better off at the temple, and our husbands will know we are here."

Crystal turned her clay tablet over to the mistress of accounts and hurried away. She knew that Ember was right. If there were no problem, the temple was still a good place to be. But if the worst occurred, the temple was their best chance for life.

Ember tried to interest herself in the temple routine, but simply couldn't concentrate. Scorch, Carver—had they survived? What would the family do, if—

A slave approached her. "Mistress, if it please you."

She turned to him. "Yes, Crock."

"Some of us would rather fight."

"But I told you—"

"Yes, mistress. But we think that maybe the goddess really could use our help, this time. If we could go to the wall, at least—"

"Crock, your lives will probably be spared, because you're noncombatants. But the moment you take up arms, if by some mischance the commander allows it, you'll be subject to the same strictures as the men. That means death or—"

"Or slavery, mistress," he said, smiling. "It isn't as if we have much to lose."

"But with us, you are enlightened slaves, scheduled to earn your freedom before too many years. With them, you would have no such assurance."

"That is true, mistress. But we are already slaves—and if they win, we will be *their* slaves. They won't honor the credit we have earned with you. Our lives will be disrupted, at best. At worst, only our women will survive, unpleasantly. We're better off with you. So we want to help you win."

Ember was touched. She didn't want to tell them no outright, so she temporized. "Let me check."

She went to talk with those of other temples. Their slaves had similar sentiments. The news from the field was worsening; the city would be under siege within hours. If the walls did not hold, all was lost.

Ember returned. "I will take any of you to the wall who wish to help in a noncombatant role, assisting our defenders. If we repel the invader, any who have served well will be freed and granted citizenship. But be aware: half of you may be dead, even if we win. That wall is apt to be a hazardous region."

"We know," Crock said grimly.

"Go to the morning keg and fill your mugs. There won't be slaves to bring you your rations from the goddess."

They laughed. They went for their ale.

Soon they were ready. "Crock, you will be my second-in-command, in this noncombatant effort," Ember said. "You will relay my orders. That means that when I say we shall march to the gate, you will yell it loud, and give any additional orders you deem necessary to accomplish that mission, and report to me that it is being done. If we approach in impressive order, the gatekeeper may allow us to mount the wall and assist the defenders there."

"We understand." Slaves were considered to be worthless for combat, so they had to demonstrate otherwise. In the guise of being noncombatants.

"To the gate—march," Ember said.

"Gate—march!" Crock bawled with enthusiasm.

The slaves started off. At first they shuffled in normal slave fashion, but Ember picked her feet up high and set them down hard, and Crock emulated her, slapping the pavement with his feet. "March—so!" he cried. "In step with me. Show whose god you are serving!" They picked up their feet, and soon the ground reverberated with their cadence. They were showing something seldom permitted in slaves: pride.

They came to the next temple. More slaves were waiting there, eager to join. "Fall in!" Crock bawled. "Match the step!"

By the time they reached the gate there were more than a hundred slaves keeping the step. They came to a prideful halt.

Ember approached the gatekeeper. "You are shorthanded. I bring noncombatant reinforcements. They will need tools and instruction, but they will serve well."

"Slaves?" the gatekeeper asked incredulously. "Slaves never bear weapons."

"Of course they don't," she agreed smoothly. "They are here merely to assist the soldiers, as they did when they brought the ale this morning. Perhaps this time they can bring other supplies, or serve in other ways."

"This is highly irregular. Slaves are not to be trusted."

"I trust mine. The will is there. They know they are better off with us than with the enemy. Indeed, they know they will be freed, if they serve well. Give them their chance."

"We might as well just open the gate to the enemy!"

She cocked her head at him. "How long has this shift served since relieving the prior shift?"

"Too long. But—"

"How long before the next shift comes?"

His lips drew tight. He knew, as she did, that there was no relieving shift; all the remaining men had gone out to battle. The men would soon be useless because of sheer fatigue.

"Let each of your men become a leader," she said. "Let him order the slaves. Naturally he will not direct them in the firing of arrows, the throwing of bricks, anything like that. They will do what he requires, obeying without thought. When he knows they are ready, he can rest for awhile, recovering his strength. That way we will have fresh, alert men on the walls, instead of suicidally fatigued ones."

"But slaves! Who ever heard of this?"

"I will go up and stand on the wall near the gate," Ember said. "I will depend on their goodwill."

"The first enemy arrow would take you out!"

"Not if the defenders are apt."

He hesitated, uncertain. These were trying times.

She made up his mind for him. "I will stand aloft!" she cried to the slaves. "You will help the soldiers protect me—and the goddess of ale—and the city." She started up the ramp.

"Follow her!" Crock bawled. Then: "Half to the other side!"

Ember reached the top. "Go two to every soldier on the wall!" she cried. "Learn from that soldier. Help him in whatever way he directs. I want no sluggards defending me." She walked to the place where the wall rose up to handle the gate, and stood there in a partial alcove, arms spread, her robe flowing in the wind. "These are noncombatants," she called to the soldiers. "They will do whatever you say, so long as they touch no weapons." She knew that the wind up here was making her words hard to distinguish, so that misunderstanding was possible. But she had officially done her part, remaining true to city policy.

The slaves moved out. Some could be recognized because they had served the ale, earlier. The soldiers hesitated, but realized that there was no help other than this. They began the instruction. Ember saw some making throwing motions, demonstrating how to hurl a brick down without losing one's balance and falling after it. Some were lifting bows, demonstrating the angle and pull required to find the range. Many were putting spare helmets on the slaves, and such armor as was available. The misunderstanding was in full swing. The slaves would not be able to perform as well as real soldiers, but the enemy would not know that, and might be daunted by the number of heads on the wall.

Meanwhile the returning column was approaching the gate. There were too few men there. Ember spied the figure of Carver, but not that of Scorch. In that moment she knew the worst. But she refused to let her horror be known. She stood proudly on the wall, looking out.

Already the enemy was coming. Those ranks were solid instead of intermittent. Light glinted from the massed shields. This was surely doom.

They marched to just beyond arrow range. Those on the wall had the advantage, because their elevation gave them more distance. But they lacked the numbers and the energy of the attackers, as well as the experience. Only some unusual occurrence would save the city from conquest.

But first the enemy had to breach the wall. They would try to do this by battering down the main gate. They would have a battering ram: a huge heavy log they would run with, crashing its end into the gate and bashing it open or down. Once that gate had been breached, they would simply charge into the city and lay it to waste.

But they couldn't do that if the men carrying the ram were shot down. So the archers on the walls would try to take down those men. If the men could not bring the ram, the gate would not come down, and the city would not fall. The challenges on either side were straightforward.

There was a period of organization. Then a peculiar formation moved toward the gate. It looked from a distance like an enormous desert insect with glistening scales. Perhaps a weird thousand-legger. It crawled across the ground, jerkily, its parts not quite coordinated. What was it?

Soon enough, she was able to piece it out. The bug's central spine was the battering ram, an enormous log mounted on several sets of wheels. On either side of it were the brute men who pushed it forward. Beside each pusher was another man, who held his shield up over the pusher's head and back. In this manner the pushers were protected from the arrows of the defenders, so that the ram could reach the gate.

However, the shields would be less effective when the range shortened, and less still when it was time to get the ram moving swiftly enough to bash down the gate. The shieldmen would have trouble protecting both themselves and the pushers.

Ember saw several of her slaves aim large bows and shoot their arrows out in high arches. Why weren't the experienced bowmen doing it? Then she realized that this was because the ram party represented an excellent chance for practice, for learning to shoot the arrows effectively and finding the range. Few could aim accurately at the extreme range, but it was possible that some arrows would score randomly. Especially if there were enough of them. So the slaves practiced—and on occasion a pusher or his protector did fall.

As the formation came closer, the slaves improved. Then the experienced bowmen joined them. Suddenly a swarm of arrows sailed down, and a number of enemy men fell.

The enemy retreated, dragging away their wounded and dead. They left the great ram-log sitting on the road. It was safe there; no one from the city would go out to fetch it, because then they would be at a disadvantage. But they had won the first encounter by stopping the men around the ram. Some of the slaves were cheering.

Ember knew it wouldn't end there. Indeed, soon more men came out. This group carried linked shields that could be arched over the heads of the pushers, making them almost impervious to arrows from above. It was apparent that these were more experienced troops, and would be harder to stop. Perhaps the prior group had been mostly slaves, sent to test the mettle of the city defenders. So slaves had been killing slaves.

The new group formed around the ram, and it resumed motion. Arrows rained down, but no men fell. The protection was tight.

But as it came close to the gate, the defenders started throwing bricks. These were not building bricks, but large, ragged ones with many projecting corners. They had more mass than the arrows did, and when one struck a shield, the shield bearer felt it. The shields lost their placement, and a few arrows were able to get through to score. But not enough; the ram continued to move forward. As it got close, it gained speed, making it harder to score on.

Then the slaves on the wall closest to the gate went into another type of attack. They heaved up big bags of sand and flung them out to land on the shields. This time the shields were crushed down to the ground, their bearers caught beneath them. The sheer weight of sand and the speed at which it struck were breaking down the formation. Whenever a shield went down, the pusher was exposed, and the arrows of the experienced bowmen quickly brought him down. But this defense was limited, because only those right next to the gate could hope to reach the battering ram, and it was hard to heave the heavy bags far enough out. So the ramming crew was battered, but not destroyed.

Still, it was enough to slow the progress of the ram, so that it was likely to lack the force needed to break down the gate. The enemy force retreated a second time, forced to leave a number of dead behind. The defenders had won again. There was another cheer. But Ember was sure that this was not the end of it. The battering ram was now close to the gate, and if another crew were able to get to it, the gate would not last long.

A third mission came forth. But it did not go for the ram. This time the shield bearers protected bowmen, and the bowmen got close to the wall—and fired up at the defenders. Ember realized that they had decided that they could not move farther without reducing or eliminating the defenders, who it seemed had put up more resistance than expected.

The attack was devastating. The enemy archers were experts. Every arrow seemed to find its target. Suddenly slaves were slumping, arrows embedded in their bodies. Inexperienced, they had forgotten that they could be targets, too.

The survivors quickly got behind the solid projecting outer rim of the wall. But that single sally had taken out perhaps a third of them.

Ember realized, belatedly, that no arrows had come close to her. Had the enemy archers realized that she was only an unarmed woman, so they hadn't bothered with her? If so, so much for her heroic stance. But probably they just hadn't shot accurately enough. Yet. She had been lucky.

In the brief period of panic and dismay on the wall, the enemy quickly resumed its formation with the battering ram. "The ram!" Ember cried as the thing started to move. "Stop it!"

This time an arrow did come for her. It stung her right hip. She reeled, almost falling off the wall before dropping to her belly. Then the pain surged forth from her hip.

She heard a crash, and knew that elsewhere in the world the ram was pounding the gate. Their defense had faltered. The city was about to fall.

After that she faded in and out, hearing the commotion in the city as the enemy troops ravaged it. She had done what she could, and her loyal slaves had helped, but it had not been enough. There were not many men left to kill, but she heard the screams of the women being raped. She hoped one of them was not Crystal.

"Ember!"

She came alert. It was Carver, Crystal's husband. "Hide!" she cried. "Before they kill you!"

He smiled. "They don't kill old women. They ignore them as being neither desirable nor dangerous. Come; I will help you down."

Now she saw that he had shaved his beard, making him woman-faced. He wore the voluminous robe of an old crone. He had marked his face and hands to look spotted and aged. Smart young man!

He lifted her and put an arm around her. They walked. Ember's right leg was stiff and caked with blood from her wounded hip, but she could tell that her wound was not mortal. The arrowhead seemed to have been deflected from the bone of her hip, gouging flesh and falling away. Pain was her only problem, and she clenched her teeth against it, knowing that otherwise it would be death she faced.

They were the only people on the wall now; further attempts at defense had become pointless when the gate went down. The enemy men didn't care about the wall, as long as there was no attack from it; in due course they would man it with their own bowmen and sandbaggers, defending the city from other enemies.

They made their way down to the ground inside the city. Men wearing the badge of Umma seemed to be active everywhere, burning, looting, pillaging, and killing any who protested. The two seeming old women hurried out of their way, and were duly ignored. Already the activity was winding down; there was only so much loot to be taken, and only so many young women to be raped.

There wasn't even much rubble in their section of the city. The men of Umma were not destroying buildings they expected to take over and use themselves. Carver helped Ember along the narrow, winding street and finally into her house. This was the one Scorch had bought when they came to Girsu, in the upper-class district. It was rectangular, with two stories and a central open courtyard. It even had its own little shrine, for the goddess Ninkasi, next to the storage room where barley and ale were kept.

He brought her to the courtyard, because that was cooler than the chambers, and she lay on a mat, staring at the sky. "I'll fetch the others," he said.

She faded out again. She was aware of Crystal, and of four-year-old

Flower, tending her as the fever came. Carver was in and out, still using his old-woman disguise. But not Scorch.

In her fever dreams, Ember saw her husband again and again. As a young man, whom she had vamped and married when barely nubile, because he worked with fire. And because his eyes were green, like hers. She had tried desperately to persuade him that she was old enough for him, and had succeeded. Then Crystal had come, and Scorch had been good with her, showing her the things of the world. He had been there too when they had traveled from their old town to Girsu, where there was better employment. And when Crystal had grown up and married Carver. And especially when Crystal had wanted to become a scribe: Scorch had talked with friends and worked hard behind the scenes, as had Ember herself, and together they had managed to get her into the apprenticeship training. She had been the only female in her class, and might have washed out if the increasing power of the temple had not protected her. But Ember could not have helped enough, if Scorch had not supported her fully.

Now he was gone, and her overriding emotion was remorse. He had been such a good man, always supportive, even when she had been caught in a bad situation and gotten herself raped. They had never spoken of that, later, but he could have divorced her for it, had he chosen to. She owed him everything—and had never really delivered. Because always in the back of her fancy had been the nebulous image of her ideal man, the one to whom her true love belonged. She had never truly given herself to Scorch—and now could never do so.

When the fever faded and her injury started healing, Ember revived and took an interest in the condition of the family. There were now four of them, in three generations; Carver, Crystal and Flower had joined Ember in her house. Their situation was desperate. Their store of food had been exhausted, including a few dates Carver had salvaged from their share of the city's garden plot, and there seemed to be no good way to get more. Carver, garbed as an old woman, was unemployable. If he assumed his true form, he would be immediately killed. The extent to which males were being hunted down after the conquest was unusual; normally conquering armies collected their booty, slaves and the icon of the fallen god and returned to their own city to enjoy the spoils. But the conflict between these two cities had festered for 150 years, and the king of Umma, Lugalzaggisi, seemed to have larger ambition.

Crystal, now twenty-two years old and attractive, could not admit she
was a scribe; the conquerors were routinely killing or deporting all local
officials. Neither could she go out to beg, because any Umma soldier
who saw her would simply haul her to his home as a concubine. Little
Flower had to remain completely hidden, because any child was subject
to induction into the slave corps; the best slaves were those who were
started young, so that any resistance could be beaten out of them.

That left Ember. As priestess, she had had power, but now the temple
was out of business, replaced by the conqueror's male god, and Ember
had to hide her identity. The brewery was actually attached to the main
temple of Ningirsu, the patron god of Girsu; Ninkasi was a minor
goddess, despite the importance of her ale to the folk of the city. The
Ummites would tear down the idols of Ningirsu and replace them with
those of their god Shara, son of Inanna, hero of An. Thereafter the
Lady Who Fills the Mouth would serve Shara, if they allowed her temple
to remain at all. More likely they would raze it along with the main
temple, once they got organized, and build their own brewery. Meanwhile Ember, as an anonymous old woman, was worthless. They
certainly would not want her for raping or for slavery. What could she
do?

She must have been thinking about this during her fever, because it
was as if she remembered Scorch coming to her and telling her that the
welfare of the family depended on her. She had to organize things so
they could survive and even prosper. "But how?" she asked the
memory, and had no answer.

As she struggled with it, an answer slowly formed from the chaos of
her fever and grief. Their reduced family had skills; the thing was to
organize them for survival. If they worked together, they could do it.

She explained it to them. "By ourselves, we are useless. We all have to
hide our real identities, lest we be punished for being male or literate or
young or a temple official. We dare not show our skills openly to the
conquerors. But we can make use of them if we are circumspect, and if
we work closely together."

"Mother, are you running another fever?" Crystal inquired anxiously.

"Let me explain. The Umma folk have the same need of our skills as
our own administration did. A city doesn't run itself; it needs trained
personnel, from garbage haulers to temple builders. Right now the

Umma soldiers are in a destructive frenzy, but when they start getting hungry because there are no gardeners and thirsty and dirty because no water flows in the public troughs and bored because there are no dancing girls, they will settle down and let the old personnel operate unhampered. They will want servants, and they will have to feed them if they want any enduring loyalty. They will want new clothing, and they will have to pay for it if they want it made well. They will want jewelry, and they will have to pay for that too. The time of rapine and pillage is brief; they have to stop soon, or there will be nothing left, and they will find themselves alone and mired in filth. So they will change. What we have to do is determine what they will need, and what they will pay for, and have it ready."

"Every surviving old person in the city wants to be a servant," Crystal remarked sourly. "The young ones can't risk coming forward, for the same reason we can't."

"Yes," Ember agreed. "So we have to decide what we can provide that others can't. We have among us an administrator, a scribe, and an artisan. Our skills remain, but not our employments. Scorch could have had immediate work, forging weapons and armor for the conquerors. But managing and scribing are problematical. That leaves Carver."

"I worked for the temple too," he reminded her. "I don't dare practice my skills of sculpture in wood, metal or stone."

"Your skill is one thing, your sculpting another. We need to find a new application for your skill."

The others looked at her blankly. "How can he sculpt without sculpting?" Crystal asked.

"By calling it something else. There is unrecognized art in many things. Such as the ornate handle of a good pickax, or the design of a house."

"I don't know how to—"

"But you could make a very fancy seal," Ember said.

"A seal! That's tiny!"

"Yes. You would have to take time to work with fine tools, to make very delicate pictures for the seal. No two seals are ever the same, and a truly fancy seal should be valuable. One made from metal, perhaps. I think the conquerors would pay well for custom-designed seals."

Carver nodded. "I think I could do that. But I can't go and talk to a conqueror."

"You can't. But Crystal could."

"He'd enslave me for concubinage!" Crystal protested.

Ember nodded, reassessing it. "Yes, that risk remains. Later, when things are settled, a young woman may be able to go safely, but not yet. Then I will have to do it. Old women are safe from that."

"But if anybody recognized you—"

"We shall have to hope they don't." Ember considered. "We must have some sample wares. What do we have for making seals?"

"I have my tools at home," Carver said. "I could carve something in wood. But I don't have the equipment to make fire-hardened brick, or to melt metal."

"The conquerors do. If we sold to them, they might even provide the materials. It is skill we are selling, more than things. But first we must have some items. See what we can cobble together for the first offerings. Fetch your tools, Carver, and anything you might be able to use."

He went out. Ember stirred herself. "Now I must do my part," she said.

"Your part, Mother?"

"I must fetch food, so we can survive until we make our first sale."

"But what can you do? You are still weak from your injury, and anyway—"

"I can go out and beg," Ember said.

Crystal was shocked. "No one in our family has ever begged!"

"Then it must be time to start. Crystal, you must come with me. Bring your clay and stylus."

"But—"

"Flower, you hide here," Ember told the child. "Show yourself only to your father, and tell him that we hope to be back soon with food."

"Yes, Grandmother," Flower agreed.

Ember had Crystal rub ashes into her hair and on her face, to gray her into age. Then, well-cloaked, they went out. Ember felt somewhat unsteady, and her injury hurt when she walked, but she refused to be governed by it. She stepped along briskly.

They walked out of the city, which was now quiet. The conquering soldiers had pretty well worn themselves out with their violence and debaucheries, and now were recovering. Ember saw that normal pursuits were resuming, as she had known would be the case. That was

good. The city had fallen, and new rulers governed it, but its ordinary
activity had to continue.

Beyond the city were its outlying settlements. The irrigated fields
grew barley, wheat, beans, peas, and flax, and the farmers were carefully
tending them. To one side were herds of sheep, goats, and cattle, kept
out of the wrong fields by fences and alert herding. Peasant shacks were
scattered throughout. The enemy troops had not bothered to ravage
here, because they knew that agriculture and animals were the heart of
the region's food supply. As long as the farmers served the new order,
they would not be molested.

Ember made her way to a village she knew, where a prominent farmer
lived. She approached the farmer, knowing him by sight. "Kind sir, we
two old women come to beg barley from you, that we may bake for our
supper," she said.

The man stared at her. "What have you in trade, woman?"

"Only goodwill, and our record of the debt, which we will repay when
we can."

The farmer realized that something unusual was happening here.
"Let me see your face, woman."

"If you recognize me, I am dead," Ember said. She drew back her
hood, showing her face clearly.

The farmer's eyes widened. He did recognize her, for they had done
business many times when he brought his barley in to the temple. "You
are a stranger, old woman, but I have a soft heart. I will not give you
barley, I will give you bread. Come to the house."

They followed him to the house, where the farmer's young slave girl
gave them a large bag of bread. Crystal made an entry on her tablet,
impressed her signature seal, and offered the clay document to the
farmer. It was still soft, but would harden as it dried, firming the record
of the debt.

"Keep the record yourself," the man said gruffly. "You can read it, as
I can not. Return here when you need more bread."

Ember nodded, and lifted the heavy bag. Her hip flared, and the pain
made her stagger. She was weak and tired.

"My slave will carry for you," the farmer said quickly.

Ember did not protest. The slave girl heaved up the bag and began
walking toward the city.

"Wait!" Crystal protested. "It is not safe for a young woman, on the city streets."

The farmer considered. Then he nodded. "We must make her old." Together they rubbed dirt and ashes in the girl's hair and across her face, to her chagrin, making her old and ugly.

"The Umma men steal pretty young women to be their concubines," Crystal murmured to the slave. "They beat them if they protest."

Wary comprehension came. Not only did the girl cooperate, she adopted a stoop, making herself as old as possible.

They walked to the city. Ember continued to tire, and Crystal helped her increasingly. As they entered the city, the slave girl helped too, despite her load of bread, so that Ember was supported on both sides. They looked like three ancient, worn, feeble women staggering for whatever hovel home they had. Others gave them plenty of room.

Carver was waiting when they returned. "You got bread!" he exclaimed, smelling it.

Ember collapsed on her mat. "See the girl off," she told Crystal as she sank into semiconsciousness. By the time she was ready to assume full awareness, the slave was long gone.

The bread helped enormously. They tried to ration it, so as not to have to return to the farmer any sooner than necessary. But two days later the farmer's slave girl came on her own to their house, bearing another bag of bread. "May the gods forever bless your master," Ember told her gratefully as Crystal marked the tally.

Carver worked diligently, carving tiny intricate patterns in wood. Each was a model seal, that could be pressed into soft clay to make the distinct mark of its owner. Seals were normally made of hardened clay, but were relatively crude, because clay was not readily carved. The best ones were incised in stone, but they lacked the right kind. The wood would have to do.

When there were six good models, Ember set out on the next stage of their venture. She took the models to the house of the local captain of the Umma guard. "My man is infirm, but he can carve well," she said. "He could make you a seal like one of these, if he had the materials. Or to conform to any other design you specify."

The man peered at the models, impressed. He was interested. "What price?"

"Merely your favor, O great leader."

The man nodded, understanding her perfectly. "Bring him here."

Ember returned to their house. "He will see you," she told Carver. "Make yourself old."

"I will not be able to deceive him," Carver said nervously.

"No more than I deceived the kind farmer," she agreed.

Crystal remained at the house, with Flower. Ember and Carver, in the aspect of an old woman and an old man, walked to the captain's residence.

It was evident that the captain's first penetrating squint told him that Carver was much younger than he pretended to be. But the man did not challenge him. Instead he presented Carver with a nice block of soft wood, suitable for carving. "Make this design." He showed a crude sketch on the surface of a clay tablet.

Carver settled down with a will. It was soon clear that he was quite competent. But the design was intricate, and the completion would take time.

"Take it home," the captain said. "Bring it back complete, tomorrow. My man will see you there."

An Umma guard appeared. He marched beside them as they walked the wide street, and then the narrow street. When they reached the house, the guard took his spear and used its head to scratch a mark on the outer wall of the house. Then he departed.

"Why did he do that?" Carver asked, alarmed.

Ember smiled. "We now have the captain's favor. Any person who molests this marked house, or the folk in it, will soon enough feel his ire. We will also be allowed to do business with others, selling our seals to them for what the market will bear. Just as long as we keep his favor, by providing him or his household with any good seals they wish, as gifts."

Carver shook his head in wonder. "You know more than I do, Mother!"

"I have lived longer, son."

They were in business. Ember knew that they would soon be able to repay the kind farmer, and she knew exactly how. The next time the slave girl came, she showed her several model seals. "Take these to your master, and tell him to keep the one he prefers, or to describe the kind he would like."

Soon it was safe for Crystal to accompany Ember to the captain's house. He recognized her nature as readily as he had Carver's, but she was a member of a favored enterprise, so he let her be. That meant that all of his soldiers let her be also. She was now able to carry her scribe tablet openly, and on occasion the captain even asked her to read or record something for him. He was of course unable to read the marks himself, but his ability to get them interpreted when necessary gave him increased power.

The falling of the old order had been disastrous for the family, but it was finding new security by accommodating the new order. This was the way of survival.

Indeed, the city-states of Sumer were giving way to kingdoms, and those who adapted well to the new order were to prosper. The hegemony of Umma lasted only briefly, being conquered by the Akkadians from farther north, under Sargon. Thereafter Sumer was to become a smaller part of larger kingdoms and empires, such as Assyria, Babylonia, Persia, Alexander, Arabia, and Turkey. The region is now incorporated in the modern state of Iraq. Its present significance on the global scale is not great, comparatively, but it is remembered as the region of the world's first urban, literate civilization, older than Egypt, Crete, India or China, and possibly the source from which all other civilizations drew their inspiration.

CHAPTER 13

EMPIRE

Shelley's poem "Ozymandias" describes the way a mighty king of kings might have been lost to history, and all his works forgotten. Shelley could have been thinking of one of the earliest and greatest empires of Asia Minor, which flourished for several centuries and disappeared almost without trace. Only more recently have ancient tablets been found and translated, revealing its true extent.

The migrations of barbarian peoples was constant, pushed by changes in weather and by the power of enemies, and gradually the Indo-European tribes from north of the Black Sea expanded into new regions. Among these

253

in the second millennium B.C., *three to four thousand years ago, were the Hittites. They came to Anatolia, conquered the highly cultured but divided residents, and set up their capital at Hattusa. They had perhaps three significant advantages that enabled them to carve out one of the more powerful empires of the day: horses, which had enabled all the Indo-Europeans to prosper; iron, which made superior weapons but was in extremely short supply at that time; and enlightened law, which enabled them to integrate other cultures without having to obliterate their special ways.*

One of the major powers the Hittites encountered was the north African kingdom Egypt, intent on building an empire. Finally, about 1300 B.C., *Ramses II of Egypt marched north with a force of 20,000 men to establish Egyptian supremacy in the Levant. The Hittite ruler Muwatallis went to meet him with a similar force. They met at the trading city of Kadesh, in what was perhaps the greatest military clash of the times.*

O F course there were constant reports from advance scouts and spies, so they knew approximately where the enemy was at all times. That allowed them to travel in relative comfort, wearing light clothing instead of battle dress. The horses were not pushed unduly, which meant that the war chariots were not banged about. That in turn made light work for Stone, the chief ironsmith with the expedition. He was there as a specialist rather than a combatant, though he would have to fight if the army ever was truly pressed.

Stone was performing a routine check of one of the leaders' equipment, when one of the commanders approached the chariot. The man's metallic skirt and curl-pointing shoes helped signal his status; he was in formal dress despite the rigors of the mission. "We need to refresh our supplies before we engage the enemy," the officer said to the charioteer. "The king has asked me to go out and reason with the natives, who are nominally part of our territory. I need to take a supply wagon and a chariot. Are you ready to go?"

"I'm missing my spearman and shieldman," the charioteer protested. "I'm having the smith go over my wheels."

The officer glanced at Stone. "Is this chariot ready to go?"

"Yes, sir," Stone replied. "But my job would be easier if the warriors didn't insist on driving the chariots recklessly cross-country, striking rocks and muck. It is only a thin rim of metal around the edge of each wheel, and it dents readily."

The officer smiled in a way that made Stone realize he shouldn't have complained. "We shall give you a taste of the fieldwork, smith. Take up the shield and board this chariot." And to the charioteer: "I will carry the spear. We now have a full crew for the mission. Fetch your horses."

The charioteer shot a dark look at Stone for getting him into this mischief, and went out to the pasture field to find the horses. Stone knew better than to protest again; he was no trained shieldman, but he understood the principle. He knew the officer would never go out with inappropriate personnel if there were any real danger. But it probably would not be a completely pleasant ride.

Soon two vehicles moved out: an empty supply wagon that still seemed surprisingly solid, and the chariot, in which the three men stood. Stone found it precarious. The chariot barely had room for their legs, but it supported them up past the knees, so that they could not fall. But suppose there were an accident and it tipped over? He had learned a lot about chariots during this campaign, having been impressed into service because he was a metalworker. He was actually a copper, silver and gold sculptor, but they needed metalsmiths for their chariots and armor, so he had been taken as a smith. He did actually have the required competence, and was doing the job; he just wished he could have stayed home with his lovely wife Seed and his six-year-old son. He found little appeal in roughing it on the campaign trail, though he was about as well off as anyone here. They wanted to be sure that the expertise was handy for spot repairs.

They were not moving rapidly, which was a relief. Stone wasn't sure how he would keep his position while protecting himself and the other two with the large shield he held. It wasn't big enough to protect all three simultaneously. He was on the right, with the charioteer on the left; he would have to angle it across to help them, and then he would be exposed himself.

"You seem uncomfortable, smith," the officer remarked. "This is not slow enough for you?"

"I have no complaints, sir," Stone said tightly. He did not want to give the officer any further pretext for a demonstration.

"You would like the Hurrian chariot. Just two men, no shield. One to drive, the other to attack. They depend on mail coats for protection. They're the best horsemen in the world."

But the Hittites, Stone knew, had learned from the Hurrians, then excelled them. Indeed, the Hittites had later crushed the Hurrian kingdom of Mitanni. That suggested that it took more than horsemanship to prevail in war. But Stone kept silent.

They reached a settlement. The wagon came to a halt, while the chariot went slowly to the center of the group of houses. The officer hailed an older man who emerged from the largest house. "Hey, elder!" he called in Hittite. "I have come to speak with you."

The man looked confused. The officer changed to Amorite. "We need to fill this wagon with food for our troops," he said. "Gather your villagers to load it."

The man glanced at the wagon, shrugged, and turned away. He reentered his house.

Stone kept his face straight. The village elder was evidently dismissing the officer's request out of hand. It was a gesture of contempt.

"Ah, see how you treat me," the officer called to the house. "I make a reasonable request of a friend, and I am greeted with disdain. Even so was it between our great King Mursili and the kingdom of Arzawa. I beseech you, let our acquaintance not come to such an unfortunate pass."

What was the man up to? Stone was having trouble deciding whether the officer was joking, or a fool. The natives were not going to give up their hard-foraged supplies without a fight, or at least evidence of a significant threat. They might be considered part of the Hittite Empire by the Hittites, but not by themselves.

Stone glanced at the charioteer, who was smiling wryly. He had evidently seen this sort of encounter before.

There was no response from the house. The officer tried again. "I ask you to emerge and give the directives to your people, so that this unfortunate misunderstanding can be at an end. Mursili himself would not have been more generous."

Generous? Stone stifled a smile of his own. He knew history too. The kingdom of Arzawa had been destroyed and made a direct part of the empire.

When there was only silence, the officer shrugged. "Then I must take reasonable steps. I declare this village to be a vassal state of the Hittite

Empire, subject to our laws. Since you did not join us voluntarily, you are liable for penalties. Your supplies are forfeit, and your people subject to serfdom. You will emerge from that house and serve the new order without further delay."

The officer waited a moment. There was still no response. "I regret to see it come to this," he said. He glanced over to the driver of the wagon. "Remind this person of the penalty for insubordination to the empire," he said.

The driver got down, reached into his wagon, and brought out a smoldering torch. He waved it in the air, causing it to brighten into a blaze. Then he walked to the house and touched the torch to the overhanging edge of its thatched roof.

The fire climbed the roof rapidly, spreading across the house. In a moment the man dashed out, screaming. A young woman followed him, her tunic and long hair flowing behind as she ran.

"Well, I am sorry," the officer said, unmoved. "You were impolite, so I reluctantly took steps, even as Mursili did. Now I suggest that you obey the directive I gave you, before there are further consequences."

The man ran through the village, shouting in Amorite. The girl tried to follow him, but the wagon driver got out and intercepted her, clamping a hand on one of her slender wrists. He hauled her to the chariot.

"Yes, I will take this maiden as my chattel," the officer said. "Take her to the wagon and hold her for me."

Stone opened his mouth to protest, but stifled it, knowing that it was both out of turn and pointless. The officer was making his point, to the villagers and to Stone himself. This was war, and spoils were taken in war. Now Stone had a better notion just how the warriors had come by the items that had turned up along the march here.

He watched as the wagon driver hauled the girl to the wagon, where he tied her with a rope about the waist. She did not protest, apparently realizing that she would only make her situation worse. Though her tunic covered most of her body, it was evident by the way she moved that she had the health and beauty of youth. Perhaps she was the headman's daughter, leading a privileged life until this moment. Stone felt sorry for her; she surely had done nothing to deserve the fate she faced.

Meanwhile the headman was attracting attention. People came out, listening to him and staring at the fire. But they did not report for labor within the Hittite Empire. They charged the wagon and chariot, wielding clubs.

The officer sighed. "I see we shall have to make a further demonstration. Be ready with your shield, shield bearer."

The charioteer signaled the horses, who leaped into action. Stone had to brace his legs hard as the vehicle swung about. The horses charged the villagers, who scattered. One did not get out of the way quickly enough, and was knocked to the ground by the shoulder of one of the horses. Stone saw that the Amorites were terrified by the swiftly charging chariot; its effect was as much psychological as physical.

The charioteer guided the horses in a trot. They looped around and oriented on the village again. The chariot stopped. The officer surveyed the situation, satisfied.

The villagers were in complete disarray. The fight had left them. The headman's house stili burned, unattended.

"Proceed to your storehouse," the officer called. "Load the wagon."

This time the villagers obeyed. They walked to the house where their supplies of grain and silage were. They began bringing out the storage crocks.

Then other men appeared. These were more fully armed, carrying swords or spears as well as clubs. There were about ten of them. They were evidently Amorite soldiers, alerted by the fire and commotion. Immediately the villagers' attitude changed. They turned to face the chariot, picking up their clubs.

The officer shook his head with mock reproach. "These are extremely slow learners," he remarked. Then he faced the wagon and shouted: "Reserves, emerge."

Stone's jaw dropped as the loose cloth covering of that wagon parted and a number of armed Hittite soldiers piled out. Some had spears, some had swords, and some had bows. There were three of each type of warrior. No wonder that "empty" wagon had seemed so solid!

The bowmen struck first. Their arrows brought down three of the enemy soldiers, who had no chance to fight back at a distance. Then the spearmen and swordmen moved forward to engage the remaining Amorites, in disciplined formation.

The Amorites still outnumbered the Hittites. They lined up, about to charge, so as to get into fighting range before more arrows brought them down.

The chariot moved. It sliced toward the unprotected Amorite flank.

The remaining enemy soldiers fled.

The chariot halted again. It hadn't actually engaged, this time; the mere threat had destroyed the enemy will to fight. "Now—" the officer said, turning to the villagers.

The men threw away their clubs and resumed work. Soon the wagon was loaded.

"Excellent," the officer said, stifling a mock yawn. "Men, the town is yours."

The soldiers broke ranks, charging through the village and into the houses, seeking whatever plunder was to be had. This was how they were paid: after they had done their duty by terrorizing or killing the enemy, they were allowed to keep whatever they found. Stone had known the way of it, but never seen it in action in the field.

"Meanwhile, let's see what we have," the officer said. The chariot moved over to join the wagon, where the woman sat with her head bowed and her dark hair across her face, her indication of shame. The villagers quickly moved away from the wagon, which perhaps was part of the officer's purpose. He was not only inspecting the captive, he was guarding the goods while the soldiers were having their fun. He seemed casual, but his hand remained on his spear, and his eyes constantly quested through the area. Stone was coming to appreciate how *un*careless the man was, despite his cavalier attitude. "Lift your head, girl; look at me. Tell me your name."

The woman did not respond. In that she resembled the headman. "Now, is that the way to treat your new master?" the officer inquired, smiling grimly. "Surely you do not wish to displease me."

"I will make her do it," Stone said quickly. The woman reminded him of Seed, when he had first met her, and he wanted to prevent her from being hurt. He hung the shield on the chariot and jumped down to approach her.

The officer shrugged nonchalantly, satisfied to have Stone's active cooperation. "Cause her to show her face."

Stone stood before her. "He will beat you if you do not obey," he murmured urgently in Amorite. "Please, humor him."

The woman lifted her head and shot him a glance through her falling tresses. Her eyes were dark brown, almost black, as was her hair. Then she brushed back her hair and faced the officer. Her face was comely. "I am called Honey-from-Bees," she said.

"Cause her to show her body," the officer said with seeming indifference.

Honey hesitated. "Please, he will have them tear off your tunic and make you go naked," Stone said. "It is better not to oppose him, so that he forgets about you for awhile."

She drew open her tunic, showing her breasts. They were small but well formed, and her body was pleasantly slender.

"It's good enough," the officer said as if bored.

Stone walked back to the chariot and resumed his place. Now he was glad he had been brought along, because he feared that the woman would have been brutally treated otherwise. Perhaps she still would be, but at least he had helped ease her transition to captivity.

In due course the soldiers returned with their booty: jewelry, tools, cloth, and knives. No women; these must have fled when the trouble started. Stone was relieved.

There was no longer room on the wagon for the soldiers, because the supplies took up the space. So the soldiers walked ahead, carrying their spoils and making sure there was no other opposition. Then came the wagon, with Honey as part of the supplies, and finally the chariot.

But now the natives recovered enough to make some resistance. Stones were hurled from the cover of the forest.

The chariot veered off the trail, charging first one side and then the other, but didn't go quite far enough. The rocks kept coming. One crashed into the chariot; others passed overhead, making Stone reach nervously with his shield.

"I wonder whether we should ride a bit faster, over rougher terrain," the officer remarked musingly. "If it wouldn't dent the wheels too much."

Stone knew he was being teased, but he appreciated the point. "Yes!" he agreed.

The charioteer, responsive to signals Stone didn't see or hear, caused the horses to jump forward. Suddenly they and the chariot were plunging faster and farther. The natives, surprised, tried to run out of the way, but several were caught. The officer knocked one on the head with his spear. Soon the rocks stopped flying.

They returned to the main camp. "I have to see about the distribution of the supplies," the officer said to Stone. "You have a fairly stationary occupation. Keep the girl safe with you until I return for her." He handed Stone the end of the cord that tied her.

"But—" Stone started, caught completely by surprise.

The man smiled again. "If I don't return, she is yours. That should be fair recompense for your effort."

Stone knew that it was useless to argue with this man. "I will try to keep her safe for you."

So it was that Honey-from-Bees was put in his charge. Stone took her with him as he resumed his inspection of chariots. "If I leave you in my wagon, someone else might take you," he told her. "I can protect you only if you are close. I mean you no harm."

She nodded, understanding well enough. This was the heart of the enemy camp; she needed safekeeping.

He completed his inspections and returned to his smith wagon. He fetched food from the mess wagon. It was no problem to get extra for Honey, because Stone knew the personnel, and was considered to be of officer status himself because of the value of his work. He explained that she was the officer's captive and needed to be maintained in good condition. There was no argument.

The officer did not come for her that day, evidently being busy elsewhere. Stone made a place for her in the wagon among the tools and gave her a blanket. But there was an awkwardness. "I do not wish to keep you tied, but if you run away, I will be to blame, and when they catch you they will kill you, and probably also your father. Do you understand?"

"I will not run," she said listlessly.

"I will take you to the latrine trench," he said. "I will turn my back. You have promised not to run."

"I have promised," she agreed.

When he turned his back he half feared that she would pick up a rock and strike him, so as to make a break. But she did not, perhaps understanding the futility of it. Then he took her back to the wagon, where she climbed into her place and disappeared under her blanket.

Stone made himself another place and buried himself under another blanket. He thought of Seed, still so lovely at the age of twenty-three, eight or ten years older than Honey, and wished he were home with her. Had it been like this for Seed, before Blaze bought her for Stone?

Next day as the army prepared to resume travel, Stone spied the officer. "I have Honey," he said. "You did not return for her."

"She is more secure with you," the officer said indifferently. "If there is a problem, mention my name."

Stone was inclined to agree: the woman was better off in the wagon of a noncombatant than with a chariot officer. Soon enough the battle with the Egyptians would occur, and then no one could be sure what would happen.

They proceeded to the fortified Hittite client town of Kadesh, but did not enter it. The army stopped north of it, without making full entrenchments. They were by the River Orontes, so they could restock their water. But why didn't they go ahead and enter the city, which was friendly and which they had come to defend? Stone, uncertain whether this was to be a pause or a camp, took Honey and went to the command wagon to inquire. He encountered the officer.

"I think I have two matters to inquire about," he said. "I need to know how long we will be here, so I can set up to inspect and repair chariots if that is in order. Otherwise I would prefer to set up in the city, where there will be superior facilities."

The officer gazed at him in a disquieting manner, seeming to be distracted. Then he spoke. "Yes, we shall be camping here," he said loudly. "Make your preparations." And in a much lower tone: "But do not dismantle any chariots, and remain ready to move on short notice."

"But—" Stone broke off, recognizing the man's expression. Something was afoot, and what seemed nonsensical was likely to have a surprising point. The officer's feigned indifference could hide extremely specific tactics. Just as the "empty" wagon had been loaded with soldiers, a trap for the unwary. "Yes, sir. And this woman, your captive—"

"Is she causing you mischief?"

"No, but—"

"Watch her another day. It is not convenient for me at the moment. I will take her off your hands in due course."

Stone nodded, privately relieved. The officer might or might not treat Honey decently after he raped her. This gave her one more day as a person.

He returned with her to his smith wagon. "Thank you for taking care of me," Honey said.

"I wish I could take you back to your village," Stone muttered. "But you know I can not."

"I know you can not," she agreed. "Why do you treat me so well?"

"My wife is beautiful, as you are. She was a slave before I married her. She—had been used. You remind me of her in these respects. I wish I could protect you from what she suffered."

"I wish you could," she agreed. "I will cause you no mischief."

Stone set up his wagon to give the appearance of activity, but did not set up his forge. Honey helped him. He realized that it might look as if he were instructing her, which could account for his failure to actually do solid work. He gave her some tools to carry and started on a routine inspection tour.

"This is a ruse," she murmured. "This time it is not my village, but the Egyptians who are being tricked."

"It must be," he agreed. "But I don't understand how it works."

"What kind of woman is your wife?"

Stone laughed. "If I start to talk about her, I will talk a long time! She is everything to me, and I live for the hour I return to her."

"How long have you been married?"

"Nine years. We have a six-year-old son. We were fourteen when we married."

"Oh, she was my age when you married!"

"Yes."

She did not pursue the matter, but his thoughts did. It was as if he were seeing Seed again, with the vantage of his added years. Honey was not quite as pretty as his memory of Seed, but that might be because his youth and fancy had enhanced Seed beyond reality. Honey seemed too young for marriage, while Seed had seemed ideal. Perspective made the difference.

Suddenly the order to move came. Stone and Honey, forewarned, hurried to the smith wagon and quickly packed it up for travel. The horses were brought in and hitched, and they joined the column moving out. Honey now sat up front with Stone, without being bound.

But they did not travel south. Instead they turned east—directly into the river. The grumbling became loud: why were they fording the river, getting their things wet, when the city was right at hand?

Soon the word spread: the Egyptians were rapidly approaching Kadesh from the south. In fact they were about to bypass it to the west, instead of attacking it. The Hittite army was moving swiftly to get out of the Egyptians' way. What madness was this?

"The madness of soldiers hidden in a wagon," Honey said sadly. "The Egyptians would be ready to fight, if they knew how close the Hittites are."

"They seem to think we're far to the north," Stone said. "But why would they get that idea?"

"Because of those two deserters we sent," the officer said, passing on his horse. "They reported that our army is afraid to meet them on the field, so is retreating to the north. So the Egyptians are hurrying to intercept us before we can escape."

There was a shout of laughter, which even Honey joined. Afraid to meet the enemy in battle! Here was the most formidable Hittite army ever assembled, with contingents from a dozen vassal states ranging from Mitanni down—and it was afraid to fight? What fools the Egyptians must be, if they believed that.

Stone now understood some of what had been keeping the officer busy. They had been setting up this trap for the enemy—and the enemy was marching right into it.

In fact, as it turned out, the Egyptians were so eager to pursue the supposedly fleeing foe that they had divided their army into four divisions, with the Pharaoh in the lead one, Amon. The Hittite army remained unified, massing to the east of Kadesh as the Egyptians passed to the west. They kept the city between them, so that the Egyptians remained unaware.

The Egyptian's Amon division made camp north of the city, where the Hittite temporary camp had been. It seemed to be waiting for the other units, now strung out far behind, to catch up.

Then the Hittites forded the river south of the city, this time going west. The chariots cut into the second Egyptian division, Re, and cut it apart. The Egyptians were caught completely by surprise. The remnants of Re fled to the north and south, pursued by the chariots.

Meanwhile the rest of the Hittite army was fording the river. Stone brought his wagon across without difficulty; the river was shallow here, and the crossing place had been buttressed by extra sand scraped across.

Immediately he had work to do. Several chariots had suffered breakage in their wheels or axles, from the violent action. Stone readied his tools and approached the closest, which had a jammed wheel.

Honey stifled a scream. The wheel was jammed by a battered human body. One leg had become wedged, and the rest was an almost unrecognizable mass of abraded meat.

Stone took a long crowbar and wedged the leg out. He checked to be sure the wheel was free. "Go ahead," he called to the driver, who hadn't realized the exact nature of the problem.

The other repairs were incidental. He pounded one wheel rim back into proper place, and replaced a wheel that had broken. Honey was getting good at locating the tools he needed quickly.

Now the action was to the north. The chariots had pursued the Egyptian remnant to the large Amon camp. The Hittite phalanxes were pursuing and closing in. They outnumbered the Egyptians and were in good order, while the enemy was surprised and disorganized. They were trying to break camp and resume fighting order when the Re remnant charged through, interfering with their effort and throwing them into worse disarray. Only the Pharaoh's formidable bodyguard troops stood their ground.

Stone and Honey watched from the rear as the divisions of the Hittite army swarmed up to surround the Pharaoh's unit. The remainder of both the Amon and Re divisions were driven off to the north. "It's a rout!" Honey exclaimed, almost seeming to enjoy it.

Stone looked south. In the distance the third Egyptian division was coming, but it was so far back that it was evident that the battle would be over before it arrived. "A victory, certainly," he agreed.

"What is that?" she asked, pointing to the northwest.

Stone looked. "Maybe another remnant of the Egyptians." But he was in doubt.

As the wagon forded the branch of the river that flowed from west of the city, one rider came back. It was the officer. "All well here?" he inquired.

"All well for us," Stone agreed. He smiled. "I don't suppose you wish to take your captive with you now."

There was a bark of laughter. "What would I do—use her for a shield? Keep her just awhile longer, smith."

"What is that?" Honey asked the officer, pointing, as she had before.

The man looked. "I'm not sure—and it is my job to be sure. I will investigate." He signaled, and several other horsemen joined him. They rode out toward the mysterious formation.

Meanwhile Stone saw that the Hittite units had entirely surrounded the Pharaoh's force. They were about to crush it, attacking from all sides, and kill the Pharaoh or take him prisoner. The final victory was close. He took his wagon in that direction, knowing that there would be more for him to do as soon as the Egyptians were destroyed.

But the Pharaoh did not simply sit there. His troops launched a desperate counterattack. They drove toward the river, where the Hittite flank was thinnest. Their chariots forged into that line, their bowmen firing arrows at a range the Hittite spears could not match. The Hittites were pushed back into the river.

There they stayed, as Stone's wagon approached. The fighting was so heavy there that Stone could not make out the details, but the fact that it was not moving across the river meant that the Hittites were holding the Egyptians, and soon their other units would close on the Pharaoh's rear and destroy him from behind.

Then something happened. "Why are they milling about?" Honey asked.

Stone peered at what had been the center of the Egyptian camp. "The fools!" he exclaimed. "They're looting the camp!"

"Isn't that what soldiers do?" she asked without seeming malice.

"But they have not yet finished with the Pharaoh! As long as he remains free, he is dangerous. They must not let their attention wander from him."

Indeed, the Hittite officers were screaming at their men, trying to restore order. But the mercenaries, paid only by plunder, were too eager to be first at the best.

Seeing this, the remnants of Amon to the north re-formed and charged back toward the camp. There was fierce fighting as the Hittite unit at the north side turned to engage them. But that unit was now weakened by the desertion of its own plunder-seeking men, and in trouble. Stone, having reached the camp so he could be of service to the several stalled chariots he saw there, abruptly had to reverse course to get out of the way of the renewed fighting.

The Hittite units to the west and south moved to support the one to the north. But they, too, were incomplete, because of the indiscipline of the looters. Nevertheless they still outnumbered the Egyptians, and were bound to prevail as they restored their organization.

Except for one other calamitous break. The formation Honey had seen to the west now charged the camp. It was another Egyptian force, Canaanite by their markings: phalanxes ten ranks deep and tightly ordered. They attacked the Hittite force on the western side of the camp, which was ill prepared to meet them. The Canaanites were fresh, while the Hittites had been amidst battle and were facing the wrong way. The Canaanites broke through them, much as the Hittites had broken through the traveling Re division before.

Stone watched in dismay as the complexion of the battle changed again. The Hittites were now at a disadvantage, and were giving ground, leaving many dead. "If only they had finished off the Pharaoh when they had the chance!" Stone moaned. "Then the Egyptians would not have rallied, and the Canaanites would have been too late."

"I know the feeling," Honey murmured. Then: "I don't think we can get out this way."

He had been hoping she wouldn't notice. For the Canaanite division had cut off their retreat to the west. They were going to get caught in the midst of the battle.

What was he to do? If they remained here, the onslaught of the Canaanites would catch them. But there didn't seem to be any feasible escape route.

"Maybe if we follow the Egyptians," Honey suggested anxiously.

Stone looked, and realized that this astonishing notion had merit. The Pharaoh's unit was at the river, trying to fight its way across, moving away from the campsite. He should be able to pass fairly close behind without attracting attention, because of the ferocity of the action in the water.

He guided the wagon east and south, picking out avenues between broken chariots of either side. If he found a hole in the fighting, or if the Pharaoh's unit was finally defeated, they would be able to get free.

But the Egyptians showed no signs of defeat. They were fighting like demons, and their chariots actually seemed to be better in close battle than the Hittite chariots. That was amazing and frightening. Stone kept his wagon moving, hoping for fortune.

"The Egyptians are maneuvering better," Honey said tightly. "Are we going to die?"

"Of course not," Stone said. "Our chariots are sturdier, so move slightly more slowly, but each has one more man than the enemy does. That gives us the advantage when one of ours meets one of theirs."

But that advantage was hard to see, in the melee. The enemy maneuverability seemed to be at least as much of an asset as the Hittites' third man. Stone wouldn't have believed it if he weren't seeing it. The Egyptians were gaining.

Now Muwatallis was driven back across the Orontes. He made a stand on the far side of the river, his troops re-forming around him. He had retained a large chariot force in reserve, which he now was using to block the Egyptian thrust, ensuring that his forces could retreat in good order. Now the line was holding. But the situation was dubious at best, with evening closing and the third Egyptian division approaching from the south. Could he kill the Pharaoh before that other division joined the fray?

Muwatallis did not try. He took the expedient course, and sounded a retreat. His unit and the others moved toward Kadesh, entering it. They did so in disciplined manner, not allowing the Egyptians to attack their rear, but they did withdraw.

The Egyptians did not really try to pursue. They began to draw into their camp, which was now being vacated by the Hittites. Stone hastily guided his horses into the river, hoping the wagon did not get stuck in the bottom muck. The confusion was such that Hittites were encountering Egyptians in the water and passing without fighting, each just wanting to get to safety. Stone, of course, joined the flow. Honey hunched down as if afraid that someone would discover a young woman getting away, and do something about it. She relaxed visibly as they worked their way out of the danger. Soon the smith wagon was through the water, out onshore, and then within the walls of Kadesh. They were safe for the night.

Or were they? All night the men prepared feverishly for a siege. They feared that the Egyptians would charge the walls and use ladders to scale them, or try to beat down the gates with axes. This was prohibitively costly when a city was alertly defended, but it might happen. Stone was kept busy repairing the surviving chariots, which would be used to sally in force to drive the attackers from the walls.

Honey could have lost herself in the confusion of the torchlight preparations, but she remained close to Stone. "Go to the wagon and sleep," he told her gruffly. "This is not woman's work."

"Someone might take me from there," she countered.

He could not argue with that. It seemed she still was not going to try to escape. That was probably a good decision. At least with him she had a protector of sorts.

But by morning it was apparent that the Egyptians, too, had had enough. They were not going to try to storm the city. Indeed, it seemed that their losses were so heavy that they lacked the power to take the city, defended as it was.

So it was that the Egyptians withdrew. Kadesh remained part of the Hittite Empire, making this technically a victory. Of course the Egyptians would claim otherwise. The Hittites had outmaneuvered the Egyptians, but then had lost their discipline just as the luck had turned against them. Thus their victory had become a draw. At least it had not become the disaster that had threatened for awhile.

There was one other thing. The officer did not return. They learned that he had been killed in the final action, perhaps by the Canaanites. "Did I send him to his death?" Honey asked, bemused.

"Perhaps. So you have had your vengeance. Now you belong to me, and I will set you free."

"Don't do that!" she protested, alarmed.

"Don't you want to return to your father?"

She glanced at him with an inscrutable expression. "Yes. But I may not. If some other soldier does not make me captive the moment you free me, I still may not rejoin my village."

"Why not? There will be no Hittites here, after we withdraw to the north."

"Because they will believe me to have been despoiled, and will not accept me. They will kill me for having collaborated with the enemy."

"But you have not done that!" he protested. "You had no choice but to obey your captor."

"They will not believe that."

He saw her point. It was believed that all female captives were raped, unless they submitted voluntarily. It was considered to be the woman's fault, regardless. Only the chance of the officer's delay and death had saved her. Honey had been exiled from her village the moment she was taken captive.

"I could take you to my city," he said. "But I don't know what you would do there."

She faced him. "Could I not remain your slave? I would serve you loyally, for you have been kind to me."

"I never intended to—"

"Or you could take me as a concubine. Perhaps I could give you children to augment your family."

"I never—"

"Whatever you wish," she said. "Only please don't throw me to the wolves."

Stone was stumped for an appropriate response. "Maybe there will be something," he said awkwardly. "I will ask my wife."

She smiled, reminding him how very pretty she was. "Thank you, Stone."

As it turned out, he could not have returned her anyway. Muwatallis, irritated by the sight of Amorite standards among his enemies, decided to teach the Amorites a lesson on the return trip. He destroyed a number of settlements and enslaved their populations. One of them was Honey's home village. She had nowhere to go. If he freed her, she would probably be captured by another, probably crueler master. That was clear to both of them.

❁

It was a relief to be released from service, with his stipend and the added favor of the king. Stone brought his smith wagon north through the great Hittite Empire, dropping off soldiers and servitors as they passed their villages. This was mutual convenience: Stone had transportation and food, while the riding soldiers provided protection from any possible brigands along the route, and lent their muscle to shove the wagon out when it got mired in a mudhole. Honey had no privileged position; she had to fix the meals for them all. But she was herself protected, because she belonged to Stone, and it was his wagon. She rode near him and slept near him, and remained unmolested. Not, however, ignored; had Stone not been a firmly married man, he would have taken her up on her offer to be his concubine. Even as it was, he was fighting back temptation. Only the constant thought of his lovely, loving, loyal wife sustained him.

Stone lived in the former capital of the empire, Hattusa, beautiful in its mountainous setting. It was magnificently defensible, which was fortunate, because the Kaska warriors close to the north had never been properly pacified. Only truly strong ramparts sufficed, and the city had them. There was a formidable gorge on the east and a deep valley on the west, so that attackers would have to try to charge up steep slopes before even encountering the wall. The wall itself was twice the height of a man, and four times as thick, fashioned of massive stone blocks intricately fitted together. Stone worked in metal, but could appreciate the quality of the stonesmiths, his namesake; they had done a phenomenal job.

The site was excellent in other respects: it was close to the seven springs that never ran dry, so that the city never went thirsty. The nearby forests were excellent for both construction timbers and fuel for hearth fires.

"Oh, it sounds so wonderful!" Honey said enthusiastically. "I have never seen anything like that!" He suspected that her brightness was artificial, but her evident interest in his description was nevertheless flattering. She did not want to be dumped alone and defenseless in a strange city, and he understood that; otherwise her attitude might have been different. Still . . .

They rode the wagon up into the mountains, slowly ascending through the forests to the south until they reached the open region that surrounded the city. This was no accident; it would have been folly to allow potential enemies the close cover of trees. Now, above the stone glacis, they saw the outer wall, and close inside it the far larger inner wall with its parapets and crenellations. A ramp and two sets of steps led up to the great gate with its carved stone sphinxes.

Usually Stone didn't bother with either of those. He simply used the postern: an open tunnel which slanted through the ground under the walls, giving easy access to the city. In time of war, these tunnels allowed Hittite soldiers to charge out to attack a besieging enemy. There was no need to conceal these posterns or their purpose, because any enemy troops who tried to enter them would be at the mercy of the defenders.

He yielded to a sudden impulse. "Take the wagon through the gate," he told one of his riders. "I'm going to show Honey the postern."

Without a word the man moved forward to take the reins. Probably he figured that Stone wanted to get Honey out of sight of others for awhile so that he could enjoy her body before returning to humdrum homelife. Why not? She belonged to him.

They jumped off the wagon, and he showed the way to the stone-rimmed hole in the sloping ground. "Our special passage," he explained, guiding her in.

She was duly impressed. "What a long tunnel! The light is so far away!"

"It passes right under the walls," he agreed. "Don't worry; it will not collapse. See, the stones are carefully arched."

"Yes, I see," she agreed, impressed again. But she hesitated, not far into the passage.

"But if it frightens you, there is no need to go through it," he said. "I thought you would like it."

"Oh, I'm not frightened," she said. "Not when I'm with you." Yet still she hesitated.

"Then what is the problem? Here, I'll lead the way."

"I just thought, perhaps—" She shrugged.

"Thought what? I don't understand. Do you prefer not to enter the city?"

"It's not that." She evidently came to a decision. "I had thought you might want to do this." She put her arms around him and drew him in for a kiss.

Startled, Stone found himself reacting. Then he drew away. "I never sought to force my attention on you. I said I would ask my wife."

"Yes, of course," she agreed. Perhaps she was blushing in the gloom.

They went on through the tunnel and emerged within the city. Soon the wagon made it through the gate and came along the road. They got back on. The soldiers remained silent, but there were knowing smiles.

The city lay spread before them, for they had entered at its highest part. Nearby was a walled enclosure within the larger walled city, made of stone and mud brick. "Those are the temples of our gods," Stone explained as Honey looked. "They have the best place, of course."

"Of course."

They passed the large nice homes of the leading citizens, each on its own level terrace. Beyond these was a more impressive complex, walled off and almost projecting into the great east canyon. "The King's Citadel," Stone said. "This is no longer the capital city, but the king still resides there when he visits the city on his annual tour of the religious sites of the empire."

"It is amazing."

Farther downhill, where the ground leveled somewhat, flat-roofed houses were crowded together near one of the most impressive structures. "We live near the Great Temple of the Storm God, our city's patron," Stone explained.

"I must worship there," Honey said. "If they allow slave women?"

"They allow women. You will surely be free."

There was a fair amount of traffic in this vicinity. Men in simple tunics were carrying large earthen jugs, while women carried baskets. "Slaves bringing water from the springs," Stone explained. "Women going shopping."

They parked the wagon at Stone's metalsmith shop, where workers hurried out to unload it and take care of the horses. Stone took Honey along a narrow alley toward his home. Water coursed from waste holes in the walls of the houses and flowed on down the street, requiring them to step carefully. There was the smell of hot olive oil. "We will be eating soon," Stone said, reminded of his stomach.

"But first I must meet your wife," Honey said nervously.

Stone's indecision remained as they came to his home. Honey had proved to be increasingly convenient to have near, and he liked her very well. But what would Seed think? He was tempted once more to take Honey at her word, and make her his concubine, but the thought of his wife still prevented him. Yet would Seed believe him, or Honey's assurance? He did not want to do anything to upset his wife, and he feared that this would, no matter what.

Meanwhile it was good to see the tunics and pointed shoes of Hatti again, and to be free of the onus of military duty. He would have been completely happy, if only it were not for the problem of Honey.

Seed met him at the door. She was beautiful in a brightly layered day-robe, and her hair was exquisitely coifed. A jade-green comb set off her lovely green eyes. Obviously she had prepared for his return. He had hoped somehow to be able to broach the matter to her alone, but there had been nowhere to park Honey. He had to do it in the baldest way. "Seed, this is Honey, my Amorite slave by right of plunder. I give her to you, to decide whether she should remain in our household, and how she might serve there."

Seed pursed her lips. "A concubine?" she asked in Amorite.

"I—"

Seed turned to Honey. "This is by your choice?"

Honey shrugged. "I do not protest it. He saved me from much pain and mischief."

"You have not been raped?"

"No. He protected me from that. Neither did he take me when I was willing."

Seed shook her head, bemused. "Come inside, to the courtyard. I will talk to you further." She looked at Stone, her glance seeming curiously compassionate. "Then I will talk with you, my husband."

That was what he had feared. What should have been a passionate, delightful homecoming had been rendered into a strained dialogue.

Stone went to his private chamber and cleaned himself. He changed into a clean Hurrian shirt, which was a long woolen tunic decorated with brocade. He put on his long-toed shoes, which he had left at home rather than take on the campaign. He took a sharp bronze blade and shaved the growing stubble from his face. It was some time before he was done, and he did not rush it. He wanted to give Seed time to draw her conclusions.

In due course she came to find him. "Ah, you look handsome again, my husband," she said.

"And you are beautiful," he said with feeling. But he did not approach her.

"I have talked with Honey. She's a lovely girl. She says it really is true: you protected her, and did not use her yourself."

"Yes. But I don't know what to do with her. She did not want to return to her village."

"She knew it would be futile. She was tainted by her capture. And she wanted to stay with you."

"I was a noncombatant. It was safer. The officer who captured her was killed in battle."

"It is more than that, Stone. You are a decent man, without ill will toward others. You would never mistreat her. When her world ended so abruptly, you were the one she could trust. Without you she would have had nothing to cling to. I understand the way of it. It would be unkind to cast her out."

"She said I could take her as a concubine, but I knew she meant she would not fight me," Stone said, feeling awkward. "I would never take a woman on that basis. In fact the only woman I ever wanted was you."

Seed shook her head. "I must tell you something. You know I was not a virgin when I came to you."

"I never cared about that! When I first saw you, and you smiled at me—the only thing that made Honey appeal to me was the way she reminded me of you. Except for her eyes."

"Perhaps more closely than you realized," she said soberly. "The girl is not a virgin, Stone."

He was taken aback. "I assumed—I mean she was living with her father—"

"He was not her father."

He stared at her. "Not—?"

"He owned her. Her family expiated its debt to him by giving her up to him. You treated her better than he did. That is why she did not wish to return."

"I never realized!"

"You did not inquire. You merely assumed the best of her. She liked that."

"I did not know her at all." Stone was bemused.

"She knew *you*. That was all that was necessary. Now you must decide whether you wish to have her for a concubine."

"Oh, Seed, you are the one I love! I was just trying to do right by her."

"You have no desire for her?"

"She reminded me of you!" he repeated defensively.

"As I was when I first came to you," she agreed. "I am older now."

"Nothing has changed. I never wanted to go on the expedition or to take booty, and the girl was just chance."

Seed looked unhappy. "I think I would have preferred it if you had made a mistress of her and sold her before returning home."

Stone was appalled. "I would never—"

"I know. So we must deal with this now. I must tell you how it was with me before I met you—and after."

Stone felt a chill. "After?"

"I was like Honey. My world had been lost. One man was kind to me. I clung to him. But he was married, and he would not marry me. I knew that. So I gave him all I had to give, and took from him all he would give me, and I loved him and learned from him. Then I was brought to you.

If I pleased you, it was because of what I had learned from the man I loved. I loved him still, though I knew I could never be with him again. He was the one I would have married, had I had my will. Even after I married you, I wanted him."

Stone knew that his mouth was hanging open. "You did not love me?"

She gazed at him, and the tears were flowing in twin streaks. "Oh, Stone, I love you now! But I knew him before you, and it took time. You were always good to me, and I never had any complaint of you, and I bore you your sons. That other man is gone from my dreams now, and you are in them. But I wronged you in my heart, for a time."

He was stunned. "I never knew."

"I never wanted you to know. I did my best to love you, knowing you were good. Knowing you were better for me than he could have been. And you believed the best of me, as you did of Honey. That was part of your goodness."

"You were so ardent," he said. "I thought you loved me as I did you."

"It was guilt that drove me. I knew I was not worthy of the love you gave me. Until finally I believed, and then I loved you as I had loved him."

Stone grasped at a decision. "We must forget the past. I want only you, as you are now."

"But I must expiate the past," she insisted. "Now you may serve me as I served you. Take her as your concubine, and have the joy of her youth and beauty. I have no right to stand in your way."

"I can't do that!" he protested. "I never knew the injury you thought you did me, and I have no wish to return it in kind. I want only you and your love."

"You have both, Stone. But you can have her too. You must consider it carefully, for she will gladly give you what I gave my lover. She is young and fresh and ready to love you."

"I can't consider it! We must free her and send her away."

"In a city that is strange to her? No, we must keep her here. So you must decide. Have no fear; I will see that she is treated well. I have already fed her; she is eating in the courtyard."

He realized that she was serious. She had loved another man, so she was giving him leave to love another woman. There was a logic there, but it was alien to him.

"I will consider," he said. He walked out of the room, and out of the house, deeply troubled.

Stone did not return to the shop. Instead he went to the storm god's temple, to make an offering and seek enlightenment. But the god did not speak to him.

He walked on past a section where new buildings were under construction. He had to detour to avoid a great wooden beam being hauled into place. The thatch roofs and mud-brick walls were constantly wearing down during the winter snows, and in summer it could be easier to rebuild the structures than to repair them. Stone's own house had been rebuilt ten years before, and before he died it would have to be built again.

He passed doors through which he could glimpse the assorted artisans of the city: potters, leatherworkers, stone chippers, weavers, and jewelry crafters.

His feet took him to the shop of his father, Blaze, who was a ranking ironsmith in the city. Iron was the most precious of metals, because of its hardness; it required a special forge to heat it so that it could be shaped. Blaze was old, forty-eight, but still well able to work the divine metal. He had always been there when Stone needed advice or support.

As it happened, the forge was still heating when Stone arrived, so Blaze had time to converse. "I am glad to see you back, son," he said as he poured a jar of water into a stone basin. This was for quenching, which was one of the secrets of ironworking. Without it, the iron turned out less hard than bronze. With it, iron could become the hardest of metals, excellent for knives and weapons. It was a secret every apprentice swore to keep, even from other metalsmiths, so that iron would remain useless to foreigners even if they knew how to smelt it. "I heard that you acquitted yourself well on the campaign."

"I fixed the chariots," Stone said. "I got a captive girl. But now I don't know what to do with her."

"Sell her or give her to your wife. What is her age and appearance?"

"She is fourteen and beautiful. Seed says I should take her for a concubine."

Blaze turned serious. "There is trouble between you and Seed?"

"She told me that she loved a man before me, so I should have leave to love another woman. But Seed is the only one I want."

Blaze shook his head. "Seed has a rare understanding of the passions of men. The captive is fourteen? That can be a nice age for a woman."

"I don't know what to do."

"I can't advise you, son. You are more honorable than I."

"I am full of doubt!" Stone protested. "The girl is beautiful and willing, and would be easy to love. But I have no wish to hurt my wife. Now to have Seed tell me to do it—I don't understand her attitude."

"I loved a woman other than your mother, once," Blaze said. "Yet Bunny was constant, and in time my love returned to her. Men are less constant than women."

"You loved another?" Stone asked, amazed.

"She was beautiful and willing, as you describe this captive girl. She wanted to be with me, and I lacked the gumption to deny her. So I can not tell you not to do it, imperfect as I am."

Stone had sought iron for his spine, and instead had found what he had never suspected. "How can this be, and I never knew?"

Blaze laughed. "Naturally I did not proclaim it to my family and neighbors. Your mother was the only other one who knew, and she never spoke of it. I think if you take this captive girl, Seed will not speak of it either. It is this way in many families; accommodations are made. You are free to do as you wish."

"I don't know what I wish!"

"You're a good man, son. Better than you know."

"What does that mean?"

Blaze tested the forge, found it still not hot enough, so inserted some more charcoal and made sure his bellows was ready. Then he stood back and looked pensive. "You know the story of Telipinu, of course," he remarked, gazing into his fire pit.

"The god of agriculture and fertility," Stone agreed. "Are you saying that I should pray to him for guidance?"

"Perhaps. Do you remember how Telipinu, indignant because of a frustrating incident, was so distracted that he put his right shoe on his left foot, and his left on his right, and wandered away?"

"Of course. During his absence everything went wrong with the world. Fog seized the windows, smoke clogged the houses, and the logs were stifled in the fireplaces, for nothing would burn well. Because these things related to his powers. But what has that to do with me?"

"Everything was stifled, because of his anger and his absence," Blaze agreed. "Misfortunes abounded, until the other gods knew they had to go to find him and bring him back. But none of them could locate him."

"Until the insignificant little bee took up the search," Stone said. "And the bee accomplished what the gods had not, and found him sleeping in a distant meadow."

"But still he would not come back," Blaze said. "In fact he was angry at the bee for finding him. He sent further plagues upon the land. He diverted the flow of rivers, and shattered whole houses. Things were worse than ever."

"Until Kamrusepa, the goddess of magic and healing, came to him," Stone agreed, enjoying the rehearsal of the story, however familiar it was. "She offered him the essences of cedar, figs, ointment, malt, honey, cream and other delicacies. 'Let your soul become sweet and your heart smooth,' she implored him. 'O Telipinu, give up thy rage, give up thy anger, give up thy fury!' And she embraced him, and her body and manner charmed him, and he realized that he had no reason to remain angry. So he returned with her, and all was well again." Stone shook his head, perplexed. "But how does that relate?"

"Do you remember what made Telipinu angry, in the first place?"

"Of course. He had discovered a wonderful nymph girl, but his father the storm god had admired her also and taken her from him. Telipinu could do nothing but depart in anger. But I still don't see what—" Stone broke off, making a connection. "He realized that it wasn't that important! He did not have to punish everyone, when there was a goddess like Kamrusepa. He could just accept things the way they were, and be satisfied."

Then the forge was ready, and Blaze had to go to work. The mark on his forehead became more pronounced as he exerted himself. But no further dialogue was needed; Stone had the key to his resolution.

Stone walked home, his emotions still in turmoil, but clarifying. He had come to this problem so innocently, and discovered things he would have preferred not to have known about his wife and his father. Both had had affairs! Certainly he would not discuss this matter with his mother, lest he learn even worse news. But he could simplify the situation, and be at peace.

He entered his house and returned to his room. Seed was there, as if she had never left. She smiled, but there seemed to be a strained quality about it.

"I talked with my father," Stone said. "It happened to him too. He had an affair. I never knew. So I have no reassurance, only further doubt. But perhaps a resolution, thanks to Kamrusepa."

"How do you feel about your father's revelation?" she asked tightly.

"How can I feel anything? It was his business. I don't even know the girl."

She remained oddly strained. "Perhaps one like Honey."

He shrugged. "Perhaps. He indicated as much. It doesn't matter. It was no business of mine."

"But you're his son! Surely you have feelings about it."

Stone considered. "If my mother forgave him, so can I. He remains my father. A girl like Honey—I can see the temptation. Anyway, it's over, and should be forgotten. That's the lesson of Telipinu and Kamrusepa: I must accept what I have, and be satisfied, not asking for more. It is already more than enough."

"But you have Honey. Will you take her?"

"No! Seed, I want only you. I always have."

"Though I transgressed against you, as your father did against your mother?"

"I forgive you too! I have no wish to quarrel with anyone. Let Honey take care of our sons, who will surely like her. Let her help you in whatever ways will make your life better. Please—can't we forget all this, and be as we were?

Slowly she smiled, the tenseness dissipating. "Yes, I think we can, now. Let me attend to just one thing, and I will return to you."

She walked out of the room, leaving him perplexed. He heard talking elsewhere in the house. Then, after another pause, Seed returned.

She was beautiful. She had loosened her hair and donned a light robe, and her face was painted with rouge. "We are alone in the house now," she said, smiling.

"But—"

"I sent the boys shopping, with Honey to watch them, as you suggested. That was an excellent idea of yours, Stone."

"It was really my father's idea, I think. But I meant only for her to help you in the house."

"The market is as safe as the house."

"But they're children, and she doesn't know the city!"

"She's not a child, and they do know the city. They will get along perfectly."

He realized that it was so. He was forgetting to accept what offered without getting upset. "She can be their nursemaid, wherever they may be. She seems to be of good conscience."

"Yes. Now I will give you what you declined to take from her." Seed threw off her robe and stood beautifully naked, her body glistening with fine, scented oil. She was older than she had been when he married her, but maturity had only added to her splendor. She was, to his eyes, the most wonderful creature alive.

"Oh, yes!" he agreed. "You are Kamrusepa to my Telipinu! Your body is malt, honey, cream, cedar and all things sweet and smooth, and I love you always."

"Kamrusepa!" she said, surprised, then pleased. "Yes, let me be that to you, always."

And soon any remaining frustration was abated amidst his wife's remarkable passion. The empire of the Hittites was a great thing, as was the profession of metalworking, but it was his family he truly cared about.

Egypt claimed the battle of Kadesh as a victory, but historians consider it a draw or a net victory for the Hittites, who kept the city and the region. But after that encounter, both powers declined, and in the next century the Sea Peoples—probably tribes driven from Crete and the coast of Anatolia by the invading Dorian Greeks—attacked Egypt and so weakened the Hittites that its empire was overrun by former vassal states, the Phrygians and Luvians. The Hebrews were said to have escaped Egypt at this time, commencing their history as an independent people. Soon the vacuum was filled by the expanding power of Assyria.

The origin of disciplined ironworking is unknown, but the Hittites seem to have been the first people to do it systematically. When their empire fell, the closely guarded secrets leaked out into adjacent areas, and the use of iron spread. In time it would cease being a rarity and became a staple throughout the civilized world.

CHAPTER 14

IRON

Meanwhile the effects of civilization were extending westward across the Mediterranean Sea. The Greeks traded and colonized widely along the northern shores, while the Phoenicians were as extensively active along the southern shore. Thus there was the Greek Syracuse near the toe of Italy, and the Phoenician Carthage across on the northern coast of Africa.

But one culture seems to have achieved civilization without being part of the spheres of either Greece or Phoenicia. This was that of the Rasenna, in northern Italy. The Greeks called them the Tyrrhenoi, while others called them the Etruscans, or Tuscans. They had a language of uncertain affinity, a

283

literature which has been lost, and a high level of civilization. The people seem to have migrated from central Europe anywhere from three to four thousand years ago, and to have started their cultural rise about 900 B.C. Some historians suggest that they started as a remnant of the Hittite Empire, and the timing of their rise fits. But so few of the distinctive Hittite attributes carried across that this seems unlikely. Their shoes may have been similarly pointed, and their burial vaults bear some resemblance to the Hittites', and the Etruscans used griffin and other Eastern motifs in art. But their language was not Indo-European, and there is a general cultural continuity in the archaeological remains, suggesting that they evolved locally. They may have borrowed what they chose from adjacent Greek colonies, including the general layout of their cities and the Greek alphabet in their own script, but they developed their own distinctive style of architecture and art. They were a sea power and a land power, extending their influence throughout northern Italy and to some settlements along the southern coast. Yet soon after their time of greatness they were destined to be eclipsed by an unlikely and relatively primitive city-state on their fringe.

The time is about 650 B.C., in central Italy.

EMBER looked out and saw the storm rising from the south. It was singularly dark and turbulent. "Flower!" she said. "Where is Flower?"

Crystal looked up from her design. "She went to the vineyard to practice her music. Probably she dawdled there; she likes the blossoms nearby."

"I had better go fetch her. I don't like the look of that storm." Indeed, she felt the tic starting in her cheek. That was one of the few things she had never been able to control.

"We can send a slave," Crystal said. "Kettle likes her; he'd be glad to go." That wasn't his real name, of course; it was a fond nickname used only within the household. It had come about because Kettle's father was their longtime kitchen slave, forever scrubbing pots, so he had been nicknamed Pot. When they had adopted Pot's somewhat slow-witted little boy, he had had to work closely with his father, lest he blunder. Thus he had become Kettle. Now the lad had grown into a great strapping young man, still somewhat simple but an excellent worker when closely directed. He was devoted to Flower, with whom he identified because she too had come on the scene as a child, and though normally amicable, he could become dangerous when she was threatened. But he had to be watched, when with her, because he would do absolutely anything she fancied, and her childish fancies were not entirely to be trusted.

"No, they're busy, and I'm free at the moment." Ember smiled. "Besides, I like the blossoms too."

Crystal laughed. "Mother, you're fifty-two years old; how can you be childlike?" Etruscan women were many things, being the social, political, and spiritual equals of men; it behooved them to maintain appropriate decorum in public. But notions of decorum differed. Ember remembered when they had had a Greek visitor, a client for fine bronzework. When told he would have to consult with the scribe, Crystal, he had inquired where to find her. "Oh, she is having sex with Carver," Kettle had said blithely. "They should be finished shortly. I'll go see." He had then done so. Ember had happened on the scene at that moment, and seen the look on the Greek's face. She had had to admire such a rare combination of horror, embarrassment, outrage, disgust, and shock. It had been good for the best laugh of the nine-day week, when she later told the others; Flower had literally rolled on the floor. Yet it had been true, and another Etruscan would merely have smiled tolerantly at the slave's slight betrayal of his master's business. Kettle's mistake had been in failing to treat the Greek like the rigidly conventional uptight foreigner he was. Nevertheless, there were limits, even within the family: it bothered Crystal when her aged mother failed to act her age.

"It comes with age," Ember called over her shoulder as she hurried out, teasing Crystal about it.

Even in her urgency, she admired the niceness of the villa she was passing through. Carver's excellent talent at fine metalworking, Crystal's finesse with the accounts, and Ember's own acumen in arranging new contracts had integrated to make theirs a remarkably successful business. From the depths of despair when her husband had died, they had made a new family life, better materially than before. So the villa was well constructed, aesthetically laid out, and comfortable. They no longer had to bother with the complications of city life; their slaves went to Veia daily for the family supplies. She broke into a run as she left the garden by the house. The storm was looming rapidly, doing its best to reach the vineyard before she did.

She was glad that she had maintained her health despite her age, so she could still run without being instantly winded. She was not yet ready to wait on the gods in the afterlife.

The vineyard was on a slope beyond a slight green valley. The path curved gracefully around the rocky outcroppings and avoided the forest, never losing the way. But already the cold gusts were reaching out from the storm, catching at her braid and tunic. It reminded her of the wind on the sea, though it had been long since she had been aboard a boat, and she was not at all eager to repeat the experience. The first fat drops of rain spattered the ground around her. She wasn't going to get her granddaughter back to the house in time. They would have to seek shelter in the pavilion at the top of the hill just beyond the vineyard.

She reached the vineyard, breathing hard. There was the girl, standing among the grapevines, facing into the wind, her hair billowing behind her. Eight years old, not yet showing the aspects of a woman, pretty as only a child could be. In that instant she reminded Ember of Crystal, as she had been at that age, eagerly exploring everything, even deep caves, returning breathlessly to tell of her adventures. And of Ember herself, forty-four years ago, or was it that many thousands of years ago, meeting a boy—

"Grandmother!" Flower called, spying her. "Isn't it wonderful? I think I summoned the storm with my playing!" She held up her flute, which was actually a double instrument, with merged mouthpieces, one played by each hand. Thus it was possible for one person to play a harmony. Flower was getting good at it, having the sharp hearing of her age. But there was no time for that at the moment.

"It's dangerous, child," Ember said severely. "We must get under cover immediately."

"Awww—let's just take off our clothes and get wet."

"I don't think we had better."

"Kettle would," the child said brightly. "Why didn't you send him?" But Flower's mischievous look showed that she knew why not: Etruscan women were not supposed to disport openly with slaves. Had it been Kettle, they would have run naked through the rain, but not told anyone else, and any other family members who noticed would have pretended not to see. Ember had anticipated something like that, which was another reason she had come herself.

The odd thing was that she was tempted. Had there been a time when she had gone bare? It almost seemed that there had, a very long time ago, in the childhood of the species. Then the storm rumbled and brought back her senses. What could she have been dreaming of? "No, child; it's dangerous. Come to the pavilion. Hurry!"

Flower did not protest further. The strength of the storm was pushing them, its wind whipping by their faces, making it hard to talk. Thunder was crackling in the distance, coming closer. The grape leaves were tugging at their vines, barely holding on. This was no passing shower.

They dived into the pavilion just as the rain turned heavy. The water tried to catch them by slanting in, and when they stood at the far side, the wind curled around and carried the wetness in from behind. "Oh!" Flower exclaimed, laughing.

The sky became dark. The fury of the storm seemed to orient on the pavilion, trying to blow or wash it away. The branches of nearby trees waved back and forth as if demented. The rain came down in sheets, pounding on the tiles of the roof. Vapor seeped up from the ground. It was as if they were in a tiny world surrounded by chaos. "Isn't this fun!" Flower exclaimed.

Thunder boomed almost overhead, deafeningly. Flower screamed and leaped into Ember's embrace, no longer enjoying the experience of the storm.

There was a sharp crack by the vineyard, followed immediately by another horrific thunderboom. Flower buried her head in Ember's bosom, trying to hide from the awful sound. Indeed, Ember was frightened herself. She had always liked fire, and been drawn to it, and had worked with it, helping her husband and then her son-in-law. But lightning was uncontrolled fire, and dangerous. She wished they had been able to get back to the house instead of being trapped out here. Suppose it struck the pavilion?

A bolt struck a tree to the side. The trunk burst open as the sound smote them. Ember hugged Flower close, terrified herself. Were the gods out to destroy them?

The gods! What had she been thinking of? She should have prayed to the local god the moment she realized that the storm would catch them. "O god of this mountain," she cried into the wind. "I beseech you, I beg you, I plead with you, spare us! If we have offended you, tell us how, and we shall make our best amends."

Flower heard her, and joined her muffled prayer. And after a time the wind abated and the rain slowed. But they could still hear the thunder in the distance, and knew that the storm had neither passed their region nor spent its fury. It had eased off here, for the moment. Their god had interceded.

Then something strange happened. A light approached, not following the path as might be the case if Carver had come with a lantern, but bobbing between the trees. It drifted toward the pavilion. It was a glowing ball, floating over the land at about the height of the head of a man, but there was nothing supporting it. It was just there, like a ball of windblown seeds.

Ember and Flower stared at it speechlessly. The thing came close to the pavilion, and for a moment Ember was afraid it would come in and touch them, but then it moved to the side. It circled the pavilion and wafted on beyond. It hovered for a moment by the edge of the vineyard, then veered into the forest and disappeared.

The rain intensified again, but without the strong wind. The thunder did not come close again, and no lightning was visible. The two of them remained without moving, afraid to do anything that might attract the attention of the storm to them.

Finally it eased to the point where it seemed safe to return to the house. They went quietly along the path, looking nervously to the sides, but there was no trouble.

They reached the house and told their story. Crystal and the slaves were amazed. If Flower had returned with such news, she would not have been believed, but Ember had never been one to imagine things. She had of course never told others of her dream fancies of other realms.

"We must consult with a diviner," Crystal said. "This must be a message from the gods."

"From the god of this mountain," Ember said. "It was he to whom we prayed."

Carver agreed. It was known throughout Etruria that all things in the world occurred by the express design of the gods. It was man's place to fathom that design and act accordingly. The gods did not deign to speak plainly to lesser beings, any more than an adult explained everything to a baby, an animal, or a slave. But the gods did on occasion give signals, and those who were most attentive and apt at understanding those signals were bound to prosper. This was why some were successful in love, business, and reputation, while others failed. He who could not or would not heed the gods deserved his fate. Ember's family had always been careful to seek information on the will of the gods, and retained an especially close rapport with the god of the mountain on which they lived.

They sent a slave to bring a lightning diviner, a *fulgurator,* from the city, for the art was highly specialized and an entrails reader would not do in this case. Soon the man arrived, knowing that there would be good payment for a true interpretation. He was old and bearded, unlike the majority of Etruscans. He listened carefully to Ember's narration, showing no emotion, but she could tell that he was surprised and impressed by the bright ball.

Then he questioned Flower. "Now, do you understand, child, that you must tell the exact truth?" he asked her.

"Oh, yes," she agreed brightly. "A person must never lie to or about any god."

He nodded. "We can never deceive the gods, but we annoy them when we try to hide anything from them. Did you see anything your grandmother did not?"

"No, sir. She saw more than I did, because she was less afraid to look."

"But you heard the thunder, as the clouds collided to release the lightning?"

"Yes, sir."

"How many close thunders did you hear?"

"Three, sir. Then the lightning ball came."

"The lightning ball," he agreed, smiling at her quaint childish term. "How much thunder did it make?"

"Oh, none, sir. It was quiet."

"Yet we know that thunder is always associated with lightning. Why then do you call it a lightning ball?"

Flower's hand went to her mouth in chagrin. "Oh, that's right! I just thought—it was so bright—I don't know what it was."

He smiled. "It was ball lightning. This is a very rare, an extremely rare phenomenon. I have never seen it myself, though I have watched thousands of lightning strikes. I have heard of it only twice before, and both times it was significant." He turned to the others. "I believe I understand the meaning of what you saw. Here is my augury: this was no local god, but Aplu himself, god of the sun—and of music, and of prophecy. He came not to hurt or threaten you, but to advise you. He came to the one playing music, in kindness, for her tribute to him. The three close lightning strikes were a warning to you—a warning of danger. Had I been there, I could have analyzed the particular types of strikes and spoken far more specifically. But Aplu perhaps knew you were not diviners, so gave you a clue that could not be mistaken. He sent you a messenger to show you the way."

Suddenly it made sense. Of course the god knew their limitations. So he had used the lightning mainly to get their attention and impress on them the importance of the warning. But what could the soundless ball of lightning mean?

"There is great danger for you here," the diviner continued. "You must depart, and quickly, if you are to save yourselves. Within three days, by the number of the strikes."

"But where can we go?" Ember asked, dismayed. "Everything we have is here: our villa, our business, our friends."

"The ball lightning showed the way. You must go in the direction it showed. That was down the river."

"But there's nothing downriver!" Crystal protested. "Just a few peasant villages, and mostly foreign at that, and finally the great bleak sea. Everyone knows that civilization stops at the river."

"I realize that. But Aplu knows. He has shown you. Whether you heed his message is up to you." The diviner got up to depart, pausing artfully to allow Ember to fetch his payment.

After he left, they discussed it. They all agreed that this was disaster, but that the message of the god could not be ignored. Obviously Aplu could have destroyed them with one lightning strike; he had carefully avoided doing so, then sent a harmless but obvious signal. They had to believe him. So they would pack up and go down the river. Within three days they would be gone. It would be a horribly busy time, but it was necessary.

On the third day they were worn, short of sleep, but ready. Their slaves had brought their belongings to the pier and stood by, ready to load them on the boat. The family members were in the city, bidding parting to their many friends and visiting the temples of Tinia, Uni, and Menrva, the major gods. Ember tried to keep the tears from her face; she had never wanted to leave this great and wealthy city. But the omen of the lightning could not be denied. They had to go.

The boat came down the Tiber River and docked. They heard its bell. It would be on its way again as soon as its cargo had been exchanged, and if they were not there, their belongings would go without them. They hurried down the main street toward the river.

They were in good time. The slaves had explained the situation, and their things were aboard. Now Ember had just two things to do: settle with the captain, and settle with the slaves.

The captain was easy enough. "For passage to the next significant city, for four of us: this mirror." She held up one of the finely wrought bronze mirrors Carver had made. The captain, a veteran trader, simply took the mirror, knowing that it was an excellent bargain. He well might sell it before getting under way, for the Etruscan women loved to admire themselves. Their admiration was of course justified, for they were as a rule beautiful, in part because they paid attention to their appearance. They were always well dressed, with fine jewelry and stylishly draped mantles.

The four slaves were more difficult. The routine was simple: Ember had simply to state before suitable witnesses that each was free, and give to each his or her slave token, signifying self-ownership. But neither the family nor the slaves wished to part company. They had discussed it, and agreed that it was not feasible to take slaves to another city, where rules might differ and it might be hard to support them. So they were to be freed and allowed to make their own ways in Veia. Despite the pain of the separation.

Ember went through the ritual of freeing for each in turn, and hugged each. Then Carver, Crystal and Flower hugged them also. Flower was openly crying, and so were the slaves. The slaves had been with them for a long time, and were much like family members. Ember knew that no food would taste as good, when not prepared by the women, and no house would seem as clean. But the four should be able to make their way in the city, being free; they did have useful skills.

Ember had one pleasant surprise at the end. "We have made an arrangement for you to remain at the villa until the new owner takes possession. You may use its facilities, in exchange for taking care of it. When the owner comes, in a month, you may then undertake service with him, or depart, as you wish. By then you may have found better situations elsewhere."

"Oh, thank you, mistress!" the elder woman cried. "That will be so much better than the common barracks."

Then they boarded the ship, taking seats in the passenger section. The journey would not be difficult; it was the new city that concerned Ember. All the rules would be different, and perhaps the language too. Worse, it was likely to be uncivilized. They had wealth, but what would it avail, if brigands ran free?

"What is the next city?" Flower asked worriedly. "Is it nice?"

Ember tried to put the best face on it. "It is across the river, a town that is expanding into a city. So there is room there for skilled artisans. It is called Ruma."

"I don't like it," Flower decided.

Ember had to laugh. "None of us do. We all know that Veia is the jewel of Etruria. But perhaps we shall be able to help make this primitive foreign town into something better."

In due course the boat set sail and moved away from the pier. The current took it, so that the oarsmen hardly had to strain. It moved smartly along. They watched the buildings of Veia pass to the rear. Then they went beyond the great outer wall. The city did not end there, of course; it had long since outgrown its walls, and there were more temples outside. But in time of war the populace would withdraw to the center city for safety.

"Practice your flute, dear," Crystal suggested, to divert further questions.

The girl brought out her double flute and played. The harmony trilled, and soon the rowers were keeping time to the beat of it. The captain approached. "Maybe sell her to me, to be a mascot for the boat," he said jovially.

"You couldn't afford her," Carver responded, smiling. "She eats too much."

The captain shook his head with mock regret. "Too bad. My boat will go slower without her."

They saw the salt road, which was the main route by which the precious salt that was the principal source of Veia's wealth was transported. There was traffic there, as the wagons hauled the salt for export. Then there were the huge tunnels, used to divert the flow of the Tiber for irrigation and return water to the river for swamp drainage and protection against flooding. It was said that no other city had as fine or extensive underground water ducts, carved from solid rock. The irrigation enabled Veia to grow crops for a longer season than usual, because there could never be a true drought.

Ember sighed to herself. How could the wonders of Veia ever be matched in the cultural hinterlands? Yet they would have to make do.

How had they offended the local gods? For only a significant offense could account for the abrupt finality of their dismissal from their home city.

She had no answer. Troubled, but lulled by the gentle motions of the boat, she drifted into a lethargy.

The scene shifted. The outlines of the boat and men assumed preternatural brightness, being outlined in faint fire. The water of the river beyond glowed. The banks and trees became unnaturally clear, as if her old green eyes had sharply improved. Everything was beautiful.

Ember realized that she was having a vision. Sometimes it happened. She pounced on her opportunity, knowing better than to let it go to waste. *O Aplu, how have we offended thee?* she thought forcefully. For despite the word of the diviner, she was not at all sure that they weren't in trouble with the gods.

A swirl of vapor appeared in the distance. It came toward the boat, then lifted to hover on the deck before her. No one else seemed to see it, but that was to be expected; it was her vision, not theirs.

The vapor remained, shimmering, whirling, but not otherwise active. It waited.

She realized that she could not simply sit and wait for it to communicate. She had to ask.

"O messenger of the god, how have we transgressed?"

The swirl remained, unresponsive. Apparently it would not speak to her in a human voice. She realized belatedly that this made sense; it was after all merely the stuff of clouds and fog. She had to address it in a manner that facilitated its response.

"O messenger, give me a signal. Can you answer yes?"

The vapor suddenly puffed out, becoming larger. Then the surplus mist flaked away, and the swirl was as it had been before.

That must be its way of saying yes! All she had to do was phrase her questions so that it could agree.

But that meant that she would have to become more specific. She would have to run through a list of possible transgressions, and that could take a long time. She wasn't sure how soon the messenger would become impatient and depart.

So she tried for a quick simplification. "*Have* we transgressed?"

There was no response. That might mean that the god was not angry, or it might mean that she had not properly phrased the question. She needed to narrow it down quickly.

"Is the god happy with us?"

There was no response. Again, it might mean that she had asked the wrong question.

"Is there some purpose—something Aplu wishes of us?"

Now the flare. So it was neither anger nor pleasure on the part of the god, but a signal that something had to be done. Ember was relieved. She had thought that the family had lived a righteous life, but their sudden expulsion from Veia had shaken her certainty. Yet what could it be that the god wished of them?

"Does it have to do with our profession—metalworking?"

The vapor flared. Now she was getting somewhere. It wasn't that they had erred, but that their expertise was needed elsewhere.

"They need bronze artistry in Ruma?"

There was no response, so she continued. "Gold? Silver? Tin? Copper?" Still no response.

Ember was at a loss. What other metal was there? Surely not—but she would have to ask. "Iron?"

It flared.

"But we don't work in iron!" she protested. "It's a crude metal, difficult to work, and it rusts. It is better suited for swords than artistry. The problems of procurement, transport, inferior malleability—"

But the messenger of the god had faded out. The scenery was back to normal. The vision was over.

"Oh, no," Ember breathed, chagrined.

"What is it, Mother?" Crystal inquired.

"We must bring iron to Ruma," Ember said heavily. "That is what the god wants of us."

Crystal stared at her, horrified. So did Carver.

Only Flower was pleased. She put aside her flute. "Iron's fun! It pulls things in."

"It is pulling *us* in," Ember agreed glumly.

They reached the town of Ruma in the afternoon. Ember saw the wide expanse of cornfields on either side of the river; this was a fertile region. But indefensible: the land offered free approaches from every side. This would therefore never be a significant city, because the moment it developed any aspiration, another city's army would march in and loot or destroy it. It did have a wall, but modern siege techniques would make short work of that. Ember had a notion of such things.

The boat came to the main pier, and they got off. They had to carry their own things, because of the loss of their slaves, and this town was evidently too primitive to have regular harbor slaves to serve the public need.

In due course they were in an inn. It wasn't of the quality of those found at Veia, but of course nothing was, here. It was adequate, and at least they would get a meal and a night's rest before the labors of finding a permanent residence.

Next day turned out better than Ember had expected. Though the majority of the residences were thatched mud huts, she discovered a fair number of quality stone dwellings, and more were being constructed. Ruma was not in Veia's league, of course, but it was a large community, verging on a full city. In fact it had a king, Ancus Marcis, who had expanded the domain considerably. This might be a better place to set up a metalworking practice than she had thought. A growing community was good, because it lacked the entrenched upper class that dominated in an established, stable city.

They found a suitable new stone house by one of the main roads, excellent for its access to transport. Ember was able to obtain it for what she thought was a bargain price, until she realized that real estate values were of course lower in a region like this. In a few days they were moving in their belongings, and Flower pronounced it good, because there was a courtyard suitable for blossoms. The little girl was the one they had worried about, because she was less able to understand the disruptions of moving.

Carver began setting up his shop in the shed to the side. "I'll start with copper and bronze," he said. "It will take time to get into iron. I'll need a hotter forge, and water for quenching, and an anvil. And a supply of iron bloom."

Crystal checked her scribe notes. "There is no iron foundry in Ruma. We may have to smelt it here."

"That is a more serious operation. I can do it, if I get the ore, but I'll need more than a bronzeworking shed."

"You shall have it," Ember said. "Crystal, exactly where is the closest iron mine?"

Crystal checked again. "The Tolfa Hills, across the Tiber River. They are under the control of the city of Tarchna."

"We have had dealings with Tarchna," Ember said. "That's a center for Etruscan bronze. I should be able to deal with them. The problem will be shipping the ore here." She considered. "If we have to deal with an Etruscan city, I had better clear it with the king of Ruma first. I don't want the natives to be suspicious of us."

She wasted no time seeking an audience with the local king, Ancus Marcis, a Sabine. Ember had had dealings with Sabines, too; they were one of the Latin tribes of the inland regions. So she would address him in Latin.

But she ran into a complication. It seemed that women were not held in the same regard in backward Ruma as they were in civilized Veia and other Etruscan cities. When she requested an audience with the king, the clerk refused to schedule her. She had to haul Carver in and prime him on protocol. "Make sure you acquaint him with our potential usefulness to this region," she said. "They probably don't have the expertise for dental work, and their nobles should appreciate our capacity for false teeth carved from ivory and held in place by bridges of gold. Then there should be greater acceptance of our mission to bring ironworking here."

In due course Carver had his audience with the king, who was indeed interested in the dental potential and welcomed his effort to bring iron to Ruma. Transporting the ore? A good wagon would be provided. But there was another complication: the heavy forests between Veia and the Tolfa Hills were viewed with superstitious dread by these folk. They would not go there. The king himself did not share this folly, but he was realistic about the capacities of his subjects. They would have to arrange their own transportation after all.

Ember sighed. Establishing an iron foundry was not the simplest of operations to begin with, and this was already getting more complicated.

They decided to divide the family for this purpose: Carver and Crystal would remain in Ruma to complete the establishment of the house and shop, preparing a sample artificial tooth and dental bridge, while Ember and Flower journeyed to Tarchna to arrange for the importation of iron bloom. That would give the little girl the thrill of more traveling, while leaving Crystal free to work effectively. It was no burden for Ember, who liked Flower, and often had greater rapport with her than Crystal did.

They arranged for passage on another trading boat going upriver to Veia. Flower was delighted to revisit her familiar home city, and Ember shared her feeling. How much nicer it would have been, if only they had been allowed to remain there! Ruma was just too crude in style, technology and attitude, with its hovel-like buildings and the way it treated its women like second-class citizens. It was a relief to get away from it for a time.

At Veia they rented a wagon with two strong horses. "You'll need a slave with a strong arm to handle these," the proprietor warned her. "They like to move."

"We'll manage," Ember said. She took the reins herself, and guided the horses past the man's dubious gaze.

The horses were indeed frisky, and Ember's arms were soon tiring, holding them back. Fortunately she did not have far to go: she guided them to her former villa.

Kettle charged out. "Miss Ember!" he shouted as Flower leaped off the wagon to hug him. "You've come back!" In a moment all four were there.

"We're only passing," Ember explained. "I have business in Tarchna. But it's not a trip for women alone. I wish to hire two men to handle the horses and wagon, and to guard us from brigands along the way."

"We'll do it!" Kettle exclaimed.

But Pot was more restrained. "We're free now, Miss Ember. What do you offer for hire?"

Ember brought out two fine bronze weapons, a sword and a long dagger, and held them out to take. "You remember when Carver made these? Use them in our service, and when we return they are yours to keep."

"Oh, no, Miss Ember!" Pot protested. "One of them would be more than our service is worth."

"This is not kitchen work," she replied grimly. "We shall be hauling iron, which is heavy. And while I am old and worthless, my granddaughter is not. I would not want her to fall into the hands of rough men."

"What rough men?" Kettle demanded, taking the sword and lifting it threateningly.

"Put that thing away before you lop off someone's nose!" Pot snapped at his son. Then, looking at Ember, he nodded, and took the dagger. "We will guard her—and you—with our lives, Miss Ember."

"I am sure you will," Ember said, smiling. The thing about hiring these men was that she knew them well, and could trust them; she and Flower would be able to sleep without fearing their guards as much as their enemies.

They spent the night at the villa, and started off early next morning. Pot drove the horses, with Ember riding beside him to give directions, for he had never been away from Veia before. Kettle and Flower rode behind, pretending that the wagon was a ship and the landscape was a fabulous sea; each hill was a big wave they had to navigate.

The road wended up and down, but mostly up, for they were going into the hills. On occasion they encountered a wagon going the other way; then they had to pull to the side at a wide place to let it by, exchanging greetings with the other drivers. But mostly they were alone, passing through the crop fields of the city.

Then they entered the forest. Large oak, elm and beech trees crowded close to the trail, and the land was deeply shaded. This was the region that the Rumans feared, perhaps because they lacked the protection of the Etruscan gods. Ember wasn't worried about the supernatural, because she was here, really, by the directive of a god: to bring iron to the hinterland. It was only man she had to fear, and her concern had been alleviated when she hired Pot and Kettle.

As they climbed higher, the oaks gave way to pines, and the forest closed in even more tightly. There was an odd quietness about such a forest; perhaps the pine needles damped out the sound. Pot and Kettle began to look around nervously. They would not admit to the kind of primitive fear that uncivilized folk had of deep wilderness, but they nevertheless felt awe in the ambience of this somber region. That began to get on Ember's nerves, though she was no superstitious barbarian either. "Flower, why don't you play your flute?" she suggested.

The girl, getting bored with scenery no matter how novel, was glad to oblige. She brought out her double flute and practiced the scales. Then she played melodies, and the harmonies went out through the trees of the forest and became enhanced. Flower would one day be a fine musician; she was already quite good with the flute.

When the child tired of playing, Ember filled in with a story. It was of course familiar to them all, but that was part of the point: its familiarity was comforting. It reminded them all that the gods were in charge and would not allow civilized folk to come to harm here.

Long ago, Ember explained, the people lived close to the land. They planted wheat, made wine, herded swine, and enjoyed sex, much as has been the case since. But they had one significant flaw: the gods were a mystery to them. They were unable to read the true signs, or to interpret the true omens. Thus they were blind to the fundamental nature of existence. They did not understand destiny. They did not know greatness. So they suffered for their ignorance, thinking that floods and droughts and fires were random events that they could do nothing about.

But the gods were tolerant of this naivete, and in due course gave the people a chance to learn the truth. After all, even as a child grows and learns, so does a primitive people mature and gain wisdom. The gods decided on a region, and then on a man in that region: he would be the one they first contacted directly. His name was Tarchon, and he was until this moment an ordinary farmer.

One day Tarchon was plowing his field when his plow suddenly cut deep into the earth. Startled by this mishap, he tried to right his plow, but it dug deeper yet. So he halted his ox and stared down into the furrow, thinking that perhaps he had run afoul of some nether root.

He found no root. Instead there seemed to be some sort of opening in the bottom of the furrow. From this something was emerging. It was round and hairy. Amazed, the farmer sought to brush the dirt off it so that he could see what it was. It seemed to be some kind of ball.

Tarchon's amazement expanded into shock. On the ball was a face. It was a human head! In fact it was a small child, emerging from the cleft of the furrow like a baby from the cleft of a woman. The earth was giving birth!

"Well, don't just gawk, Tarchon," the child said, spying the farmer. "Help me get out of my mother."

Numb with astonishment, Tarchon put his hands carefully on the child's head and pulled him up. The little body slid out with a sucking sound, and the earth closed up somewhat beneath him, still leaving a deep furrow. The farmer set him on the turf beside the furrow, and fetched water to wash the mud off. He turned out to be a handsome boy looking about two years old.

Tarchon cried out with this miracle so loudly that his wife and children came to investigate. They too were astonished when the farmer explained how he had found the lad. "But who is he?" the wife asked. "Surely his mother misses him."

"No, I remain close to my mother," the boy said, patting the ground. "It is my father who sent me to you. Now don't waste time; bring your lauchumar here so I can educate them."

"The clan kings? But they won't listen to a mere child like you," the farmer protested. "In fact, they won't listen to me, either."

"I am more than a mere child," the lad said, frowning with such authority that all of them were impressed. "Tell the lauchumar that Tages is here, and will not wait overlong on their convenience."

Tarchon, impressed anew, hastened to tell his clan king of this news. The lauchumar was not pleased to be disturbed from his gaming with dice. Back in those days, remember, the authorities did not know about the signals of the gods, so whiled away their lives with entertainments. Today, of course, they understand much better—and love gaming and amusements just as well. "If this is some ruse to waste my time, I will have you boiled in olive oil," the lauchumar muttered warningly. "I have better things to do than rescue lost brats."

Nevertheless, the lauchumar followed the farmer back to the field. Immediately the child spoke. "Now pay close attention, lauchumar, because I will not repeat myself. Make sure you write everything down, so that you can duly inform the others."

The clan king opened his mouth to protest, but withheld his reproach, because the child was so self-assured and spoke so effectively, at an age when few children were speaking more than isolated words.

"I am Tages, son of Genius and of Earth, sent to inform you mortals of the ancient wisdom," the child said. "Listen to my chant, and heed my message, that you may become civilized and prosper. First I will deliver the book of the Netvis."

Tages then chanted the text of that sacred book, and the lauchumar hastily wrote it down, because it was quickly apparent that this was indeed great wisdom. From this book the people learned how to interpret the signs in a sacrificial liver. Ever after, their priests would know how to sacrifice sheep and read the messages of the gods in the steaming livers. This became one of the pillars of human understanding of the gods, respected throughout the world.

Meanwhile, the news of this remarkable event was spreading, and a second lauchumar, from another clan, arrived to assist. This was fortunate, because the first lauchumar was exhausted from his task of recording the book.

To the second clan king Tages chanted the book of the Frontac. From this book the people learned how to read the gods' messages in the lightning and the thunder. They learned how to face south to determine whether the lightning came from the east or west, and how to note the precise point that the bolt issued from the heavens, for that indicated exactly which god had loosed it. For a number of gods could hurl lightning bolts, and there were eleven directions from which they could come. Each bolt could be benign or malignant, depending on the god and the situation, so it was essential to identify it correctly. Normally, however, only Tinia, the chief god, threw bolts to be dreaded. His first thundering was merely an alert, and his second a good omen. But the third could be disaster, and such a signal could never be ignored. The date of a lightning strike was important, too; any bolt could be clearly understood, if it occurred on a key date. Thus the precise calendar of portents was vital, and Tages presented this too.

A third lauchumar arrived, and he also was needed. Tages chanted the words of fate, and the words of salvation, and the words of expiation. The lauchumar collected these in the book of ritual, which every priest had to know thereafter.

At last the last chant had been chanted. The child-sage ceased speaking, and silence fell on the land. The lauchumar and the multitude of common people who had assembled by this time took a breath.

Then Tages's eyes glazed. He fell forward into Tarchon's deep furrow, dead. The earth filled in, covering him over, and it was as if the field had never been plowed. The messenger of the gods was gone.

The lauchumar and the people held a ceremony of mourning, for they knew that a great entity had visited them, and delivered his supremely important message, and died on their behalf. Because of Tages, they now understood the gods, and they understood destiny, and they had the vision of greatness.

They built a city on that spot, and it became the first and greatest of the League of Twelve Cities. They named it for the farmer who had plowed that fateful furrow that birthed Tages, thus determining the site of the miracle. Thus Tarchon's name became enshrined in that of the city of Tarchna.

"And it is to this city we are now traveling," Ember concluded. "We shall be seeing it tomorrow."

After that they moved through the deep forest with greater confidence. How could they be frightened by the very forest whose glade had been the site of such a significant event? Surely the gods regarded this region with continuing favor.

In this manner they came without event to Lake Bracciano, a huge expanse of water. "Ooooo!" Flower exclaimed, awed and thrilled. "So wide! So pretty!"

"We'll camp beside it," Ember said. She understood the child's delight in the water, for she shared it. Sometimes she dreamed she was on a boat or raft, crossing water so wide that land could not be seen at all. That was both frightening and tempting, and she had never understood where the dream came from, because she had never done such a thing. Getting seasick on a ship had been bad enough. "You and Kettle can gather wood for our fire."

There was an outdoor hearth under the shade of a large maple tree, because this was a frequently traveled road. Ember started a fire in it while Pot watered the horses and turned them loose to graze in the brush and turf near the water's edge.

There was a scream, then a splash. Flower had fallen into the water. But in a moment Kettle was in after her, picking her up and carrying her to the shore. Seeing them that way, Ember was surprised. She tended to think of them as two children, because intellectually they were, but physically Kettle was at least double the girl's mass.

They came to dry out by the fire, Flower naked, Kettle in a simple short skirt, by his father's directive. Then Ember brought out a dry tunic for the girl. All too soon Flower would become a woman, and have to leave the joyous freedoms of childhood behind.

They ate the evening meal, consisting of the more portable types of food Ember had bought in the city: bread, cheese, dried swine meat, apples, and thick sweet wine. It wasn't exactly a feast, but it sufficed. Ember could see that the men felt awkward, and she realized why. "Eat, friends! You are no longer slaves and I am no longer your mistress; you are hired freedmen, and I am a traveler. There is no impropriety in my doing some work with my hands, or in your eating in our company." Then they relaxed and ate well.

There was still some light left in the day, so Ember set up a popular game. She had Kettle hammer a wooden pole in the ground. On this she balanced a little wood chip. She drew a circle in the dirt, around the pole and an appropriate distance from it. She gave each person a cup of water dipped from the lake. "Now we shall pretend that this is a bronze disk," she said. "And that it is wine in our cups. The one who wins three falls first gets the remainder of the real wine." She set out the prize: the wineskin.

Flower, being the youngest, had the first turn. She took a sip of water and blew it out toward the chip. She missed, not getting high or far enough, and the water splatted on the ground.

Kettle was next. He was the tallest of them, and had considerable power of spit. Too much: his shot passed over the chip.

Pot's shot was better. The spit passed close to the chip, but did not quite touch it.

Then it was Ember's turn. She made a perfect strike, and the spit knocked the chip to the ground. "One for Grandma!" Flower cried, clapping her hands gleefully.

In the second round Flower got both elevation and distance, but still missed. Kettle lowered his sighting and missed just to the side. Pot scored, knocking the disk down. But Ember scored again, so was still ahead, two to one.

In the third round no one scored.

In the fourth round Kettle scored, and so did Pot.

In the fifth round Flower finally managed to hit the disk. She jumped around, fabulously excited. But Pot also scored, winning the wine.

"Congratulations, champion," Ember said, handing him the wine-skin.

Pot shook his head knowingly. He understood that she had missed deliberately after the first two rounds, giving the others a chance. She had had decades of experience in this popular game, and had long since become more proficient than any child or slave could be. The point had been to have a bit of fun, and it had been that for the other three.

They slept on the wagon under blankets, lulled by the sounds of the night. This, too, seemed oddly familiar to Ember, though she could not place any similar event.

Next day they continued through the hills and forest, and by evening reached the city of Tarchna, where Ember rented a house and stable for the horses. On the day following she took Flower and visited the residence of a former business supplier, to explain her need. Unfortunately she learned that there had been a change in management, and the new master did not know of her family or business. He was a gruff, stout man, not far her junior, and evidently impatient with the interruption of his day. "What do you want, woman?" he demanded.

"I need a regular supply of iron bloom, for my daughter's husband to work. He is a skilled metalsmith, expert in bronze and gold but also competent in iron. We just have not done much in iron before. But now we have to."

The iron master squinted at her. "Who are you, an old woman, to come make such a demand of me? How do I know you are not wasting my time?"

"I am Ember, of Veia," she said evenly. "We have long purchased copper and tin from Tarchna, for our bronze. Check your records. Now we wish to purchase iron."

He scowled. "Ember, eh? Well, then, you can just call me Slag. Look, woman, we have orders elsewhere for iron. Come back in two months."

"Two months!" she exclaimed. "I need it now! I have a wagon to carry it with me."

"One wagon? This is evidently a small operation."

"We are just instituting it, in Ruma. We will doubtless use more as we get established."

"Well, return when you are established."

"We need the first iron to *get* established, Slag, as you must know. We have to show the king what we can do."

"He is right to be doubtful, woman. Iron is not a metal a person just decides one day to work. Stick with your bronze."

"We can't. We had a thunder signal from Aplu, who told us to bring iron to Ruma. We will continue with bronze, and gold, but also will honor the god's directive."

The man sighed, evidently not wishing to directly interfere with a mission dictated by a god. "I just can't see Aplu sending a woman to do a man's job."

"I know metalworking," Ember said. "I could do it, if I had the youth and muscle required."

Slag laughed. "You think that's all it takes? Get out of here, woman, and let me get to my work."

Ember could not entirely condemn Slag for his attitude. But she had to have that iron. "Suppose I make you a wager," she said.

"A wager? Woman, I bet on the wrestling matches, not on iron."

"Let me direct your workers at the foundry. Let me show you what I know. If I prove I know iron, you will sell to me."

"If you prove you know iron, I'll *give* you what you make!" he said, laughing again.

"It is a wager," she agreed evenly.

"Grandma, is this smart?" Flower asked nervously.

"It's necessary," Ember said.

Slag led the way out of his shop. "Come on, woman; I have a foundry nearby. We shall have the proof of this in short order."

They followed him to his foundry outside the city. It was a barren area, with a pall of smoke. There were piles of dry wood nearby, and a kiln where the wood was processed into charcoal. There were also wagons loaded with iron ore. It was evident that there was a lot of business here.

Slag brought them to a small smith shop made of wood and thatch. He summoned two workers. "Do what this woman says," he told them. Then he stood back and waited.

Ember surveyed the premises. There was a bowl-shaped pit rimmed by stone, large enough for a family to bathe in. It was like a forge, on a larger scale. It would do.

"Fetch charcoal," she told the workers. "Fill the bottom of the smelting pit."

They went out, and returned with bags of charcoal, which they dumped into the pit. "That's enough," Ember said in due course. "Now fetch hematite."

They brought in bags of the iron ore, and dumped these on top of the charcoal. "That's enough," Ember said. "Now bring more charcoal."

Slag nodded, becoming persuaded that she did know what she was doing.

"My granddaughter could do it," Ember said, noting his nod. She couldn't resist bragging.

"Could she? Perhaps she should try it."

Ember smiled. "Flower, you take over." She hoped the girl remembered and understood what she had observed in Veia.

The girl was surprised, and not at ease, but she realized that Ember was trying another ploy. "Fill it to the top," she said.

When the pit was filled with charcoal, and mounded over, Flower called a halt. "Now light it," she said. "From the bottom." She had seen her father do this often with the bronze forge.

When it was burning, and the fumes were rising evenly through the charcoal and ore, Flower turned to the tools in the shed. "Set up the bellows."

Slag interceded. "What bellows?"

Flower pointed to the goatskin bags lying by the wall. "That bellows." Then, becoming bold: "Do I have to show you how to work it?"

Slag smiled. "Yes."

Flower went and got the bellows. She dragged the solid mechanism to the burning pit and got it into position. She used rawhide strips to tie its opening to a set of clay pipes near it. Then she fitted the pipes into a heavy clay tube. She shoved this through a hole in the stone rim of the fire pit, keeping the bellows itself well clear of the fire.

"Why are you doing that?" Slag asked.

"To blow up the fire," Flower answered. "Because it will never get hot enough to smelt that ore into iron bloom by itself. It wouldn't even melt copper."

"Enough," Slag said. "You have made your point, Ember. I will sell you iron."

Ember nodded. A lot of work remained, but she knew that iron was coming to Ruma.

Iron did indeed come to Ruma, which was known by the natives as Roma, and later as Rome. It borrowed freely from Etruscan culture, especially with respect to the sophisticated methods of handling water, and spread that civilization as its power increased. The city grew rapidly under vigorous kings, some of whom were Etruscan, until it rivaled Etruscan cities. Because they never united against Rome's territorial ambition, the Etruscan cities were overcome one by one. Rome in time became a republic, and then a significant empire, uniting most of the peoples of the Mediterranean region. Its impact on human history was considerable, and vestiges of its Latin language are widely spread today.

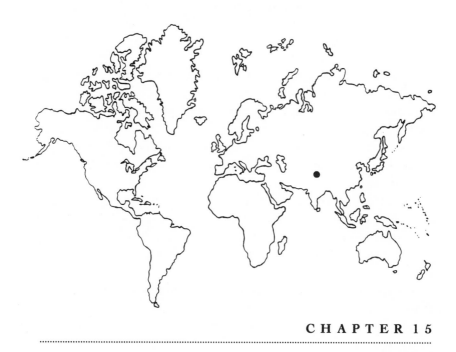

C H A P T E R   1 5

SILK

In the year A.D. *87 the Roman Empire circled the Mediterranean Sea in the western side of the Eurasian continent. The Han Empire was of similar size on the eastern side. Between them wended the Silk Road, an extremely long and treacherous network of trade routes that persisted because of the wealth it generated. From the west came fine bronze statues, glass, and alabaster vessels; from the south came ivory plaques; and from the east came lacquerwork and garments of silk. Such items were of immense value, and were coveted by the steppe peoples of central Asia. Control of the Silk Road was a source of constant friction.*

309

At this time the westernmost outpost of the Han Empire was at the town of Kashgar, where caravans from the east met those of the west and traded their goods. The king of Kashgar was Chung, who was a protégé of the formidable Han general Pan Ch'ao. But Chung had become greedy, and rebelled, seeking the riches of the Silk Road for himself.

Pan Ch'ao had defeated him in battle and driven him out of his own city. Chung's situation was desperate. But he had a plan.

O H, my husband, my love, I am afraid," Seed said as Stone finished his meal of mutton. "Let me go with you."

Stone knew there was no chance, but he tried to put her off gently. "Who would take care of Tree?"

"He can stay with Blaze and Bunny," she said. "He's ten; he can almost take care of himself. Anyway, he likes their wagon. All the smithy tools are there."

She was right, but it was not enough. "Chung is going into Kashgar to make submission to the Chinese tyrant," he reminded her. "His allies from the hinterlands must go too. I count, as a Hsiung-Nu horseman; Chung wants to show his good faith by bringing in a metalsmith too. So I'll take some simple examples of my art and instruments, and make an offering to General Pan Ch'ao, and join the feast. I'm just a token figure, really. After the ceremony of submission you will be able to come into the city. But not until the agreement has been cleared. You are too precious to risk during the hostilities, which technically remain until the ceremony is done."

"Then let me try to protect you in what way I can," she pleaded. "It is you I fear for. I have a bad premonition about this day."

"Foolish woman," he said, smiling though he felt it too. He did not care to admit his fear that things were not as they seemed.

"Let me garb you in armor," she said. "A hard leather jacket, leggings, a stiff collar—"

"What are you thinking of!" he exclaimed. "Are you trying to weight me down so that I fall off my horse? No one wears such things!"

"And a bronze plate inside the jacket," she concluded, fetching the items. "In fact, it can be one of the offerings, conveniently carried. And bronze bands around your arms, and iron wristlets. Don't take them off until you have to present them."

"This is ludicrous!" he protested. But she kissed him, and pleaded with him, until he suffered himself to be garbed as she desired. She was twenty-nine years old, but still beautiful in his eyes; he would do anything she wanted. So under his loose, calf-length linen robe, held in place by the belt with its iron buckle, was the much larger bronze plate that covered his entire belly and chest. Under the cloth gathered at the wrists were the metal bands and wristlets, and within the wide-legged trousers, strapped at the ankle, were more bronze bands. She made him wear boots of the heavy combat kind, instead of the ones with comfortable soft leather soles. There was even a copper bowl under his conical fur cap. He felt like a clanking freak.

Then he donned his short fur cape, mounted his gelding, and rode out to join his assembled clan. The horse hesitated, until Stone spoke reassuringly to him. "Yes, I know I feel like a stranger, with all this metal on my body. But how can a man argue with a woman?" The horse shook his head as if in agreement, so that his long mane flung out before settling to rest against his forelegs and knees.

Stone saw his father's tent. On impulse he guided his horse to it. Blaze came out to meet him, his forehead mark ruddy in the cold air of the morning. "On your way, son?"

"On my way," Stone agreed. "But my wife is not easy about this mission, and has me loaded with bronze." He tapped his belly, making the plate under his clothing sound.

"Your wife is a good woman," Blaze remarked.

"I feel like a fool."

"Women do make fools of men. But humor her. She has uncanny instincts."

"This mission bothers me," Stone said.

"Our leaders have a notion what they are doing. Humor them too. Get on your way, lest you be late."

Somehow that helped reassure him. Blaze evidently knew something about the matter, and felt confident, and Seed's caution evidently didn't concern him. There was nothing to do except get on with the mission.

Stone was the last to make the formation, because of the delay occasioned by his peculiar additions. The horde commander frowned, but let it pass; Stone had done good work for him and other leaders. Allowance had to be made for those who were not top fighters. Stone would have been glad to have been left out of this whole march, and the military folk knew that. In fact he would have been happier yet to be back on the steppe, not involved in any of the eternal quarreling over the Silk Road. But when his Hsiung-Nu Horde had come here to ally with Chung, Stone and his family had had to come along. He did not pretend to like the politics of the day; the horde had been promised good booty from the Silk Road, so had come.

They rode to join Chung's minions. These were impressive with their large horses towering over the horde's big-headed, short-legged, bushy-tailed animals, and their spears and swords. Of course a nomad warrior on a small horse could put an arrow through a spearman from a distance, no matter how big the other's horse. The hordes were matchless in open territory. Their composite reinforced war bows were especially effective on horseback, because their arms were of different lengths. The long arm was up, and the short one down, so as not to interfere with the horse. Specialists crafted them, and bowmakers were highly regarded; good bows were handed down the family lines as heirlooms. Blaze had one, which would in time be passed on to Tree, because Stone would not care to try to use it. But much of the local fighting was in or near towns, with narrow streets inhibiting the animals, and houses getting in the way of arrows. No nomad liked fighting in a town. That was almost as degrading as this dirty business of surrendering. Whatever had possessed Chung to give up the fight, when he had such an effective fighting force remaining? Even Stone was disgusted by a quitter.

An officer rode out to meet the horde commander. Stone thought it was only to clarify the position the horde was to take in the formation, but it turned out to be far more serious. "As most of you already know, we are not going into Kashgar to make submission, but to feign it," the commander announced after a moment. "We will have a banquet, and make our presentations. Then, when the enemy has been lulled, we will turn on him and destroy him."

Now, this was different! A cheer rose from the ranks. No nomad liked the idea of surrendering. Instead there would be mayhem and plunder. Perhaps only Stone was not enthusiastic. He was troubled by several things. What of the honor of the horde? It was part of a deal for surrender; was it right to change that to treachery? And this meant there would be fighting, for even when caught by surprise, the Chinese forces could be tough campaigners. Especially in the cramped confines of the town. Much blood would flow. No, Stone did not like this development at all. It would have been better to meet the Chinese in good, honest battle out in the countryside. Even a loss would have been honorable, then.

He was also bothered by the discovery that just about every man here except himself had been told ahead of time about the true nature of the mission. They were all armed for battle, while he was only haphazardly prepared, thanks mainly to his wife's premonition. Why hadn't he been told?

He had a suspicion about that: because they knew how readily his wife fathomed every nuance of his emotion. If he had known the plan, she would have divined it too. In fact she had just about done so, when he *hadn't* known. So their caution was justified, aggravating as it was. He wished he could get far away from here, for personal shame as well as his disgust at the treachery of the plan.

But he had no choice. He had to do as his horde did. At least, as a metalsmith, he might not have to participate in the slaughter. Even if he did have to contribute to the deception.

They rode to the city. The warriors were well armed, their bows sheathed from their belts in front of their left thighs, their quivers of arrows across their backs, ready to be brought out rapidly from the right. Most wore sheep's-leather armor, with some of the leaders having scale armor of bone or metal. Stone himself had metal armor, of a sort, thanks to his wife's concern. It would never do in a battle, but might help if a stray missile hit him. Her premonition had been good to this extent: there was danger. The best place for a noncombatant to be was as far from a battle as possible, lest someone make a mistake.

They entered the town. If the Chinese were concerned about the size of the party, with its bows, swords and lassos, they gave no evidence; the gate was open. Perhaps the Chinese general was happy to have the bulk of his enemy's forces here, so that he knew there were not others waiting in ambush outside. Trust was seldom complete, and Pan Ch'ao had proved to be one of the most cunning and ruthless officers the Chinese had sent out to the steppes. He had been more than a match for the local kingdoms. Now, with nomad allies, perhaps it would be different for Chung. If only the advantage didn't have to be gained by treachery!

Kashgar was dominated by a great stone tower, the place for rendezvous of caravans. Today instead of traders and goods there were armies. The Chinese had pitched a large open tent in a central square, and had set up a great banquet. Tables were loaded with food, and young women were bringing more. This was to be a real celebration. Stone could well believe that the Chinese were eager to have peace; the fighting had continued for decades, disrupting the trading caravans and therefore interfering with the wealth they generated. Now he almost felt sorry for the enemy; they had opened the town in good faith, and were to pay a brutal price for their naivete.

General Pan Ch'ao was there with his Chinese guard force. Chung dismounted and went with his top officers to make his false submission. After the banquet, the warriors would quietly go to their steeds and mount; then the lancers would charge the Chinese and destroy them in one efficient action. After that it would be just a matter of mopping up the leaderless forces of the enemy, and the town would be theirs. Stone realized that the deception was hardly necessary; there were fewer Chinese than expected. Their forces must have been depleted by the recent campaign, so that they depended increasingly on their allies, the Wu-Sun. The Wu-Sun were not a match for the Hsiung-Nu in the open, but could be formidable in restricted territory. Yet there weren't many Wu-Sun here either. They were fairly readily identifiable by their fair skin and bright eyes, contrasting with the complexions of the Chinese. This town was far less effectively defended than they had realized.

Chung dismounted with his officers and approached the general. The two groups met in the open tent, and Chung kneeled, making his submission. He gave up his sword. Pan Ch'ao accepted it and nodded graciously; their words could not be heard from beyond the tent.

Then Chung signaled Stone. Stone dismounted and walked to the tent, carrying some of his offerings. He gave a beautiful gold cup he had crafted to Chung, who in turn gave it to Pan Ch'ao. The general turned to Stone. "Your work?" he inquired in accented Hsiung-Nu. "It is very nice. In China we appreciate fine workmanship. You will work for me hereafter." He made a signal, and a man approached, carrying a package.

"As you wish, General," Stone said, bowing. He felt the large plate in his shirt. Was it time to take it out, so that it could be presented?

"And as a token of our association," the general continued, "here is my gift for you: a silk robe for your lovely wife."

Stone was startled. "You know of my wife?"

"By reputation. She is said to be among the most beautiful women of any age. You are a fortunate man."

"Uh, yes," Stone said, disgruntled. It was said that the general's spies kept him constantly informed, but Stone had never imagined that they gleaned information like that.

"But first the wine," the general said affably. He raised a hand, and immediately several girls brought wineskins and goblets. They poured each goblet full, gave it to each man present, and quietly retreated.

Soon all of them were drinking. Then, as they turned to approach the banquet tables, the general made a small signal with one hand. It was only chance that Stone saw it; he had been looking for some way to return to his horse, because he felt distinctly out of place in this exalted company.

Two Chinese took hold of Chung by the arms. His wine slopped from the goblet. "What—?" he started to ask.

Then a third man drew his sword and swung it at Chung's neck. The two at his arms ducked out of the way. The sword passed through Chung's neck, and his head fell off his upright body. The men let go of his blood-spouting body and let it drop.

Suddenly there was mayhem. Stone was struck in the belly. It clanged. He looked down to see a Chinese sword glancing away from it. The man had tried to kill him! The sword had passed right through the package with the silk gown Stone was holding. So much for the general's offer of employment.

The gown was spilling out of the package like a collection of entrails. The man evidently did not yet realize that the thrust had not been effective; he was already turning away, ready to stab the next victim. Stone grabbed the silk, strung it out between his hands, and flung it over the soldier's head. He crossed his arms, drawing it tight, a garrote. The soldier's eyes grew large as he struggled for breath. His sword dropped to the ground.

The soldier sagged. Stone reached down to take the fallen sword. All around him Chinese were slaughtering Chung's men. More Chinese were pouring from hidden places, and, Stone realized, mounted Wu-Sun were charging the Hsiung-Nu from the side, lancing them before they could get oriented.

Stone ducked down and fled the tent. In the melee no one noticed.

He ran to his horse, which was being ignored because it was riderless, and fairly leaped to its back. If he could ride away before anyone realized—

A lasso caught him from behind. Before he could react, it drew tight and yanked him off the back of his horse. The horse bolted and Stone took a hard fall on his back, gasping. He was amidst a pile of slaughtered brethren. Only his stiff collar had saved him from being throttled.

The Wu-Sun who had lassoed him charged across, his lance coming down to skewer him through the chest. The point shied across the hidden plate, delivering a rib-crushing blow but not killing him.

"What is this?" the rider grunted, surprised. But then he spied another Hsiung-Nu trying to flee, and quickly reoriented to catch that one. He jerked the lasso free and galloped on.

Stone realized that any effort to escape at this point was futile; it was the escapees the Wu-Sun were after. So he tried to play dead, hoping that there would be a later change in the situation. He got a handful of warm blood from the nearest corpse and smeared it across his face and chest, then lay still. If this didn't work, they would kill him anyway, but it was his best chance. He settled into as still a position as he could manage, trying to look safely deceased. Unable to do anything else, he thought about his situation.

The carnage continued. There were many more Chinese and Wu-Sun than there had seemed to be; now it was clear that they had been in hiding. It was also clear that General Pan Ch'ao had not been fooled by Chung's pretense of submission; he had simply struck first, reversing the ploy. So it was Chung who was finished, and the Chinese would remain in power in Kashgar and the region, controlling the silk trade. Somehow it seemed fitting. The art of politics was the art of betrayal, and the general had proved to be better at it than the nomads.

He thought of Seed, his lovely wife. What effrontery the general had had, to spy out the fact of her existence and compliment him on her, all in the effort to lull Chung into a false sense of security! Did Pan Ch'ao intend to capture her and make her serve him? She would never do that. She had confessed, once, to having an eye for another man, before she married Stone, but she had never since strayed. Stone had come to realize that that other man had done him a strange kind of favor, because all that she had learned from him she had used to make Stone happy. She had been his constant love and support, and he knew that much of what he was he owed to her. The rest he owed to his father, Blaze, and his mother. A man who did not like to fight was not normally respected among the nomads, but they had made Stone be respected for his artistry with bronze and iron. Because of them, he had had the best of lives.

Oh, how he longed to return to Seed! To take her deep into the hinterland with their horses, sheep and children, and just exist among their own kind, far from the barbarities of the civilized folk. And if he managed to escape alive, that was exactly what he would do. They would bring up their son on the wonderful steppes, and Tree could marry a good steppe woman. As Stone had married Seed.

Actually Seed had come from one of the towns of the Silk Road, and been taken by Blaze in a routine raid. Recognizing her beauty and worth, Blaze had brought her home for Stone. Oh, she had indeed been silken from the outset! She had long since lost the desire to return to the town life, and had become a full nomad. But perhaps her support for his metalwork stemmed in part from her town experience; she appreciated nice things, especially the ones he made for her. He was sorry he couldn't bring the general's gift of silk back to her; she would have loved it.

His attention returned to the activity nearby. Some Hsiung-Nu had remained mounted, and some had managed to recover their horses. These were putting up a desperate fight despite their poor order. Outnumbered and in a bad position, they did what they could, beating a slow retreat toward the town gate.

Which was now closed and guarded. Stone heard the cries of consternation as troops of Chinese archers ambushed the horsemen. Escape was illusory; Pan Ch'ao had closed his trap.

But it did mean that the action had moved elsewhere. No one seemed to be watching the corpses near the tent. Cautiously, Stone lifted his head and looked around. Then he took the sword of one of the corpses and got to his feet. Maybe he would be able to take out one more enemy man before he himself was killed.

Where could he go? The town was hostile territory, and the gate was closed. He could neither hide nor flee. Had his emulation of death merely postponed the reality?

Then Wu-Sun cavalrymen returned. Apparently the mopping up had been completed, and now they were coming to rob the bodies. Stone threw himself down among the corpses again, having no other recourse. This might buy him a bit more time before the end.

The Wu-Sun rode up. They shouted orders. Now slaves came out from the houses. They would do the dirty work of stripping the bodies for their masters.

Stone realized that his case was hopeless. If he remained here, he would be discovered when they stripped him. If he tried to flee, they would see him and kill him. All he could do was wait for the inevitable.

A wagon came up. Already the slaves were throwing the stripped bodies onto it, proceeding efficiently. The victors didn't want the town to stink of corpses. Stone happened to be in the first area they were processing, perhaps because it was central. Otherwise he might have been able to wait until night, and sneak away in the darkness. On such erratic fortune his life depended, ironically.

The bodies apart from him were done, and then the ones near him. Stone watched through slitted eyes. It was almost as if this were happening to someone else. He could observe objectively because he had no hope. He saw to his surprise that the slaves were naked, both male and female. Then he realized that this was because the masters feared the slaves would steal some of the booty. Naked, they could hide nothing of any consequence on their bodies, so did not have to be closely watched. Indeed, the supervisors were not watching; they were sampling the feast on the banquet tables, drinking the wine and joking among themselves. The slaves were simply ripping open the clothing of the bodies, checking for valuables, and piling the booty by the side, under a corner of the tent. This must be the general's territory for plunder; everything taken near the tent went to Pan Ch'ao, not to the warriors who had made the kills. So there was no greedy attention; it was just a chore.

This meant that another possible break for Stone had been eliminated. Wu-Sun warriors might have taken occasional breaks from the job, or quarreled among themselves about the division of spoils, or gone in a group to eat, so that no one of them would be left to steal from the others. But the slaves would work right through, not having the options of resting or quarreling or eating.

Now it was his turn. A young woman took hold of his robe and tore it open. There lay the bronze plate. Surprised, she lifted it out, admiring it. Then she set it aside and undid the belt, so as to check for whatever might be hidden in his lower clothing. In so doing, she touched his belly. She paused.

Stone knew why. It was because she felt his warmth. His body should have cooled by this time. She was about to realize that he was alive.

She looked at his face. She put her ear to his mouth, to listen for his breathing.

"I am not dead," he whispered. "My plate protected me."

She stared at him. She put her hand square against his neck, feeling the pulse there. She seemed uncertain how to react.

"Nor even wounded," he whispered. "I pretended to die, so that I might return to my wife, who is as lovely as you, and was once a slave, like you. I love her."

She put one hand to her hair, in a mannerism startlingly similar to Seed's, as if assessing who might be more lovely. This girl was not beautiful, being rather too plain of face and spare of body, but surely loved the suggestion that she might be. Now she had to decide whether to tell the warriors that one enemy body was alive, and sacrifice the one who had complimented her, and be the cause of one more death, or to let him be.

"I would have done the same for you," Stone whispered.

That decided her. She passed her flat hand across his face, as if closing the eyes of the dead. Then she checked the rest of his clothing, removing his good cape, armlets, bracelets, collar and shoes. She stood and deposited these things in the pile, then spoke briefly to a male slave. She went on to the next body.

Two male slaves came. One took hold of Stone's arms, the other his legs. They lifted him and carried him unceremoniously to the wagon. Then they swung him and heaved him up onto the pile of bodies in the wagon. He landed, rolled, and came to rest sprawled amidst cool, partly naked corpses. Already the smell was hardly sweet, though the bodies had hardly begun to decompose. His emotion was not horror; rather it was relief. His ploy with the slave girl had worked, and she had told the males to keep the secret. He had been processed through as a corpse.

He lay unmoving, afraid that any twitch could be observed. Soon another body was tossed up, and it rolled and came to rest partly on him. That protected him somewhat.

As evening came, a driver hitched up two horses and got on the front of the wagon. Someone else joined him. He drove down the street, which seemed to have been cleared of bodies. The front gate opened, letting the wagon out. It rolled on through, leaving the town behind. There was another horse leading the way, Stone realized; he heard its hoofbeats ahead, now that the noises of the town were gone. That would be either a Chinese or a Wu-Sun warrior, directing the operation.

The wagon left the road and cut across a field. The wheels bumped across stones and ruts, making the piled bodies bounce. Stone would have extricated himself from the pile, jumped off, and run, but he was afraid the horseman was watching. He could yet be hunted down and killed, if he were spied alive. If only the wagon had gone out alone! But of course there was a supervisor along, and the driver would take along a slave to dump the bodies off. No free person did any work that he could make a slave do. So Stone bided his time, hoping for his chance.

As he waited, he realized that even if he got free without trouble, it would not be easy. He was not heavily clothed, after losing his cape and boots, and the night was already cooling, and it would be a long trek barefoot to rejoin his clan and family. Assuming that they remained where they had been. More likely they had gotten news of the slaughter, and were moving out, fleeing the wrath of the Chinese. He would likely perish of exposure, exhaustion and hunger, trying to reach them as he was.

Yet what was there to do but try? Perhaps he could forage for food and clothing, and get by. If only he had been able to save at least a knife, so he could kill a sheep and have meat and fur for a crude shawl. But his life and blood-soaked robe and trousers were all it had been possible to salvage, thanks to the kindness of the slave girl he had flattered.

The wagon came to a gully and stopped. This was where they would dump off the bodies, for the wolves and vultures and ants to feed on. He hated the thought, but he might be able to salvage something from those bodies. Any remaining tatters of cloth, or anything that the slaves might have missed. It was gruesome, but possible.

The horseman spoke, in a language Stone couldn't follow. The ones on the wagon answered. Stone stiffened. One was a female voice! The driver had brought along a woman.

And the woman was a slave. She came to the rear of the wagon and began pulling at bodies. One slid as she tugged at a foot or arm, and finally rolled off, hitting the ground with a thunk. She hauled at another, bringing it down. Then she put her hand on Stone's bare ankle. She squeezed, feeling its warmth, then let go.

It was the slave girl he had spoken to! He couldn't see her, but only she would be so sure of him. She must have volunteered to come along for this distasteful chore, replacing one of the men. She knew about him. What did she have in mind?

Meanwhile the man was working similarly on the other side of the wagon. The horseman was silent, perhaps watching.

Another body slid, rolled, and thunked down. And another. Stone was now mostly uncovered.

The slave girl moved to the side, and more bodies fell. He could hear her grunting as she labored to get them down, for each was heavier than she was. The driver helped her with some. Every so often the horseman would rap out a command to make them hurry, when they seemed slow.

She returned to Stone's side. He saw that she was now wearing a cape, being no longer naked. No danger of stealing anything here! She paused, reaching inside her cape—and brought out a knife. Was she going to kill him herself?

She laid the knife down beside him. Then she hauled on another body, grunting again. She was letting the horseman know how hard she was working. And she hadn't let him know that there was a live body here. One that was now armed.

Stone grasped the knife. It would be invaluable for his foraging. But first he had to get away from here. He did not want to hurt anyone.

The girl and driver hauled off the last body. Only Stone was left. Now he had to go. Should he let them just haul him off to thunk on the ground, and lie there with the other bodies? Or should he jump down and run, hoping that the horseman wasn't looking?

He decided on running. He rolled himself to the edge of the wagon, and got ready to move.

But the girl was there before him, blocking his way. She shook her head quickly no. She made a gesture with two hands, as of drawing a bow.

Oh. The horseman was a bowman. Stone could not hope to escape an arrow. So he would have to go the dead meat route. Now he could see the man astride his horse, facing away, not deigning even to watch. But any good steppe warrior could track by sound as well as by eye. He would know the moment anything unusual happened.

The horseman spoke again, urgently. He was of the Western physical type, large, with the edge of a red beard showing. The girl did not haul Stone down. Instead she grimaced and went to the horseman. Stone saw the man dismount and turn toward her, grabbing for her cloak. No question what he wanted. She was a female slave, bound to do the man's bidding, if he owned her. But that did not seem to be the case. She must have gotten him to agree to let her take a male slave's place by indicating that she would be amenable to his desire. Now it was time to deliver. Apparently a female slave could deal on her own to that extent, agreeing to pleasure a man without telling. If a man raped another man's slave, he would be in trouble with the owner, so this was worth his while.

Stone turned his head, risking a look at the wagon driver. This was a male slave, perhaps one of those who had lifted Stone to the wagon. That would mean that he knew of Stone's condition. The man was staring at the scene by the horse, his face frozen with repulsion.

Suddenly Stone understood. The driver and the slave girl were lovers! The girl had helped Stone, and she had brought him a knife. Now he knew what she wanted of him. Her own escape, and that of her lover! If he ran away now, while she was distracting the horseman, not only would he be leaving her to something she did not desire, he might be getting her in worse trouble. He doubted he could run away without being spotted, even when the Wu-Sun was focusing on the girl. If he did, the horseman might make a body count, and realize that one was missing. Then the slaves would have to try to explain how they had lost a body. That could cost them their lives, on a day like this.

The warrior tore open the girl's cloak. But as his head turned, his blue eye caught sight of Stone, still on the wagon. He grunted with surprise, pushing the girl away and reaching for his bow. She grabbed hold of one end, preventing him from using it. He struck her, knocking her to the ground. He lifted his bow, reaching for an arrow. The male slave stood frozen, not daring to act even in this extremity, or perhaps knowing the futility of the attempt. Slaves were not noted for initiative.

Stone had no further choice. He scrambled up on the wagon and lunged for the bowman, using the height of the wagon to give him a high takeoff point. He leaped right into the bow with its lifting arrow, stabbing forward with his knife. Then his body struck the man's head and shoulder, bearing him down. There was a horrible scream.

Stone scrambled, trying to get free of the Wu-Sun before the warrior got organized. Then he realized that the man was not fighting him. The knife had driven deep into his chest, and he was dying.

Stone reached, took hold of the hilt of the knife, and pulled it out. The warrior twisted on the ground, blood spouting from his chest and his mouth. Stone could not stand to let even an enemy suffer needlessly. He jammed the knife into the man's throat, stopping the blood from going to the head, and death followed immediately.

He looked up to see the slave girl watching. "Take his clothes," she said. "And the wagon. And us. You said you would."

It was true. Stone had meant it only as flattery, but it constituted an offer. She had done her part; in fact she had done more than enough. While her lover had gone along, passively. Stone would have wondered about that, if it hadn't been so similar between him and Seed. She had always been the one to take action, while he had always gone along. Only when he was alone and in trouble, as now, did he take firm action—and even so, he had really been following the slave girl's lead, once she decided to help him. She might not be as lovely as Seed, but she was similar in the other respect. Her lover had chosen well—or perhaps been fortunate in the woman who chose him.

He gave her the knife to clean and keep, and got to work on the Wu-Sun's clothing. There was a toughened leather vest which would have stopped the thrust of the knife, if the man had not opened it in preparation for his encounter with the girl. There was a military hat, and good boots. The man was larger than Stone, so it was easy to use the clothing. He wiped off some of the blood by rubbing the vest on the turf, and put it on.

When he was dressed, he did something else he found distasteful. He used the warrior's knife to carve into the man's face, mutilating it beyond recognition. Then he hauled the bare body into the gully, and piled two other bodies on top of it. Now it would be difficult to tell that this had not been another enemy cavalryman. Others would not know the exact body count. They would assume that the warrior had gone elsewhere, perhaps even stealing the wagon and slave girl.

Stone mounted the horse and took the reins. The girl and her lover got on the wagon, as they had been before. They started off. It was now dusk. They would have to ride through the night, but Stone knew the way, even in the dark.

Stone spied another wagon, with its accompanying horseman. He barked a command, and the empty wagon drew to the side to let the loaded one pass. The other Wu-Sun warrior saluted him and rode on. Stone breathed again. They resumed their motion, and soon left the established trail, heading for Hsiung-Nu territory.

Stone had a strong feeling of déjà vu, as if he had done something like this before, though he was sure he hadn't. He had never been in an actual battle, and never brought home slaves to free. Yet, somehow, it was as if he had.

That reminded him of what he had to do. He turned to the couple. "You are no longer slaves, as of this moment," he told them. "I will take you to my clan, where you may live as free people if you wish, learning our ways, or you may go elsewhere. My family will help you as much as you need. I know my wife will, because she remembers. You will be safe from molestation. You have given me my life; we shall give you yours. Is this fair?"

"Yes," the girl said, and smiled. They rode on through the night, satisfied.

The Hsiung-Nu had once had an extensive steppe empire, but the determined actions of the Chinese generals of the Han Empire fragmented them into factions and set them to warring against each other. They were of diverse racial stock, Mongolian, Turkish and Iranian. Some of the western clans may have merged with other steppe fragments to form a new people, called the Huns, who lived in the region of Lake Balkhash and west, still menacing the Silk Road. They were at this stage unknown to the inhabitants of Europe, but this was to change.

Later the expanding empire of the Eastern Goths—Ostrogoths, originally from the Scandinavian region—encroached on the territory of the Huns, provoking them into conquest. The Huns destroyed Goth power and drove many other tribes before them. These tribes entered the Roman Empire, and were responsible for breaking it apart. The Huns themselves invaded Europe. They were in the end repulsed, but the Roman Empire never recovered its former power, and Europe was set on a course which became recognizably modern.

Thus it may be said that the civilized Etruscans led Rome into empire, and the uncivilized Huns drove it back into barbarism. History, however, is more complicated than that.

CHAPTER 16

T'ANG

Perhaps China's greatest dynasty was the T'ang (Tang), which originated in A.D. 618. It was founded by Emperor Kao Tsu of the Li family with the capital at Changan (Chang'an or Ch'angan) on the Wei River in north-central China—one of the great cities of history. There were about one million people within its walls, and another million outside them. It was laid out as a perfect rectangle, to reflect the shape of the land of the gods, six miles east–west and five miles north–south. The streets were laid out in perfect parallels, with the central thoroughfare leading from the main entrance on the south, the Vermilion Gates, north to the Imperial City in the center. There were more

327

than one hundred neighborhoods, centers of business, art, religion and residence.

The emperor was called the Son of Heaven, and was regarded as virtually divine. The politics of the Imperial court were, however, somewhat less loftily laid out.

LOTUS Flower stood before the Kan-yeh-ssu convent, daunted. This was a wing of a Buddhist monastery, holy and beautiful, but also formidable for a girl of twelve.

"It will be all right," Ember reassured her. "It is an honor to serve in the Son of Heaven's household, and you will learn much. It is also an excellent business connection—and we do need that."

Lotus knew it. Her mother Crystal was a scribe with a small printing shop, and her father made beautiful print blocks for it, and her grandmother Ember did her best to run the business efficiently. But they were Buddhists of northern lineage, of a minor Shansi clan, in a time when Confucianism and the Four Great Clans were dominant in government. Consequently their once-successful business had dwindled, and if they did not soon find Imperial favor, they would be impoverished. This service of Lotus's represented an avenue to such favor. It was this responsibility, as much as the job itself, that frightened her.

"Oh, Lotus, we wish we did not have to do this!" Ember said, hugging her tightly. "But it will only be for a year, perhaps, and we know you will be well treated. Never forget how we depend on you."

"Never," Lotus agreed, trying to stifle her tears. Then they went on into the convent.

The head nun was gracious. She wore a saffron robe and a cap over her head. "Yes, we expected you," she said. "You must understand, this is highly unusual, but it is the will of the Son of Heaven."

"We understand," Ember said. "My granddaughter is discreet."

"An excellent quality." The nun turned to Lotus. "You are to serve the Lady Wu Zhao, who has been recalled to the palace, though she is presently a nun. She was until two years ago a courtesan of the Son of Heaven, and retired here when he died. You will obey her implicitly, and never speak of her business to others. Do you understand?"

Lotus forced her tongue to operate. "Yes," she said faintly.

"I will take you to meet her. If she finds you acceptable, you will return here to bid parting to your grandmother, then will remain with the Lady."

"Yes," Lotus peeped.

She followed the woman down a hall to a plain chamber. There stood a woman in a saffron robe, with a hood pulled close about her head to shroud her face. Lotus hastily bowed—and lost her balance, almost falling. Horrified, she righted herself. She hadn't even been introduced, and she had already made a mistake!

"Please," the woman said to the nun. "Let me talk to her alone for a moment."

The nun withdrew. The woman approached Lotus. She drew back her hood to reveal finely formed features. "You are Buddhist? Shansi? Of good family?"

Lotus, too choked to speak, nodded her head.

"And you feel shame."

Lotus nodded again.

"I am to appear at the Son of Heaven's court," the woman said. "See my head." She pulled her hood off so that her full head was exposed.

Lotus stared. The woman was completely bald!

Zhao smiled. "It is the style of a Buddhist nun. Did you not know that?"

Lotus struggled, and managed to speak. "Yes, Lady. I just thought—"

"That I would grow my hair back, when I left the nunnery. Certainly I will. But that will take time. Meanwhile, should I appear before the Son of Heaven like this?"

"I—I don't know, Lady."

"Would you like to appear before him so?"

"No!" Lotus said. Then, embarrassed again: "No offense, Lady."

"None at all. Therefore you understand my problem. I would like to have a good wig, to appear in public, until my hair grows back. Do you think you could get one for me?"

"I—my grandmother could, I think."

"But I would prefer not to have this widely known. Do you understand?"

"Yes, Lady."

"Here is money. Get me a wig, without anyone knowing whom it is for." The woman gave her several coins.

Lotus looked at the coins, startled. They were gold. She had never seen so much money at one time. "Yes, Lady," she said. "I—right away?"

Zhao nodded.

Lotus clutched the coins and turned away. In the hall she encountered the head monk. "She rejected you?" he asked, disappointed.

"No, I—I have to see my grandmother about something. Something I forgot." She hurried on down the hall, leaving the monk staring after her.

In the front chamber she found Ember and went quickly to her. "Grandmother, she needs a wig. Can you get it?"

"A wig? Why, I don't know—"

"She gave me this to buy it." Lotus showed her the gold coins. "She—she doesn't want it known."

Ember took the coins. "Wait here, Lotus." She gave her a hug and walked quickly out of the chamber.

Lotus remained where she was, fidgeting. She was afraid that the monk would come and ask her exactly what it was she had forgotten. She thought she shouldn't tell him, but as a Buddhist herself she wasn't sure it was right to hide anything from such a high person. Was she doing right by concealing her mission?

She saw a statue of the Buddha in an alcove. She went to stand before it. She bowed, this time managing not to stumble. She focused on the figure, meditating. *O Enlightened One,* she thought. *Show me the way.*

The statue seemed to blur before her. *Follow the Eightfold Path.*

She focused on that. The Eightfold Path required right view, which she took to mean that she should look at the problem in the right manner. But what was the right manner? All she could think of, in this case, was to trust the preference of the Lady Zhao and do what she wished. That made the other requirements of the Eightfold Path fall into line: Right intention—she really wanted to do the right thing. Right speech—she was saying nothing. Right action—she was getting the wig. Right livelihood—she was taking a special job and thereby maybe helping her family. Right effort—she was trying to do the right thing. Right mindfulness—oh, she hoped that was what this was. And right concentration—what she was doing now.

You are a child, the Buddha's thought came. *You have much to learn. But*

follow the Middle Path, avoid extremes, and you will in time find enlighten-
ment.

"Oh, I will, I will!" she breathed. "I'll try as hard as I can!"

She bowed again. The statue returned to clear focus, and she knew the interview was over. But now she had confidence that she was doing the right thing.

She turned to face the center of the chamber. The monk stood there. He was as forbidding as before, but now her fear of him was muted. Buddha was with her.

Then her grandmother returned. Lotus realized that more time had passed than she had realized. Her communion with the Buddha had seemed brief, but could have been extended. Time did not have the same meaning to the Buddha.

Ember gave her a package and two coins. Then she hugged Lotus again. "I will try to see you at the court, or your mother will," she murmured. "I know you will do well, my child." Yet her reassurance was belied by the tiny twitch in her cheek, which appeared when she was under tension.

Lotus stifled her tears again, then went bravely back down the hall to the Lady's chamber. She knew it would be some time before she saw her grandmother again, and longer before she saw the rest of her family. But it seemed that it was going to be all right.

The Lady Zhao seemed not to have moved in the interim. Lotus went up to her and proffered the package. "Here—my grandmother got it. And here—she did not need the other two coins." She opened her hand to proffer them too.

Zhao accepted the package and coins. "Your grandmother is an honest woman," she remarked.

"Oh, yes, Lady!" Lotus agreed enthusiastically. "And my mother, too. She is a scribe."

"But I think not a wealthy one."

"Business has not been good," Lotus agreed.

"There are those who would have kept the coins."

"My family never cheated anyone!" Lotus said hotly. Then, realizing that she had spoken intemperately, she blushed. The Lady only smiled.

Zhao opened the package. Inside was a fine dark wig with remarkably natural-looking hair. Zhao stood before the mirror and put the wig on her bald head, adjusting it. "Yes, this will do," she agreed. "Your grandmother has excellent taste."

She turned, and Lotus saw her full face, framed by the locks of the wig, and two braids trailing down her back. "Oh, you are beautiful!" Lotus exclaimed.

"Thanks to you—and your grandmother," Zhao said. Then she removed the wig, becoming bald again. "Wrap this and carry it for me."

"You aren't going to wear it?" Lotus asked, surprised.

"It would not be expedient to wear it here," Zhao said. "But when we depart these premises, I will don it, knowing its quality."

"Oh." Lotus set about wrapping the wig, making sure not to damage any of its fine hair.

"Tell me of you and your family," Zhao said.

"We aren't special. I'm Lotus Flower—"

"Ah, you are of the T'ien-t'ai persuasion of Buddhism, then."

"Yes, Lady. How did you know?"

"I am long familiar with the Lotus Sutra. There is hidden meaning in the texts that can be understood only by subjective interpretation and meditation. How could I fail to recognize a child of the Lotus?"

"Oh. Yes, of course," Lotus agreed, embarrassed to have forgotten this aspect of her name. "And my mother is Crystal, and my father is Carver, and my grandmother who brought me here is the widow Ember. We have a printing shop, and my father carves the letters and the pictures for the print blocks."

"So your mother is literate. Can you read too?"

"Some," Lotus agreed shyly. "But there are so many symbols."

"Each with its own meaning," Zhao agreed. "Just as each person has her own meaning."

"She does?"

Zhao laughed. "Are you not an individual, little Lotus? Different from any other girl?"

"Oh. Yes. I'm myself. But I'm no one."

"Can you keep a secret, Lotus?"

"I didn't tell anyone about the wig—except my grandmother," Lotus said quickly. "And I know she didn't, either."

"I mean a secret of past experience. You are ten?"

"Twelve," Lotus said. "I am small for my age, and—and not yet a woman."

"Old enough to have discretion, I think. I will tell you my secret. When I first came to the Imperial palace as the Son of Heaven's concubine, I was not a lot older than you. Barely fourteen. My cousin was a favorite, and she got me in. I was very shy, like you."

"You were a—a what?" Lotus asked, thinking she had misheard.

"A woman for the Son of Heaven's bed," Zhao said. "Did they not tell you about that?"

"They said you were a Lady of the court."

Zhao smiled. "A courtesan. I see your confusion. Such ladies of the court serve the sexual will of the master. But here is one secret: there were many other concubines, and I was young and inexperienced and beneath notice. The Son of Heaven never used me—not in nine years, until he died."

"Never? Then why did he keep you there?"

"The Son of Heaven must never lack for company. Had he had a whim, he might have taken me. I had to be ready, along with all the others, just in case. That is the way of the typical concubine."

"It must have been dull."

"Yes, at times. Extremely. But I was well cared for, and I learned the secrets of beauty and performance from the others, and perhaps the prince liked me."

"The prince?"

"The Prince of Jin, the Son of Heaven's third son. He was three years younger than I. Younger than you, when I first saw him. Now he is the Son of Heaven Kao Tsung. He has recalled me to court."

"Oh, then he did like you!" Lotus agreed. "That's nice."

"Very nice. Now I am to be his concubine. And you will be my companion, helping me make my way at court."

"Oh, I don't know anything about the court," Lotus protested. "I've never even been to the palace."

Zhao smiled. "That is I think one reason I can trust you. You were not brought up in the ways of court intrigue. You are a simple Buddhist girl, straightforward and innocent."

"Yes," Lotus agreed.

"But you will learn. I want you to listen always, but speak only to me of what you hear. Especially if it should concern me."

"People will talk of you?"

"Very likely," Zhao said, with an obscure expression.

"Well, I should be able to do that. I like you."

Zhao smiled. "And I like you, little Lotus. I think we shall be friends."

"But I'm only a common girl," Lotus protested.

"So was I, once. Come, let us contemplate Buddha while we wait for the carriage."

"The carriage?"

"To take us to the palace. Have no fear, Lotus, you will ride with me, and you will live with me at the palace. You will answer to no one else."

"That's nice." Lotus didn't mind doing things, but didn't want to be confused about to whom she should answer.

They contemplated Buddha together, facing the little bronze statue on a shelf on the wall. Lotus was glad the Lady Zhao was a Buddhist; it made it ever so much easier. But of course that was no coincidence; the Lady had asked for a Buddhist child. She wanted someone she could trust.

The monk appeared. "The Imperial carriage is here."

Zhao gathered her cloak and hood about her. She approached the monk. She kissed him on the mouth. Then she moved on, leaving him standing much like a statue. Lotus followed, carrying the package. She realized that she had just seen something she should keep secret. So she pretended not to notice.

Outside, the carriage was waiting. It had four large wheels and an arching canopy. Zhao swept up to it, and the driver drew open the canopy for her. She mounted the set of steps before it, and Lotus started to follow.

"You walk behind!" the driver snapped at Lotus, making her jump.

Zhao paused. Her head turned to orient on the man, her eyes seeming almost to glow within her hood. He stepped back as if struck, though she had spoken no word. Then she moved her fingers, signaling Lotus forward, and Lotus climbed the steps to join her.

They got into the carriage, where there was a padded bench, and sat beside each other. The canopy aperture fell closed. They were isolated within the silken enclosure. "You will separate from me only when *I* tell you to," Zhao murmured. "Ignore all others."

"Yes, Lady," Lotus breathed, gratified.

The carriage started, its wheels crunching over the pavement. Lotus found the motion pleasant. She had seldom ridden in any wagon, and never in anything as fancy as this.

Zhao held out her hand. Lotus put the package in it. Zhao opened it and carefully donned the wig. "I have no mirror here. You must be the judge: is it satisfactory?"

"It's a little to the side," Lotus said.

Zhao adjusted it until it was right. Now she was beautiful again.

"But won't they know, at the palace?" Lotus asked. "I mean, because all monks and nuns are shaved?"

"They will know, but also know why I use it. I am no longer a nun. This is the symbol of my liberation."

"If I may ask—why did you go to the nunnery, Lady?"

"When the Son of Heaven died, his entourage of wives and concubines was disbanded. Some went home to their families. Some died. I was in an awkward position, because the prince liked me."

"But wasn't it good for him to like you?"

"Not when I was pledged to his father. So there were those who thought perhaps I, too, would be better off dead, so as to provide the prince no distraction as he married and set up his household. So I thought it expedient to retreat to a place where I would be no threat to anyone, and I went into seclusion and entered training to be a nun."

"I thought no monk or nun ever returned to ordinary life," Lotus said.

"They seldom do," Zhao agreed. "But exceptions are made, especially by the will of the court."

"The Son of Heaven must like you a lot, to summon you back."

"Not exactly. I am sure he does not object, but it was the Empress Wang who summoned me."

"The empress! His wife? *She* wants you to—to—?"

Zhao laughed. "Lotus, we of the north are generally monogamous, and rightly so, unlike those tasteless creatures of the south. But the court is its own custom. The empress can hardly be expected to constantly attend her husband in bed, in the manner of an ordinary wife. How could she get her rest, and how would she keep him from becoming bored? Especially when she gets with child? So the Son of Heaven maintains a staff of concubines, perhaps one for each day of the month, to satisfy his every whim. I will be one among many, as I was before."

"Oh, so he won't actually use you."

The Lady made her obscure smile. "I wouldn't say that. The empress wishes him to use me, so as to distract him from another courtesan who may be gaining too much influence. She remembers that he did like me, and hopes that he will like me again, and lose interest in the other woman."

Lotus had trouble working this out. "There is a concubine for every day of the month, and each is lovely and talented and eager to share his bed, but he doesn't notice them, yet you who were ignored before must distract him from his favorite?"

"That is the case, Lotus. Do you think I can manage it?"

"Lady, forgive me if I affront you, but if he knows you are bald—"

"A challenge indeed," Zhao agreed. "Yet I shall try my best to please the empress in this respect, to vindicate her judgment."

"Lady, I am afraid for you!"

Zhao met her anxious gaze. "May I share another secret with you?"

Lotus was nonplussed. "It is not for me to give you permission for anything, Lady!"

"Oh, but perhaps it is, if we are friends. There is no difference of status between friends."

"There isn't?"

"When we are alone, we are friends," Zhao said firmly. "When we are among others, we are not. That is one secret."

"It is?" Lotus feared she was being mocked.

"And the other secret is that I, too, am afraid for me. If I should fail the empress, after she has gone to the trouble to pry me from the nunnery, my head might alleviate her embarrassment."

"You must succeed!" Lotus exclaimed, freshly alarmed.

"The Buddha willing, perhaps I will."

They rode the rest of the way in silence. Lotus's mind was in turmoil. The Son of Heaven's wife herself had summoned a Buddhist nun to the court to distract her husband from another concubine. What a strange business!

The carriage stopped moving. They had arrived at the Imperial City. In a moment the driver came around to draw open the canopy. Zhao stood and stepped out, and Lotus followed closely.

They were before the main palace, a huge elegant building built of precious wood, with many upcurving roofs, overhanging balconies, and bright red support posts. It was so impressive that Lotus simply stared, her mouth slack.

Zhao gently touched Lotus's chin, lifting it up to close her mouth. "It is impressive," she agreed. "But we will not live here. This is only for my rendezvous with the empress."

They walked up the massive central staircase. It seemed to take forever, because of the scale of the building. Lotus had never expected to come this close to the palace, let alone enter it.

At the top of the steps they turned to the side and followed a walkway to a smaller building that was part of the palace complex. Here a truly regal woman awaited them: surely the empress!

"No, only a matron," Zhao murmured, anticipating her thought. "The Empress Wang would not sully her hands on such business directly."

So it was. The woman outfitted them both with far more decorative gowns, so that Lotus looked like the daughter of a king and Zhao looked like a queen. Indeed, Zhao's splendid figure now manifested in a way it had not within the nun's cloak, and Lotus began to understand how she could hope to win the favor of the Son of Heaven away from another woman. She was the most beautiful woman Lotus had ever seen.

Zhao smiled, and achieved the impossible: yet more loveliness. "I was going to ask your opinion, Lotus, but I think you have already given it."

"Oh, yes, Lady!" Lotus breathed. "In all the world, there can not be a woman more splendid than you!"

Zhao's mouth quirked. "Thanks to your wig, perhaps."

"Oh, no, Lady! Your face, your body—" She broke off, realizing she was being teased.

They proceeded to the residence of the concubines. This was a series of separate chambers, with a concourse leading to a larger common room. The surrounding grounds were parklike, a delight to see, with decorative fruit and nut trees and shaped shrubs. It was a considerable contrast to the crowded and often dirty alleys of the city where Lotus had lived. Elegant young women walked through these grounds, conversing with each other or congregating at tables for games. Each seemed lovelier than all the others, but none as lovely as the Lady Zhao.

A servant guided them to one chamber among many. There was a nice bed for Zhao, and a corner with cushions for Lotus to sleep. "This is our room," Zhao said. "Now that we have taken possession, no other person may enter without my permission. Should you be annoyed by someone elsewhere, come here and she will not follow. In my absence, only you have access, and only you will have authority to allow entrance by any other, even if she be a Lady."

That was comforting. Lotus tested the pillows and found them soft. There were silken sheets folded on a table, and a basin and water pitcher. Zhao saw her glance, and explained. "The basin is for you; I will be bathed by the servants in the main bath. In fact you will attend me there, but you will not bathe there. This is protocol."

"Of course," Lotus agreed, relieved. The last thing she wanted to do was show her naked body in public, because it was as yet almost undeveloped. The Lady Zhao would naturally be proud to show her perfect body.

"Under the bed you will find a covered pot," Zhao said. "This is for you also. We shall pretend that I have no natural functions, so when I use it you will take it out to the refuse dump as yours."

"Yes, Lady," Lotus agreed. "But don't folk know that ladies also—?"

"Common women have urine and feces. Royal women are above that sort of thing—especially in the presence of royal men." She winked. "A Son of Heaven's concubine has only two orifices: her mouth to be kissed, and her vagina to be penetrated. All else is completely pristine."

Lotus nodded. Appearance was all-important here. It was her job to maintain the Lady's appearance in whatever way was required.

"I must show you around, but we shall pretend that you are merely attending me as I take my air."

"But a servant could show me where things are," Lotus protested. "You don't need to take the trouble."

Zhao smiled. "There are nuances of protocol. By showing myself with you, I identify you clearly as mine, discouraging any others from interfering with you. Also, sometimes the servants play jokes."

"Jokes?"

Zhao smiled reminiscently. "When I first came here, largely innocent of the ways of the court, I let a servant show my helper-girl around. The servant showed her the empress's private lavatory as the place to dump her pot."

"Oh!" Lotus covered her face with a hand, feeling the embarrassment of such a miscue.

"Fortunately the empress was experienced and tolerant. She posed as an elder servant and explained to the girl that this was a confusion, and showed her the correct place. It wasn't until a month later that the girl saw the empress at a public function and recognized her for what she was. Then she fainted."

"So would I," Lotus said sincerely.

"But the new empress is much younger, and her humor is slight. Such a miscue could cost a girl her head."

"Oh!" Lotus repeated, horrified in another way.

"Have no fear. I will see that nothing untoward happens to you. I have the fortune of having been here before, and of learning the ways."

"Oh, I'm glad!" Lotus breathed.

Zhao took a walk around the premises, remarking on the small changes which had occurred in the two years of her absence, and greeting several servants by name. She ignored the other concubines.

"But aren't any of them friends of yours?" Lotus asked.

"None. All the concubines are new."

"Then why are you—I mean—" Lotus faltered, realizing that she could be treading on forbidden territory.

"It is highly unusual. But the empress believes that an experienced woman is required to do the job she desires, one who knows the ways of things. And the Son of Heaven did like me. When the ordinary does not suffice, the extraordinary must be tried."

By the time they returned to their room, Lotus knew the locations of the dining chamber, lavatory, bathing pool, kitchen, maintenance servants' quarters, and storage rooms. She would have no trouble finding her way.

"Soon it will be time for the evening meal," Zhao said. "I will eat at the main table, while you will eat at the servants' table to the side. You will watch, and if you see me lift my hand to you, you will come to me immediately. Beware lest others try to distract you so that you miss my signal. I would be obliged to punish you, lest I seem unduly soft-hearted."

"I will watch constantly!"

"No, Lotus. You must watch elsewhere, not seeming to orient on me. But frequently your errant gaze will pass my way, and I will time my signal so that you can catch it without seeming to. Then, after just enough of a pause so that it seems you have missed it, you will rise, turn, and come to me as if it is your own decision."

"I—but why, Lady? I am your servant." ·

"Have you ever seen a cavalryman on his horse?"

"Yes, sometimes, when they pass on the street."

"Have you seen him stop or turn or change pace?"

"Yes."

"Have you seen or heard any signal between the man and his horse?"

Lotus paused, surprised. "No, Lady. It was as man and horse were one."

"Yet it was the man making the decisions, and the horse obeying them."

"Yes. I wonder how that happens?"

"The knees. The shift of weight. The horse feels the signals." Zhao met Lotus's gaze. "Even so must be the signals between us. Others will know that you obey my signals, but will seldom see the communication between us. That is a mark of sophistication. Similarly, if there should be something you need to do or to tell me, you will signal me, thus." The woman made a tiny gesture with one hand, by her hip. "By that token I will know, and will respond."

"But it is not for me to—"

"If the man signals the horse to gallop forward, but the horse sees a deep pit in the road that would cause him to stumble and perhaps fall, hurting his master, what does the horse do?"

Lotus had to think about that. "Balk, perhaps. He has no way to tell his master."

"But you are not a horse. You can understand things, and communicate them. It may be that you will know something that I should be warned about. But it is not your place to speak out of turn. Then you must signal me, so that I can cause you to speak in turn."

"Yes, Lady," Lotus agreed uncertainly.

"Let us rehearse it. Assume that you know that the Son of Heaven is walking behind me. I am talking with another person and do not see him." Zhao faced the wall and gestured as if addressing another Lady.

Lotus looked at the shrouded entrance panel as if seeing someone, then formed her hand into the key signal. But Zhao didn't see her. Lotus started to reach out to touch the woman's hand, but realized that that wouldn't do. So she managed to nudge around until she stood before Zhao, and repeated her signal. Zhao glanced at her, made another gesture as if addressing the other person, then turned as if coincidentally. And immediately went into a full, graceful obeisance. She had spied the Son of Heaven.

"But I never got to tell you!" Lotus protested.

"Your signal was enough. I knew you would not work so hard to get my attention if it wasn't important."

"Yes," Lotus agreed, relieved, though it had all been make-believe.

"Now you will use the pot and empty it," Zhao said.

"Oh, I don't need to—" Then she caught on. She scrambled to fetch the pot from under the bed and set it up for the Lady to use. In due course she took it to the dumping site and emptied it, and rinsed it with water so it wouldn't smell. She returned, and Zhao smiled approvingly.

Then they went to the meal. Lotus accompanied Zhao to her place at the main table and saw that she was appropriately seated, then went to the servants' table. There was a big tub of boiled rice, and some vegetables. Lotus took a bowl and put rice in it, then found a place to sit. She brought out her chopsticks.

"You must be new," a girl about her own age said.

"Yes," Lotus confessed shyly.

"New servants sit over there." The girl pointed.

Lotus looked in that direction. There was another table, with no one sitting at it. "Oh—I didn't know." She picked up her bowl and walked to the other table.

Then she remembered to look around. It was well she did so, for just then Zhao signaled. True to her instructions, she took no obvious note, instead continuing to the table, where she set down her bowl. Then she turned and walked to the main table.

"I am not sure the seasoning is right," Zhao said, holding up her own bowl of much fancier rice. "Taste it for me, Lotus."

Lotus dutifully dug a small bit out with her chopsticks and brought it to her mouth. It was the best rice she had ever tasted. But as she was about to say so, she saw Zhao's tiny motion of the head: No.

"I—I think not," Lotus said, hoping this was the proper response. What was the Lady up to?

"Are you sure? Try a larger portion."

Lotus took a larger portion. She savored it. But again there was that trace shake of Zhao's head: No. "This is not right for you, Lady," Lotus lied obediently. "It is too strong."

"I suspected as much. You take it. I will take a better one."

"But, Lady, I already took a bowl for—" But that trace No stopped her. "I mean, may I fetch you a new bowl, Lady?"

"No, I will have one brought directly from the kitchen," Zhao said. "You return to sit with the others, not by yourself. Leave the other bowl."

Lotus went back to her first table with her new bowl of rice. She realized that Zhao had done her the favor of giving her a much nicer meal than she would otherwise have had. But why had the Lady made her return to the wrong table?

"Hey, you aren't supposed to be here," the other girl said as Lotus sat down.

"I answer only to my mistress," Lotus said with a firmness she hardly felt. She began eating the fabulous rice.

The other girl shrugged, making no further protest.

Before Lotus finished the bowl, keeping an eye out for any further signals from Zhao, she saw several other women enter the dining hall. They were concubines, by their elaborate dress. They sat at the table where Lotus had been sent. Suddenly she understood: it had been a joke! She had been sent to one of the tables reserved for the ladies. Her bowl still sat there, a reminder of her possible breach of etiquette. Zhao, alert for her welfare, had saved her from that hideous embarrassment.

One of the concubines, seeing the bowl, evidently took it for a sample. She tried a mouthful of its rice—and in a moment was coughing and running to another table for water.

Lotus, momentarily baffled, suddenly realized what had happened: the other girl must have dumped some hot sauce into the rice. So that not only would Lotus sit at the wrong table, she would call immediate attention to herself by choking on the first mouthful. What spiteful mischief!

But she gave no indication that she knew. She merely made careful note of the other girl's appearance, so as to recognize her henceforth. Perhaps there would come a time for a return of the favor.

Later, back in their chamber, Lotus ventured an unsolicited comment. "Thank you, Lady, for saving me from humiliation."

"Ah, you realized." Zhao smiled. "Sometime you may save me from similar."

"I hope so, Lady."

"Go to the kitchen and fetch me a tasty pastry."

"But you've just eaten!" Then Lotus caught herself. "Yes, Lady." She went out along the halls to the kitchen. "My Lady Wu Zhao wishes a sweet pastry," she told the matron who intercepted her there.

"Ah, she's up to her old tricks," the matron said, fetching a pastry and wrapping it.

"Tricks?"

"That woman may be the smartest concubine ever to inhabit this palace. She knows every little device. Such as eating only sparingly in public, so as to appear to need little or no sustenance. As if she is some ethereal creature. So she must take the rest of her food in private."

"Oh." Lotus had never thought of that.

"After this, don't announce it. Just come here, and I will recognize you and give you what you need."

"Thank you." Lotus took the package and left. She was learning things at a great rate.

Zhao smiled when Lotus told her of the encounter. "Yes, I know her of old. You can trust her. But be wary of others."

"I learned that today," Lotus said, thinking of the episode at the dining hall.

"Yes. But you responded well. Every day will be easier, as you master the nuances of distrust."

They settled down to sleep. Lotus's mind was awhirl with the new experiences, but she concluded that on the whole she liked her new situation. Certainly she liked her mistress, Wu Zhao.

Next day Zhao began introducing herself to other concubines, in seemingly casual fashion. Many of them were accompanied by their servant girls, who remained always close but behind and quiet. The Lady always wore the wig in public, but was quite free about admitting that her hair was not her own and that she had come from a nunnery.

One concubine was especially pretty, and very polite. Her name was Hsiao Liang-ti, informally known as Liang. But Lotus was startled when she saw the woman's servant. It was the girl who had tried to embarrass Lotus at the dining hall!

Her hand twitched, making the signal. Then she realized that this was hardly relevant to Zhao's interests, and straightened her fingers. Fortunately Zhao hadn't seen it.

But moments later, when they were alone, Zhao inquired. "What was it?"

"I—think nothing. I didn't mean to signal."

"Let me judge."

"Well, that woman—her servant is the one who sent me to the wrong table and put hot sauce in my rice."

"The Lady Liang's girl?"

"Yes. But that shouldn't concern you, Lady."

"Oh, I think it should, Lotus. Liang is the Son of Heaven's current favorite."

"Oh! The one you are supposed to displace?"

"The same. So I think it was not coincidence that her girl was there to tease you. Your embarrassment would have been my embarrassment, for having a seemingly stupid or clumsy girl. Liang knows I am a threat to her."

"I never thought of that. I thought it was just because I'm new."

"This is not as innocent a realm as it may seem. I will of course continue to be polite to Liang, as she is to me. You must be similarly polite to her girl. But never trust either of them."

"I never will!" Lotus agreed with such fervor that the Lady smiled. Some lessons had more impact than others.

Two days later a eunuch came with the news that Zhao had been summoned to the Son of Heaven's bed for the night. Zhao masked her joy at this assignment and assumed a cool demeanor. Lotus accompanied her to the Imperial palace, perhaps the most splendid structure in the city. Zhao was dressed in a fine silk gown with gold stitching and a décolletage that showed so much of her breasts that it would have been dangerous for her to breathe, let alone lean forward. Only her hair was not fancy, being the same wig.

An armed guard waited at the edge of the concubine complex. Without a word he set forth, leading the way. Others in the vicinity feigned indifference; the Son of Heaven's business was not their business.

They entered the grand palace, passing many guards and servants within it. It was apparent that the Son of Heaven was well protected, and that the various personnel knew exactly what was going on. Should an unauthorized person attempt to intrude, he would not get far at all.

Lotus had thought there would be some formal meeting place, where she would be quickly sent back to the room in the concubine quarter. Instead they were brought directly to the Imperial bedroom. There stood a handsome young man in an informal robe.

The moment he saw Zhao he strode toward her, opening his arms. She swept into his embrace. It was as if they had been lovers for years. So ardently did he kiss her that her wig was dislodged, falling askew on her bald head. When he saw that he laughed. "The nunnery!" he exclaimed. "I almost forgot! Oh, Zhao, it is good to have you back."

"You know I always loved you, but could not speak," Zhao replied.

"How well I know! But now you are mine."

"I am yours," she agreed. "But if I may—I must have my girl take my wig, before it gets in the way."

"Your girl?"

"Lotus. She is the daughter of Crystal, a scribe who has done occasional commissions for the court. They do some very nice printing. Lotus has been a fine companion and help to me. She got me this fine wig."

"Oh. Of course."

Zhao removed her tilted wig and gave it to Lotus. "Go to the outer chamber and wait there," she said. "A servant will attend you."

Lotus nodded, awed by the presence of the Son of Heaven, and backed out of the bedroom. As the curtain fell closed she saw the two embracing again, most passionately. The Son of Heaven certainly did like Zhao!

The servant was an older man. "Sit down, girl," he said. "Have you eaten?"

"Yes." Lotus looked around nervously. "She told me to—to wait here."

"That's right. She will be with him the night. You may lie on those cushions and sleep, if you wish."

"I—yes. But not yet." She did not want to say that it bothered her to be alone with a strange man.

"Be at ease, girl," he said as if reading her mind. "I am not a man. I'm a eunuch. I will not molest you."

She stared at him, astonished. She did not know what to say. But she had to say something. "I don't know exactly what to do."

"Then sit at the table here and play me a game of go."

"Go?"

"Don't you know the royal game of enclosing?"

"I—I have heard of it, but never played it."

"Then it is time to learn. Do not be afraid of me, girl. I serve the Son of Heaven. I would cut off your head if he told me to, but that is not his business tonight. I am here to see that no one intrudes, and at midnight I will be relieved by another with the same mission. I am bored, and go is the game to distract one's mind. Let us make our introductions: I am Old Coal."

"I am young Lotus," she said, smiling.

"Here is the game," he said. "Here is a place for you."

Lotus joined him at the table, sitting on a cushion to get enough height. There was the go board, a grid of nineteen lines square. Beside it were two bowls of pebbles, white and black. "The game is best learned by playing," the man said. "Take a black stone and set it at any intersection on the board."

Lotus took a black stone and set it in the closest corner.

"Now observe: your stone has two freedoms. Two directions in which you might build. I will remove one of them." He set a white stone next to it. "Now if you do not protect yourself, I will remove your other freedom, kill your stone, and take it from the board, and you will have nothing."

Lotus considered, and put her next black stone on the place of her second freedom. "Ah, now you flee," he said. "I must work harder to enclose you, for a chain must be captured as a unit." He put another white stone beside his first, starting a chain beside hers. "But if you make a mistake, I will still get you."

"But what about all the rest of the board?" Lotus asked.

"It is there to be played on. It is not the stones that count, in the end, but the amount of territory you control. If I kill your first two stones, I control a territory of two points. That is not enough to win."

Lotus was getting the idea of it. She shifted to the center of the board, where she had more freedoms, and the battle took shape. She soon lost the game, but remained fascinated, and started another, playing with greater savvy. "Ah, you learn quickly," the man said, concentrating.

While they played, they chatted. Lotus told about her family's printing business, and the man told of his family's farm to the north. He also said something about Zhao.

"There is a story about her. Perhaps it is not true. Certainly I would not credit it."

Lotus pretended nonchalance. "What is it?"

"She was a concubine for the Son of Heaven T'ai Tsung, the father of Kao Tsung who is now the master of all, but she was not in much demand at the time. Yet it is said she did not retire a virgin."

"She didn't?"

"Mind you, this may be fanciful, and I would not impugn the good name of my master the Son of Heaven for anything."

"Naturally not," Lotus agreed, catching on to the way of such narrations. "Nor would I impugn my mistress, Wu Zhao. But I like to know what is said of her."

"I merely mention what some unkind person bruited about. It is that some call her the Fox Woman."

"The Fox Woman? She does not resemble a fox to me."

"This is a story of China's illustrious past. The Fox Woman of folklore is one who assumes human form and preys upon unsuspecting men by stealing their vitality and leaving them in sexual exhaustion. For some reason such men never seem to protest such treatment."

Lotus had gathered enough of the passions of men to appreciate why. Their appetite for sex was almost insatiable. Thus a woman with an even greater appetite would be in rare demand. "There was such a creature in China's past?"

"During the Han dynasty there was one who came to be known as a fox woman. She was Wei Tzu-fu. It is said that she was a servant who waited on the Son of Heaven while he changed his dress. That is to say, while he did what all men and most women must do every so often, that no other can do for them. In that state of dishabille he observed the form of her body, and was so smitten that he stood up straight, as it were, and 'favored her' on the spot. She became a concubine and later displaced the empress herself."

"But that was in the Han dynasty," Lotus protested. "What does that have to do with Lady Zhao? Did she seduce the Son of Heaven?"

"Not the Son of Heaven. The Son of Heaven's young son. He was only twelve at the time, but eager to know the ways of the flesh, yet hesitant to approach a woman. It is said that the Lady Zhao happened to be in the vicinity when he changed his dress, and perceiving the standing sign of his dawning manhood, arranged to acquaint him with that which he most wished to know. She was then fifteen, and as lovely as a new temple, and perhaps somewhat miffed that the Son of Heaven took no notice of her. It is said that the lad was most grateful, and thereafter eagerly sought more instruction of that nature.''

"Of course it is only a story," Lotus said, intrigued. "Yet they do seem to be well acquainted, considering their recent separation."

"Yes. That is surely coincidence." His tone suggested that it was no coincidence at all.

They continued playing the game, conversing about other things. Lotus was enjoying herself greatly.

Another man entered the chamber. "It is midnight; my relief has arrived," Old Coal said.

"Already?" Lotus asked, surprised. "The game is not finished."

Both men laughed. "There speaks a true go player," the first said. "She plays for hours and doesn't notice."

Lotus realized that it was true. The time had passed unnoticed while she was taken by the game, and it was long past her bedtime. Go was a great discovery.

The replacement finished the game. Lotus lost again, but by a lesser amount. Then, reluctantly, she went to the cushions and retired for the night.

She dreamed of go, of enclosing and being enclosed. Black stones warred with white stones, constantly.

"Wake, girl," the man said. "They are stirring."

Lotus scrambled up, logy from insufficient sleep, realizing that the rest of the night had passed. She had to be ready to serve her mistress.

Soon Zhao emerged, looking radiantly fulfilled. Lotus approached with the wig. The woman donned it, then moved on out of the chamber. Lotus followed.

Back at the private chamber, as Zhao let her pretense expire and her fatigue began to show, Lotus broached the awkward matter of the story of the Fox Woman. "You asked me to listen, and to tell you what is said of you, but I fear you will not like it, Lady."

"The Fox Woman!" Zhao said, laughing. "How apt!"

"Apt?"

"That was just about the way it happened. But it had to be secret, of course, for I was pledged to his disinterested father. What we did would have been called incest. I did like him, though he was three years my junior, and we passed many happy hours together. He certainly was virile, for his age." She stretched languorously. "Still is."

"That was why he liked you?" Lotus was amazed by this admission. She had feared that Zhao would be furious with the story.

"That was why. At one time he was quite smitten with me. But we knew it couldn't last, and when his father died and the girls were sent away, I had to retire to the nunnery. Mind you, I am a sincere Buddhist, but I would have preferred to remain with Kao, had I had a choice. I thought he had set me aside when he assumed the burden of being Son of Heaven. But then he visited me at the nunnery, and I knew he had not forgotten."

"He visited you there?" Lotus wondered if she was being teased.

"Yes. And the empress learned of it, and realized that I might represent the tool she needed to pry his interest from Liang. I think she was right."

So it seemed. It was evident that even with her head bald, the Lady Zhao had captivated the Son of Heaven.

They went to the morning meal. Many heads turned when they entered the dining chamber. Liang's head did not turn; she faced sullenly ahead, knowing who had displaced her the past night.

Lotus got her meal, and sought the table where Liang's girl sat. "I think my mistress got something yours did not, last night," she remarked innocently, and was gratified by the other's glare of wrath.

After breakfast Zhao and Lotus retired to their room, where both slept much of the day. It didn't matter that others would know why they had lost sleep; in fact it was a matter of pride. A concubine who returned from the Son of Heaven's bed well rested obviously hadn't interested him much.

After that Zhao joined the Son of Heaven more often than not, and sometimes by day as well as by night. Once the Son of Heaven was playing a game of go with a noble, and it was Zhao who sat by his side for all to see. She was certainly accomplishing the empress's mission. On this day there was a royal dog, whom Zhao held for awhile, then passed over to Lotus to hold. He was a frisky animal, eager to make the acquaintance of everyone, and she had to clasp his collar quite tightly to be sure that he did not stray.

But she did get to look at the go board. Soon she saw that the Son of Heaven's position was not good. The other player was making canny moves and gaining territory. The Son of Heaven seemed likely to lose, but of course could not complain, for it was a fair game and he had to demonstrate good sportsmanship. There was probably a considerable wager riding on the outcome, for the wealthy and powerful liked to make things interesting.

Then Lotus caught Zhao's signal. But what did it mean? She didn't know what to do.

Zhao's eyes moved to the dog. She made the signal again. Was Lotus doing something wrong? But she was holding the animal tightly.

Then she understood. She hoped. She let go of the dog's collar. "Oh!" she cried in simulated dismay. "He got away!"

Indeed, the dog rejoiced in his freedom. He bounded forward— right up onto the go board itself, scattering the stones. He licked the Son of Heaven's face, then jumped playfully away. Several servants chased after him.

The game had been ruined. Zhao jumped up. "Oh, you bad girl!" she exclaimed to Lotus. "You were supposed to hold that dog tight!"

But the Son of Heaven restrained her. "It was an accident," he said. "The dog is strong. The child did the best she could. It behooves us to be generous. We shall play again tomorrow." He looked straight at Lotus for a moment, and his mouth quirked. Then he got up and walked away, and Zhao walked with him. Lotus followed, her eyes downcast.

For a moment there were no other courtiers near. "Your girl is responsive," the Son of Heaven remarked to Zhao.

"I am sure I don't know what you mean, O Illustrious One," Zhao murmured.

The Son of Heaven understood perfectly—and kept the secret. As would Zhao and Lotus. It must never be known that the mishap that had saved him from the embarrassment of a loss had been no accident.

Next day Crystal came to the palace. The Lady Zhao brought Lotus to see her. Lotus flew into her mother's embrace. "I'm so glad you could visit me!" she exclaimed.

"But I didn't come to visit you," Crystal said, surprised. "Your father was summoned here to receive a commission for a printing job. An excellent one. It seems we are in favor now. I merely accompanied him to the palace, where I was told someone wished to see me separately."

Then Lotus understood. It was the favor of the Son of Heaven, coming as swiftly and effectively as his disfavor. Zhao had arranged it, of course.

But all was not perfect. Resentment grew as it became apparent that the Lady Zhao was now the Son of Heaven's favorite concubine. Lotus was snubbed by a number of the other girls. The court was a cauldron of ambition and scheming for favor, and whoever was successful was the target of much jealousy.

One evening as Lotus went to the kitchen for a pastry for Zhao, she was intercepted by a kitchen hand. "So," he said, catching hold of her arm. "Someone sneaking in to steal food, eh? Well, we'll just put you in the pot and cook you for tomorrow's dinner."

"I'm coming for the Lady Zhao," Lotus cried.

"A likely story." He hauled her into a storage chamber. "Now let's just peel the fruit, shall we?" He ripped off her tunic.

Lotus shrieked and struggled, but he was far too strong for her. The noise of the nearby kitchen drowned out her screams. He stripped her naked and gazed at her slight body. "Not much, but might as well make use of it while it's here." He opened his garment to reveal his huge terrible member.

He was going to rape her! The realization brought an odd calmness to her. She was in awful trouble, and if she wanted to survive, she had to stop acting like a foolish girl and start thinking the way Zhao would. She had to be canny.

She pretended to faint. The man, undeterred, set her on the floor and let go of her arm so he could separate her legs.

The moment her arm was free she grabbed for his hand with both of hers, and put her mouth to it. She bit him on the side of the hand, as hard as she could. He roared, caught by surprise. In his momentary distraction she scrambled out from under, got to her feet, and launched her body out the door.

She ran as fast as she could back to her room, oblivious to everything except her need to escape. For the moment she had forgotten that she was naked, but it didn't matter; she just had to get far away from the brute man.

Women and girls stared as Lotus charged past. Then she reached her room and dived in, finding her place of safety at last.

Zhao sat up on the bed, startled. "Lotus! What happened?"

"The man—he—he—"

"Come to me, child," Zhao said, opening her arms. Lotus flung herself into them, sobbing uncontrollably. The Lady held her, stroking her hair and murmuring comfort.

After a time, Lotus calmed enough to tell her story. Then Zhao's questions began, as she dipped the sponge and used it gently to clean Lotus's face and body. Lotus, distracted, didn't think to protest this menial chore being performed by the Lady. "Did you recognize him?"

"N-no. He wasn't one of the kitchen regulars. I tried to tell him I was on your errand, but he wouldn't believe me." She winced as the sponge cleaned a bruise.

"Would you know him again if you saw him?"

"Oh, yes! But please don't make me go near him!"

"Which hand did you bite him on?" Now Zhao was brushing out her hair, which had become sadly tangled.

Lotus had to pause to work that out. "The—his left, I think. My right side. That was where the door was, and I just wanted to get out it and away."

"Lotus, I must leave you for a bit, but I will return soon. Remain here. Lie on my bed."

"Oh, I couldn't!"

Zhao smiled. "It isn't as if I have very much use for it, anymore. Use it whenever I am not here, and entertain your friends as you please. This is my directive."

Lotus could not demur when it was phrased that way. "Yes, Lady."

Zhao disengaged, straightened her gown and wig, and quietly departed. Lotus lay on the bed, her shuddering gradually subsiding.

"Lotus." It was a soft call from outside.

Lotus recognized the voice of one of the girls who hadn't snubbed her. "Come in, Bamboo."

The friend parted the curtain and stepped in. She was tall, thin, and lanky, with large joints, accounting for her nickname. She was the opposite of Lotus, who was small, but the two had found each other because they were both Buddhists. She paused as she saw Lotus on the bed. "My mistress sent me to inquire what happened."

Lotus realized how presumptuous it looked for her to be on the bed. "My mistress told me to use the bed when she wasn't here," she explained. "The other—I think I would rather not discuss it."

"My mistress says she just saw the Lady Wu Zhao forge out of the complex like an armored horse," Bamboo said. "She said she had never seen her so angry."

"My Lady's been here only a month," Lotus pointed out. It was good to talk to a friend; it made the world settle back into its ordinary place.

"Ah, but the Lady was here before. My mistress is the niece of one of former Son of Heaven T'ai Tsung's concubines, so she knows. She says even in the old days the word was that it was bad to cross the Lady Zhao."

Lotus was alarmed. "Oh, I hope I didn't cross her by getting in trouble! I just went for a pastry for her, and this man—" Then she was telling the story after all.

"A strange man," Bamboo echoed. "He must have been sent."

"No, I think he was just new to this kitchen, and didn't know me."

Bamboo shook her head. "Everybody in that kitchen knows you, Lotus. It is said that fortune smiles on whoever smiles on the Lady Zhao's servant."

"Oh, that can't be!" Lotus protested, embarrassed.

"It's because the Lady takes care of her own, and she has the ear of the Son of Heaven. That was clear in the first three days, and clear even before then to the smart ones."

"It wasn't clear to me," Lotus said, bemused.

"Because you remain innocent. If the Lady Zhao should lose her status, many who smile on you now would ignore you."

"Many already ignore me!"

"Many of the rest. But you must know that there is malice behind some of those smiles. Many are jealous."

"Oh, Bamboo—are you jealous?" Lotus asked, upset.

"No. I learned early that my feelings have no effect on my body or my fate. Only on my outlook. So I keep them positive. I know that you would be just as nice if you were the servant of any other Lady."

Bamboo paused, collecting her thoughts. "But I was not speaking of other servants. I meant other ladies. They hate you because they hate the Lady Zhao. I think someone arranged to have that man there. And that the Lady Zhao knows it. That's why she's angry."

"Oh, I can't believe—"

Bamboo put her hand on Lotus's hand. "Believe, my friend. But also believe this: there are those who do not hate you or your mistress. They accept the way of things. My mistress is one of them. She bid me tell you that if ever you need help, and the Lady Zhao is not near, come to her and she will do what she can."

"Oh, thank you for that," Lotus said gratefully. She found that she was hungry for reassurance.

Bamboo left. Lotus knew that the girl would tell her mistress everything, but didn't mind. Once the story was out, she herself would not be required to tell it. She realized, too, that things happened often enough, and that any lone girl had to be wary of any strange man. She had been foolish to think herself charmed, and now she realized that she was indeed also countercharmed. That man had been too determined, too sure of himself. A new man would have been cautious, until he knew the way of things in this section.

Zhao returned, carrying a new tunic for Lotus. It was finer than her old one. "I must go to join the Son of Heaven tonight," Zhao said. "If you wish, you may remain here."

"Oh, no, I must serve you!" Lotus cried, jumping up.

"As you wish. Perhaps that is best." The Lady now seemed completely composed; there was no sign of alarm or anger, only sympathy.

"My Lady, may I speak?" Lotus asked, suddenly hesitant.

Zhao sat on the bed and gave Lotus her whole attention. "Of course, my friend."

"I love you." That was all, but Lotus meant it. There were good things and bad things throughout the world, but the Lady Zhao was the best.

"And I love you, Lotus. I mean to protect you better than I have before. Come." She opened her arms again.

Lotus hugged her, feeling wonderful. Nothing more needed to be said.

Then they went together to the Son of Heaven's quarters, carrying their chins high, as if nothing had happened.

The eunuch Old Coal was there, as usual. As usual they played go. And as usual they talked with seeming casualness while they pondered their moves.

"It is said that the servant of a prominent Lady was molested today," the eunuch remarked.

How could he know so quickly? "Almost," Lotus agreed. "She managed to escape."

"It is said that the Lady is angry."

"Perhaps she was, but no longer."

He lifted his eyes to give her a straight look. "It is too soon to say that. It is said that a search was made for a man with a bitten hand, and that there will be blood across the sand before her anger abates."

"Oh, my Lady wouldn't—" But his gaze held, and she felt a chill. Old Coal had served in this palace for decades, and knew the way of things.

"It is said that perhaps even now there is the sound of a man howling under the torture."

"Torture!"

"It is said that they wish to know who sent him, and he does not wish to tell. But he will tell." Old Coal set down his stone with a certain force.

Lotus shuddered. She almost thought she could hear faint screams of agony.

Next day the Lady Zhao was summoned again, at noon. Lotus went with her—and discovered that it was actually Lotus they wanted. For they had the man who had accosted her, bound, his head hanging. He was alive, but no longer seemed to care whether he remained so.

"Is this the man?" an officer brusquely inquired.

Lotus forced herself to look more closely. "Yes," she agreed faintly.

The officer raised his huge bright sword. "Now witness the fate of all enemies of the Son of Heaven."

Lotus screamed and turned away. The Lady Zhao caught her. "Not before ladies," she said sharply to the officer. She guided Lotus away.

Behind them there was a sound, possibly like the splitting of wood or the cleaving of tough meat. Then a thunk, as of something striking the ground. Lotus buried her head in Zhao's robe.

Then she realized what another consequence might be. "Lady—did he tell—?"

"Of course. We know who sent him."

"Will she—?"

"Of course."

"Oh, please, Lady, no!" Lotus begged tearfully.

Zhao squeezed her shoulders. "You ask this?"

"Please, please, no more blood! No more torture!"

"Of course, dear."

That was all. But by the time they returned to the concubine quarters, the Lady Liang and her servant were gone. It seemed that she had been abruptly dismissed and sent away in disgrace. No one spoke of her thereafter.

Lotus loved the Lady Zhao. But now she also feared her. She was chagrined to have been the cause of this horror, though she knew that the same thing would have happened if any other girl had served Zhao. All she could do was try to blot the whole episode from her mind.

That was not difficult to do. Life at the court was far from unpleasant. The Lady Zhao attended the Son of Heaven increasingly in the day as well as the night, seeming much like an empress. Often she arranged to let Lotus have nice things, such as a serving of wine-soaked fish which the Lady deemed to be too much for her delicate stomach, or a sherbet made of iced milk and rice. Lotus ate like an empress—in the guise of protecting her mistress's faint appetite. The Son of Heaven allowed it, and even on occasion passed along some of his own supposedly imperfect food. He seemed pleasantly amused by the closeness of the Lady and the servant girl.

Once, Lotus was left holding the dog again, as the Son of Heaven and Lady Zhao played the board game of backgammon. The Lady was good at it, as she was in all intellectual matters, but somehow arranged to misplay when she threatened to win. The Son of Heaven glanced at Lotus. "This time you won't need to loose the dog; she does the job herself." Lotus tried to look blank, pretending not to understand the allusion, but the humor boiled up and forced her to avert her face for a moment. The Son of Heaven merely smiled. It was evident that he enjoyed teasing her.

"If you come to like my girl any better," Zhao murmured to him, "I will be in fear for my position."

Lotus, appalled at such an implication, blushed so deeply that the Son of Heaven laughed. Yet this banter covered the fact that even as the Lady Zhao's natural hair slowly grew back, so was Lotus's young body developing. Within a year she would be a woman. That would spell the end of her service at the court.

Once Lotus got to go on a cruise along the Grand Canal. This waterway had been dug forty years before, and periodically the Son of Heaven cruised it in his barge, leading an entourage of boats stretching back farther than the eye could see. This time the Lady Zhao accompanied him in his lead barge, and Lotus attended her.

Zhao was splendidly dressed for the occasion. She wore a headdress of iridescent peacock feathers so elaborate that she was able to forgo the wig. A comb of jade fastened it in place, and a pin in the shape of a kingfisher. Her sash was sewn with pearls, and fitted her waist so closely that Lotus knew she dared take no deep breath. Her silken gown was embroidered with silver and gold, and even her slippers were separate works of art. She seemed almost to shine like the moon, her beauty radiating and reflecting from her surroundings. Perhaps she drew more attention than the Son of Heaven himself, but he was oblivious; it was evident that he was so completely taken with her that he cared about little else. The empress was not present; Lotus wondered whether this was significant. It seemed that Zhao was succeeding in her mission almost too well.

The boat was magnificent. It was twenty times the length of a man and fashioned in the form of a ferocious dragon, with the giant head high in front and the tail curling up behind. The dragon's mouth was so big it could readily have swallowed a man, with teeth as long as a man's forearm, and it was colored with bright red, gold, and blue. There were four deck levels, with the lowest for the oarsmen and the highest, within a square pavilion, for the royal party. They stood and looked out across the green rice fields of the empire, where the workers had been given leave to line the banks of the river and cheer the royal party on.

Taken as a whole, it was a glorious experience for Lotus. But she could not help noticing that both the Son of Heaven and Zhao looked bored. It seemed that this was a show for the masses. Lotus, of course, was one of the masses; she knew the glorious memory of this excursion would remain for the rest of her life.

In such manner, Lotus's year of service progressed. By this time the Lady Zhao's hair was long enough to serve as a base for considerable decorations, and the wig was no longer used. She was seldom in the concubines' quarters. Increasingly she was served by the Son of

Heaven's staff. The Son of Heaven drew upon the concubines only when Zhao was indisposed, and sometimes it was Zhao who selected his company for the night. She had come a long way from the nunnery.

Meanwhile Lotus learned from her mother's occasional visits that the printing business of their family prospered as never before. Ember had to hire and train new staff to keep up. Zhao's favor carried as far as her disfavor.

At last it was time. The arrangements were made, and a carriage came to convey the damsel Lotus to her home. The Lady Zhao came to bid her farewell. They embraced; then the Lady proffered a package. "It is the wig," she explained. "I thank you for its use; now it is yours. I hope you will remember me when you use it."

"But I don't need to use—" Lotus caught herself. "I will always think of you, great Lady," she said formally. "You have given me the most wonderful year of my life."

"It has been good for me too, perhaps for not quite the same reasons," Zhao said. "But I always trusted you, Lotus, and valued your friendship. Perhaps you will come with your father, on occasion, when he does further business with the court, and we can see each other in passing."

"Oh, yes, Lady!" Lotus exclaimed. Then, tearfully, she got into the carriage and waved parting.

Yet it was also good to get home. Lotus had missed her mother and father, and especially her grandmother Ember, who had had much of the burden of her care. Now she would be with them again, no longer as a child, but as a young lady. She had learned much of Lady protocol during her service at court.

When Grandmother Ember opened the package, after the tearful reunions, there lay the wig—wrapped around a dozen gleaming gold coins. There was enough wealth there to ensure that even if the family business faded, it would be long before they were in financial difficulty. The Lady Wu Zhao had indeed been generous in her friendship.

Wu Zhao's rise continued. Three years later she displaced the Empress Wang herself as principal consort. The Son of Heaven had a stroke in 660, and Zhao became the virtual ruler of China. In 690, following the emperor's death and the forced abdication of her two sons, Zhao ruled outright in her own name, becoming the only female Son of Heaven in the history of China.

She was highly competent, and the T'ang dynasty prospered. She was finally deposed in 705 at age eighty, when ill, and the dynasty faltered until her grandson Hsüan Tsung came to power in 712. Some consider her to have been a scheming, perhaps brutal woman, but the evidence is mixed, and she was loyal to her precepts and her friends. She did much good for Buddhism in China. No following ruler possessed her level of competence. The dynasty itself endured until the year 906, followed later by the Sung dynasty. But the T'ang dynasty was arguably the greatest age of China. Thanks, perhaps, to a woman.

C H A P T E R 1 7

LITHUANIA

In 1207 Genghis Khan (variously spelled; one variant is Jenghiz Qan) assumed power over the Mongol horde and began the expansion of his steppe dominion, which was by the end of the century perhaps the largest unified land empire of mankind's history. (The later British Empire was scattered around the globe.) China fell, and Europe was saved from similar conquest only by chance: the Great Khan Ogadai died as the Mongols, having defeated the powers of eastern Europe, were about to move west. Thereafter, the Khanate of the Golden Horde retained power in what is now Russia, and to the immediate

west assorted principalities developed along the coast of the Baltic Sea. Among
these were the Teutonic Knights and Lithuania.

The Teutonic Knights, also known as the Knights of the Cross, or
colloquially as the Whitecapes, were as Crusaders determined to convert the
pagan Lithuanians, whom they called the Saracens of the North, to Christian-
ity. In the process they seemed to be equally determined to carve out and settle a
territory for themselves. The Lithuanians objected to both aspects. Consequent-
ly there were some battles, one of which occurred on the Gulf of Riga in 1270,
between the Teutonic Knights and a faction of the Lithuanians called the
Samogitians. It was not considered to be historically significant, but it does
show the nature of the rivalry.

T REE saw them coming: mounted knights whose white capes were
emblazoned by crosses, and whose helmets were adorned by
peacock feathers. Whitecapes, marching north!

This was the force he had been sent to locate. He lingered only long
enough to get a fair notion of the size of the dread force that Master
Otto had raised. Tree had taken refuge in the thatched-roof wooden
house of a sympathetic family, pretending to be a lowly serf. In fact he
was the son of the Lithuanian metalworker Stone, and grandson of the
patriarch blacksmith Blaze. Their homestead was threatened by the
encroachment of the warlike Christians, so they supported the action
against them. The plan had been to advance into the Teutonic territory
of Livonia at the same time that Master Otto's army was moving south
into Lithuania, cutting him off from behind. Otto had learned of
this—he had spies too—and turned to intercept the Lithuanians. But
they had crossed the frozen Gulf of Riga to take plunder and camped on
the island of Oesel. They would strike out from there wherever Otto's
army wasn't, wreaking havoc before moving back south to Lithuania
with their plunder. But they needed to keep track of the location of
Otto's army.

Now it was evident that Otto had gathered reinforcements, and was
about to pursue the Lithuanians across the ice. This was an unexpected
move, and Tree had to hurry to notify his countrymen lest they be
caught at a disadvantage. On such information the fortunes of nations
could hinge.

But as Tree set out across the snow, a Whitecape knight spied him.

"Ho, varlet!" the man cried. Actually Tree didn't know the Crusader's language, but knew that this was the sort of thing they cried.

He did the expedient thing: he immediately fled into the forest. The great oaks and beech trees had always been a comfort to him; he had been named after them, and wood was his destiny. The branches interlocked overhead, forming a natural canopy, and thickets filled the spaces below. In summer ivy grew everywhere, making it impenetrable to those not versed in its ways. In summer Tree would have disappeared in an instant, feasting on berries, mushrooms, apples and pears while the pursuers floundered hopelessly. But this was winter, so that the forest was somewhat gaunt, and the snow made tracking all too easy.

But winter had its tricks, too. The snow had fallen several days ago, so there were a number of trails left by animals and hunters and firewood gatherers. Tree ran to one of these, then ran back along it, toward the main road. He touched his bracelet charm for luck and ducked behind a large beech as the horseman galloped into sight. Sure enough, the knight followed the trail forward, pursuing a spot quest just about as pointless as his crusade. Christians were not the smartest of creatures.

Tree returned to the road, drew his gray sheepskin coat more closely about him, and continued toward the coast. He passed a young woman in a brilliantly woven shawl and skirt. She turned her head and smiled at him, her face framed within her kerchief. She was about his age, and pretty.

Oh, how he wished he could stay and talk with her. His contacts with girls had been limited. In fact, his main emotional experience was the crush he had had on the pretty slave girl who had cared for him and his brother when he was young. But she had in due course earned her freedom, and had married and moved away, leaving him desolate for a time. How nice it would be to get to know a real girl! But his mission was too important to allow for dalliance. So he smiled back and went on without pausing. Probably it had been an idle flirtation on her part anyway.

Then he heard the sound of horse hooves behind. The knight was returning. Tree ducked back into the forest before the man could spy him again. The Christian was suspicious, justifiably; the natives would not be avoiding them. Tree would have to stay off the road, and that would slow him, but it was the safest course. The Crusader might be dull, but not so dull as to let Tree give him the slip again after being spied.

Fortunately he did not have far to go before the terrain changed, and the day was fading. In the darkness he would be free to travel as rapidly as he could.

Tree came at dusk to the verge of the Gulf of Riga. Now it was time for his secret weapon. He opened his knapsack and brought out his skates. These were ox shins cut down to size, with leather thongs, and metal rims. He used the thongs to tie these firmly to his shoes. Then he got to his feet and stepped out onto the frozen sea.

He took a moment to get his balance and start his motion. He had converted his shoes to skates, and the property of skates was that they were more effective on ice than were shoes. Ordinary skates were made of animal ribs or shinbones, as his were, but his canny grandfather Blaze had added a unique touch by binding sharp iron rims to them. This made it possible for Tree to skate harder and faster, for the iron bit into the hard ice better than bone did. He could move far more rapidly on the ice than a man afoot. Not only that; it was easier, because he could slide between pushes. Now if a Christian saw him, it would hardly matter, provided the man were beyond bow range. Not even a metal-shod horse could catch him, because the horse would still have to run, not skate.

However, Tree had a fair distance to go, and the ice was not perfectly smooth. He could afford to skate no faster than he could see, lest he run afoul of a broken hump or even a break in the ice. Fortunately it was a clear night and there was a bit of moonlight.

Tree skated north into the night. He steered by the stars, orienting on the Great Bear. Even so, his navigation was not perfect, and it was dawn by the time he reached the isle of Oesel and saw the tents of the Lithuanian camp near the houses of the town. That was a relief, because he was now so tired he didn't know how much farther he could go.

He located the section of his feudal chief and skated there. The archers, not recognizing him, aimed their crossbows at him. "Hold!" he cried. "I am Tree, the scout, and I have important news for the chief!"

The chief appeared. "What did you learn, Tree, that brings you here beforetime?"

"Master Otto has gotten reinforcements and is coming after you!" Tree said. "He may start crossing the ice today!"

"Come with me," the chief said gruffly. He led Tree to the tent of the commander of the Samogitian force.

Tree made his full report, including his estimate of the origin and number of Otto's reinforcements, and their likely schedule of advance. The commander shook his head gravely. "They've got us trapped," he said. "They'll have forces guarding the east and south shores of the gulf, to ambush us if we try to flee there. They'll overwhelm us here if we stay on land. We'll have to fight them on the ice."

"On the ice!" Tree exclaimed, amazed.

"Go get your sleep before you collapse," the commander told him.

Tree was glad to do so. He untied his skates, which were clumsy on land, and sought his unit. It was actually in a group of houses which had been taken from the natives. The army had come here for plunder as well as to damage Christian power in the Baltic region. Houses represented temporary plunder; if their occupants didn't flee, the men were killed, and the children and younger women taken as slaves. That wasn't merely Lithuanian policy; it was universal with armies. The Christians did the same when they raided Lithuania, though they pretended that they were merely seeking converts to their noxious religion. There was his grandfather Blaze, still hale at sixty-four, with his smithy tools mounted on sleds. Tree ate some smoked boar meat and disappeared under a heavy blanket in a room of the house. He hardly even dreamed.

Late in the day he woke to find Blaze busy hammering out strips of iron and cutting them into bits. "The commander was impressed with your travel on the ice," he explained. "You made better time than he thought possible. Now I'm making cleats for some of our shoes. There's not time to do the job properly, but perhaps it will help."

Meanwhile there were constant councils of war, as the leaders made plans for the engagement. They knew they would be outnumbered and that the Teutonic Knights would have superior cavalry. There were those who claimed that these Crusaders were the finest fighting forces known. Tree wasn't inclined to argue; stupidity was a great asset for a professional fighting man. But they had never fought on ice before, and that just might change things. After all, hadn't the Lithuanians routed the Christians thirty-five years before by fighting them in a swamp which incapacitated the enemy's horses?

It was actually two more days before Master Otto's army closed on

Oesel. That gave the Lithuanian army plenty of time to rest and prepare, as well as to continue with the business of burning and pillaging the rich native settlements. Most of the soldiers did not care to mess with the cleats, but some did, because the cleats enabled them to move with greater confidence on the ice. A number were practicing their swordcraft, to see how it worked on the ice. Others were scrounging for cord and thong, which they attached to the baggage sleds. What were they up to?

"To tie the sleds together," Blaze explained briefly. That didn't make much sense, so Tree let it go, not wanting to appear stupid.

Tree skated out across the ice again, searching for evidence of the enemy. When he found none, the first day after his sleep, he returned with relief to make his report. Privately he hoped that the Christians would not come at all, though that would invalidate his prior report. He just did not relish the notion of battle.

In the evening they ascended a hill, where they made a fire from the eternal flame, beneath the highest oak tree. They prayed in a group to their god Perkunas. There was only one white-robed virgin priestess there to sanctify the ceremony, because women were a nuisance on any military expedition, but she tended the altar and gave them courage. They also addressed the unseen sacred serpent who was in the groves below the hill. All was snow and ice, but they knew the spirit of the serpent was there.

Tree's confidence was enhanced by the ceremony. He knew little about the weird rituals of the Christians, and didn't care to. No priestesses? No sacred flame? He had heard they even regarded the serpent as evil. Obviously they were crazy.

After the ceremony there was a surprise. Blaze brought the priestess to their house. "Keep her out of mischief," he told Tree.

"But she's the virgin!" Tree protested, astonished.

"Precisely. The commander is trusting me to protect her from molestation, and I am delegating you. You should understand her well enough; she's your age." He went off to his smith works.

Tree stared at the lovely girl. It was almost as if he had known her before. "I—I don't know what to do," he said.

She lifted a hand in a graceful acknowledgment. "I am called Candleflame. All I need is a place to sleep where I won't be seen." She spoke in the dialect of the Estonians, but he was able to make it out.

"You can have my bed," he said quickly. "In our house—I mean the one we are using here."

"I must not take your bed," she said gently.

Tree found himself blushing. "I didn't mean—"

She smiled. "I know what you didn't mean. I mean I would not care to deprive you of your bed. Take me to your house and I will make up one of my own."

"Yes, of course." He showed her the way, his embarrassment giving way to fascination. He had never before been this close to a virgin priestess, and was amazed to find that she was much like an ordinary girl. Also that she was Estonian, rather than Lithuanian. The Estonians had always been enemies.

"I think I should explain my situation," she said as they walked. "I have lived here on the isle of Oesel, but I must not remain here longer. Our people were converted to Christianity against our will by the Danes and Swordbrothers. Oesel is now considered to be a bishopric allied to the Teutonic Knights. But in our hearts many of us remain true to the flame and serpent. So we are not as much your enemies as we once were. We have a mutual hatred of the Christians."

That explained a good deal. But not quite enough. "We came to plunder," Tree said. "Your town is burning. Why should you help us in our worship, after that?"

"It is true that we do not like to be ravaged. But we have already been ravaged by the Christians, not only when they conquered us, but when they forced their awful religion on us. You Lithuanians merely ravage us physically, and you will not remain here long. And you spared my family, when we explained that I had religious training and was willing to sanctify the ceremony of the eternal flame."

"But then won't the Christians punish you, when they return? For collaborating with us?"

"Yes. So I can not return to my family. They will say I was taken as a slave by the raiders. But I will instead be taken to a temple and cared for there, and allowed to become a priestess in Samogitia. This is better for me, and for my family."

Tree realized that there had been an element of duress in this deal. But it had saved her family from the horrors of being burned out, and perhaps worse. "My grandfather Blaze is an honorable man. He will see that the deal is honored. I will help all I can."

"Thank you, Tree." She smiled, and it was as if a ray of warmth speared into his heart.

They reached the house, which was now empty. Candleflame searched out straw and a blanket and made herself a private bed, while Tree shored up the hearth fire. Then he retired to his own bed, but sleep was slow to come. The girl was a virgin priestess, never to be intimately touched by a man lest she lose her special spiritual power, yet she was also a pretty girl and inherently fascinating. His guilty imagination brought her to his bed. If only she weren't what she was!

Blaze tramped in later, flopping on the other bed in the room. Tree was glad for the presence of his grandfather, to whom he almost felt closer than to his father. Blaze was gruff in public, but always listened in private, and never belittled Tree's concerns. Others said that Tree took after his grandfather almost more than his father; that pleased Tree, but his mother never spoke of it.

In the morning Candleflame was up early, seeing to the hearth and making wheat porridge for them all. "But you shouldn't be doing that!" Tree protested, scrambling up. "You're a priestess!"

"Who is an ordinary girl by day," she responded. "Our religious rites have always had to be secret; yesterday was the first time I was able to perform them openly. If the Christians had ever suspected—"

"Still, in Lithuania—"

"This isn't Lithuania. But you will take me there. Until then, I will manage as I always have."

Blaze woke. "And we shall treat you with the courtesy we accord any Lithuanian woman, and defend you from the dread Christians," he said. "We shall have to be going out, but you must remain here at the house, hidden."

"I thank you for this sanctuary," Candleflame said, and served out the porridge.

After breakfast Blaze headed out to do his smithy work, and Tree donned his skates. "What is that?" Candleflame asked, staring at them.

"Metal-rimmed skates," he replied proudly. "Blaze made them for me."

"Oh, now I see. Bone skates, with metal. Those must be very special."

"They are. With them I can skate faster than others can." He paused, realizing that she seemed knowledgeable on the subject. "Do you skate?"

"Yes. It is useful, here on the island, in winter."

"Maybe Blaze will make you skates like these. Then—" But he balked at the continuation, fearing that he was overstepping his bounds.

"Then we could skate together," she finished for him. "That would be nice."

Wonderfully nice! Because he was good at skating, instead of awkward as he was in the rest of life. Even though there was no future in it, on skates he could interact on an even basis with a girl. He realized that his grandfather had had something like this in mind when he agreed to board the priestess. He had found a way to give Tree experience with a young woman without embarrassment.

That day Tree went out on the ice, as before, and this time he spied the enemy. He skated quickly back, readily outdistancing them, and made his report. The Lithuanian army mobilized for action. The time had come.

"But what about me?" Candleflame asked as he and Blaze prepared to vacate the house. "I can't stay here. Suppose you got killed?"

"A battle is no place for a girl," Blaze said gruffly.

"Maybe she could dress like a boy," Tree suggested.

"Yes! That is my best protection," Candleflame agreed. "Then I can go out with you, and no one will know."

"And I'll have two grandsons to run errands," Blaze said. "Very well. Get changed and join me at my sled." He moved out.

They ransacked the house, finding suitable clothing. Candleflame had to do some quick cutting and sewing to make a sheepskin cap. When she bound her flowing fair hair up and back, and covered it with the cap, she did look much like a boy. "But add some dirt," Tree said. "Boys are slovenly."

"Not all of them." She gave him a fleeting smile, another dart to his heart. "But the point is well taken. Put some dirt on my face, to make it right."

"But I mustn't touch you!"

She laughed. "You may touch my face, Tree. That will not cost me my virginity."

Oh. Tree rubbed his hand on the floor, then carefully grimed her face, making her look suitably disreputable. The crude male clothing entirely concealed the contours of her body. But she still looked beautiful to him.

Then they went out to join Blaze. "Stay close by the sled," Blaze said
gruffly. "This is not going to be fun. You have knives?"

Tree did, of course, but Candleflame didn't. Blaze dug one out of his
collection of iron. "If anyone comes at you, lad, use it this way," he said.
He held the knife at waist height, then made a sharp thrust forward.
Candleflame winced, but when he gave her the knife, she made a similar
jab at the gut of the imagined man. "But your best strategy is simply to
stay clear," Blaze concluded. "Hunker down on or behind the sled, and
don't move. Dead men don't get attacked."

Tree put on his skates, so he would be able to move well on the ice.
But others had little trouble, for the surface was rough and pitted, with
scattered humps, making it seem like a mountainous terrain.

When the Crusaders came into view, the Lithuanian cavalry rode out
on the ice, hauling the sleds. Tree and Candleflame rode the sled with
the tools. It would be their job to defend that sled as well as they could,
though neither was a trained soldier. Tree was far from sanguine about
it, because it was apparent that Master Otto had a force approaching
twice the size of their own. Yet ten years ago the Lithuanians had
defeated the Knights, when the enemy's allies had had a difference
about the division of plunder and had deserted on the battlefield. Of
course that was unlikely to happen again. Disaster was threatening.

Yet Candleflame's presence soon distracted Tree from his own
concerns. He was worried about her. She was so much more vulnerable,
and so much less experienced in the brute business of war. He had to try
to protect her, however he could.

Then, before engaging the enemy, the Lithuanians dismounted. They
led their horses back behind the sleds. Blaze came to stand with his
horse a short distance away. "Lash our sled to the ones on either side,"
he snapped. And, as an afterthought to Candleflame: "Remember, men
don't scream."

Good point. If Candleflame got frightened, and made a piercing
feminine scream, everyone would know.

The two of them used the cords to lash the sleds together, as others
were doing all across the ice. Now the sleds were making a barrier across
the ice. Suddenly that aspect made sense. That would be a real
impediment to the enemy cavalry, and to the enemy archers too.

Meanwhile the Lithuanian archers were lining up behind the barricade, ready to fire from this cover. Tree and Candleflame finished their job and got down behind the sled.

Her pale face approached his. "I'm terrified!" she confided.

"So am I," Tree answered honestly, and was rewarded by a wan smile.

They saw Christians hold council, then move into attack position. Their cavalry charged across the ice directly at the barricade. Chips of ice flew out from under their horses' hooves. The force seemed irresistible. Candleflame put both hands to her face, as if to stifle a scream.

The Lithuanian crossbows let fly. Tree heard the swish of their massed release, like a sudden wind overhead. He peered past the sled, hoping to see a devastating effect. How nice it would be if every Christian were struck through the heart and fell immediately dead, ending the battle! The armor of the mounted knights was strong enough to withstand ordinary arrows, but crossbows, though slow to draw, had more power and accuracy. A number of knights were cut down before they got close enough to engage. But not enough. The great majority continued their charge directly toward Tree and Candleflame. The horses loomed horrifyingly large, like irresistible beasts about to trample everything under their awful hooves. Even the vapor snorting from their big nostrils looked ominous.

Candleflame's face turned toward him. It was drawn, and tears were brightening her eyes. She was terrified.

He put his arm around her, and she huddled against him. Again he knew that his own fear was muted by the need to allay hers. "They can't reach us," he said, hoping it was true.

The knights came right up to the sleds. Unable to hurdle them, they tried to halt—and their horses' hooves skidded on the ice, causing a number of them to spook. The ice groaned with the weight, and Tree felt it give way somewhat, but it was too thick to break. That was a relief—or was it? Who would suffer more, if they all got dunked in ice water?

There was a noise from behind. Tree looked back. "Our men are coming," he told Candleflame.

Indeed, the Lithuanian foot soldiers charged up to the sleds, clambered across them, and surrounded the floundering cavalry. They drew their swords and cut down the horses before the Crusader foot soldiers at the flanks could get there. Blood flowed out across the ice, and the agonized squealing of the horses was dreadful. Tree hoped the blood wouldn't reach their sled; he didn't want Candleflame to see it.

But she did. She winced. "Those poor horses!"

Then the soldiers cut down the stranded knights. "That's Master Otto!" Blaze exclaimed, recognizing the dread standard of the enemy leader. Tree saw the man being hacked at from three sides, and in a moment he went down. His knights tried to rally to his defense, but they too were cut down. The Lithuanians' practice on the ice, and perhaps the cleats of some of them, gave them the advantage. The ice was littered with Christian bodies: ten, twenty—there must be fifty or more of them, killed before they could be rescued by their own troops. What a victory!

Then the enemy flanks arrived. Their strength was too much, and they scattered the Lithuanians. The battle was turning the other way despite the decimation of the knights. Tree saw the Lithuanian soldiers being mobbed, their blood joining that of the hated Christians, and their formation was broken up. Soon the Christians were pursuing the fugitives across the ice, and cutting them down without mercy. Blood was congealing on the frozen surface. Tree cowered down on his sled, hoping no enemy would realize that he and Candleflame were there and slay them. Only Blaze remained upright, at his age not expected to be a combatant, but determined to defend his sled regardless.

But the Christians had made another tactical mistake. Their forces were now being scattered, because of their pursuit of the fleeing Lithuanian flanks. Their formation had dissolved. The Lithuanian center forged across the sled barrier and attacked those out-of-position Teutonic flanks from inside. Suddenly a second massacre was in the making.

Candleflame recovered some of her poise. She lifted her head and saw the carnage before the sleds. "Oh, I don't like battle!" she said fervently.

"Neither do I," Tree agreed with similar emotion. "I wish this were over. And maybe it will be, soon."

But it wasn't over. The Crusader cavalry was tough and competent. It managed to regroup despite the harassment. Then it launched a series of attacks which took the attention of the Lithuanian center. Now the advantage of the horsemen counted solidly, and they inflicted heavy losses. The Lithuanian army was pushed back over the sleds in one place. Then it was pushed over in another section, as the knights gradually achieved control of the center. Then it happened by the smithy sled. "Get away from here!" Blaze cried. "We can't hold the line."

But it was already too late. A knight charged near the sled. His sword swept down, severing the cord, and the sled lost its connection to its neighbor and began to slide out of place. Candleflame emitted a stifled scream.

Faint as it was, the knight still heard. His horse turned, and he oriented directly on the girl. Then Tree realized that it wasn't just the sound. Her hair had worked loose under her cap, and was falling down around her shoulders in a yellow tangle. She was being unveiled.

The knight advanced. For the moment, despite all the activity around them, the scene seemed to be reduced to just the four of them: Blaze, Candleflame, Tree, and the dread Christian. The three had tried to stay out of actual combat, but the fourth was a creature of violence. In his blood-smeared armor, on his sweating horse, he was a fiend ready to destroy two of them and carry away the third for eternal damnation.

The horse charged at Candleflame. She threw herself down, sliding across the ice. Blaze leaped for the knight, but was knocked aside by the horse's shoulder. Tree found the knight's leg right by his face.

Tree's knife was in his hand. He thrust it at the leg. It slid off the leather armor. He thrust again. This time it found a crevice and penetrated. He rammed it in as hard as he could, feeling it cutting into flesh.

The knight vented a vile-sounding Christian oath and turned on him, lifting his sword. Tree knew he could not retreat quickly enough to avoid that weapon. Instead he dived forward, under the horse. He slid by the fidgeting hooves, afraid he was going to get stepped on.

Then the horse leaped away, bearing its rider. Tree realized that somewhere in the melee of violence and sound there had been a call. The knight had had to move to rejoin his formation, lest it get scattered again. They had escaped, perhaps by the intercession of the gods.

"Tree!" Candleflame cried. "You've been hurt!" She skidded toward him, heedless of the gore on the ice. She dropped beside him and put her arms around him.

"I'm all right," Tree said dizzily. "Don't—don't compromise your-self by touching me."

"Oh, I don't care about that, after this! You were so brave, stopping that evil knight from getting me. Then you went down, and I was so afraid—"

Blaze approached. "Get back to the sled, and tie it to its neighbors," he said. "This day is not yet done."

Embarrassed, they let go of each other and did as told.

Now it was getting dark. The battle had gone on all afternoon. The Teutonic Knights had command of the center, the Lithuanians were scattered and disorganized, and the sled wall had been breached and severed in several places. But the mounted knights did not like to fight in the dark.

The Teutonic flanks had also had enough. Their commander, himself wounded, ordered a Christian withdrawal. The cavalry prevented the Lithuanians from harassing the retreating soldiers, then retreated itself. The Lithuanians were left holding the field, such as it was.

Tree, safe by the sled with Candleflame, relaxed. The Lithuanians had won the battle! But it was already evident that their side had lost twice as many men as the Christians had. It had been a costly victory—and but for the complication of the ice, it would have been a loss.

Nevertheless, they were the victors, and the spoils were theirs. The men went to work stripping the dead and dividing the booty. In due course they hauled their own dead soldiers to the land and labored to bury them. The Christians they left out on the ice, naked, as befitted their ilk. Then they marched for home in good order.

Tree knew he had not done anything especially noble or outstanding. But Candleflame thought he had, and she seemed to be changing her mind about being a virgin priestess. The experience of the battle had been horrible, but now his prospects in life seemed wonderful.

The uneasy relationship between Lithuania and the Teutonic Knights continued, with each having more success elsewhere than against each other. In the course of the following century Lithuania expanded south and east, largely at the expense of the weakening Khanate of the Golden Horde, until it reached from the Baltic Sea to the Black Sea. Then it joined with Poland, by a royal marriage in 1386, became nominally Christian, and for the following century was perhaps the dominant country of Europe. Eventually the growing powers of Russia and Germany squeezed it from east and west, and before 1800 it was partitioned between them and disappeared. Both Lithuania and Poland were restored to existence in the twentieth century as separate countries. In this manner a small and insignificant country grew large and powerful over the course of five centuries, and finally shrank again. Today its onetime greatness is largely forgotten.

CHAPTER 18

KUBA

The civilizations of the continent of Africa have been generally disparaged by those who destroyed them in their quest for ivory, minerals and slaves. Though technologically behind the peoples of Europe and Asia, the Africans had their own cultures and arts. One such was the group of tribes others call the Kuba, or "people of the lightning," in the Congo region of central Africa, in the period between A.D. 1500 and 1800. The lightning was not that of the storm, but of the flashing of their complicated, deadly throwing knives used in war, a terror to opponents. Yet the Kuba culture was civilized and generally

377

peaceful. At least one Western historian, Leo Frobenius, a German anthropol-
ogist, considered Kuba to be the acme of native African culture. It had a
formidable oral tradition, including a listing of some ninety former kings, a
body of laws, and a sophisticated court system replete with an appeals process.
None of this derived from contact with the white man, a strange creature
known only by the legends of neighboring tribes. About 1620 there was a
question of succession, because of the king's lack of male heirs. It was settled by
negotiation and compromise, as were most issues.

RAFFIA Flower, perhaps I have a good marriage for you," Crystal
said as her daughter chewed on a fat roasted grub.

Flower grimaced. "I don't want a good marriage, I want the *best*
marriage." She was sixteen, and knew exactly what she wanted, except
for the dull details. She was pretty enough to have some reasonable
hope of getting it.

Crystal smiled, used to this. "How about the king of Kuba? Then you
could feast on sweet bananas instead of tough plantains, and have
warthog venison every day instead of fish."

Flower laughed, thinking it a joke. "And all the palm wine I need to
make me silly! Mother, he's already got eighteen wives—one from each
clan of the Bushoong—and dozens and dozens of concubines from the
insignificant clans. Besides, he's old; he got daughters older than I am."

"I was not speaking of King Shyaam," Crystal said evenly. "I was
speaking of his heir."

"What heir?" Flower demanded. "He has sired only girls. I think
something's wrong with his manhood."

"But he has broadened the laws of succession to allow any legitimate
son of a royal wife to be the heir. I was at the council where that was
confirmed."

"Anyway, we don't know who'll be the next king, because he hasn't
designated his heir." Flower started cleaning her abdomen, so that her
small ceremonial clan scar showed more prominently. It would never do
to have someone mistake her for the wrong clan.

"Ah, but we know who will be designated," Crystal said.

Flower looked at her, surprised. "We do?"

"His cousin Mboong aLeeng."

"The Hawk? But he's not like King Shyaam at all! They don't even get along with each other. He's a fierce warrior, a terror with the lightning. King Shyaam never fought a war."

"Nevertheless, Mboong will be the one. I happened to be near when it was being discussed; I think the king does not know how sharp my hearing is. How would you like to marry him?"

Flower considered. "Well, he's older than I am, and violent. I might have trouble managing him."

Crystal smiled. "Especially with seventeen other major wives competing to manage him themselves."

"Well, I would be the First Wife, of course, since I'm of the Nbong clan. My word would govern."

"You would send him to the others only for sex, not advice," Crystal said, this time suppressing her smile.

"Yes. That's what they're for, after all."

"And all this time I thought it was to give all the tribes fair representation."

Now Flower had to smile, sensing the humor. Men were notoriously hard to manage, even those with single wives. "But it doesn't matter. Mboong's not going to notice me, and I'm not going to chase him."

"I think he will notice you," Crystal said seriously. "Because he will need you."

Flower glanced down at her full brown breasts and loosely wrapped skirt. "He can get the same from any number of women who will be glad to marry him the moment his status becomes known."

"It is your mind he will need. I know this man, Flower; he is strong in combat, but weak in knowledge. The council will not confirm him unless he proves himself by reciting the King List."

"Oh, that's right! He'll have trouble with that. There are more than ninety names and histories."

"That's right. So he will have to learn them well. And whom do you think he will learn them from?"

"Why, the chief historian, of course."

"Who is of a different clan, and not partial to warfare. How patient do you suppose he will be when Mboong stumbles frequently?"

Flower tittered. "He might even slip Mboong some wrong information, to make him mess up. I wouldn't trust the historian from any farther away than I could kiss him."

"And Mboong wouldn't even care to kiss him," Crystal agreed. "So where else can he turn?"

"I suppose he'll have to come to you," Flower said thoughtfully. "You know the kings, though it's not exactly your job, because of all the songs and praise poems relating to their mothers and wives. You have access to the palace and knowledge of the King List because of your position as chief singer. Why, even I know—" She paused, realizing something.

"I have business enough to hold me," Crystal said. "But you are free. You have learned much of the King List from me. You could teach him, and no one would know."

"Why shouldn't anyone know?"

"Because no king or future king would humiliate himself by taking instruction from a woman."

"But then how could—?"

"He might, however, romance a prospective bride from a prominent clan."

Flower considered the prospects. "He would say it was romance, but his interest would be in the kings. However, by the time he learned all the kings—" She inhaled.

"Precisely. If you can not make a man notice you when you have him alone for prolonged periods, then you may have to scale down your ambitions."

Flower nodded. "I will have to review the kings myself, because I never tried to learn them all."

"Speak to your grandmother Ember; she knew them all before me."

"Yes, I will do that." Flower jumped up and ran out of the house.

The capital city of Nsheng was huge and spacious. It would be about all a girl could do to walk the length of it in a day, yet it was completely surrounded by a palisade: a wall of sharpened stakes higher than she could reach. Within this extensive enclosure the city was aesthetically laid out with wide streets, plazas and marketplaces, so that no line of sight became dull because of its length. The main avenues were blocked by public buildings of various heights and widths to mask the approaches to the main plazas. Trees were placed with an eye toward enhancing horizontal lines and further reducing the monotony of too great an unobstructed view. The architects had understood that the proper way to experience a city was to move through its streets, rather than to stand still and view it as if the observer were a statue. Flower loved it, and was sure there was no other city like it in the world. Certainly not among the tribes around Kuba.

She approached the house of her widowed grandmother Ember. Its walls, like those of most buildings, were fashioned of wickerwork and decorated like mats. They were movable, because every few years the entire city was moved to a new site. It had happened three times in Shyaam's reign as king, and would continue to happen under his successor. This kept the city perpetually fresh and vigorous as well as beautiful.

Grandmother Ember was an ancient sixty-eight years old, an age Flower found difficult to imagine. Surely she had seen all the ages of mankind! It was amazing that she was still so spry. Perhaps she had been toughened by helping her husband with the ironworking, before he died. She had developed a bit of a twitch in her cheek, but her eyes were still sharp.

She listened with interest to Flower's case, then set to work rehearsing her on the missing kings and histories. There was more of it than Flower had realized, and it was harder to get it all straight than she had expected. But the appeal of the notion of being First Wife to a future king made the effort worthwhile.

In due course Mboong aLeeng did inquire, in the guise of other business, and Crystal did refer him to Flower, suggesting that the appearance of a romance would effectively mask his real purpose. He was quick to appreciate the potential. Thus it was that he came to her house in a formal manner, to obtain her father's permission for him to court her. He was a highly athletic and reasonably handsome man, black of skin and blue of skirt, a redoubtable warrior, and of royal lineage; such a suit could hardly be declined. Carver had of course been given the word, so he would have approved the matter anyway.

Flower, taking pains to appear somewhat diffident, took a walk with Mboong. This was important; it meant they were being seen alone together in public, and therefore were considering marriage. Not all such couples did marry, of course; when either of them was seen with someone else, the people would know that the romance was over.

When they were out of sight of others, in a parklike section of the city, they settled down and reviewed the list of kings. Mboong was really ignorant, but eager to learn, and Flower took pleasure in telling the earliest of the stories about the kings:

✪

Back in the earliest ancient days, the whole region was an impenetrable forest. The Kuba lived as a small tribe under their chief Lukengo, together with the more powerful tribe of the Bieeng on the left bank of the Lulua River. One day the chief of the Bieeng demanded tribute from Lukengo. He refused, saying that he was equal to the Bieeng chief, and not his subject. This led to an impasse, because the two tribes were related by blood and did not wish to fight each other.

Finally they found a means to decide who among them should be paramount. Lukengo and the Bieeng chief would each fashion a copper plate in a special shape. Then the chiefs would throw their plates at the same time into the Lulua. The one whose plate floated would be the victor, and recognized as the greater chief. So they retired to make their plates, so as to be ready for the contest on a later day.

But on the evening before the day of decision, the Bieeng's young wife overheard her husband and his tribesmen planning to cheat. They had taken palm wood and covered it with such a thin layer of copper that it was too light to sink. Now, it happened that the woman was from the Kuba tribe, and her blood called her, and she knew she could not allow this to happen. So during the night she stole the false plate and ran with it to Lukengo. She told him about the planned deception, and showed him the plate as evidence. Lukengo was deeply annoyed by this, for he had made an honest copper plate. But faced with this evidence of his opponent's cheating, he decided to reverse the ploy. So he gave the woman his plate and told her to return it to the place she had found the false plate. So the young woman took his plate and substituted it for the one she had taken. Then she retired, and her husband never realized what she had done.

Early next morning Lukengo came to the bank of the Lulua with all his followers and called for the Bieeng to come and participate in the contest. The Bieeng chief was embarrassed, for he had slept later and been upstaged. He took up the plate and hurried to the river. Then the two of them threw their plates out into the broad river. Lukengo's plate floated, while the Bieeng chief's plate sank. Lukengo declared himself to be the paramount chief of all the people, and the other could not refute him.

However, Lukengo remained disgusted with the way the other chief had tried to cheat, and decided not to remain his neighbor. He crossed with his people to settle on the right bank of the Lulua. There he founded a kingdom in the middle of the forest, with himself as the first king. In time he extended his rule to the tribes of the northeast and became a greater king.

However the Bieeng chief discovered what his wife had done, and was very angry. She fled his vengeance, going across the river to seek refuge with Lukengo. Seeing her thus in daylight for the first time, he realized how pretty she was. He owed her a debt of gratitude. So he rewarded her by marrying her himself, and made her his First Wife. He issued a law that in remembrance of her patriotic deed his followers should be allowed only monogamous marriages with Kuba girls. Hence every Kuba man may have only one legal wife from his tribe. His other wives, whose number is not limited, have to be slaves.

❁

Mboong nodded. "She was surely beautiful," he agreed, contemplating Flower's torso. "She surely deserved her reward."

"To be his first and only wife among the Kuba," she agreed. "As is the custom for Kuba men."

"But not for Kuba kings," he reminded her. "A king must have many wives, as well as slave concubines."

"But only one First Wife, who must be of the Nbong clan."

"True." He gazed at her body a moment more, then returned to the work at hand.

They drilled on the other kings and their histories. But Mboong had a problem. "I would not criticize the record," he said, "but parts of it don't seem to make much sense. It's as if some of it repeats, and some is missing."

"You're right," Flower said. "I was distressed about the same thing, but my grandmother explained it to me. You see, what is important is not what actually happened, but what is authenticated by consensus. True history has to be properly interpreted. Only then is it part of the official record."

"But some of the history differs from itself," he protested. "I mean, one story of Lukengo tells how they threw anvils into the river, instead of copper plates, and then the water turned red, yellow, and white, and the trees shook and a giant crocodile appeared. Lukengo stood on its back, and rode out across the river. How can we explain such differences?"

Flower shook her head. "We don't try. We accept them both, as different ways of seeing history. The validity of one does not necessarily exclude the validity of another. It is the same with the stories of the first man, Woot, and his sister."

"I have never understood that, either."

"I'll try to explain it." Flower concentrated, for this was very difficult material, that somehow seemed to make much more sense when Grandmother Ember explained it than when Flower thought it through for herself. "Woot was the first man, and his sister Mweel was the first woman. So they longed for each other, because there was no one else. Yet it was not right, and Woot was stricken with leprosy and had to leave the primeval village. His sister would not let him go alone, however; she went with him to live in the forest. Mweel tended him, and loved him, and became a wife to him, and so the children were born. From them sprang all the clans of the Kuba. Finally he became well again and they left the forest and brought the children with them. Then the Pygmies saw them, and asked how Woot could have an incestuous relationship with his sister. Woot was so ashamed that he fled upstream. But he was also furious, and he caused the primeval village to burn to ashes, and the streams around it to dry up and break open. The game animals who had been companions of man in this early paradise fled into the bush. Mweel stumbled against a burnt tree stump while fleeing, and felt a soothing tickling in the wound. She investigated, and lo, it was salt. In this manner she discovered salt, which has been of great value to mankind ever since. When Woot left, he took the sun with him, plunging the world into darkness. A spell lay on the country, and it was blanketed in perpetual night. Mweel could not see to tend her children. Twice she sent messengers to Woot, to plead with him to return and to bring back the sun, before he relented and restored light and fertility to the country."

"Yes," Mboong agreed. "That one I know. But—"

"I'm coming to that. There is also the story of Ooto, who was the sun, and Iselenge, who was the moon. They were children of one mother. They migrated with many people and came to the country between the Lulua and the Kasai rivers, south of our present country. All of them spent the night in a huge house, with the couples sleeping together and the unmarried men sleeping on one side and the unmarried women on the other side. But in the darkness Ooto quietly crossed and stayed instead with Iselenge. She would have told him to go away, but she did not wish to shame him, and so he slept with her. But the rats could see them together in the night, and a rat approached and said to Ooto: 'You are a chief. Your sister is also a chief. How can you sleep with either your sister or another chief?' The rat was giving him the opportunity to admit his error, and to retire to the side of the house where he belonged. But Ooto merely replied, 'I have no other woman,' and would not desist. The rat, seeing that Iselenge declined to protest, chided him: 'This is evil of you.' After a time Ooto felt the shame of it and went with other people across the Kasai River where the Pende people lived, pretending to know nothing of what had happened. Iselenge remained in the big house with their children. But they could not endure without the daily presence of the sun; they became ill in the arms and legs, and many died. So Iselenge sent a fly across the river to Ooto to plead with him to return, but he refused. Then she sent a dog to beg him, but he would not. Finally she sent a turtle, and Ooto sent the turtle back with the message 'I will come tomorrow.' But he did not, for the shame had not left him. A week passed, and Iselenge and the children continued to suffer. So she sent the dog back again, threatening to send the rat next, and this time Ooto replied, 'I will come tomorrow, when the cuckoo sings.' And, mindful of his sister's threat about the rat, who knew too much, Ooto did return on the morrow, and everyone became healthy again."

"Yes," Mboong agreed. "Woot and Mweel were brother and sister, and Ooto and Iselenge too. It is much the same story. But the details differ. Why should that be?"

"It *is* the same story. But through the two we can appreciate much more about the nature of history than we can from either alone. Because they are recognizably similar, yet different."

He shook his head. "My mind feels like solid palm wood. Surely the two versions only generate doubt, because of the confusion."

Flower cast about for a way to clarify the point, and suddenly had a notion. "Look at your eyes," she said.

He laughed. "We must go to a pool to see our reflections, for that. I can only look *from* my eyes."

He had a point. "Then look at mine. You see I have two." She met his gaze. "Suppose I had only one eye. Would I be able to see as well?"

"No." He closed one of his own eyes. "I can see all of you, but not quite as well."

There was a sound nearby. Someone was approaching. Flower had to smile. "They will think we are staring at each other for love!"

"Then let's give them reason." He closed the distance between them and kissed her.

Flower, caught by surprise, was not completely thrilled. Yet it was supposed to look like a romance, and she did want to marry him and be First Wife, so she took advantage of the occasion to give him the kind of kiss he might not have experienced before.

When the kiss broke, Mboong seemed somewhat shaken. She knew she had impressed him. But she did not want to appear eager. After all, the romance was supposed to be only a pretense, until she was able to make enough of an impression on him so that he would decide to marry her. So she returned immediately to business. "When you look at a tree in the distance, how can you tell how far away it is?"

Mboong looked at a tree. "Well, I have to know, because there might be an animal there I wanted to kill." He brought out his *shongo*, which was the deadly throwing knife with blades projecting in a special pattern.

"But could you tell its distance with only one eye?" she asked.

"Why not?" He closed one eye. "It remains as far away as it is."

Her nice analogy wasn't working. Flower tried again. "With one eye, could you tell which flowers on the ground are closer?"

"Flowers?" He closed one eye, and hurled the shongo. It neatly clipped a daisy from its stem. He walked down to recover both the knife and the flower. "Here it is for you," he said, proffering the blossom.

"Thank you." She took it and tucked it in her hair, and smiled winningly at him. "You have the accuracy of a great warrior." Indeed, she was impressed. But her mind was distracted. How was she to make her point?

"What does this have to do with history?" Mboong inquired sensibly.

She tried again. "Close one eye and look at my hands," she said. She put them together, one before the other, and stuck up one finger from each. "Which finger is closer to you?"

He looked, one-eyed. "They're the same distance."

"Now use both eyes," she said, not moving her hands.

He opened the other eye. "Why, the left one is closer. I hadn't realized."

"Because your two eyes can tell distance better than one eye alone." She rearranged her hands, and he played the game again. Sometimes he was right, sometimes wrong, with one eye.

Soon he was satisfied. "Two eyes are better."

"Because each sees the same thing, but not quite the same," she said. "So you can tell the distance. Now remember the stories: they are the same, yet different. When you look at them, and try to understand them, you can get a deeper insight into the depth of history."

Mboong considered that, concentrating. In a moment he brightened. "Yes! Suddenly I see the meaning of it! Woot and Mweel, Ooto and Iselenge, the Sun and the Moon, husband and wife, brother and sister—they were like us, but also so much more! They were great spirits, yet also man and woman, with the passions and weaknesses of our kind. We know them as we know ourselves, yet they were greater than we are." His face shone with the revelation.

Flower was greatly relieved. The analogy barely made sense to her, but it had worked for him.

Time had passed, and they had to return to her house. "We shall talk again tomorrow," Mboong said. "You are very clever, and pretty too. I will kiss you a second time." He proceeded to do so. Flower was satisfied to cooperate.

Inside, Crystal was unsurprised. "You seem to be making progress."

"I am. I think he's interested. It would be a good marriage."

"You are in doubt?"

"He just doesn't really excite me. When he kisses me I'm bored."

"With seventeen other wives, you won't have to be bored by him often."

"True. As I said, it would be a good marriage."

But, unsatisfied, Flower went to talk again with Grandmother Ember. "I can marry a king, but it doesn't seem enough," she said. "What is wrong with me?"

Her grandmother smiled. "You may suffer from my affliction. I always longed for a special man, a perfect one, even when I was married to your grandfather Scorch. Scorch was a good husband and a tolerant man, and I had no complaints of him, yet I could not abolish that private longing. I know, and always knew, that there was no such man; still I dreamed of him. But I had the sense to get on with my life, and it has been a good enough life. You must do the same."

"But suppose there *is* a perfect man for me?" Flower asked. "And I married another before I met him?"

"If you wait for perfection in manhood, you will never marry," Ember said indulgently. "Leave perfection to your dreams; that is the only place it can be. Even my dream man wasn't quite perfect physically; he had a scar or mark on his forehead."

Flower was not entirely convinced, but neither was she sure that her grandmother was wrong. All she could do was continue her present course, and hope that her emotion would come to agree that her plan was as wise as her intellect suggested.

Next day she took Mboong through more kings and histories, and kissed him again. He was definitely interested, but oddly reserved. It was almost as if he, too, had doubts. She dismissed that notion, of course; what was there for a man to doubt about? Flower knew that her face and body were as good as any, and it was a rare man who could see beyond those.

Finally she had him so well rehearsed on the kings that it was clear he would be able to perform for the council, and be confirmed as the designated heir to the kingship. He was also quite smitten by her, and kissed her so often it threatened to interfere with her instruction. He would quickly have had sex with her, if she had let him. Yet still he hadn't asked her to marry him.

So she had to tackle the matter herself. "Don't you want to marry me, Mboong?"

"Yes, I do," he agreed sadly.

"And make me your First Wife?"

"Yes. I love you and desire you more than anything."

"Then why don't you ask me if I am willing, and then talk to my father?"

"I can not."

"You can't? I don't understand."

"Because I did not want you to understand."

What was this? She hardly expected subtlety in this or any man. "What didn't you want me to understand?"

He looked miserable. "That I can't marry you."

"You can't marry me! Why not?"

"It is hard to explain."

"I should think so."

"I didn't know you would be so attractive. It was supposed to be a mock romance. But every time I kissed you, I liked you more. I should have told you, but then you would not have kissed me anymore."

"Why not, if it was all a pose?" she asked sharply.

"Because I knew what you wanted."

"What did I want?"

"To be First Wife. You did not care about me as a man, you just wanted me to care about you, so I would marry you and then leave you alone when distracted by the other wives."

Her jaw dropped. He had defined her interest perfectly.

"I knew I was a fool," he continued. "But you were so winsome, I could not stop. So I didn't tell you."

Flower's head seemed to be spinning. "Tell me what?"

"That I must marry another woman of your clan, and she must be First Wife."

"But you have not been seen with any other woman since being seen with me."

"True. She is not beautiful, and I have no desire for her. There is no courtship; indeed the family does not want the betrothal known until they choose to make it known. But I must marry her."

"But why? I—you understood me correctly, but I would do whatever you wished. I would give you a male heir."

"And perhaps you would even come to love me, in time," he agreed sadly. "But it may not be."

"I just don't see why you should have to marry a woman you don't like."

Mboong looked away. "King Shyaam does not like me. But he has been unable to sire a male heir, and I am his cousin, his mother's sister's son, his closest eligible kin, and competent. So he must designate me his heir. But he is making me pay. The woman's family is loyal to him, and supports his policies. So he requires me to marry her, as a condition of the designation. I know he is not bluffing; he can reach farther out for an heir if he has to. So I had to agree, and I will marry her, though I love you. If I do not, I will not be king, and you would not be the wife of a king, and would therefore lose your interest in me anyway. I have no choice."

"Yet how could you have courted me, while being betrothed to this other woman?"

"The king is pleased to see me dance on a string, loving elsewhere, knowing that nothing can come of it. The woman's family cares only that she will be First Wife, with her sons given preference for subsequent heirs. They may even be pleased to show their power by requiring my attendance when it is obvious that I lack desire for it. All this I knew, and I resolved that the romance between you and me would be mere mock. But you won my heart despite my cynicism and yours. My folly is that I knew the likely pain of it, and pursued it anyway. Your kisses were too sweet to resist."

He was right. He could not marry her. Yet, ironically, his present honesty moved her deeply. "I think I can't fault you, Mboong," she said heavily. "You were right, that I would not have encouraged you if I had known. If you wanted my attention, you had to do what you did. Now that you know the kings, we shall have to separate. But I was at fault for leading you on, and now if you wish to have your will of me before we part—"

"No. The mischief is already more than enough. I will simply depart."

"I will not protest or charge you with a wrongful act. I feel guilty for my part in this."

"Your guilt is not more than mine. You have done the job; you have prepared me for the recitation of kings. I owe you the marriage you sought. I can't pay. I thank you for your offer, which I most desire to accept, and I decline it."

Flower found herself with mixed feelings, but the better part of the mixture was relief. She flung her arms around him and kissed him with more passion than ever before. Then she separated and walked away. He let her go.

Flower, distracted, did not go home. Instead she went to Grandmother Ember for solace. "So I can not be First Wife," she concluded. "Nor wife at all. What am I to do?"

"The world is not lost," Ember replied. "You must do everything you can to see that Mboong is the next king of Kuba."

"What do I care if he's king? It won't do me any good."

Ember sighed. "I was sixteen once; I remember. Take my word: what is important at sixteen is not as important at a later age, and no one knows the future. Some things you must do because they are right to do, and trust to the moon to reward you. You must arrange to be at the confirmation council, to help Mboong get through without shame."

"But only a few chosen women besides Mother, as the chief singer of the king's harem, can attend, and she doesn't speak there unless a man asks her a question."

"Nevertheless, Mboong may stumble in the pressure of the recitation. He is a fine warrior, but not bold academically. Your presence will surely help him through."

Flower stared at her grandmother suspiciously. "You're up to something."

"It is the nature of old women."

So Flower, perplexed, returned home. "How can I be at Mboong's confirmation council?" she asked her mother.

Crystal looked at her. "What has happened?"

Flower told her, as she had told her grandmother. Then she told of Ember's reaction.

"Your grandmother was always one of the canniest schemers," Crystal remarked. "Did you hear how she lured your grandfather into marriage when she was thought to be too young to manage a man?"

"Many times. I used similar ways to lure Mboong. But what is Grandmother thinking of?"

Crystal pondered a moment. "I think I am feeling ill."

"Oh, Mother, I didn't know!" Flower said, alarmed.

"In fact, I think I will need some assistance when I attend the confirmation council, lest I embarrass myself in public."

The import dawned. Crystal, too, could be canny. "I will go with you, to help you."

"That's sweet of you, dear."

So it was that Crystal, abruptly infirm, brought her daughter along for support. Flower was awed by the council. It was assembled in the main chamber of the king's palace, and the powerful men of Kuba were seated in their bright belted skirts, holding their distinguishing staffs, wearing their feather badges of rank. How impressive they were in their somber grandeur!

She also saw a number of works of sculpture, some of them made by Carver, her father. There were statues commemorating King Shyaam and the heroes of the past, and horrendous masks, wood carvings, and a number of shongo knives.

King Shyaam entered and took his seat, which was below that of his mother. He was most impressive with his elaborate skirt and belt. He was, according to the history of kings, the son of a slave. He had gotten great wealth as a trader, and finally managed to become king, but the tinge of illegitimacy still clung to him. That meant that though he was widely popular, he still had to heed the concerns of the council, and not everything went his way.

Shyaam glanced at his mother, for she alone had the privilege of speaking before him. She, as Flower understood was usual, elected not to speak. The privileges of women were nominal rather than actual, though mothers and wives did have special powers over the men to whom they related.

"I have selected Mboong aLeeng to be my official heir," the king announced. "He will be king after me."

This was no news to the members of the council; the word had spread ahead, as it always did. In fact, they had probably required the king to make this designation, because Mboong was both the closest male kin and the best qualified. The king had delayed, hoping to have a male child, but now he was old and no child born after this would be of suitable age by the time Shyaam died. So they signaled their approval by raising their belts.

"But is this man worthy?" the chief historian inquired, following the ritual for this occasion. "Does he know the lineage and histories of the kings of our land?"

"About that he shall have to satisfy you himself," Shyaam replied.

"Then let him enter and demonstrate his knowledge," the chief historian said.

At this point Mboong entered, resplendent in his skirt and belt. He came to the center of the chamber and looked around. Flower saw his eyes widen a trifle when they passed her; he had not known she would be there. Then he faced the chief historian. He began to recite the lineage of kings.

But Grandmother Ember's concern proved to be well founded. After the first several kings, Mboong hesitated, evidently having lost his place. It had happened several times when Flower was drilling him.

The particular king he needed had been known for introducing a new kind of nut to the diet of the tribe. Flower slowly lifted her hand to her mouth, and bit down as if breaking open a nut. In a moment Mboong's gaze passed her, and he saw her unobtrusive pantomime. Immediately he spoke, naming the nut-king and continuing with his history.

Twice more during the recitation Flower cued Mboong on particular kings. Then he finished the last several with flair, knowing that he had passed his examination of worthiness.

The chief historian nodded. The heir apparent had proven himself.

The council meeting was done. The men departed. Flower helped her ailing mother to make her way out. It had been an interesting experience.

As they left, Mboong stepped from the shadows. "I will remember," he said, and went on as if merely passing them.

Flower understood then that time would prove that memory. The business of Flower's family would prosper because of the favor of the king, and in due course Flower herself would be appointed chief singer, allowing her mother to retire. She would achieve a position of considerable prestige, and remain free to marry whom she wished. Grandmother Ember had known.

Mboong aLeeng's reign was considerably more violent than that of his predecessor; there were a number of wars. But the Kuba did well, and maintained their special identity through to the present. Many legends came to clothe the reigns of Shyaam and Mboong, making them archetypes of the peaceful and warlike aspects of tribal history. In terms of global politics the region was incorporated into the Belgian Congo, which today is the nation of Zaire. But the people of Kuba remember their history, which is unique to them in detail and manner.

CHAPTER 19

INDIA

The British Empire at its height was the most extensive known to man, in global terms, embracing territories in Europe, America, Africa, Australia, and Asia. But its most valuable was India, including what are now Pakistan, Bangladesh, Ceylon, and later Burma down through the Malay Peninsula, and it carefully safeguarded the strategic points of the routes there. Thus Gibraltar, South Africa, Suez, the Gulf of Aden and other spots became British and remained so until the twentieth century. British soldiers and merchants were everywhere, but their relationship with natives was not always easy. In 1857 several units of the Indian army revolted against the British

395

domination; that was put down, but British cynicism increased. Worse was to come in the following decade.

S TONE laid the letter on the table. "Tree, your grandfather has agreed to make the arrangements for your keep during your time in England," he announced. "We shall arrange passage for you next year, and you will start classes there in 1866."

Wood nodded. He couldn't stop his father from calling him by his given name, but elsewhere he could get away with a nickname. Stone had arranged a good thing for him, and he was duly appreciative. This meant that he would be able to have the two years of schooling in England required to prepare him for the rigorous examinations for qualification for the Indian Civil Service, or ICS. He also liked the idea of having closer contact with Grandfather Blaze, whom he had met only twice but regarded as a great old man. He hadn't seen Blaze since he was twelve, six years ago when the elderly couple had visited India, so it was certainly time.

"I shall try to uphold the standards of the family, Father," he said.

"I should expect so." Stone turned away, dismissing him.

Wood left the room. He knew his father cared, but like most upper-class Britishers he found it almost impossible to express anything as common as family closeness. Grandfather Blaze was entirely different, being expressive and warm, as was Grandmother.

He found his mother working in the garden behind the bungalow. She loved gardening, and had many exotic as well as local flowers and shrubs growing. At the moment she was among her ginger plants. "Grandfather Blaze has agreed," Wood told her. "They'll board me in England."

She set aside her trowel and brushed herself off. She was forty-one years old, but still by his unobjective judgment a lovely woman. "Oh, that's wonderful, Woody!" she exclaimed, hugging him. "I know you'll love England." She was as expressive as Stone was inexpressive, though in public she managed to appear properly reserved.

"It is a relief," Wood admitted. "I feel at home here in India. At least with Grandfather Blaze I'll have someone to make that foreign land bearable."

"Why, England isn't foreign!" she protested, laughing. "It's our homeland. You were born there, Woody. You need to refresh your interest in your true culture."

"But this is the land I love, Mother. Almost everything I remember is here. I know some of the dialects about as well as I know English."

"Then it is high time you reviewed English," she retorted. It was clear that in this respect her attitude was one with his father's.

Out of sorts, Wood took his tennis racket and went to the club for a workout. His family was not wealthy, but every Britisher had the privileges of the dominant group, and all the considerable entertainment facilities of Calcutta were available to him.

At the club he passed several British women. He ignored them, and they ignored him. Their mutual aversion had long since been recognized. He regarded them as spoiled, snotty creatures without depth, and they regarded him as what was termed "turning native." It was true; he had come to value the cultures of India, and had respect for many of its people, and he couldn't stand those who looked with disdain on the natives. So the gulf between him and most other children of British officials in India was too deep to be conveniently bridged.

Today he spied a newcomer. The man had a racket, but looked uncertain. Wood approached him. "Are you looking for the courts? I'm going there myself."

"Actually, I was looking for an opponent," the man said. "I arrived a few days ago, and I'm not familiar with the people here."

"As I said, I am going there. If you care to play against me, I'm of middling competence."

"That's my case exactly!" the man agreed. He held out his hand. "John Duncan, here."

"Wood Stone," Wood replied. "No, it's not a pun, other than that foisted on me by my parents." He shook the hand.

They walked on toward the tennis courts. "Everything seems so strange here, no offense," John said. "For example, I never saw an elephant before, yet here they are commonplace. Such huge creatures! Every person seems to have several servants, and can't do anything for himself. But I'm used to doing for myself, so I said no thank you. But I find that does leave me a bit lost."

"Next year I must go to England, to complete my education," Wood said. "I expect to be similarly lost there."

"You have not been there?" John asked, surprised.

"Not since I was six years old. I remember it, but not well."

"Ah, your family never returned! That's unfortunate."

"I have not thought it so. I like India."

"But you must give England a chance! There is no country in all the world like it."

They came to the courts and changed to playing uniforms. Native boys came out to tend to their balls and provide towels, refreshments, and enthusiasm. "Why, this is just like a club in England," John said, surprised.

"I wouldn't know," Wood said. "Perhaps when I am in England, I shall be able to play, and recover a sense of home."

John laughed, thinking it a joke. They proceeded to the play. They turned out to be well matched, both being in the middle range and neither being too proud to look foolish on a point. John had a strong serve that gave Wood some trouble at first, while Wood had a drop shot that continually caught John playing too far back. Their first set went to several deuces before John put it away 10–8.

Several others had gathered to watch. Now two young British women approached, lovely in their well-fitting sport outfits. "May we join you?" one asked John. "We would love to make it a doubles game."

Wood was disgusted. He knew the girls. They were good enough players, for their gender, but that was because they seemed to do very little else in their limited lives. He regarded them as decorative nuisances.

"Why, I don't know," John said, taken aback. "I'm new here, and don't know the conventions." He looked at Wood. "Are such things done here?"

Both girls shot Wood warning glances. They had come to move in on a new prospect, and didn't want him interfering. Since he did not want the kind of scene that could erupt if he balked them, he yielded gracefully. "Here in India we have smaller communities than perhaps are the rule in England. Men and women do play together on occasion, especially when there are not otherwise enough to make a group."

"By all means, then, let's play," John said.

One girl joined John, and the other joined Wood. "Just keep your mouth shut," she muttered.

They played a doubles set. The girls were in decorously long sleeves and long white skirts, but it was amazing how clearly their limbs and torsos manifested, especially when they reached for far balls. John was plainly impressed, as he should have been, for the display was for his benefit. Once, Wood's girl managed to crash into him when trying for a ball she shouldn't have, and he had to support her lest she fall. "What are you trying to do?" he asked as he set her upright, knowing that she had no interest in him.

"Watch and learn," she replied.

Not long later John's girl did the same with John. Somehow their supposedly inadvertent entanglement became more like an embrace, with her body making lingering contact with his. Then she flashed him a brilliant smile. "Thank you so much for preventing my fall," she told John.

After that Wood saw that John watched her, unobtrusively, not with distrust but with interest. She had made an impression on him. Wood's girl had set it up by demonstrating how such innocent contacts could occur.

After the set John's girl suggested that they retire for some refreshment, and John was happy to agree. They went as a foursome to the refreshment counter. Thereafter they broke into two couples, at the girls' instigation, and separated as such. That had been the girls' objective from the outset: to attach one of them to the new man, who should be good for some entertainment before he became too familiar.

"You know, you're not a bad sort, when you behave," Wood's girl remarked. "Would you care for some croquette?"

Wood knew that the offer included more than that, if he had a mind for it. The British women of Calcutta were nominally completely proper at all times, and the older ones were busy enough to comply, but boredom brought some of the younger ones to sometimes notorious private behavior. Wood understood this, but remained turned off, because he knew how utterly shallow this girl was. She considered it a virtual crime to know or care anything about the natives; her life was completely isolated from theirs. By her estimation, an Indian existed to serve a British person, completely and without protest, and deserved no other life.

"I think not," Wood said, and left her.

❂

Another day John saw him in the club and approached him. "I say, I didn't mean to break up the tennis without giving you a chance to even the score," he said apologetically.

"It was a good match as it was," Wood said. "Don't be concerned."

"Please don't take offense, for I mean none, but you seem different from others I've encountered here."

Here it came. "How so? No offense, of course."

"You have character."

Wood laughed. "How could you tell that, from a tennis game?"

"It isn't what you said, but what others have said of you. They intend, I fear, disparagement, but I take it otherwise. They say that you have gone native. Meaning that you seem to care more for the concerns of the natives than for the prerogatives of the British echelons."

"They're right."

"I respect that. I believe we shall be unable to benefit the natives if we don't learn their ways."

"Not all their ways are nice by our definitions," Wood said wryly.

"How so?"

"For example, the Hindus have *sati,* literally 'true wife,' which is the practice of throwing a widow on her husband's funeral pyre. We have outlawed it, but not with complete success."

"Certainly we outlawed it! You can't approve of such a practice!"

"No. I merely recognize that it is part of their culture. There are, by my definition, both assets and liabilities of it. They view some of our customs with similar disdain."

"Oh? What—"

"We don't regard the cow as sacred, or the pig as unclean."

"Oh, yes. That triggered the Sepoy Mutiny eight years ago. Because the grease on the cartridges for the Enfield rifle contained tallow which was said to come from a number of animals, including pigs and cows, and they had to bite into it to open the end and release the powder. No one at the time clarified that the source was actually mutton fat. That was certainly a mistake."

"It was more than a mistake," Wood said. "Suppose you had to bite into a cartridge heavily smeared with polluted sewage and excrement? So that you feared dysentery as well as being absolutely disgusted? To a

Muslim pig's fat is similarly disgusting, and to a Hindu the touch of cow's fat on the lips would be worse. In fact it would be an abomination for which we have no parallel, because of the sacredness of the animal. Imagine eating fat rendered from your own deceased father, perhaps. It would damn a person spiritually. Our disregard for such sensitivities brought much mischief."

John nodded. "I appreciate that now. There is more I have to learn about India, that I think was not adequately covered in my lessons in England."

Wood shrugged. "We are as a class largely indifferent to the concerns of the natives. I'm not. That damns me in the eyes of my associates."

"Not in my eyes," John said firmly. Then he extended his hand.

Wood took it, gratified.

❂

In the following weeks John was occupied studying local language at the College of Fort William, so that he could pass his examinations before being posted to the field the following spring. He found it difficult. "I have no trouble with the ordinary aspects of education," he confessed to Wood. "But I never was sharp at foreign languages, and these of India have me baffled. I'm not sure I'll ever get it."

"That's odd," Wood said. "I never had any problem. I suppose it's because I grew up here, and listened to the natives speaking among themselves when I was a child. I just seemed to pick it up naturally. What I fear are the sciences and pedagogic aspects."

"I wish we could exchange parts of our minds," John said.

They discussed some of the things that John found most confusing, and Wood clarified them for his friend. John made better progress. "I don't know where I would be, without your help," he said candidly.

Then disaster came. "I'm being posted this autumn!" John said, stricken. "I'm not ready. I expected to have until spring, but it seems that something came up, and my professor recommended me. I fear it is your fault."

"My fault? I have tried to help you."

John smiled. "Exactly. I have improved so much, after a shaky start, that it impressed my professor, who believes I have a special talent for native dialect. I tried to tell him that I have gotten special tutoring, but he thinks I'm being modest. It's a good assignment; it means I will be commissioned sooner than otherwise. But I am distinctly unready. I fear I will make hideous blunders."

Wood realized that he did indeed bear some responsibility for his friend's situation. He knew that John did not yet have sufficient command of Indian dialects or nuances of culture to handle himself well. "I shouldn't have interfered," he admitted ruefully.

John was immediately contrite. "I was not serious, Woody! Without your help I would have been completely lost at sea. I simply didn't realize that I was making a better impression than I deserved. Oh, if only I could have your advice on the circuit!"

Wood considered. "I wonder whether that's possible? I'm not busy until I embark for England next year. I love India, and would be glad to see as much of it as possible before I have to leave it. But I also would like to learn more of England before I go there, so as not to be in the same trouble there that you are in here. You could surely prepare me for that, if we had time together to talk. Do you think I could go along as an interpreter?"

"An interpreter!" John exclaimed. "That's ideal! I must see if it can be arranged."

They worked on it. Wood told his father the situation, and his responsibility in the matter, while John made a clean breast of his concern to his professor. Stone agreed that there was perhaps an aspect of duty involved, and the professor preferred not to be embarrassed by a faulty recommendation. Subtle strings were pulled, and in due course Wood was approved as an additional translator and deputy for the posting. This was to Orissa, the district just southwest of Bengal. Wood was familiar with it, having ridden and hunted often enough in that direction. Despite its proximity, it was relatively undeveloped, densely populated along the coast, with no train lines passing through it, and much of it was accessible mainly by horseback. A Britisher unfamiliar with the terrain and language would certainly have trouble getting along there.

They took the coach to the provincial capital of Cuttack, where they obtained horses from the local stable for the ride to the country. All along the way, Wood pointed out significant aspects of the geography and the inhabitants, while John responded with aspects of Victorian England. Queen Victoria herself, he said, just wasn't the same since her consort Prince Albert died, but the country and empire as a whole were doing well. One preposterous yet interesting thing he had learned about in college was the radical and perhaps heretical theory promoted by one Charles Darwin, that all living creatures were somehow related, having propelled themselves forward from lesser origins by a process called evolution. "I don't believe it, of course," John confided. "Yet I must say, I enjoy seeing the clerics outraged. Imagine man actually descending from the apes!"

Wood had to laugh. Such a notion would certainly offend the churches, both Catholic and Church of England. And it did have a certain tempting rationale. He had often wondered just where man had come from, and an instant creation from whole cloth didn't quite satisfy him. Evolution from apes? What a jolly heresy!

John, as subdivision officer, duly reported to his deputy commissioner to be given his assignment in the field. Wood stood behind him, expecting a good deal of harrumphing and considering before being told that they would accompany an experienced officer to learn the ropes. The reality was startlingly different.

"You're it, eh? Strap on your pistol and come with me." The commissioner marched out of the building, leading them to another house where a number of natives stood waiting. "This is your court," the commissioner announced, gesturing to a table. "These are your assistants." He indicated four turbaned, bearded men wearing *dhoti,* untailored cloth wound around the waist and legs. "Now get to work."

John was taken aback, understandably. "To work, sir?"

"You didn't come here to sleep, did you? Clean up this mess so you can move on to your next station." The commissioner marched away.

John took his seat in the rattan chair at the end of the table. Wood went quietly to stand behind him. No one challenged this arrangement; these were after all two British gentlemen. John did know the procedure; he had described it to Wood. He just hadn't expected to be thrust so suddenly into it, with no testing period or detailed instructions.

The *peshkar,* or "bringer-forward" clerk, snapped out words so rapidly that Wood knew John couldn't understand them. But this was what he was here for. "He says these are the cases on Your Honor's file, and what are your orders?" Wood translated quietly.

"Let's get on with it," John said briskly in English, as if merely not deigning to use the native dialect. He was putting up a suitable British front, and he was good at it; the assistants were impressed.

The peshkar looked at his papers and spoke rapidly again. Wood realized that the man was probably doing it deliberately, hoping to embarrass the new officer without actually being disrespectful. But that wouldn't work in this case, because Wood understood perfectly. "The clerk is reading out the first case," he murmured in John's ear. "The clerk has considerable power, because he decides the order in which cases come forward. You can of course overrule him if you feel he is being unfair."

"I know that," John murmured back somewhat edgily. "What's the case?"

"The prisoner is accused of stealing thirty stalks of sugarcane, worth about one penny, from a field in the night. There are witnesses to testify."

"Ah," John said, relieved. He proceeded to try the case, being duly satisfied that the man was guilty, and assigning a suitable penalty. This aspect he understood; it was only the swiftly spoken native dialect that confused him.

So it continued. There was a seemingly endless list of chores which, taken as a whole, were at best dull. Occasionally Wood's ready translation enabled John to pick up on an irregularity that the clerk might have hoped to slip through, and John quickly corrected it. It was evident that he was making a good impression.

As the day waned, John called a halt. "We will resume tomorrow morning," he announced. "See that the papers are in order."

The clerks bowed respectfully and departed with their papers. John stood and entered the main part of the house. "Where the hell's the privy?" he asked Wood. "I'm ready to burst."

Wood smiled. He had not realized, and so surely the clerks had not. John had seemed like an iron man, a machine dispensing justice.

They found the privy. Then John lay down on the bed to rest. "Tell the cook we'll eat in an hour," he said.

Wood did so, and also ordered a man to pull the *punkah* cord. This cord passed through a hole in the wall and was attached to a framework with a damp blanket above the bed; the cord made this move back and forth, generating a cooling draft. He also directed another servant to pull off His Honor's shoes and socks. Such personal services, he explained to John, were standard when the British were on duty among the natives. John pretended to be at ease with them, despite his preference in doing for himself, so as to make the proper impression. Wood sat in the nearby chair and rested himself.

He was of course not John's servant, but they had discussed this and decided that it would be easier if he appeared to be so, or at least a lieutenant who spoke for the senior officer. That way John would seldom have to attempt the native dialect, and could seem to ignore what was addressed to him so that his lieutenant could relay it with proper form. His ignorance would be covered by his seeming arrogance. So he was putting on a show at the moment, demonstrating his complete command of the situation—as Wood had quietly suggested. Impressions counted for a lot, and the lack of arrogance could be taken as weakness.

So it went. In three days John wrapped up the caseload at this station. Wood had to admit he was good at it; the man was a natural administrator. Perhaps his professor had selected him for that rather than for the seeming finesse with language. Wood was learning already, preparing for the time when he himself would return to India to do similar work.

Now they went out on the circuit. They were equipped with horses and guns and servants and clerks and even an armed escort. They would live in tents during the tour, and inspect everything from roads and bridges to police stations and records of field and crop allocations. This was, by British standards, roughing it, but it was a far easier haul than that of the servants.

They traveled about ten miles to a suitable campsite near the village and made camp. For the next two days they rose at dawn to ride out on inspection, covering a school, a sanitation site, a disputed court case from the prior month, and the vital *patwari*'s papers. These formed the basis for all land revenue—that was to say, taxes—and were extremely important and sensitive. Late each morning they returned to bathe in the tin tub behind the tent, and dry with towels hung over the tent ropes. There was nothing like a sun-warmed towel! Then a big meal serving as breakfast and lunch. In the afternoon there were petitions and new court cases to be heard, including disputes arising from the morning's inspection. John did his best to be fair, and Wood's accuracy with the language enabled him to grasp the nature of each case quickly. It showed here, too: John was making an excellent impression.

The late afternoon and evenings they had to themselves. They rode out hunting, searching out quail, partridges, peacock and hares.

Peasants appeared unasked, and made themselves useful by beating the bushes for game. "I know the natives don't love us," John murmured. "Why are they volunteering?"

"They want your attention," Wood replied. "They aren't on the official lists, perhaps being out of favor, but they have concerns. It is best to treat them with courtesy, to make a good impression."

"To be sure."

"They may demur, at first, but they do want service," Wood said. "You will have to ask them more than once. It is the protocol."

"Got it. Thanks."

After bagging several quail, which were eagerly fetched and brought in by the peasants, John addressed the matter. "I say, can I do anything for you chaps?"

"Oh, no, sahib! We just want to help."

"Come now. You have done me a service; perhaps I can do you one. It is only fair, after all. What's on your mind?"

"Your Honor, my brother—he was horribly beaten last night, for stealing a hammer, but he was innocent." Wood murmured a continuous translation, so that John seemed to understand directly.

"Who did steal the hammer?" John asked briskly.

"Nobody, Your Honor. It was misplaced, and was found an hour later."

"There are witnesses to attest that it was never stolen?"

"Yes, Your Honor."

"Bring your brother to my court tomorrow, and I will make it right."

"Oh, thank you, thank you, sahib!"

So it happened. The man was not on the clerk's list, but Wood kept an eye out for him and brought the man and his brother personally to the head of the line. John entered a judgment against the beaten man's master and ordered that the man be given two days of rest with pay. This the clerk duly noted; it would be done.

One problem was that many farmers were unable to make their full tax allotments, because the monsoon rains had been low that summer, and the crop correspondingly poor. Fortunately there were reserves of grain to carry them through. John settled it fairly: "Your tax shares will be reduced this year, but correspondingly raised next year to make up the difference, assuming that the weather improves." They were satisfied with that; next year was far away.

But privately John was concerned. "Does this happen often? Suppose there's low rainfall next year, too?"

"There would be a famine," Wood said seriously. "But there's no need to worry; there hasn't been a famine since 1801."

"Nevertheless, it isn't good to deplete the margin. We must make sure that the reserves are restored."

At the third village the local patwari's papers were in good order, and the verification was relatively easy. The man's name, approximately translated, was Whittler, and he issued an invitation to the officer to do him the honor of coming and dining at his house. This caught John by surprise. "Allow me a moment to consider," he said. "Is this regular?" he quietly asked Wood.

"Not exactly. Such invitations are made, but normally declined, because of the potential for abuse."

"Abuse?"

"The host normally proffers a valuable gift. This might be considered a—"

"A bribe! We'll have none of that!"

"But in Indian culture it is standard. In the past, I understand some officers have accepted such gifts, enriching themselves."

"Well, I shall simply decline any such gift."

"That would be awkward to do. It's part of the ritual. You might give the impression that you had taken offense, or that the gift was unworthy. It would be better simply to avoid the whole thing by declining the invitation."

"Well said." John returned to the patwari. "I regret that my business prevents me from accepting your kind offer, but I thank you for it."

The patwari did the unusual thing of repeating the offer. "But we would so very much like to have you!" Wood translated.

John hesitated. "The truth is, I don't want to make a fool of myself; I don't know the nuances. But he strikes me as a good man, and I don't want to distress him. I suspect there is something he wants to broach unofficially, and I doubt it is ill intended. Is there an alternative?"

Wood pondered. "I suppose you could delegate me to attend in your stead. I wouldn't mind a good Indian meal."

"But the gift—"

"Maybe we could give them a gift ourselves. This isn't usual, but they wouldn't refuse it, and it might balance things out."

"Excellent. What do we have?"

"There is some nice jewelry I brought from Calcutta. I had thought to trade it for something, if I saw anything I wanted, but there's no need. I might present it to his wife."

"Note its value, and we'll try to get you reimbursed." Then he returned to the patwari. "I remain unfortunately busy, but my second officer can speak for me. If you care to extend your invitation to him—"

The man was happy to do so. So Wood fetched his jewelry and rode home with the patwari. There was indeed an unofficial concern. "The auguries are poor," the man said. "I fear that the harvest next year will be bad, and I am concerned for the people here. I do not wish to alarm anyone, however. If such a thing occurs, do you suppose grain could be shipped in from a more distant region?"

"I will ask the officer about that," Wood said. "Certainly we would not wish to be caught unaware." He remembered that John had already spoken of restoring the reserves, so this was an easy promise to make.

"Perhaps I worry unduly. But I would feel easier if I knew that preparations were being made, just in case."

"This seems sensible to me, and I'm sure my superior will agree." Quite sure.

"But I would not care to burden my family with such an apprehension."

"Understandably. I shall not mention it again tonight."

"Your understanding is much appreciated." The man hesitated. "If I may make a personal remark . . ."

"Be welcome, no offense taken."

"You seem unusually conversant with our customs and language, for an Englishman, considering your age."

Wood laughed. "My father has been stationed in Calcutta for a dozen years. I grew up here, and learned the local ways. I regard India as my home."

"Yet others have grown up in such manner, and not been interested in our ways."

"I confess to being somewhat of a rogue among my kind. I do feel more at home, sometimes, with the people of India than among the spoiled children of the empire."

"I never heard you use the word 'black' in all your dialogue and translations these past two days of our business, even during the trying times."

Wood looked at his tanned arms, then at the patwari. "I suppose there is a difference of color. I think too much is made of it."

"We Hindus are accustomed to the strictures of caste. Color becomes another caste."

"I do not care to discuss my differences with the system of castes, lest I become offensive. I am to that extent an Englishman."

"Your philosophy seems consistent to me."

They rode on, and soon arrived at the patwari's house. This was made of stone and wood, with a thatched roof, and was fairly large, because the servants' rooms were part of it. The patwari's mother, wife and daughter came out to greet them, three generations. They wore flowing formal dresses made from khadi, the hand-spun, handwoven cloth of India.

"This is Heaven-sent Sahib Stone, lieutenant to Sahib Duncan, who was unable to attend," the patwari said, introducing Wood to his family. "This is my mother, the widow Ember, my wife Crystal, and my daughter Ginger Flower." The three women bowed to Wood as they were introduced. The elder was stately with her bound hair and conservative white dress, her green eyes reminding him of his grandfather Blaze. The middle woman was comfortable in quiet blue. The young woman was comely in a golden jacket and green skirt, with lustrous dark hair.

"I am pleased to meet three such charming women," Wood said. He met their gazes, briefly, in turn. The eldest woman seemed to have a slight affliction of one cheek, perhaps a consequence of age. But when he came to Ginger, something passed between them. It was as if a small spark jumped, and her face was illuminated by it, becoming abruptly beautiful. As if he had just met the woman he was destined to love. As if he had known her before. Déjà vu, inexplicable yet gloriously powerful.

Wood shook himself, and Ginger blinked, evidently suffering a similar confusion. No one else, he hoped, had noticed this curious connection.

"Now allow me to present you with a token of our esteem," the patwari said. He brought out a fine hunting pistol in its case.

Wood was taken aback. He had expected a gift, but not one of this value. The family circumstance could have been seriously reduced to afford the purchase of such a weapon. It must have been obtained with the expectation that the officer himself would attend, instead of his lesser assistant. "Oh, I could not accept—"

"Ah, but we insist," the patwari said graciously. "It is a symbol of the regard in which we hold you and the service you represent and the empire of England."

Wood could not decline a gift phrased in that manner. Reluctantly he accepted the pistol. Then he brought out the jewelry he had brought. "I regret I have nothing to offer that even approaches the value of what you have given me," he said. "But allow me to present your mother with this bauble." He held up the pearl necklace. It was of course far more than a bauble, but still not of the level of the pistol.

"Jewelry is not for withered old women," the widow protested. "Give it to my daughter instead."

Wood turned to the patwari's wife. But she, too, protested. "When would I wear such a fine necklace? Give it to my daughter."

He turned to the daughter. She in turn opened her mouth to protest similarly, but their eyes met again, and she was unable to speak. Wood, shaken, forced himself to act. "Ginger, you must accept this necklace, as a token of my great respect for your father, though it can only diminish the loveliness that is already yours." Never had a formulaic utterance had such truth! He stepped toward her, lifted it, and put it over her head to rest on her shoulders. Her great eyes stared into his, like pools through which he saw all the stars of the eternal night sky. "I love you," he whispered, unable to help himself.

Then he hauled himself away, hoping he had not shamed himself too badly by an evident lapse of protocol. The eyes of both other women were on him, and he knew they knew, but they were silent. What had happened to him?

The dinner proceeded, with Wood given the place of honor at the head of the table. The food was surely good, but he hardly noticed it. There was polite dialogue, but he could never after remember it. For him there was only one thing, and that was Ginger, whose eyes he dared not meet again.

As they were finishing, there was a commotion outside. A servant went to investigate, and returned to report that a farmer had a grievance about his land revenue assessment.

"Oh, he thinks I am the officer," Wood said. "I lack the authority to help him."

"I will send him away," the patwari said, rising.

In a moment the sounds of arguing were heard. It seemed that the farmer did not choose to believe that there was no help here. He wanted the officer to come out. The patwari, of course, was adamant that the guest not be bothered.

"Perhaps we should retire to the courtyard, to avoid the noise," Grandmother Ember suggested. Mother Crystal nodded agreement. Daughter Ginger rose gracefully and led the way. Wood followed, realizing that the women would not precede him, except for the one showing him where.

The courtyard was nicely laid out. There was a small pigeon loft in one corner, a miniature family Hindu temple in another, and a fountain in the center. Around the fountain was a jasmine garden with a pleasant stone walk through it.

Ginger showed the way to a bench behind the fountain where they could sit. She sat decorously facing slightly away from him. He sat facing slightly toward her. Suddenly he realized that they were alone; the older women had not followed them into the courtyard.

"I think perhaps I owe you an apology for presumption," he murmured.

"By no means," she replied. "It is extremely forward of me to be with you like this."

"No, not at all! I relish your company. I mean I should not have spoken as I did."

Her eyes fixed on the fountain. "You were being humorous?"

"Never more serious! There is something—the moment I saw you—all the rest of the world peeled away, and it was as if I had known and loved you through all eternity. But of course I realize that it was completely improper for me to—we are of different cultures—I deeply regret causing you embarrassment. I fear I offended your mother and your grandmother, who remain silent only so as not to shame a guest in their house. So I apologize for this lapse, and will depart as soon as—"

As he spoke, she turned toward him, her eyes coming to meet his. Her face was very close. Then, abruptly, she kissed him, cutting off his speech.

The globe of the world stopped its motion. The sun, moon and stars halted in their orbits. There was nothing in the universe but her lips and her faint ginger scent.

At some point the kiss must have ended, because he discovered they were separate. Yet his world had changed. Now he knew that not only did he love her, she returned the sentiment.

"I am the one who must apologize," Ginger said. "In addition to the concerns you mention, there are more serious ones on my side. I wish I could have acquainted you with them before we met, so that you could have avoided this encounter."

"Many things of my life I have regretted in the past, and many more I may regret in the future, but I have no regret about meeting you. I never shall."

She shook her head sadly. "I am—in your vernacular, damaged goods."

"This cannot be! Surely you don't plan to trek to the purifying water of the River Ganges with the old women and drown yourself there, or be buried alive in the riverbank."

"I might as well, for I am worthless."

"To me you are priceless!"

"I must explain. I was married at age three to a boy of good family. You would call it a betrothal, for we both remained at our homes, awaiting the proper time for consummation, but it was valid for us. When I was ten he was killed in an accident. I am therefore a widow, by our custom, and can not remarry, lest my entire family be shamed and rendered untouchable. I am therefore a burden to my family, and only my father's generosity and my own cowardice prevent me from going to the river. I had no right to approach you, but was unable to resist."

"That I much understand! I know the Hindu convention. But in this respect I am completely British: I do not subscribe to it, and indeed regard it as a barbarism. I find no fault in you on such account."

"Yet the fault exists."

"Not in England."

"This is not England."

"Ginger, I know this is impossible. But I think I will die if I do not see you again."

"I, too." There was a tear at her eye.

"There must be a way."

"I fear there is not."

There was the sound of the patwari's voice in the house. "Well, I finally got rid of him. Where is our guest?"

As if drawn together by elastic bands, they quickly kissed, then stood and walked sedately around the fountain to rejoin the others.

"You have a beautiful daughter," Wood said. "Your garden was kind enough to show her to me."

There was a peep of mirth, probably from a servant. Then Wood realized what he had said. In his distraction he had garbled what should have been routine, and made it worse.

The patwari looked disgruntled, evidently not knowing how the women had arranged to leave the two of them alone. He could not have afforded to show approval if he had known, for this was an extremely irregular business. So he ignored the matter, and the dialogue proceeded into inconsequentials.

All too soon Wood found himself riding back to the campsite. Now at last he was alone, having resolutely declined company for the return trip; he knew the way.

What had come over him? He had caught his first glimpse of a lovely girl his age, and plunged into love with her. How could this be explained? He had met girls before, many of them, some with excellent face and features, and had never reacted like this. This one was native, and tainted by the reckoning of her culture. Love made no sense at all. Yet it was undeniably true.

All he knew was that he had to see her again.

He reached the camp, dismounted, and turned the horse over to a servant. He entered the tent.

John looked up. "My God, man—what happened to you?"

Startled, Wood checked his suit. Everything seemed to be in order. "I'm not sure I understand."

"Not your clothing. Your face, your manner. You look as if you'd seen a real live ghost."

Oh. "Perhaps I did."

John squinted at him. "Your face is slack, your pupils dilated, and you're moving like a zombie. If I didn't know better, I'd say you were in love."

Wood sighed. "I am."

John gestured, and the servant in the tent departed. Then John told his story. He had thought to keep it to himself, but it was too much to hold, and he needed the input of a dispassionate perspective.

John shook his head. "Naturally I don't believe in reincarnation or any of that rubbish, but this almost makes me wonder. Do you suppose you knew her in a prior life?"

Wood had to consider this seriously. "I don't think so. There's a phenomenal familiarity, but not that specific. It's more as if she fulfills an archetype that I wasn't aware I was looking for. And that I fulfill one for her. But this defies rationality. The world doesn't work that way."

"It seems rational to me. I've always harbored the notion that somewhere in the world the perfect woman awaits me. Of course I expect to settle for somewhat less, but it's a suitable dream. Your archetype notion is apt. So you found the perfect girl for you. Of course there may be a complication. The British Empire does frown upon that kind of mingling with the natives."

"And the natives frown upon that kind of mingling with the barbarous conquerors," Wood agreed. "If I had the luxury of being rational, I'd reject the notion out of hand."

"Tomorrow I'm due at the next village. I admit it will be a struggle, but perhaps it is time I made my own translations. You could remain here a few more days."

"I appreciate the offer. But I can't just ride up and visit her, as may be the case in England. Her family can not properly allow her to see me."

"But if I understand it correctly, she is already unmarriageable by their conventions. Shouldn't they want to find a placement for her elsewhere?"

"What they may want bears little relation to their situation. If their daughter violated the cultural restrictions, their entire family would be shamed, and the man would lose his position as patwari. Poverty and desperation would ensue. I would not want to be the cause of that, and neither would Ginger."

John shook his head. "You certainly don't pick your problems small! Well, officially I must know nothing of this, but as a friend I'll be glad to do what I can. Just let me know what that might be."

"Thanks. But I fear there is nothing."

○

But fate provided something. A week later a messenger came from that village: rabid predators were ranging the fields at night. The peasants were terrified, and dared not enter the fields. Immediate help was needed.

"Rabid, my eye!" John muttered. "There's been no rabies here in a decade, according to the records. It's probably one panther who's gotten canny about raiding where people are vulnerable. A rabid animal doesn't confine its activities to night."

"I agree," Wood said. "But once peasants get a notion, dynamite will hardly blast it loose. You will have to return to shoot the panther."

"With my schedule here? I can't afford the time." Then John looked cannily at him. "But I think *you* can. Take a good rifle for the job. Go there in my stead, stay at that patwari's house, and do the job. I think I've got the hang of the routine, and I'm picking up more of the dialect; I should be able to muddle through for a few days on my own."

And maybe he could see Ginger again. It just might work. "I am on my way, as directed," Wood said with a smile.

John threw him a mock salute. "I know what a chore it is. I will put in a favorable report."

He probably would, too. Wood mounted and set off immediately.

By nightfall he reached the village. The villagers and the patwari welcomed him. "I shall find a place to stay, and hunt for the panther in the morning," he said.

"But the creature ranges only at night," the patwari protested. "And you'll have no beaters by day; the men are too frightened of the ghost panther."

"Ghost? I thought it was supposed to be rabid."

"Ghost to the field workers. Rabid to educated folk."

Wood reconsidered. "Then I shall go out now, hoping to intercept it. I shall however need a fresh horse."

"It will not come out until later, well after dark. Come, you must eat with us, and rest somewhat before the ordeal."

That made sense. "Thank you. But no gift; this is business."

The patwari smiled. "No gift. Business."

Wood joined them. They had already eaten, so he was given a private meal. Ginger was the one who served it. Wood knew this was not quite proper, but gathered that the women had spoken rather firmly to the man, who perhaps by no coincidence had business in the village at this time. The women, he realized, were on his side.

Which was curious, for normally women supported the system as avidly as the men, despite their inferior place in it. Maybe they did have some hope that they could place an otherwise unplaceable daughter. Or maybe they had recognized her love and supported her in it, however foolishly.

"Have your sentiments changed?" Ginger inquired in a whisper as she set curry before him.

"Is anybody watching?" he asked in return.

"No."

Their faces met for a kiss.

That was all, but it was enough. Their eyes maintained the dialogue.

As he ate, Ginger told him of the various incidents of the panther. There was a pattern to its marauding, so it was possible to make a good guess where it would strike this night. The reason they thought it rabid was that it was not afraid of people, and would chase them in the darkness. Wood agreed that was unusual, for panthers normally avoided man. But it might make it easier to catch.

"Sahib, I fear for you," Ginger said.

"Call me Woody. This is the kind of thing that comes in the line of duty. I'm just glad I was able to see you again."

She smiled. "Grandmother Ember says there's something about you that stretches back thousands of years. That the gods brought you here."

"I worship the Christian God, but I'll accept any help your gods have to give. Do they offer any way for us to be together all the time?"

"Grandmother says the gods will find a way, if they choose."

"I would give anything for that!"

"I want only to be yours. But I must not shame my family."

"And I must not shame mine."

After he had eaten, not daring to stretch it out unduly, he went outside. A fresh horse was ready for him, a dark mare, and there was a good outdoor lantern. There was also a long spear, of the kind employed for pig-sticking. Good enough; he knew how to use one of those. He checked his rifle, and mounted. He also carried the ornate pistol the patwari had given him, subtly complimenting the man by showing its importance to him.

He rode to the likely region. The horse was familiar with the territory, and had no trouble finding her way by night. The stars and moon were bright. Now if he could just encounter the panther and get this nasty business over with, perhaps he could see Ginger again before departing.

The mare snorted, reacting to something. It could be the panther, for she was not a spooky horse. He lifted the lantern, trying to see something.

A pair of glowing eyes lurked ahead.

Wood brought out the rifle. He aimed between the eyes, but hesitated. Suppose it wasn't the panther? He didn't want to kill an innocent animal. So he shouted. "Scat!"

The eyes disappeared. So much for that panther; that could have been a wolf, fleeing the sound of man. He could have killed a wolf without compunction, but the guilty tracks had plainly been panther, and there was no sense wasting his shot with a pointless killing.

He rode on. Again the horse reacted, this time more strongly. There was the bleat of a frightened sheep. This was a more likely prospect.

He lifted the rifle again and rode toward the sound. But he was afraid of hitting a sheep, and scaring away the panther, so he put it away for the moment and took up the spear instead. He did not expect to score with this in the dark, because he would have to be close to the creature, but it would keep him from firing foolishly. He would bring out the rifle again the moment he was sure of his prey.

There was a growl to the side. That was the panther! He kept a firm grip on the reins so the horse would not spook, and oriented on the cat. So it attacked people? He doubted it; for one thing, a panther could run faster than a person, so should have caught what it went after. But now was the time to find out. "Here, pussycat!" he cried.

The growl became a snarl. There was a pounding as the creature came toward him. Now he saw the dark hump of it bounding along. In his distraction he had not brought out the rifle again, and now there wasn't time. What folly! He held the mare steady and aimed the spear, bracing for the shock of the hit.

The panther leaped up, going for the man instead of the horse. His spear was not quite on center; the animal's shoulder knocked it aside and the thing's great claws raked into his thigh, ripping the cloth. The horse spooked despite the reins, and the cat fell down. Wood let go of the useless spear, brought the horse around, and realized that there was no time or range for the rifle. Instead he grabbed for the pistol.

The panther leaped again. Wood fired. There was a screech and the cat fell back. This time it did not move.

Now Wood's thigh began to hurt. The claws had raked his flesh, how deeply he couldn't judge. He needed to get to help before he suffered any complications. Suppose the panther *was* rabid? He guided his horse and went for the village.

He stopped at the patwari's house. "I believe I got it," he said. "I may need help dismounting."

The servants brought lamps and saw the blood on his torn trousers. They lifted him down and half carried him into the house. A woman was there immediately, and it was Ginger. "Water!" she snapped. "A knife! I'll cut this clear."

"Please leave my leg," Wood said, attempting humor. "It's just a bad scratch."

So it turned out to be: three parallel gouges, not too long. The bleeding had not been too bad. But the key question had not been answered: was the cat rabid, and had it infected him?

The patwari and several servants went out to fetch in the body of the panther. Ginger took advantage of the distraction to kiss Wood. "This is the only medicine I have at the moment," she said.

"It will do." His discomfort no longer bothered him.

Wood woke in the morning, finding himself on a cot, wearing a nightdress. They must have had servants change him after he fell asleep. There was now a compress on his thigh, suggesting that a village doctor had arrived. Probably just as well.

It turned out that he had done the job with the panther. There was a single bullet through its head. The carcass had been dragged to the center of the village to be put on display. The village doctor said that the cat was not rabid, only crazed by a festering injury on its back. Wood was a hero of the British sort, and his concern about possible infection was alleviated.

The family insisted that he rest for the day before returning to his duties with the officer. Wood, feeling somewhat logy and not eager to leave Ginger sooner than he had to, did not strongly protest.

Ginger tended him for the day, bringing him meals and diverting him with conversation. She showed him the courtyard garden again. Because servants were present, there was no further chance to kiss, or even to say anything personal, but he enjoyed the day. By evening he felt considerably better, and declared that he would ride out in the morning.

The family discreetly retired, leaving Wood to his temporary cot. He settled down to sleep, still thinking of Ginger. A shape appeared. A servant? "I need nothing," Wood said.

The shape reached out and took his hand. Suddenly he recognized Ginger's touch. "What—?" he whispered.

She leaned down and put her mouth to his ear. "We may not see each other again. I must be with you, my love."

Then she joined him on the bed. Her nightdress opened, and he felt her full bare breasts. "But—"

She put a finger across his lips. Then she tugged at his own nightdress.

She had to know what she was doing, and to be sure that no one else would enter this chamber. He accepted her judgment, and her love. In a moment they were together, naked, and merging. It was the most wonderful experience he could imagine.

❂

The tour ended in the spring. Wood did receive a commendation for his handling of the panther incident. His family was proud of him; he had performed in the British manner. His passage to England was arranged for June. He had several months to relax. But he was not happy.

His mother was quick to divine his melancholy. "What is disturbing you, Woody?" she inquired. "You should be happy with your success as a translator and your commendation. You will surely do well in England."

"I'm not sure I want to go to England, Mother."

She did not try to argue with him. Instead she questioned him, and quickly found the way to his real concern. "She is lovely, like a picture of you when you were young," he concluded. That was perhaps an overstatement, for his mother had been the most beautiful woman of her day. "I love her, and live only for the hope of seeing her again. If I go to England, that chance will be gone."

"I know the pangs and rewards of forbidden love," she said.

He was amazed. "You do?"

She touched his lips in a gesture very like the one Ginger had used. "I do not know how you may win her, but I will do what I can."

Wood had no idea what that might be, but he greatly appreciated her understanding. He hugged her, as he had when a little boy, heedless of British propriety, and was comforted.

The next news was bad. "Your grandmother has died," Stone informed him. "Your grandfather Blaze is a widower." That saddened Wood, for he remembered Grandma as a kindly old woman, always ready with a cookie and a hug. But it had been a long time ago. "However," Stone continued, "this does not affect your status there; there remains a place for you at that house."

The summer monsoon season was weak again, leading to a bad crop of millet and rice in the province of Orissa. However the magistrate at the city of Cuttack there reported no cause for concern, as there were only five more months until the autumn harvest of wheat and barley.

"The fool!" Wood seethed. He had reported the patwari's concern about future food supplies to John, who had reported it to his superior. It seemed that the authorities were doing nothing.

"Perhaps you should go there and verify the situation," his mother suggested. "Perhaps take some supplies along."

Wood was doubtful, for he lacked authority to do such a thing on his own. But his friend John endorsed the notion, and his father, prompted by his mother, grudgingly agreed. Wood was able to obtain a hundred pounds of rice and take it by coach to Cuttack, and thence by horse to the patwari's village.

Seldom had he seen such relief and gratitude on a man's face. It seemed that there had been an alarm, and people had hoarded all the grain they could find, so that the reserve supplies had quickly been exhausted. Now there was a prospect for starvation, if something wasn't done soon.

"I felt I owed you some additional gift, to make up for the great value of your gift to me," Wood explained.

"But you did that when you killed the panther!"

"That was duty. Besides, it was that fine pistol you gave me that did it. I would have been in dire straits without it, so perhaps I owe you more than I could repay."

"Ah, no, sahib! This rice is life itself. The debt is ours."

Wood stayed the night, and Ginger joined him again. Surely the family knew, but gave no indication. Perhaps they felt that Ginger should be allowed what limited happiness was offered, before she died. Possibly her presence was tacit repayment for the rice.

By May there was indeed starvation. Grain was available in other districts where the drought had not struck, but it was difficult to move it in sufficient quantities. The railroad lines did not cover this region, and in any event had not been integrated into the relief effort. Horse-drawn wagons might have done it, but horses had been butchered when the grain ran out. Oxen from elsewhere were a special problem: an ox could haul perhaps three hundred pounds of grain on its back, but it ate thirty pounds a day. Since it would have to be fed from what it carried, this severely limited its usefulness. Wood was distraught with concern for Ginger and her family.

"We must tackle this forthrightly," his mother said. "Come with me." She took him to his father. "Our son loves a native girl. He can not marry her here, but in England he could. She must go with him to England."

Stone's mouth fell open. "A native? England?"

"She will be able to help care for your grandfather Blaze, who surely is lonely now," she said. "He is dear to me, as I'm sure he is to you. This is an answer to the problem of both your father and your son. Now, will you arrange the passage, or shall I have to make an issue of it myself?"

Wood soon saw the putty that his father became when his mother truly wanted something. Stone would arrange passage for one more.

"Now go and fetch her here," she told Wood. "I believe her family will let her go, rather than have an extra mouth to feed during the famine. Take more rice with you."

Bemused but thrilled, Wood did as directed. In due course he arrived with another hundred pounds of rice masked as personal belongings so that there would be no temptation for anyone to steal it. The patwari was pathetically grateful, again, for he had distributed all of the prior bag to the needy villagers.

"But I meant that rice for your own family," Wood protested.

The patwari's mother Ember interceded. "We thought it was a temporary situation, until supplies were shipped in. We did not realize how inefficient it would be, since we had given warning."

"We relayed warning, but it seems to have been lost in the bureaucracy," Wood said. "John Duncan is disgusted."

The women directed the servants to carry the grain inside. They would try to be more careful with it this time.

Now Wood was able to speak to the patwari privately. "Sir, I love your daughter. I want to—"

"I won't listen to this!" the man cried, and stalked away. Soon he was riding toward the village, doubtless to make arrangements for the distribution of some of the rice.

Wood stared after him. He had thought this a good time to broach his request. Evidently it was not.

Ginger emerged from the house. "Ginger," he said. "I want to take you with me to England, if you are willing to go. My family accepts this. But your father—"

"Did he tell you no?" she asked.

"He refused to listen!"

"But he did not tell you no."

"No, he didn't, technically, but—"

Her grandmother Ember approached. "He must say he does not know, so that there will be no shame. Take her, Wood, and may you prosper." Then she turned her back. He saw that Crystal had done the same, along with the servants.

Wood realized that they had anticipated him, and were arranging to see nothing. Their burden of an unmarriageable daughter would simply disappear, and if the neighbors concluded that she had gone to the river, there would be no denial. There would be no shame to the family, and Ginger would be safe.

Wood mounted a fresh horse, and drew Ginger up behind him. She was now cloaked and hooded, so as to be unrecognizable. They rode slowly away.

As they left the region Ginger's father had helped, the evidences of the surrounding famine mounted. Cattle were lying in the barren fields, their ribs showing. Some were dead; others were still dying. There were few people in sight, because they lacked the strength to work outside, and most were simply lying in their houses, starving. There was a pall upon the land. Outside one village the bodies of the dead were simply piled beside the road, waiting for burial when there was strength enough for that. Children sat in the doorways of houses, gazing listlessly out. Only those families that were wealthy enough to purchase grain at enormously inflated prices were surviving well; all others ranged from hunger to death.

It was a strange world, Wood realized, in which he rode with his beloved through the horrors of the famine. His love mixed with his guilt. Had it not been for this calamity, the family might not have allowed him to take Ginger.

Yet he had done what he could. He had relayed the warning, and tried to get the officials to take precautions. Maybe, after this disaster, they would take steps to see that there was no repetition. What was needed was better roads for hauling in food from outside, and railroads to serve the region, and canals and embankments for the storage of water, so that drought did not lead immediately to crop failure and famine. He would urge John to pursue such programs with the authorities, and he knew John would do his best.

"Are there famines in England?" Ginger inquired faintly.

"No," he replied, sure that it must be true. "You will never be hungry again, my love."

"My love," she echoed, giving him a thrill that seemed to echo from thousands of years.

The famine of 1866 ravaged this region of India. By the time effective relief came, one quarter to one third of the local population had died. But stringent new measures were applied, along the lines Wood had envisioned, and future famines were greatly eased, with relatively small percentages of mortality. Only when they extended across the subcontinent did their ravages become extreme. British rule continued until the civil disobedience movement of Mahatma Gandhi eroded it in the twentieth century. Gandhi had developed the techniques of passive resistance while in South Africa, having drawn on the ideas of the Russian writer Tolstoi and the American writer Thoreau as well as Christ's "turn the other cheek" principle. The subcontinent finally became independent, fragmenting into India, Pakistan and Bangladesh. But periodic famines continued as population outran the food production, and remain a problem today.

C H A P T E R   2 0

MALTHUS

Thomas Robert Malthus lived from 1766 to 1834. He was a clergyman and economist who believed that unchecked human population increases at a geometric rate, doubling every twenty-five years, while the means of subsistence, such as food production, increases at an arithmetical rate, which is by definition slower. This, he suggested, would result in an inadequate supply for mankind, unless some reasonable restraint was exercised, or there was attrition from war, famine or disease. It has been the recent vogue to claim that Malthus has been refuted by events, because the industrial age has generated an increase of goods at the supposedly impossible

425

*geometric rate, keeping up with population. But this was done at the
expense of the world's natural resources, and those resources were being
abused and exhausted. There was also considerable loss of life because
of diseases of all types. Famines continued to occur, because though there
was theoretically sufficient food, the mechanisms of distribution were inadequate.*

*In the twentieth century there were two world wars, and the supremacy of
Europe gave way to that of America. Strife continued throughout the world,
but the principle battleground became economic, with free enterprise of the
West competing with communism of the East. Free enterprise proved to be the
superior system, and by the end of the century new economic powers such as
Germany and Japan were becoming dominant. Medical care improved,
reducing infant mortality and extending the average life span. But the
disparity in standards of living between developed and undeveloped nations
increased, the rich got richer and the poor got poorer, and damage to the global
environment accelerated. Population, unchecked, expanded enormously.*

There was bound to be a consequence.

EMBER checked her rifle carefully. It was old but clean, and she had
seventeen good bullets for it. She had not had to use a bullet in two
months, which was a good sign. "I'm ready, Carver," she said. She could
feel the slight reaction of her cheek, because of the tension.

He nodded. He preceded her out the door of the ruined building
while she covered him from the broken window. He crossed the street,
peering both ways, and made it to the wall of the building beyond. All its
windows and doors were blocked by bricks and fragments of concrete,
so that there could be no ambush from within it. He stepped into an
alcove, set his back against the wall, and lifted his left hand.

Ember saw the signal and moved out herself. She didn't expect any
trouble here, but they had learned never to take an empty street for
granted. They hadn't lost a kinsman in six months, which spoke for
itself.

She walked to the center of the street, turned, and walked down it,
watching the higher windows of the buildings on either side. They had
knocked out the stairways of all the buildings they weren't using
themselves, and set nasty snares on the lower floors, but experienced
hunters knew how to get around such things.

There was no trouble this time. Ember moved to the side of the street, near an intersection, and withdrew to another prepared alcove. She signaled Carver, who took his turn walking the street. He crossed the intersection, then covered her as she did.

In this stairstep manner they proceeded to the river channel where their algae farm was. The algae beds were broad enough so that no hand weapon would be effective from ambush unless they worked at the edge. Ember's rifle could take out any enemy who lacked a similar rifle, and the sound of her shot would bring the kinsmen running. The neighboring clans knew that. This was, in short, a reasonably safe setting.

This particular section of the river had been drained, because the alga was bad. A mutant strain had gotten into the bed and poisoned the crop; there was nothing to do but destroy it and clean the bed for a new crop. Mutation was rampant, because of the damaged atmosphere, and most wild strains were bad, but the rare good ones were responsible for their successful farm. Now the bad alga was dry, and could be scraped off and burned. If they did the job right, they wouldn't have to do it again.

Carver got to work with the scraping rack, while Ember set about making the fire. She foraged for bits of wood and dry weeds, making a pile. She moved slowly, saving her strength; at seventy-six she was simply no longer spry. She needed, above all else, to be alert.

When there was enough algae, she lit the fire. Smoke boiled up. She picked up the rifle and looked all around, because the smoke was a likely signal of human activity, and any hunters in the vicinity would take note. Fortunately the nearest hunting clan was the roach farmers, with whom they had a tacit nonaggression pact, so there should be no trouble. But such things were never certain. Only kin could be fully trusted.

Someone did come. A small figure emerged from the far-side city. Carver paused in his labor, and Ember aimed the rifle. Any sensible person would take warning and retreat, unless he thought the rifle was a bluff. That seemed unlikely, because news of operative firearms was important; Ember knew where all the other such weapons were, locally. She didn't fear them, because bullets were often more precious than lives. She was known as a defender, not a hunter, so none of the locals would waste a bullet on her without cause.

She sighted with the scope—and was surprised. It was a child! A little boy or girl, maybe only three years old, though hunger could be masking a higher age. It could not have come on its own; it would have become food for the hunters long since. Someone had sent it.

Ember studied the child. It seemed to be a girl, and she seemed healthy. A voluntary foundling. That required an immediate decision. Ember could do one of three things: accept the child and raise her as kin, reject her by sending her back the way she had come, or kill her for food.

Ember knew she could neither reject nor kill the little girl. Rejection would be tantamount to killing, because the child's family wouldn't have let her go if they had any way to feed her. So they had, in the manner of the day, given her up for adoption. They surely knew who Ember was, and that as the head of her clan she had the authority to make the decision, and that she had a tender heart. She had never killed a child.

The girl continued to walk toward her. Ember set down the rifle. She dug in her pack for some food. She brought out several small bits. When the child reached her, she extended one of these. "Eat," she said. "It's toasted roach."

The girl took the roach and put it eagerly to her mouth. She chewed it and swallowed it, spitting out the wings. Ember gave her another, which she ate as avidly.

"What is your name?" Ember inquired.

"Cobblestone," the child said carefully.

"I am Ember. I will take you home, Cobblestone."

The child nodded. She had evidently been told that this would happen. Of course they wouldn't have told her that she ran the risk of getting butchered. Ember gave her another roach. It had been a long time since she had had a child to take care of, and she rather liked the idea.

"Bogie," Carver said.

Ember looked. There was a figure where the girl had come from. Ember lifted her rifle and sighted through the scope. It was a woman standing there, lean but healthy. She lifted her arm in a wave, then turned away. In a moment she was gone.

The girl's mother. The woman had seen Ember feed the child, the signal of acceptance. The woman herself could not be trusted, for hunger was stronger than civilization, but she was unlikely to be an enemy now. Her child not only would live, she would be well fed. That was not formal kinship, but there could be fair force in informal kinship.

They completed the burning, then went home. This pasture would be left fallow for a time, then reseeded with better stocks of algae. Cobblestone seemed to understand the way of the street, remaining close to Ember and not making a sound. She should get along. They saw no other people, and no animals. The famine had cleared the land most efficiently. Only hunters and farmers survived, and the hunters were diminishing because easy prey no longer existed. The second agricultural revolution was occurring, with the farmers gradually replacing the hunters.

○

At last Ember heard the cry of the baby. In a moment Crystal emerged from the birthing chamber. "A girl. Healthy. Daisy will name her Algae."

"Of course." Ember turned to the child she had adopted at the algae farm. "Cobblestone, that's my great-granddaughter just born, who will be like a sister to you. Sisters may quarrel, but they never eat each other." The child nodded gravely. "Now I will send a message." She covered her immense relief for the safe birth by focusing on her writing pad.

Soon she had it: THE BABY IS BORN. THE FUNGUS MOTHERS WILL MEET THE ROACH FATHERS TOMORROW AT THE NEUTRAL ZONE. She gave it to the runner, who disappeared.

Then she went in to see the baby, taking Cobblestone along. Education in kinship was too important to set aside at an event like this.

Next morning they waited for the runner to verify that the neutral zone was clear. Then they set out: first Daisy Flower, carrying Algae; then Ember, leading Cobblestone. They wore their heavy, huge-brimmed hats and shoulder flares to protect them from the direct rays of the sun while showing their upper torsos, and the baby was under a small canopy. Their skirts flared also, showing their legs to the hips while similarly shading them. They wore tight vests and stockings, and wrist-length gloves and ankle-tight shoes, so that no portion of their flesh apart from their veiled faces actually showed, but its outlines were quite clear. All of them were female; that was important for this very special occasion.

From the other side two men were approaching. They wore flanged helmets, skintight suits, gloves, boots, and colored codpieces. Only their eyes showed above their cloth masks. Their outlines too were quite clear; there was no doubt about their gender. They were armed with swords, clubs, and knives, and loops of rope hung from their shoulders.

Daisy stepped under the broad roof of the unwalled neutral zone shelter first, formally taking possession. The lead man halted outside it. "May I join you, woman?" he inquired according to the ritual.

"Who are you, man?" Daisy responded.

"I am Oak Tree, of the Roach clan."

"Will you take the oath of espousal?"

"I will."

"I am Daisy Flower, and this is my daughter, Algae."

"I make the oath of espousal, to make you my wife this day, until I leave this shelter."

Daisy smiled with more than formal acceptance. "I accept your oath. Welcome to my shelter, Oak."

Oak stepped in. He spread his arms, and Daisy moved into them. They kissed, the baby and a weapon or two nestled between them. "Oh, it's happened at last," he said, evidently awed. "Our child!"

"Now we can marry," Daisy said, letting him take the baby. "Our families can be at peace."

Ember approached. "May I join you?" she asked.

"Yes, Grandmother," Daisy said. Ember stepped in.

The second man came close. "May I join you?" he called.

"Who are you?" Daisy asked.

"I am Blaze, Oak's grandfather, and head of his family."

"Then we are kin for the night, for I am espoused to your grandson, and have his child here."

"We are kin," Blaze agreed, and entered.

The two women now lined up to meet the two men, making more personal introductions. Ember faced Blaze—and the world changed. His outline seemed to be limned in fire and water, his body at once old and young. Those green eyes, that fiery birthmark on his forehead. He was the man of her dream! The one she had desired all her life, yet never found, and had thought must be an impossible fantasy. Now she knew he was real—ironically when they both were in their seventies, well beyond the age of romance.

He spread his arms, his face a mask of awe and adoration. She let go of Cobblestone's hand and spread hers. They embraced. They kissed. The universe hovered in place.

Beyond the age of what?

"How long has it been?" she asked, when she was able to speak.

"Three million years, I think," he replied. "Or sixty. I never thought to really find you."

"I knew you as a child."

"I loved you as a dawning woman, but could not have you."

"I wish you had found me then, when I was fresh and full. I searched for you all my life, but never found you."

"I wish you had found me in my virile youth, instead of now that I am withered old. I searched for you when speech was new."

"I never loved my husband enough, because he wasn't you."

"I sought you in a young woman, when my wife grew older, but didn't find you."

"I looked for you in Sumer, when I lost my husband."

"You were not among the Hittites."

"You were not in Rome."

"You were not among the Huns."

"You were not in China or Africa."

"You were not in Lithuania or England."

"I was in India, but I sent my granddaughter to England."

"She did remind me of you."

"What are you two talking about?" Daisy asked. "I was never in England!"

They broke their embrace and looked around, bemused. Both Daisy and Cobblestone were staring at them. "Would they understand?" Ember asked him.

"Does it matter?" Blaze replied.

"Have they gone senile?" Oak inquired.

Ember shook her head. "They don't remember."

"How could they?" he asked. "They are only echoes of us."

"Beloved echoes," she agreed.

Daisy frowned. "This is supposed to be the formal recognition of kinship and ending of the state of siege between our families," she said. "Exactly what are you saying?"

Blaze smiled wryly. "Let's just say that Ember and I may have met before. We are merely trying to identify the place and time of our contact."

"Well, you won't do it if you keep babbling about Rome and the Huns!"

Blaze looked helplessly at Ember. She thought a moment, then made a suggestion. "It is necessary for all of us to know each other well, so that we never henceforth mistake each other for nonkin. Let's pair off and talk for awhile. Then we can shuffle the pairs and talk some more, until we are satisfied."

"We're a pair!" Daisy said eagerly, moving into another embrace with Oak.

Blaze and Ember walked to the far side, out of sight of the younger couple, who was oblivious. Cobblestone trailed along. As soon as they were private, they moved into another embrace. "We must find a way to be truly alone," he said.

"At our age?" she inquired archly.

"You disagree?"

"Not if you don't."

They embraced and kissed again. Then they took seats, and Ember put the child in her lap. "This is Cobblestone, whom I adopted a few days ago."

"I thought I recognized her. Her mother is distant kin to us, but recently lost her man."

"We are beyond the age of making children. Will you accept her in lieu?"

"I will accept anything that comes with you, my love Ember."

"My love, my love Blaze," she agreed.

"I dreamed always of you, but never thought to find you here," he said. "Not after losing you at the Isle of Woman."

"It's been so long," she agreed. "And it's fantasy, of course. We share dreams, but our real lives have been right here in America."

He shook his head. "You are old, and so am I, yet it is as if we are also in the childhood of our species, furry and playing with fire."

"We share an imagination of history," she decided. "We fancied ourselves as characters in the history we studied, making it come alive. We were young when the species was young. Now we are old with the species."

"But you are right: our current lives in this century are what count now. I want to know you, Ember."

"And I you. Where were you born, this time?"

"In California, on the day they dropped the Bomb."

"August 6, 1945," she agreed. "The same for me, the state of New York. We were the first of the nuclear age."

"Do you remember the Korean War?"

"Not really. I was only five. But I do remember the Vietnam War."

"The Cuban missile crisis? I was afraid I'd get drafted."

"And Kennedy's assassination. I was in a college class."

"Woodstock."

"The Iran hostages."

"The fall of the Berlin Wall."

She laughed. "The birth of my granddaughter Daisy."

"The cure for AIDS."

"And the other immune system diseases like rheumatic fever and diabetes. That was a great breakthrough. It rid the world of a terrible scourge and saved many lives."

"But not as many as when they found the cure for the viral diseases," he said. "Everything from the common cold to hepatitis. I was so glad to see those frequent sniffles go."

"And the parasitic infestations," she said. "Once a quarter of the world was infected with malaria. No more!"

"It was an even greater day when they found the cure for cancer—all cancers. That used to kill more people than any of those others, especially when the ozone layer thinned and skin cancer ran rampant."

"Until they were able to stop heart and circulatory diseases. Those made cancer look small."

"And finally the brain diseases," he said. "Everything from depression to suicide. Many murders, too, because they stemmed from deranged minds."

"So everyone lived longer," she concluded. "Infant mortality practically stopped, and the number of centenarians multiplied."

"So we saw the world's human population pass ten billion much faster than projected."

"And that was the beginning of the end."

He shook his head. "The end started much earlier. Perhaps with the evolution of man himself. We thought we could breed without restraint forever."

"But we would have been all right if the climate hadn't changed," she pointed out.

"We were the cause of that change," Blaze said seriously. "We burned all the fossil fuels, we destroyed the last forests, we polluted air, earth, and sea. We overloaded the atmosphere with CO_2 and made it heat. We were lucky that the extra water in the warmer air made more snow at the poles, so that they didn't melt and raise the sea level. But that heat still changed the weather patterns, and that in turn signaled the coming end of our civilization."

"The drought," she agreed. "North America became mostly desert, while the African Sahara turned to mud. Oh what mischief! I knew trouble was coming, and I hauled my family from New York to the Great Lakes region, hoping that there we'd be assured of food. Daisy was fifteen then, and didn't like leaving her friends. You must have done much the same."

"I did, but for a different reason. I got nervous about the San Andreas Fault, and decided it was time to get away from the California coast. There had already been several major quakes, and I feared the big one was due. So we moved to Yuma, Arizona."

"But isn't that right near—"

"That's right. I hadn't really studied the matter. I didn't realize that the San Andreas Fault is actually the place where a midocean ridge is being overridden by a continent. The East Pacific Ridge had already separated the Baja California Peninsula from Mexico by opening up the Gulf of California. Now it cracked open some more terrain, extending the gulf northward. We were right at the edge of it. The earthquakes leveled the city. We happened to be camping out, so nothing fell on us, but it felt as if we were being tossed from mountain to mountain. Then we heard the roar of the water rushing into the new chasm. It was sheer luck that we weren't close enough to be dropped in."

"But I thought the midocean ridges were where magma welled up from below," Ember said. "So it made new mountains."

"It does—but first it cracks open the earth. The mountains form on either side. We were at the east side. We fled the region, of course, though flowing lava always fascinated me. I don't think I've ever been so frightened, but I had to appear confident so that the family wouldn't panic. As it was, my wife was injured, and later she died." He paused. "I didn't mean to mention that."

"My husband died thirty years ago, suddenly. I know the feeling."

"Yes. My dream was of you, but she was a good woman. The rest of us were in Phoenix when the Great Drought wiped out the crops. We had to flee the city eastward and scrounge for roots in the country. Where were you?"

"Somewhere in Indiana when the Great Famine struck. We grubbed for roots too, and rooted for grubs. We fled down the river, mainly because that was where the wild foraging was best. It was no fun time. We learned not to be choosy about our food, lest we starve."

"But at least you were away from the cities. You know what was happening there."

"I know." Ember's memory of three years ago remained vivid. "We were I think in the vicinity of Memphis when we truly came to understand what we had tried to deny." She closed her eyes, reliving the horror.

They were slowly poling their small boat down the muddy channel of what had before the drought been the mighty Mississippi River, hoping to get past the city without trouble. Strangers were increasingly hostile, wanting to rob them or worse, so they now had to consider all other people likely enemies. So far they had been able to get by without outright combat, but they had made battle plans for the time of need, and rehearsed tactics precisely.

A man stood on the bank. "Hey, who are you?" he called.

"Just a family passing through," Crystal called back. "Not looking for any trouble."

"Pull over."

"Four men; no guns," Carver reported. Guns were important, but there had been so much violence in the city when the Famine came that ammunition had run low, and of course no factories were making it anymore.

"Then we'll just slide on past them," Ember decided. "Keep poling."

Carver and Crystal did so. Daisy, at seventeen, rode in maidenly innocence in front, while Ember at seventy-three rode in old-maidenly frailty in back. The family was the epitome of harmlessness. Their boat was decrepit and their clothing tattered. Who would want to bother these ragged stragglers?

The man strode out into the channel. He carried a stout club. Clubs had become the personal weapon of choice for many, because they were easy to use, required no ammunition, and did not get stuck in the target. The family had clubs in the bottom of the boat, out of sight. "I said pull over," the man said, making a warning motion with the club.

"Aggressive," Ember murmured. "He will intercept us. Innocence ploy." For they had had to stave off molesters before, and had several battle plans to address particular situations.

The polers desisted and sat down in the boat, their hands falling to their sides—near the clubs and their concealed knives. Daisy smiled brilliantly at the advancing man. "Oh, we thought you said to pull on by. What do you want with us, sir?"

The man took a closer look at her. Daisy had a sweet face and a fine figure, not too much eroded by the lean diet of the past year. Her shawl was open in front, and her worn blouse showed more of her braless bosom than would have been proper in polite society. It was fastened together by a single large safety pin, the buttons having long since been lost. Ember had worked carefully on that blouse, tightening it just so, preparing it for the Daisy Innocence ploy.

"Uh, just to, uh, talk," the man said, catching the prow of the boat with his free hand while peering down into the pleasant valley behind the safety pin. "Where you folks going?"

Meanwhile the other three men were wading out, converging on the boat, their clubs ready. There was nothing casual about their attitude. They were husky, and evidently had not gone hungry recently. Those were bad signs.

"CM, two, three," Ember murmured before the men reached the boat. That was their coding for Combat Mode, with designated weapons. The hands of the others shifted slightly, touching their bodies. Clubs, the #1 weapon, would not be used this time. The stakes had escalated.

"Just downriver, looking for food," Daisy answered the front man innocently. "If you have any, we don't have any money, but we're willing to work."

One of the men laughed. "Oh, you'll work, all right," the front man said. Then, to the others: "Leave the girl; she's a nice piece. We'll take turns at her before we slaughter her." The others lifted their clubs.

Daisy screamed, piercingly. That was their signal for desperate action.

Daisy, Carver, and Crystal brought out their knives—the designated #2 weapons—and stabbed in concert at the men closest to them. Carver and Crystal got theirs in the bellies, and the men screamed and fell into the water. But the front man was standing too far away for Daisy to reach, though she lunged across the prow; he whipped his hand from the boat and stepped hastily back. Then, enraged, he stepped forward again, his club about to strike Daisy on the head.

Ember lifted her pistol, sighted carefully between Carver and Crystal, who remained still after their actions, and fired at the front man's face. His nose disappeared; the club slipped from his hand; he fell forward onto Daisy, who had remained down and still after her attempt. Because when weapon #3 came into play, they could not afford to risk getting in the way. Ember could hit what she aimed at, but had to have a clear target.

"Move!" she snapped. Now the others in the boat stirred, looking around, knowing that she was not about to fire again. There was the fourth man, not far from Ember herself, staring. This easy slaughter had suddenly reversed, and he had not yet taken in the change.

Ember turned and aimed the gun at him. "D-d-don't waste a bullet on me!" he cried. "I'm gone!"

It was a fair deal. Bullets were just as precious to them as to the enemy, and they had only six. The man turned and slogged away through the water, and Ember let him go.

Daisy was meanwhile extricating herself from the body of the front man, who had fallen partway across her. She was about to shove the corpse into the water, but Ember stopped her. "Leave it strewn there, where others can see," she said. "Move on out."

Baffled and repelled, Daisy obeyed. She hauled the body around so that its head was in the water on one side of the boat, and its legs on the other. That way it didn't bleed into the boat, though it did weigh down the front end. Carver and Crystal rinsed their knives in the water and put them away. Then they took up their poles again. Ember kept her eye on the river, both banks, in case any other men should appear. The sound of the shot might attract others.

But no one else sought to molest them. Surely others saw, peering from the cover of derelict buildings and piles of rubble, but elected to stay clear. That made sense, because now it was known that the family on the boat had an operative gun, and that it had already killed an attacker. As long as it proceeded straight down the channel, not seeking to land, others would let it be. This was not courtesy but common sense.

In the evening, clear of the metropolis, they did come to land, at an algae-covered broken-down pleasure pier. Huge roaches scuttled away as they stepped onto it. Beyond was the ruin of a once-elegant estate house. They verified that it was empty, and located a chamber whose roof remained reasonably intact. Here they would spend the night. They found a suitable gully for natural functions, and took turns using it, the other three standing guard.

"Now we must make a fire," Ember said. "There's plenty of wood-wreckage here."

"But won't that attract people?" Crystal asked.

"It may, but it must be risked. One of us will tend the fire, two will stand guard, and one will cook and smoke the meat."

"We don't have any meat," Daisy protested.

"We do now," Ember said grimly.

The others stared at her. "Oh, no," Crystal breathed.

"They were going to do it to us," Ember said. "We took them in fair combat. Now we must survive by their rules. We are in cannibal country."

Daisy's mouth worked. "I—I couldn't!" She looked as if about to vomit.

"Then you stand guard. I will do the necessary. Each will eat as he chooses."

Crystal and Carver exchanged a long glance. Both were lean and hungry. Both had killed on this day. They knew that it was foolish to throw away enough meat to feed them for a long time. Especially when they needed their health to fight off others who wanted to eat *them*. The body was already there.

They went to fetch it from the boat.

"And so we carved it into major segments and roasted it over the fire," Ember finished. "All of us gagged at first, but our hunger drove us. We wrapped the leg roasts in bits of canvas and took them with us in the boat. We reroasted them every few days, as long as they lasted. We were survivors in the new order."

"We were in El Paso when we learned how others were surviving," Blaze agreed. "We soon realized, as you did, that we would not survive if we were starving. It wasn't enough to scrape by on old cans of beans we dug out of the wrecks. We had to be in fit condition to fight, because our enemies were. We could only be that by eating well. That meant long pig meat. But we also protected ourselves by moving along. We followed the Rio Grande on down to the coast, using a boat as you did. We had some bad times, but we too were survivors."

"We continued down the Mississippi to the delta," Ember said. "But we weren't comfortable on the river. We wanted to find a place where we could settle down and live, instead of constantly fearing floating into an ambush." She shook her head. "How do you think the cannibalism got started? We certainly didn't seek it; we were driven to it."

"I have thought about that too. I think it started in the big cities, where there simply wasn't any food coming in. Maybe nine of ten people were willing to quietly starve to death, but one of ten wasn't. That minority was what survived, by eating the others. It wouldn't be long before cannibals were the only survivors, by natural selection."

She sighed. "I suppose so. Given a fair choice, we would have taken almost any other way, and for a long time we did. We learned to like grubs. But human meat was so relatively easy, and there was so much of it."

"And it was coming after you," he said. "But we kept looking for an alternative. For one thing, we knew that man-eat-man could not be the wave of the future. At some point the next to last man would be eaten by the last man, who would thereafter starve. So finally we came here to what used to be Houston, and realized that there *was* an alternative. We saw that the mutant bugs and roaches were prospering amidst the ruins. We realized that they could be eaten, as they have been in other cultures. So we started roach farming."

"We came here two years ago from the other direction," Ember said. "We started our algae farm."

"And we've been trading ever since," he agreed. "You provided tubs of fresh algae for our roaches to feed on, and we provided packages of roasted roaches for you to eat. Yet we never actually met, because we could never be sure of each other. We survived by trusting no one but kin, and we continued to kill those who came hunting us for meat. This was the way it had to be."

"Our contact officers met under special truce," she said. "And it seems they got along well enough."

"Yes. Now we know why. It must have been instant love for Oak and

Daisy, and not just because he was a handsome eighteen-year-old boy and she a pretty eighteen-year-old girl. They were destined for each other throughout."

"As you and I were," Ember agreed. "For three million years."

"For three million years," Blaze echoed. "Now at last we are kin, and need not hunt each other."

"Now at last we can love."

They moved back into a close embrace. Cobblestone banged her little hands together with applause. They knew that the horrors of the past five years were about to give way to a better future.

The future was not very much like the past, but all over the world surviving human beings emerged from the horror of the cannibal years with a new appreciation for the remaining health of the environment. Most of the other creatures and plants of the world had been rendered extinct by the combined effects of predation, habitat destruction, and climate, and the globe was forever impoverished thereby. But a number of species of algae, which could grow well in the marshy remains of once great rivers, and insects, which could eat that algae, survived and prospered. When the diminished remnant of mankind farmed these, he developed an excellent continuing source of food, and no longer had to eat his own kind. It was the dawn of a new era.

Yet perhaps it would have been better if man had not allowed the world to come to such a pass before he got the message.

This is the first volume of a projected series titled GEODYSSEY. That's GEO as in Geography, Geology, etc., meaning the earth, combined with ODYSSEY, as in a long adventurous wandering journey. That is what you have seen here—a three-and-a-half-million-year excursion through global history. But there is more to it than this, of course. Much more.

The genesis of this project is lost in the archaeology of my thoughts; my first actual notes date from 1966. I've always been fascinated by history and paleontology—that is, the study of former life-forms, such as dinosaurs. I just didn't realize it in school, because school is where even sex can be rendered boring, and history both natural and human is made as dull as the pedants can manage. It seems that if they can't tag it with endless dates and names of kings and wars, they don't teach it. But once I was free of school I was able to pursue what was meaningful, and history has been a common aspect of my writing. Archaeology turned out to be the region between man and the animals—the study of people by their artifacts. A potsherd may seem dull, but not when it evokes a fascinating culture. My collection of reference books on such subjects grew, and in the course of a quarter century my notion for the project expanded similarly. My notion was to employ one of the basic arts that define the nature of man, storytelling, to do what it has always done, defining the nature of man.

Some of the books I found most interesting or useful were *The Aquatic Ape* by Elaine Morgan, describing the aquatic hypothesis that I modified for Chapter 4. For general information there was *The Field Guide to Early Man* by David Lambert. Excellent, readable books on the nature of mankind are *Our Kind* by Marvin Harris and *The Third Chimpanzee* by Jared Diamond. *The Ape That Spoke* by John McCrone describes the essence of man's brain and language. Man's spread across the world is described by *The Journey from Eden* by Brian M. Fagan. Many of the creatures the world has already lost are shown in *Extinct Species of the World* by Jean-Christophe Balouet and Eric Alibert. The cave sequence of Chapter 8 is beautifully shown in *The Cave of Lascaux—The Final Photographs* by Mario Ruspoli. One of my favorite cities, shown in Chapter 11, is defined in *Catal Huyuk—A Neolithic Town in Anatolia* by James Mellaart. One of a number of historical atlases I used—I have a collection of eighteen of them—was *Hammond Past Worlds—The Times Atlas of Archaeology*. And two excellent books on the present problem are *The End of Nature* by Bill McKibben and *Earth in the Balance* by Al Gore, who as I write this is running for vice president of the United States. This list is just a sampling, by no means comprehensive, and is dwarfed by the number of texts my research assistant read. Many were borrowed from the library of the University of South Florida, where my personal papers are currently being collected. The research for a project like this is a big job, as you might imagine, and access to good and specific references is essential.

At first I had thought it could be a single novel. But as I appreciated the ramifications, the size of this projected novel grew until it was half a million words long. So I decided to split it into three volumes. Then I realized that if I started with the apes and finished in the near future, the first volume would be all pre-man, the second would be all ancient history, and the third medieval to modern history. Three different types of story, appealing to different types of readers. That probably wouldn't wash, as a series. I thought of focusing on one continent at a time, such as America, Europe, Asia, Australia or Africa. But America's and Australia's history is mostly recent—that is, the past 20,000 or 40,000 years—while Africa's is mostly ancient, the first three million years. It would also tend to make a racial thing of it, perhaps fragmenting my audience. I wanted to show mankind as a unified species. Finally I thought of making it a single, unified story, but slicing it into volumes vertically. That is, each volume would range from the start to the finish, and across all the continents, but be only a portion of the whole. Picture a layer cake, with each cut piece showing its layers from the icing down to the plate and extending from the edge to the center. No single slice contains the whole cake, but each slice samples every part of it.

This volume is like that piece of cake. I once wrote a novel with that title, *A Piece of Cake*, but that had no relation to this; it was future space adventure, and the publisher changed the title to *Triple Detente*, and so it remains. This present volume is conceived as perhaps a third of the whole, the sequels being *Shame of Man* and *Hope of Earth*. Three volumes this size would represent the half million words envisioned. But naturally it isn't that simple. Now that I have written the first volume, I am uncertain whether I can complete the story in three, so it might be a series. I am also uncertain whether there will *be* another volume, because there's an enormous amount of research and my time is always pressed. My research assistant, Alan Riggs, did a wonderful job. He was the one who did basic research on history and cultures after I set the settings, and who had to find out obscure things, such as whether daisies grow in Africa. Yes, the African Daisy is the Gerbera, a beautifully decorative import to America; we have a number in our own garden. He also checked for errors; could Ember have green eyes when she was a Black African? I wrote this novel in about six months, which is twice as long as I take on ordinary ones; it would have taken a year without Alan, or the quality would have suffered. My deadlines on other projects don't allow more time. There is also the question of market: if there aren't enough readers, it won't fly. I once wrote a historical novel couched as future space adventure, *Steppe,* ready to write others of that type if the market was there. I received many positive comments, but the sales were no better than my ordinary novels, while the research was much greater. So I did not continue that series; I became a best-seller in light fantasy instead. To put it in garden-variety terms: if you had a choice of two good jobs, and one paid twice as well while the other required twice as much work, which would you take? Fortunately I am now well enough off so that I can afford to go the route I prefer—but that choice, too, is not all that simple, because I like the fantasy very well also, and have many dedicated readers there.

So *Isle of Woman* may be a single volume, or the first of a trilogy, or of a longer series. Time will tell. At least you know its nature. Other volumes, if they come to be, will go more deeply into the relation between climate and history, the connection between important resources such as wood and the welfare of mankind, the impact of disease, and special aspects of the species and its history. They will also show other ways in which mankind may destroy itself, or manage to save itself. Overpopulation is hardly the only threat to mankind's continued existence. Nuclear war is perhaps the most dramatic of a number of ugly alternatives. There were also less devastating things I really wanted to cover here, but I had to stay within my guidelines. I wanted to get into the reason why man's penis and woman's breasts are just about the largest, in proportion, in the animal kingdom, and why we need to get vitamin C from our diet when most other animals don't, and just what did happen to the ancient culture of northern India that left the ruins of Harappa. This volume never touched on the prehistory of South America, but there is significance there too. Mankind is endlessly fascinating, in general and detail, and I want to learn it all and share it all. Perhaps I shall accomplish some of that. There are major areas this volume never addressed, such as mankind's darker nature, and it is really a simplified sanitized introductory narrative with well-meaning people in relatively normal situations. There is really little evil. That is apt to change.

The general framework of each volume will be similar to this one, covering anywhere up to four million years, touching down at human points along the way. Perhaps there will be one larger family, instead of two "male" and "female" lines of descent, and just one generation. Some readers may have noticed that the three generations age at different rates, with Blaze and Ember gaining four years per chapter, Stone and Crystal three years, and Tree and Flower two. This is to maintain the proportion as the average length of human life extends. Others may have noted the artistic echoing of elements in different chapters, such as the affair between Blaze and Seed, the emphasis diminishing as their lives across the world progress. Specific themes may be more evident in the sequels; this first volume is more of a generalized sampling, as it were introducing mankind to the reader. Assuming that we solve the population crisis by appropriately limiting our rate of reproduction, there will remain other problems almost as formidable. *All* of them have to be addressed, in reality if not in this series, or it will be like saving the patient from cancer only to have him die the following day from a heart attack. For this volume I assumed that nothing would be done, and traced the likely consequence in Chapter 20.

What, then, is the point of this volume? As is usually the case with my more serious projects, there are several. I did want to explore history, showing it the way I see it, satisfying my readers that what schools and ordinary texts do is not the only way to address this vastest of all subjects. But I also wanted to help cry warning, to show in a way that the average person can understand that mankind is headed for a crisis that can not be ignored. Mankind evolved to address the challenges of a situation in Africa hundreds of thousands of years ago, and then learned to cope with the rest of the world 40,000 years ago. The traits and abilities that enabled him to survive and prosper then are now about to drive him into disaster. Because we are crafted to respond to something immediate and dramatic, such as the pounce of a saber-toothed tiger, rather than to something dull that will happen in another generation, like running out of space for our garbage, we deal with the acute problems while allowing the chronic problems to grow. But those chronic problems, though slow, can be extremely serious. We are in the process of making the most extensive series of extinctions of animals and plants ever to occur on Earth, dwarfing the disaster of the dinosaurs, because we are not only hunting animals mercilessly, we are destroying their habitats and those of many plants. We are cutting down the last great forests. Every new house we build squeezes the natural realm a bit more tightly, and we don't even notice. We are polluting air, earth, and sea, making them turn gradually hostile to life. Yet powerful elements in our society are campaigning to continue these processes, in the name of convenience, jobs, or wealth. This is absolute folly—and we seem hardly to care.

Some readers may feel that I am being unrealistic in postulating a future in which cannibalism is rampant. Actually man has eaten man before. There is evidence that it happened in Neandertal times, and since then when hunger became sufficient. Ritual man-eating has occurred in headhunter cultures, and it became wholesale among the Aztecs of pre-Columbian Mexico, where some 50,000 people a year were ritually slaughtered and eaten; my historical novel *Tatham Mound* has reference to that, and the matter is well documented. The Donner Party of 1846–47 is infamous for surviving by eating its own when stranded by snow in the Sierra Nevada. Piers Paul Read wrote of a similar case in Chile when members of a soccer team were stranded by an airplane wreck in the Andes range in 1972. (I once received a batch of fan letters intended for him, owing to a confusion of names.) There is recent evidence that the Japanese army practiced it in World War II. Cannibalism seems to have occurred in all inhabited continents at some time, usually when hunger was extreme but also as a religious rite. Since hunger will become extreme in our future, if present trends continue, the assumption seems reasonable, as does my notion of feeding on algae and insects.

I started editing this text on my fifty-eighth birthday, August 6, 1992. That routine day I received twenty-nine letters, some packages, and the usual collection of junk mail. That was the positive side of my day. I read the newspaper and noticed how many of the items related to the theme of this project. Somalia, a country of east Africa close to the theoretical birthplace of mankind, was headlined as the "world's worst humanitarian crisis," with four million people facing death from starvation, sickness, and war. Food was being shipped in, but couldn't reach the people because of the continuing fighting; men with guns hijacked it for themselves or to sell on the black market. Meanwhile in America civil rights charges were being leveled at four white Los Angeles police officers who had been videotaped badly beating a black man, Rodney King, while arresting him for speeding. They had been found not guilty of criminal charges, that decision triggering the worst city riot in decades. Food stamps to help 20,000 needy residents after the riot had been delayed more than a month. In Europe there were charges of atrocities by the Serbs against Muslims and Croats, and the image of the Nazi death camps was evoked. Devastating fires were still raging in six American states. Saddam Hussein of Iraq was reported to have recovered the power to invade Kuwait again. Environmental damage resulting from an oil spill in the Amazon region was discovered to be worse than previously thought. The state of Oregon's tough ordering of the distribution of funds for health care so as to make it both fair and affordable was in abeyance because of a court decision. And there were reports of bad attitudes among the members of America's Olympic basketball "Dream Team," and criticism of the TV coverage of the games, and of biased judging or even cheating. In short, on this random day, ongoing mischief abounded across the world, with people suffering and dying exactly as Malthus predicted, and efforts to alleviate the situation being hindered by the indifference or active interference of others. Disharmony showed even in the Olympics, which were supposed to bring the world together in healthy individual excellence and sportsmanship. As a species we aren't learning anything, and time is running out.

I have several mental images. These are just little situations I ponder every so often. One I have used elsewhere, as a vision of a character in a novel, but it comes so frequently to my mind that I'll mention it here as well. It is a scene of two mares grazing in a fenced pasture, as ours used to do. One, more thoughtful than the other, does some computation and realizes that at the rate they are eating, they will run out before spring comes and then starve. She tries to explain this to the other horse, suggesting that they both ration their grazing so as to make the grass and hay last until the new grass grows. But the other mare ignores her, and continues to eat at the same rate. Thus both of them will later starve. What is the first mare to do?

Or picture a goat who finds himself in with a herd of sheep; he looks around and sees that the path ahead is narrowing into a corral where grim-looking men are gathered, holding shears or perhaps butcher knives. The sheep are just moving forward, each following the one in front. But they are in for a shearing or worse if they don't change course in a hurry. The goat tries to warn them of his suspicion, but they ignore him as a "doom and gloomer." He can't just cut out on his own; he is wedged into the middle of the flock, and is being borne along by the momentum of the masses. He will share their fate. Can the goat alert the sheep in time?

Or a group of people dancing on the deck of a giant pleasure ship. They are having a great time. But one boy looks over the rail and sees that the waterline is higher than it was. In fact the ship is slowly sinking in the water. Alarmed, he goes to the captain, but the captain refuses to be concerned. "It is true that we collided with an iceberg, but no significant damage was done. This ship is unsinkable. Don't generate panic by spreading a wild story." So, does the boy behave by keeping his mouth shut, or does he try to alert the passengers of the *Titanic* to the problem? Will they pay attention if he does?

Malthus was right. Our world is heading for something like this. The signs are coming clear to those who care to look. The climate is changing, bringing agricultural ruin to parts of the world. Today there is famine in Africa and shortage elsewhere. Tomorrow that famine may be everywhere. We have seen only the beginning of the most horrendous problems. All over the world our people are addressing our most immediate concerns, as we have for several million years. In the process we have made a marvelous civilization—and come close to destroying the life of the planet. Perhaps we can change course before it is too late. But will we?

I hope so.